SINFUL OATHS

SINFUL OATHS

SINS OF THE FATHER BOOK 2

ZARA JADE ASTRID

Olive Press
PUBLISHING

ISBN: 979-8-9987751-3-0 (EBOOK)

ISBN: 979-8-9987751-2-3 (PAPERBOOK)

Any references to historical events, real people, or real places are used fictionally. Names, characters, and places are products of the author's imagination.

Published by Olive Press Publishing, South Carolina, USA

Cover design by Modern Designs 139

Editing by Olive Press Publishing, LLC

First printing edition 2026.

www.publishingwitholivepress.com

Contents

Trigger Warning

Take care of yourself while reading, and thank you for embarking on this journey with me.

With love and respect,
Zara Jade Astrid

Playlist

Chapter One

Joey
1960

The dead don't stay lucky forever.

That was the first thought that hit me when Paul came barreling out of his green Cadillac Series 62 Eldorado towards me. The button to his light gray suit revealed the crisp white dress shirt underneath. His auburn colored businessman hairstyle, which he fluffed to one side, was a mess on top of his head. "Joey!" he called. "Vincent's dead."

I should've felt satisfied. *Relief.*

All I felt was unfinished business.

The sun was a merciless bastard that afternoon, burning down on us as if it knew how hot the streets were about to get. I stood near the driver's door of my black 1959 Ferrari, its polished body baking under the glare. The long driveway stretched out to the street, flanked by sprawling estates similar to ours—Angela's house next door, Lucy's just beyond hers. A few others lined either side, and at the very end of the street, looming like a landmark, stood Staten Island High School.

Paul planted himself in front of me. His eyes pleaded with

mine. "You need to lay low because you're gonna be the *first* one they question."

I heard him. He had a valid point. The only trouble was, it wasn't registering. The hatred I carried for Vincent...it drowned out logic. Drowned out common sense. The man had caused more hell than he ever paid for. Now someone had handed him his penance. But it wasn't my hand that did the writing.

"I want to see him," I said with conviction. "I *need* to see it for myself." I stepped towards the driver's side door, but Paul moved faster, blocking me before I could reach it. My brows drew tight, and a knot of irritation formed between them. Heat sparked behind my eyes, as if I could scorch straight through him and the sheer audacity in his gaze.

"You show up at that scene, everyone's gonna know you did it," He warned. "Or at least, think you did. Doesn't matter which one they run with...it's going to be World War Three on the streets."

I knew he was right. The trouble was, I didn't care.

"I was only a few hours late from doing the job myself," I hissed. "If I'd gotten there sooner..." I jabbed a finger into my chest. "...it would've been me pulling the trigger."

Paul's patience shattered like glass. His shoulders stiffened. "Snap out of this!" he barked. He had always been the calm one. In twenty years, I could count on one hand the times he'd raised his voice. "You are going to regret this. You go anywhere near that crime scene, and you'd be better off admitting to the fucking crime yourself."

I stared at him. The words finally sank through, and a strangled chuckle escaped my lips. I dragged in a breath before giving a slow nod. "You're right, Paul."

I glanced behind me. I had everything I ever wanted and more. Adriana had turned our estate into a home, while the entryway leading up to the door boasted a flowerbed that Rosa had planted. I had become Antonio's father in every sense of the word. Adriana was my wife. My health was nearly back to what it had been. My business had grown so much that I was considering specializing in luxury cars—the first luxury car dealership on the East Coast featuring only the finest American and European models. I do have a lot to lose. Or maybe, more accurately, a lot to protect.

I gave his shoulder a quick pat. "If I show up or lay low, it won't matter. I'm already guilty in their eyes. And if that's the case, I'd rather go out with the image of that unlucky bastard *burned* into my head. Let the whole damn world think I was the one who got to him first. I really don't give a fuck, Paul."

Paul blew out a huff through his nose; his lips pulled into a tight line. I had just taken my hand off his shoulder when Adriana's cherry-red 1959 Chevy Impala rolled into the driveway. She glided past Paul's Cadillac and beside my Ferrari, then cut the engine, pushed the door open, and stepped out. Her head peeked over Paul's shoulder. All I could see were her black cat-eyed sunglasses and those perfect victory curls she loved to wear. Her heels clicked against the pavement as she walked toward the hood of the car, coming fully into view as she approached us.

She wore a white A-line dress, narrow at the top and sleeveless, flaring just above her knees. She looked stunning. I hadn't seen her wear it before. It was hard to remember that Paul was furious, trying to convince me not to ruin my life, or that Vincent might have been murdered by someone else. All I could see was her in that dress; everything else faded into the background.

"What's going on?" she asked, suspicion lacing her voice.

Paul got his words out faster than I could. "Could you talk

some sense into your husband?" He held my gaze, his green eyes squinting, and lips pressed into a thin line.

Her glare burned into the side of my face as mine locked on Paul's eyes. She wanted an explanation, and I wanted to wrap my hand around Paul's throat for outing me like that. Paul jabbed a finger in my direction.

"Think about what you've got going for you, Joey. Don't throw it all away for your pride. He's dead. Go inside, have a glass of whiskey like the rest of us, and lie low, so you're not the one they suspect."

Adriana crossed her arms over her chest, cocking her hip to the side as the toe of her heeled foot tapped against the pavement in silent judgment. She tilted her sunglasses down enough for me to see the fierce glint in her dark eyes. "What's he talking about, Joey?"

My mouth went dry, and now it's going to take everything in me to hold myself back from tackling Paul right here in the driveway because the last thing I needed was for Adriana to get caught up in the middle of this. "That's enough from both of you." My voice dropped to a growl.

Paul and I held our standoff a moment longer before he finally let out the breath he'd been holding, turned on his heel, and strode past me to his Cadillac. I felt Adriana's eyes burning into the back of my head as I watched him slam the car into reverse, tires squealing as he backed out and sped off down the street.

The driveway fell quiet again. But only for a second.

Chapter Two

Adriana

My eyes bore into the back of Joey's light blue linen short-sleeve button-up. He'd paired it with cream slacks and brown loafers, one hand tucked in his pocket while the silver face of his Rolex Datejust caught the sunlight.

When he turned, icy blue eyes locked on mine. His dark hair was slicked back to perfection with Brylcreem, and his free hand clutched the back of his neck as he flashed me a toothy, nervous grin.

"What's going on? What's Paul talking about?"

His eyebrows lifted, his smile slipping into a frown as he shrugged, playing clueless. "Why don't you go inside and rest your feet? You've been out all day. Rosa will be back soon. Antonio's upstairs; he's had a long day, too."

My eyes narrowed, searching his. "I'm not going inside until you tell me what Paul was talking about, Joey." My arms folded tighter across my chest.

He stepped forward, one hand curling around my hip, and pulled me against him. The warm spice of his Old Spice aftershave—cloves, cinnamon, amber—wrapped around me, heady and intoxicating. His other hand slid to the side of my neck, his long fingers curling against my skin as he tilted my head back. His scent clung to me, as his touch seared into me.

My lashes fluttered as his thumb traced along my jaw, and then his lips brushed mine in a soft, tender kiss. The cool mint of his breath mixed with the warmth of his mouth, and I was helpless against him. His lips hovered above mine, teasing me, before he whispered in a low, raspy voice, "I don't want you stressing about anything, sweetheart. So do me a favor, go relax, and I'll be right back. Because tonight..." His smile ghosted against my lips. "...I want to see what you bought while you were out."

The thought of Joey stretched across our king-size mattress upstairs, watching me parade in lingerie, flickered through my mind. He loves a fashion show, and he never lets me take the lingerie off. *It's made to admire and worship,* he'd told me. And worship, he does, finding his way past it as though it wasn't even there.

I shook the thought from my head. "Do you really think you can just kiss me and I'll forget all about Paul?" My brow arched as I waited for his answer.

"Well, I was hoping," he murmured with a soft chuckle. The hand at my neck slipped down to my hip, and he pulled me flush against him until there was no space left between us. My arms wrapped around the back of his neck.

"You telling me it didn't work?" he teased, bending down. I thought he was coming for my lips, but instead his mouth brushed the side of my neck, his warm breath grazing beneath my ear.

"Stop it," I said, swatting his chest and stepping back to reclaim the air between us. "I want to know what you're hiding from me. Where are you going? Who's going to suspect you, and of what?"

His eyes dropped to his loafers as the palm of his hand ran over his slicked-back hair. His chiseled jaw twitched, and then his gaze lifted to meet mine.

"Vincent was murdered," he exhaled.

I blinked. "Murdered?"

"So, I'm going to meet Ben. He should be at the crime scene," Joey continued.

"Why—why would Paul ask me to talk some sense into you, then?" I stammered. "I can only assume it's because if you're seen at the crime scene, they'll think you're guilty of the crime."

"Sweetheart—"

"That's exactly it!" My voice shook with fury. "There's no amount of kissing me, sweet-talking me, or—" I sighed, "calling me 'sweetheart' that's going to make me okay with you going over there and having a target painted on your back for something you didn't do!"

He dug his car keys out of his pocket and let out a long sigh, stepping toward the driver's side door. My heart slammed into my chest with reckless urgency.

"Joey, I'm your wife," I pleaded. "You can't leave. Paul's right. You should come inside."

He took a few small steps backward, as if I wouldn't notice. His hand reached for the door handle, and I saw just how far he'd gotten. "Sweetheart, this has *nothing* to do with you. I have to go. I won't be long—"

"No!" I lunged forward, but he slid into the car, slamming the door shut behind him. I planted myself by the window, refusing to move until he came to his senses. "Joey, come inside!" I slapped the glass. He started the engine and rolled the window down enough for me to reach him. My hands gripped whatever I could. One on the windowsill, the other against the side of his neck, forcing his gaze to meet mine.

He was stone cold.

"Get out of the car!" I shouted. "They're going to think you did this! Everyone knows you thought Vincent was the one who shot you! Everyone knows you hate him!"

"I forgot to tell you...that dress looks amazing on you." His eyes softened as they traced the length of my frantic body.

I knew what he was doing. He was trying to distract me, trying to make me forget that the car was in reverse, that he was about to drive straight into the lion's den.

One hand stayed on the steering wheel, but the other reached up to cradle the back of my neck. He pulled me in, kissing me softly at first but then more firmly and demanding. His tongue teased mine, and my hands dropped as every thought of caution vanished. All I could think about was climbing in, straddling him, and losing myself to him.

"I love you, you know that, sweetheart?" he murmured against my mouth.

I continued kissing him, nodding, caught somewhere between the desire I felt for his touch and the dread of him leaving me standing here. Joey pulled back enough to let our foreheads rest together, his breath warm against mine.

"Sweetheart...I need you to move," he whispered, his voice a low coax, as he brushed a strand of hair from my face. "Please. Just step back for me. Let's not make this into something it doesn't need to be. Yeah? Will you do that for me?"

His crystal eyes searched mine, patient but insistent. I closed my eyes, knowing there was no winning a battle with Joey Romano. With a deep, reluctant breath, I pressed my hands against the windowsill and pushed myself back, letting them fall to my sides. My shoulders slumped, and I could feel the scowl etched across my face. One side of his mouth twitched upward. "Tell me you love me."

I said it on command, my voice tinged with frustration. "I love you. That's why I'm asking you to reconsider, Joey," I whined.

"I know, sweetheart. But you've got to trust me. I know what I'm doing." His gaze softened, then a sly grin spread across his face. "And the last thing I want is for my beautiful wife to be sulking and mad at me...when she looks like she could take over the world in that new dress."

I had no smile to give him. One hand stayed on the steering wheel; the other lifted to his mouth. He pressed a finger to his puckered lips, sending a floating kiss toward me. With a wink, his hand dangled on the car door, and he eased the car in reverse.

I watched, heart in my throat, as he slowly backed out of the driveway, every inch taking him and me closer to whatever awaited him on the street.

Chapter Three

Joey

As soon as I pulled onto Vincent's street, I saw the mayhem playing out in broad daylight. Five NYPD squad cars lined the curb; their red gumball lights spinning slowly, painting the brownstones in flashes of warning. Uniformed cops stood outside speaking to neighbors and Vincent's housekeeper. Yellow caution tape crisscrossed the front stoop, fluttering in the breeze, its message clear as a death knell: Vincent "Lucky" Accetta hadn't been so lucky in *this* assassination attempt.

Detectives in suits and fedoras prowled the perimeter, notebooks in one hand, Lucky Strikes in the other, as they spoke in hushed tones. I parked directly across the street from Vincent's front steps. The front door hung wide open, and from where I sat, I could see the dark puddle spreading towards the threshold. Vincent lay face down in it, his body just inside the living room. Ben was crouched beside him, studying the scene with his detective eye. A crime scene photographer popped flashbulbs in quick succession.

The coroner's wagon parked half on the curb; the rear

doors hung open. Two men in white coats stood nearby with a stretcher, their expressions carved from stone. Across the street, a pair of reporters shouted questions toward a detective who ignored them, while another scribbled furiously in his notepad. His fedora tipped low against the sun.

Whoever had killed Vincent Accetta hadn't just wanted him dead. They wanted him destroyed. This crime scene reeked of rage. Of revenge. Of someone on a mission to destroy.

"Is that the shark?" I heard a female reporter gasp. Ben's neck snapped toward me. He shot to his feet, our eyes locking as the reporters surged in my direction. "It's him! It's Joey *The Shark* Romano!"

Ben looked like the blood had drained clean from his face, and I was certain mine mirrored his. *This* was what Paul had warned me about. Now the press had me on record, standing at the scene of Vincent's murder. *Fucking spectacular.*

I tilted my head toward Ben, the smallest signal for him to meet me down the road. My foot pressed heavily on the accelerator, and I tore past the crowd of reporters. Cops kept to the scene, too busy with the body and too wary of the Shark to bother chasing me down over a traffic violation.

I parked near an empty baseball field. It wasn't long before Ben's cruiser came barreling down the street. He skidded to a stop behind me, killed the engine, and climbed out.

His NYPD detective uniform carried the wear of the day: dark wool trousers, wrinkled at the knees; a white dress shirt, collar undone and tie loosened enough to betray the pressure he was under. His navy jacket sagged where his shoulder holster pressed against it, and his badge swung heavy from his belt.

Ben slid into the passenger seat of my Ferrari, the hard lines of his uniform melting into the soft Italian cream leather. He dragged a hand through his dirty-blond crew cut, the other gripping the seat like he had to steady himself. The scent of English Leather clung to him—rich woods, warm leather, a citrus edge —filling the car until it felt like his presence swallowed the air.

A group of children, no more than six or seven, played hopscotch on the sidewalk ahead. Their laughter carried faintly in the summer air—innocent, careless—while just a street over, the body of one of the most feared men in New York bled into his own living room rug.

"And just what the fuck do you think you're doing here?" Ben growled. I turned my head, meeting those fierce green eyes drilling holes into me. His jaw was locked, a vein twitching at his temple. I let out a long sigh, leaning back into the headrest, wishing I had listened to Paul and Adriana.

"I mean, *fuck!*" His palm slammed against the passenger side door with force. "They've got you at the fucking murder scene. How could you be so *fucking* stupid?" His hand raked through his crew cut, leaving strands standing on end. Before his hand dropped to his thigh, clenching it into a fist. "I told Paul to spread the word, make sure everyone lies low. Did he not come to your house?"

"He did," I admitted, my eyes dropping to the steering wheel as my thumb ran over the stitched leather.

Ben let out a disbelieving scoff, his nostrils flaring as he shifted in his seat. "But you don't listen. Of course, you don't listen." His head tilted back; his eyes closed as if summoning patience, but when they snapped open again, they burned hotter. "You get off on making my life harder, trying to convince everyone you're just a hardworking Italian American businessman." He jabbed a finger toward me, his whole body tight with frustration. "I'd *love* to know how you think I'm going to explain this, the fucking Shark, showing up at the exact moment of Vincent's murder. The man who hated you. The man *you* hated. Yeah, Joey, that's not suspicious at all."

What could I say to this? I wasn't going to apologize, though maybe I should. Instead, I muttered, "I'll pay you for your troubles."

Ben's gaze cut to mine. A dry, humorless laugh burst out of him, laced with bitterness. "I don't give a fuck about your money, Joey. Not when it comes at the expense of my sanity." His fingers drilled hard into his temple as though trying to hold his skull together. "You're gonna drive me insane cleaning up your messes. And there's no dollar amount that's gonna keep me sane. At this rate, I'll be drooling in a psych ward, and all your money won't buy back the brain cells you've fried out of me."

The corner of my mouth twitched, and before I could stop it, a snicker escaped.

"And you think this is a joke?" Ben spat, slumping back into the seat with a violent exhale, his chin tilting up toward the car roof as his hands clawed through his hair. His knees bounced restlessly, like he was two seconds from putting a fist through my dashboard.

"Of course not," I said, pressing my lips together to choke back the laugh, threatening to burst. "Your comment was just... a little funny, that's all."

Ben's head snapped toward me, his eyes narrowing into mine. "Wait—"

My brow furrowed.

"You didn't—"

"Kill him?" I choked out in disbelief. "You really *have* lost your mind. Of course, I didn't kill him. Someone else beat me to it."

"Well, excuse me," Ben huffed. "I deliver a fucking revolver that's registered to your wife's dead husband, match the bullets to the ones they dug out of your chest cavity...and then, weeks later, Vincent's shot in cold blood, and you're sitting outside when I *specifically* told Paul to make sure everyone lays low."

I leaned back in my seat, crossing my arms. "I didn't kill Vincent. If I had, you'd be the *first* one I told."

Ben let out a humorless hum, his eyes narrowing. "True. But I suppose my work's going to be cut out for me when I try to convince the entire state of New York—correction, the entire United States—that, oh no, Joey Romano wasn't the killer. Despite being the first person anyone with a single brain cell would suspect. But no, it wasn't him. He was just devastated that his boss was killed and came to..." He paused, lifted his fingers, and snapped them in the air. "'Check it out,'" he said, emphasizing the words with exaggerated air quotes, while his voice dripped with sarcasm.

"You know that psych ward's going to be screaming your name if you don't calm your ass down," I hissed. Ben rolled his eyes, jaw tight, and fingers drumming against the leather cream seat.

"I didn't kill the bastard, though I wish I had, and I might kill the bastard who *did* do it, just out of spite for getting to the scene before I could," I threatened. "I was home, confronting my son, holding him while he cried over that bastard blackmailing, manipulating, and harassing a thirteen-year-old boy to do his dirty work. Because he couldn't take me out like a real man. *No*, he had to track down my boy on his paper route, and threaten to kill *my* wife if he didn't cooperate."

"Meanwhile, that psychotic daughter of his, Renee, worked alongside him to pry information from me, try to trick me into slipping up so Vincent could have a 'reason' to get me killed. And the real kicker? That motherfucker Hector worked with the two of them, just so he and Vincent could take me out because I'm a threat. I wouldn't be surprised if Christopher's next in this goddamn chess match."

"So now, I have to nurse a teenage boy back to health because he was convinced *I* was the bad one in this whole story. I would've killed Vincent and taken my repercussions like a real man. But I've got to keep this secret between Antonio and me, without Adriana finding out. I'm a fucking newlywed! And I've already got a secret I'm harboring. And tomorrow, I'll be in the papers *again* for a crime I didn't commit. So if anyone's going to the psych ward..." I paused, glaring at him, my voice a deadly whisper. "...it'll be me. And at this rate, it sounds like a much-needed vacation."

"Well, if the kid didn't do it and you didn't do it, then who the fuck did?" Ben muttered with his jaw pulled tight.

"That's the million-dollar question, isn't it, Benny?" I replied as my eyes scanned the street. Ben dug a pack of Lucky Strikes from his pocket, pulled one out, and stuck it between his lips. He lit it, inhaling deeply, then passed the pack to me. I mirrored his actions, feeling the smoke curl around us.

"The bastard was insufferable," he said, exhaling a long plume of smoke, letting it drift between us. "He deserved the execution-style hit he got. But you know what this means, same as I do."

Our gaze collided, and I nodded slowly. My gaze drifted toward the kids still playing hopscotch on the sidewalk. "There's going to be an all-out war between the families," I said, blowing smoke from the corner of my mouth. "And every eye is going to be on me."

"Eyes *and* fingers," Ben corrected, letting out a huff of smoke. His arm stretched along the top of my seat; the other held his cigarette between his fingers, as he rested it on the windowsill. "I hope you're ready. It might cost us both our lives just to clear your name after tonight. And if you go down...so will I."

Loyalty. It's what men like us thrived on...and died for.

"I didn't come this far to roll over and let someone else write my story, Ben."

Ben's eyes glint with a mixture of warning and calculation. "You know they'll be looking for blood. An eye for an eye, Joey. Christopher's gonna want a head on a plate, and yours is the easiest one to serve."

I knew he wasn't wrong. An underboss doesn't get taken out like this without igniting a war. All five families would be out for blood, and I was the obvious target. "Who the hell could have done this? It's got to be Hector." The words slipped out before I could stop them, spoken aloud instead of kept in the cage of my mind. "I bet they got into it, and Hector took him out."

"That's a damn good guess. My money's on him, too. If he didn't do it himself, he had someone else do it for him."

My head turned toward Ben, who flicked his gaze from mine to the dashboard window, his eyes scanning the street as if trouble would leap out at any moment. "You can't get some help from Lucy on this?" I asked. His eyebrows pulled together in fury, and his head snapped toward me. Another layer of shock crossed his face, and I noted the tension in his jaw. "Hector is her husband. She might be able to help us prove he did it," I pressed, grasping at straws.

"Have you lost your fucking mind?" he spat, holding up a hand before I could answer. His fingers twitched, and his chest rose and fell with each sharp inhale he took. "I'm *not* pulling Lucy into this," he said, his voice low but stiff.

Lucy was like a sister to me, and the love I had for her paled in comparison to Ben's. I knew that much. No woman should be dragged into this world, but could it really count if she were already a mafia princess?

"We wouldn't be involving her. We'd just be asking her to

dig a little for us," I pressed, flicking the ash from my cigarette onto the concrete outside my window.

Ben's jaw tightened, his lips pressing into a thin line. The tension radiating from him like heat. "I'm not asking her to do anything like that. Hector's barely home as it is. She'd have to go out of her way to even get close to him, and he sure as hell wouldn't confide in her. Nor would I want her going out of her way to get close to that sleaze bag."

So, I suppose, I'd have to find another way to force Hector into the light.

Chapter Four

Adriana

It's *Now or Never* by Elvis Presley rang out, the melody filling the house as the scent of baccalà in tomato sauce mingled with the crispy roasted potatoes and the tang of red wine vinegar from the side salad on the counter. I hummed along as I set out silverware on the perfectly set table.

The front door opened, and Rosa's voice chimed from the foyer. "Why hello, Joey. How was your day?"

I didn't hear his response, but I did hear his deep laugh curl through the air, and the rhythmic click of his loafers growing louder with each step toward me.

Before I could turn, his arms wrapped around my waist as I reached across the table to place a fork on Antonio's napkin. I straightened, my lungs filling with the warm cinnamon notes of his cologne, layered with a hint of cigarette smoke. He pressed a soft peck to my cheek, and I melted into him. His lips trailed down the side of my neck, his hands gliding along the curves of my body, coaxing me to surrender, to ease the tension I was still carrying from earlier.

"I like this dress. Did I mention that already?" He

murmured against the shell of my ear. The rasp of his voice sent shivers sweeping up my spine. "But you know what I'd like more than that? What's underneath it."

His large hand slid up the front of my dress, tracing past my breast, tilting my head, so our gazes met. A smirk curled on his lips as his eyes dropped immediately to mine, then to my lips. He pressed his mouth to mine, his tongue dipping in and stealing my breath.

When he pulled back, his forehead rested against mine; my back pressed against his chest. He whispered against my lips in a low and heated tone, "I told you I'd make it back in one piece. Because I'm going to sit down and eat this amazing-smelling food...and then I'm taking you upstairs. So, I can show you just how crazy you make me."

I spun around, his hands guiding me by my hips as they held me close. I lifted my arms, letting them drape over his broad shoulders, my freshly manicured fingers brushing against the back of his neck.

"I'm not even hungry anymore," he murmured, tilting his head down, his eyes glinting with desire. "Not for food, at least."

A smile broke across my face, and his hands dropped from my hips. He bent forward, his fingertips tracing the hem of my dress just above my knees, then slid higher along the backs of my thighs.

Half of me wanted to beg him to keep going, but the other half knew that wasn't happening right now. I reached behind me and swatted his hands away, letting a soft giggle escape my throat. "Stop it."

He blew out a puff of air as I stepped back from him, moving toward the kitchen to get the food on the table. "Where's Antonio?" Joey asked, his eyebrows scrunched as his gaze flicked across the downstairs.

"I've barely seen him today," I replied, checking the potatoes in the oven. "Right after you left, Enzo and Michael showed up on their bikes asking for him. I called him down, and the three of them went straight upstairs. I saw him for maybe a second before he disappeared into his room."

"Did he seem okay to you?" he asked, fingers gripping the back of a kitchen chair.

"Why wouldn't he be okay?" I said, sliding on a mitt and pulling the potatoes from the oven, placing them carefully on the counter.

Joey lifted a shoulder, his gaze drifting toward the ceiling. "Oh, I don't know. I was just wondering."

I met his eyes as I removed the mitt, setting it next to the potatoes. That flicker of guilt in his gaze didn't escape me. "Are you not telling me something?"

"What?" he choked out, shifting on his feet slightly. "I'm just asking about our son, sweetheart. He wasn't feeling well earlier, but it sounds like he's back to normal."

My eyes lingered on him for a moment longer before turning back to the food. "So, what happened while you were out?"

"Nothing," he said. "Nothing really. I just spoke with Ben and came home."

I placed my palm on the kitchen counter, studying him. Joey stood a few feet away, his hands gripping the back of a chair tucked neatly under the rectangular walnut table. White plates with gold trim, wine glasses, water cups, and a crisp linen tablecloth set the table. A brass chandelier hung overhead. Fresh flowers from the front flowerbed sat in a vase at the table's center. Heavy silk drapes pooled behind Joey's tall frame, hiding the sun as it dipped toward the horizon.

"Joey, I'm your wife," I sighed, crossing my arms. "What

happened? Why are you being so secretive about this? And you seriously expect me not to question anything?"

He rounded the table, footsteps echoing against the hardwood, and stopped in front of me. "I don't want my wife worrying," he began, his voice insistent. "Or stressing." His hands gripped either side of my face, tilting my chin up to meet his gaze. "Or to have any part of that side of me. I just want you to sit back, let me shower you with love and attention, and treat you like a queen. Sweetheart, I'm not asking for much here."

"Well, I don't think it's fair," I said, arms tightening across my chest. "How come you get to keep me in the dark just because it's messy? I live in this world with you now. Whether you like it or not, we're a team...a union."

His tongue swiped over his lips as he nodded slowly. "You're right, sweetheart. The truth is...I went over there, and it was mayhem. Vincent got everything coming to him, and perhaps more." My stomach twisted, bile threatening to rise. "They may have also seen me at the crime scene, but—"

I stepped back, horror written across my face. "What do you mean?"

"Sweetheart," he said softly, lowering his hands and brushing his thumbs along my jawline, "it's nothing to worry about. Ben will take care of it. But I'm sure they'll print something stupid in the headlines tomorrow."

"Joey!" My voice flared, hands clenching at my sides. "It's not stupid! What you did was reckless! You're entirely too stubborn for your own good! You refuse to listen to anyone, and maybe you should!"

His fingers curled around my upper arms, drawing me closer, my palms pressing against his chest in resistance. "Sweetheart, I promise, it's all going to be okay. This is why I don't want to talk about it with you. I don't want what happens out there entering this house."

"You can't be serious," I snapped, stepping back. "I'm not illiterate. I'm going to read the damn papers. I'm going to see my husband's face plastered in them and the accusations that follow."

What Joey fails to realize is that, despite his efforts to separate his two worlds, they always seem to collide. The nights he comes in the front door with blood splattered across his shirt, and it's never his. He gives me clear instructions to get it out, as if it were never there. I never ask questions. Rosa comes home telling me the horror stories of New York's rising body count. No matter how hard he tries to shut the door on one world and enter the other, pieces of both slip through, blending together into one messy, dangerous reality.

Chapter Five

Antonio

I lay back against the fluffy pillow, my arms crossed over my chest, one leg flat and the other bent. Joey's scent still clung to my shirt, reminding me of how he held me while I cried into him, trying to comfort me despite what I'd done.

The burgundy walls wrapped around me. My bed, planted in the center of the room against the far wall, felt like a king's throne in his castle. On either side, windows looked down over the front yard and the street below. Matching wood nightstands framed the bed, the one closest to me held a lamp with a brass base.

Across from me was my vanity, every comb, brush, and bottle lined up perfectly, Brylcreem included, so I could slick my hair back to match Joey's. In the nook by the wall, my desk was cluttered with last year's schoolwork, a globe, and a few encyclopedias. My baseball glove from the spring game Joey took me to sat on top, while my card collection hid safely in the drawer.

Two posters, which were gifts from Joey the night he

announced at dinner that he'd be switching the wholesale to focus on American and European cars, hung proudly on my wall. A Ferrari and a Corvette. He gave them out to every kid who stopped by *Romano Luxury Wholesale.*

In the corner near my closet sat a plush chair and Ma's old record player. Joey had given her a new one, but I couldn't toss this one out. It held too many memories.

My coverlet, ivory striped in burgundy, was smooth beneath me. I let out a long breath before Ma's voice rang up the staircase, pulling me out of my thoughts. I pushed myself off the bed and padded toward my bedroom door, then to the top of the staircase. Looking down, I saw Ma standing there, Enzo and Michael flanking her. "Joey said you had a hard day," she said, worry etched across her brows. "Did something happen on the last day of school?"

A taut breath escaped my lips, quiet and strained.

"Eh, he's just in his feelings about junior high ending and senior school starting, Mrs. Romano," Enzo chimed in, somehow knowing I couldn't find the words to say it myself. He and Michael started up the stairs.

"I'm going to start preparing dinner. If you need me, let me know," Ma said. Though I was already heading toward my room, with Enzo and Michael trailing behind.

I collapsed back onto my bed in the same position as before, arms crossed over my chest. Enzo dropped into the chair at my desk, leaning forward, his elbows on his knees, fingers interlaced, while his neck craned to look at me. "You're still alive. I'll be damned," he said, a devious grin spreading across his face.

Michael slouched into the plush chair near the record player; one leg propped, ankle resting on his other thigh, his fingers gripping the ankle. His face twisted at Enzo's joke before flicking his eyes toward me. "What he means is...what happened? You were supposed to meet us at the park so we could celebrate the end of eighth grade."

"Well, despite Joey being a man with his own laws," Enzo said in a mock broadcaster voice, holding an imaginary microphone, "Antonio has seemed to live the tale of escaping the Shark." He winked at me. I rolled my eyes, biting back a smirk. "In all seriousness, what the hell happened? I had to eat your peanuts and drink your Coke—"

"You *had* to?" Michael interrupted, glaring at Enzo. "I told you we'd bring it to him. You said there was no point in carrying a hot soda to someone."

"And there isn't, Michael," Enzo shot back. "It's criminal to do otherwise. And I swear," he swung a finger between Michael and me, "neither of you better pull a stunt like that with me. I'd rather you drink it properly, which is ice cold, with peanuts inside."

Michael rolled his eyes, sinking back into the chair cushions.

"You also missed the cigarette I stole from Val's backpack," Enzo added, a sly smirk on his face.

Michael waved Enzo off, his eyes locked on me. "Something's wrong with you. What happened? Why didn't you meet us? I saw Joey out of my bedroom window earlier, and he looked like he was arguing with Paul. I've never seen Paul pissed, but he was. Did they find out about what you did and get into an argument over it?"

"Wait, wait, wait," Enzo jumped in, his voice rapid. "Where the hell was I when this happened?"

"Well, if I had to guess," Michael said, "you were probably stuffing your face with food or stealing a pack of cigarettes from someone."

A laugh escaped me. "He found out," I admitted in a

choked breath, dragging a hand across my face. "I've never seen him like that. I...I told him *everything*."

Michael's mouth fell open, his eyes fixed on me in stunned silence. Enzo leaned back in the chair, spinning the globe on the desk with one finger. "I guess I was right," he said, shaking his head. "You lived to tell the tale of surviving the Shark... because how the *hell* were you spared after trying to kill the man?"

Michael hissed, pulling his jaw tight. "Throw something at his fucking head. He's got no self-control to say shit like that. Who says things like that anyway?"

"I only say what's on my mind," Enzo huffed. "Antonio knows I joke. He has a sense of humor, unlike the other person in the room."

Michael shot back against the upholstered chair, rolling his eyes as he grumbled, "The other person in the room has emotional intelligence."

Enzo flailed his hands mockingly, like a puppet.

"He understood," I said. "After I told him what happened, he understood. I feel guilty because he feels guilty that he didn't notice or do something to stop it. I don't even know what he could've done. But I realize he's the only father I've *ever* had, and the only one I'll ever have. I'm his son and the only son he has."

"Until your mom has another baby," Enzo muttered under his breath. Michael snapped his gaze to him. "*What?* I'm just trying to lighten the mood. And I'm not wrong, you can't seriously think Joey isn't going to knock up his mom."

I gagged at the thought.

"You're making it worse!" Michael exclaimed, glaring at Enzo before turning back to me. "Don't listen to him. Joey is your father. He's given you his last name. He treats you better than my own dad treats me. So just...let this go, leave it in the past, and ignore Enzo's sick, twisted humor. He's demented."

"I suppose you told him about Giovanni," Enzo said, ignoring Michael's sarcastic mutterings. "What's gonna happen to that idiot since he was the getaway driver?"

"Nothing," I mumbled, shaking my head.

"*Nothing?*" Enzo barked, leaning forward, his elbows pressing into his knees again. "So, he just walks freely? You know that's why he's the way he is, because he gets away with *everything*. I'm telling you, if someone doesn't knock him down a few inches, he's going to become dangerous someday. He'll never learn if he keeps skating by scot-free for all the shit he causes."

"I see your point," I said, brushing my fingers through my hair, "and if anyone wants him to pay the price for being an annoying little coward, it would be *me*. But Joey's not going to teach a kid a lesson. Like you said, he lives by whatever morals he's concocted in his head, and he doesn't break them. What do you expect him to do, anyway?"

"He could hire me to rough him up, at the *bare* minimum," Enzo said.

Michael scoffed, rolling his eyes. "Yeah, great idea, Enzo," he said sarcastically, tapping his finger against his lip as if weighing the absurdity of it. "Let Joey hire someone to beat up a *child*. Perfect. Oh, wait! His grandfather is over Joey and is looking for a way to take him out. This would really be the cherry on top. *Jesus Christ*," Michael groaned, slapping his hand onto his thigh. "Do you ever *think*, or do you just do whatever pops into your head first?"

Enzo shrugged, lifting one shoulder. "Usually, I just go with the first thought that comes to mind. Life's too short to sit there trying to come up with the '*best*' decision."

Michael huffed under his breath, shaking his head.

"Do you have no loyalty, Michael?" Enzo snapped, his eyes narrowing. "Vincent was blackmailing our best friend!" He jabbed a finger toward me. "Giovanni played a part in what happened to Joey, so he should pay for it."

"So, you think a bunch of kids can go up against a pack of made men?" Michael said, incredulous. His eyes widened, and he leaned back in his chair. "Sometimes I wonder if you even hear yourself."

"Yes, I hear myself," Enzo muttered, crossing his arms and slumping into the chair. "I'm worried about my best friend, Michael. He doesn't even look the same anymore. And fine, if nothing happens to Giovanni on Joey's account, he's got two..." He held up two fingers. "...months to get his act together. I'm not doing another four years of his bullshit, and neither one of you will stop me from kicking his ass either."

"Very mature of you. I'd expect nothing less," Michael muttered, arms crossed, his brow tight.

I pushed myself up on the bed, my legs crisscrossed, elbows digging into my thighs. "For the record, I'm not some fragile child."

"And for the record, no one forced Antonio to do what he did," Michael said, ignoring my protest. "There was no gun to his head. He made a choice, and now he's carrying the guilt. It's not hard to see that if you two would stop running off emotion for two seconds and use the logical side of your brains, life might be a little less complicated."

"I *am* using the logical side of my brain!" Enzo yelled, slamming a fist onto the desk. "And it says Vincent should be six feet under, and Giovanni should be exiled along with his mother!"

I blinked. "Um...you do know I'm sitting right here?"

"This isn't the damn Middle Ages, Enzo," Michael shot back, his voice rising in pitch. "We don't exile people in 1960."

"Alright!" I shouted over the two of them, sitting up straighter, my gaze locking on Enzo. "Enzo, I appreciate you having my back. But Joey will handle Vincent, one way or another. Karma will catch up to Giovanni. He's always been a snake in the grass, and he always will be. And if he's a little twerp when school starts back in the fall, we'll deal with him... *together*."

I turned to Michael, my chest heaving. "And *you*, yeah, *I* fucked up. I know that, okay? If anyone knows that it's *me*!" I jabbed a finger into my chest. "Do you think I don't wake up every day wishing I'd done things differently? I've been carrying this around for *weeks*. I don't need you reminding me every five minutes. I've already thought it through a hundred times over."

The room was filled with silence for the first time since they'd entered. All I could hear was my own ragged breathing and my pulse rattling in my ears.

"I'm doing my best," I whispered, softer this time. "Whether that's enough...I don't know. But I'm trying to forgive myself and fix what I fucked up."

No one knew what I was dealing with in the dark of night, the nightmares that kept me tossing and turning, the guilt that gnawed at me whenever I tried to close my eyes. Joey loved me. He treated me like a son. And I'd betrayed him. Ma didn't know what I'd done, and Joey promised she would never. He'd take it to his grave. Lie for me. Protect me. Because he loved me. *No matter what.*

That didn't make it any easier to bear. I'd betrayed him in the worst possible way.

Joey might be complicated. The papers and the news channels might call him a criminal, a monster, or whatever else they wanted, but they didn't know him like I did. He was three-dimensional, with a soft interior hidden behind a hard exterior.

Joey wasn't feared, even with the way they painted him. Nobody flinched when he walked by. Nobody feared for their lives. They respected him. How, I couldn't say. Even strangers gravitated toward him.

Joey Romano was a pillar in this strange little city, and he was *my* father.

Chapter Six

Joey

My lower back pressed against the kitchen counter, arms crossed over my chest, feet crossed at the ankles. Adriana stood across from me; a kitchen apron tied neatly around her waist, her hands fidgeting at the strings. In a hushed, almost hesitant tone, she whispered, "How...how are we going to tell Antonio?"

How do you tell a kid that the man who blackmailed him—the same man who held a gun to his face and threatened to kill us all if he didn't fall in line—had been gunned down in cold blood? Not only that, but before long, every eye in the city would be locked on me as if I pulled the trigger myself. All I knew was this wasn't the kind of conversation you had over a family dinner.

"I'll take him for a drive after dinner and tell him then," I said. I pushed myself off the counter and bridged the small gap between Adriana and me. My palms glided up and down the smooth curve of her arms, grounding myself in the only calm I had left. "I'll take care of it, sweetheart." She nodded, her eyes lingered on me.

I bent down, pecking her lips softly, before making my way up through the house, up the staircase, and down the hallway. I stopped in front of Antonio's door and knocked gently. From beyond the door, I could hear low voices, Enzo and Michael whispering about something.

Footsteps echoed softly against the floor, and then Antonio's face appeared at the door. He was still in his light green short-sleeved polo and khaki slacks, the same outfit from earlier. I had taught him how to slick his curls back, and now, with his dark hair neatly combed, he looked like a miniature version of me. I smiled as I took him in—he seemed more composed now, far from the haunted look he'd worn when confessing the horrors of the past few months.

"Dinner's ready. Come eat." I glanced past Antonio's head, my gaze landing on Enzo and Michael in the background. "Why don't you two stay for dinner?"

Michael scratched the back of his neck. "You know...my mom might've already cooked."

The only thing Lucy was known to whip up was a dirty martini strong enough to knock even the toughest guy flat on his ass. "I'll give her a call. I'm sure she'd be happy to get out of cooking for one night," I said with a smile. "Come on."

"Well, I'm starving," Enzo chimed in, already moving toward the door.

A chuckle escaped past my lips and filled the hallway as I led the way down the hall, the boys following behind. We descended the stairs and walked into the dining room, where Adriana and Rosa were setting the last of the dishes on the table. Adriana placed down the bowl of salad, her head turning in our direction, a smile playing on her lips. "Boys, are you staying?"

"Yeah," they replied in unison.

"Good," Rosa said. "There's plenty to go around."

We gathered around the table—Adriana at one end, me at the other. Enzo and Michael flanked on either side of Antonio. Rosa took the seat next to me. The smell of Adriana's home-cooked meal filled the air. The sound of plates clinking softly as food was passed around the table.

I picked up my fork, tasted the baccalà simmered in tomato sauce, and asked, "So, how was the last day of school?"

"It was great," Michael exclaimed, taking a sip of water. "We finished reading The Odyssey in English, but we have to do a book report on it and turn it in after summer break. I've almost finished mine."

Enzo leaned forward, his fork dangling between his fingers as he squinted at the back of Michael's head. "You almost done?"

Michael twisted around just enough to give him a look. "Yeah. I took notes while we were reading."

Enzo groaned, rolling his eyes before stabbing a roasted potato off his plate. "Figures. Meanwhile, Mrs. Wheeler told me I'll be pumping gas the rest of my life if I don't start caring about literature. Honestly? I'd take that over scribbling notes on *The Odyssey* and writing some stupid book report over summer break." He popped the potato into his mouth, shaking his head. "Besides, how's she even gonna know? We're not even going to the same school next year."

Antonio smirked as he forked up a bite of salad. That small smile, that tiny break in the tension wrapped tight around his shoulders, was everything.

"Pumping gas, huh?" I asked, grinning over the rim of my wine glass. "She actually said that to you?"

Enzo bobbed his head, deadpan. "Apparently, it's a crime not to understand something written a thousand years ago."

"Well," I said, tipping my glass toward him, "I won't allow it. Nobody at this table is pumping gas for a living." A grin tugged at my mouth as I went on, "Besides, The *Odyssey*'s just about a guy trying to get home. One way or another, that's all of us, isn't it? Just gotta survive the monsters along the way."

"Antonio, have you started your book report yet?" Adriana asked, her gaze bouncing toward him.

Antonio flicked his head toward her and gave a small shake. "I'll start soon, Ma." She smiled softly at him before spearing a bite of salad.

Rosa's eyes bounced between the boys. "And what are you three planning for the summer? Besides that book report, of course."

Antonio shrugged, keeping his gaze fixed on his plate as he stabbed his fork into a potato.

Enzo leaned back in his chair, stretching a hand to rake through his shaggy brown hair. "Don't worry, I'll keep Antonio busy. And we'll make sure Michael does something other than bury himself in extra credit." Michael shot Enzo a scowl, which only made Enzo smirk before he leaned forward and scooped another bite of baccalà.

"What about baseball? You boys should be practicing over the summer," I said, my fork swinging in the air between them. "So, you can win it all this season. You'd make me real proud if you did."

"You know Enzo got moved to second base," Michael announced with a smirk. Antonio snorted into his plate.

Enzo's mouth fell open. "It's because I'm quick on my feet."

"More like you couldn't throw to first if your life depended on it," Michael shot back, nudging Antonio's ribs with his elbow. Antonio chuckled, trying to hide it behind his water glass.

"Yeah, whatever, you weird brainiac," Enzo muttered, his nose flaring.

My eyes drifted from the boys to Adriana across the table.

Her smile was wide, her eyes lit up, and I felt my own lips curving to match hers. The world outside might be sharpening its knives. My name might already be passing in hushed tones. Vincent's blood wasn't even dry.

But this was sacred.

Antonio was laughing again. The boys were teasing each other like the kids they still had a right to be. I would protect this with everything I had.

Adriana and Antonio weren't just my second chance. They were my *only* chance. And God help anyone who tries to take it from me.

Chapter Seven

Antonio

I stood in the driveway, watching Michael and Enzo head down the sidewalk toward their houses, just a few steps from ours. Night had already settled in, painting the sky a dull gray as the streetlamps flickered on one by one. Enzo turned, cupping his hands around his mouth. "I'm coming over in the morning!" I nodded with a smile. Michael disappeared inside his front door, and Enzo was halfway to his when I heard our own door creak open behind me.

Joey stepped out, keys dangling from his fingertips. He tilted his head toward the black Ferrari parked over my shoulder, a lopsided grin tugging at his lips. "Come take a ride with your old man, kid."

His hand slid across my back, up into my hair, giving it a playful shimmy. I laughed and shoved at his chest. "Hey! Don't mess up my hair!"

"Excuse me," he chuckled, "you're too old for that, aren't ya? How could I forget?"

I smirked and shrugged; his arm still draped around my shoulders as we walked toward the car. He opened the driver's side door and slid in, dropping the hood before starting the engine. I climbed into the passenger seat and buckled up. "Where are we going?" I asked.

"Just for a little ride," he said with that easy smile he always flashes. "Maybe stop at Pat's for some gelato. What do you say?"

Nobody could bake Italian goods like Pat. I nodded eagerly. Joey smirked, one hand hanging out the window, the other gripping the wheel. He pressed his back against the cream seats, relaxed. When I looked at him, I still couldn't believe what I'd done to him, and that somehow, he'd chosen to look past it.

Lou Monte's, *I Know How You Feel* played low on the radio. Joey whistled along, his fingers tapping the wheel. Sometimes I think he wanted to sing, but maybe he held back because it didn't quite fit the 'mafia boss' image. The summer breeze swept through the car, ruffling my hair. We passed Rosa's old flower shop, which had been sold to Lucy. She was turning it into a beauty salon, Michael had told me. Said it was her lifelong dream, and anyone who knew Lucy knew that wasn't far-fetched.

The teal storefront sat before us as Joey shifted the car into park. *Pat's Bakery* curved in black cursive letters across the awning. An *Open* sign glowed faintly in the glass door. Through the wide windows, I caught glimpses of the black-and-white checkerboard floors. A pastel pink fridge in the corner stocked with Borden's milk—ma's favorite. A cream-colored china cabinet stood near the front, lined with tiny porcelain espresso cups and saucers. Two high-top tables flanked one wall. One occupied by an elderly couple, the other by a middle-aged pair with a squirming child.

Like most in this town, Pat had come over from Italy in the early 1900s. Now in her early sixties, she wore her black pixie cut like a crown and was notorious for mixing Jim Beam into her espresso.

Joey and I stepped inside. The couples looked up, their gazes snagging on him. Normally, their faces would brighten with easy smiles, as though Joey were some celebrity gracing them with his presence. Tonight, their eyes flickered with something else. Fear. Their smiles felt forced, stiff, and they turned back to their plates as quickly as they could. Joey strode past them with that same bright grin plastered across his face. Maybe he didn't notice. Or maybe I was the only one who did.

Behind the counter, Pat perched on a stool, one leg crossed, a spiked espresso in hand, and *La Gazzetta Dello Sport* spread open on her lap. The display case between us was stacked with temptations: golden sfogliatelle dusted with powdered sugar, flaky cornetti oozing apricot jam, biscotti lined neatly in rows, and fat cannoli shells piped with sweet ricotta and chocolate chips. A tray of fresh zeppole glistened with sugar crystals, and a pan of tiramisu sat chilled in the corner.

The air was thick with warmth and sweetness—coffee beans freshly ground, yeast from the morning's dough, citrus zest lingering from lemon cookies cooling in the back. My mouth watered just standing there. Pat's face lit up when she spotted us. She set her magazine aside and stood, smoothing over her apron that had lemons scattered across it. Joey leaned forward on the counter, his forearm resting on the granite, palm tapping it with practiced charm. "Well, hello there. If I'd known royalty were coming to my bakery, I'd have rolled out the red carpet," she cooed.

I smirked, sliding along the glass, my eyes roaming over the rows of pastries. Joey's deep laugh rolled through the bakery, but in the corner of my eye, I caught the younger couple quietly gathering their child and slipping out the door, whispering between themselves. My brows furrowed.

"What can I do for you?" Pat asked.

"Would you happen to have two cold Sanpellegrinos?" Joey said.

Pat nodded. "I do. Anything else?"

"Yeah," Joey hummed, straightening to his full height. "We'll take some gelato too. Caffè for me, and I'm sure—" His arm slipped around my shoulders, pulling me into his side. I smiled at Pat. "—cioccolato for my son."

Pat began scooping; the sound of the metal scraping the chilled pan filled the quiet. "Would this happen to be for the end-of-school-year celebration?" She asked over her shoulder.

"Yeah," Joey said, his arm still draped over my shoulders, just as the older couple slipped out of the bakery. The bell above the door jingled, and their footsteps faded into the night.

Pat turned, placing two frosty bottles of Sanpellegrino and a cup each of gelato on the counter. Joey pulled out his wallet, a picture of Ma flashing for a split second before he flipped past it. He slapped a twenty on the counter. Pat tilted her head, eyes narrowing as she leaned against the register. "Now, Joey, you know that's too much."

"Did you say it's not enough?" His brows rose as he slapped another twenty down.

Pat sighed through her nose, taking the bills and tucking them into the till. "You know, I wanted to ask you about what happened to Vi—"

Joey's smile vanished, his head shaking in rapid succession. His eyes turned cold, and the bakery seemed to drop in temperature. Pat faltered, her brows pinching, lips parting slightly. Her gaze flickered to me, and she pasted on a small smile, nodding. Joey forced a grin of his own and guided me toward the door, his hand at my back.

Back in the car, I held the gelato while Joey pulled onto the road. Half a mile later, he swung into the parking lot of *Luxury*

Romano Wholesale, stopping right at the front door. The lot gleamed under the streetlights—Cadillac Eldorados, Buick Rivieras, sleek Alfa Romeos, a cherry-red Maserati, even a Rolls-Royce Silver Cloud. Joey had no interest in "ordinary" cars anymore. He'd sold off his last middle-class ride weeks ago, replacing it with a collection that screamed wealth and taste. A new sign gleamed above the building, polished gold letters spelling it out: **Luxury Only.**

Despite the whispers of another recession, Joey's mind was set. He didn't think in terms of limits. Even at his poorest, I was sure he carried himself like success wasn't a possibility but a fact waiting to arrive. The universe, for reasons I couldn't always understand, seemed to bend to him. Joey leaned back in his seat, legs spread wide under the wheel, his gelato balanced in one hand. His eyes drifted to the flashy new sign above the showroom.

"You know," he muttered, "I think I'm going to add your name to the will tomorrow morning."

The spoon froze on my tongue. My head snapped toward him, brows knitting tight. Surely, I'd misheard. Joey's gaze flicked to mine, steady and sure, before turning back to the glowing sign. "A Romano needs to take over this place when I'm too old to do it. And the only Romano I want is my son."

Our eyes met again. My throat tightened as I swallowed down the gelato, shoving the spoon back into the paper cup. "How do you feel about that?" he asked.

"I'm surprised you would trust me to take over your empire," I muttered, stunned. "You don't have—"

"You're right." He cut me off, his voice firm. "I don't have to. I want to. Because you're my son. I want you to forget about whatever happened in the past. As Romano men, we don't harp on the past. We live in the present, and we prepare for the future. I have no empire without *you*. You're an extension of *me*."

I nodded slowly, trying to force down the knot in my throat, but it clung stubbornly.

Joey shifted, his fingers wrapped around the back of my neck, his thumb brushing against the edge of my jaw. "Look at me," he commanded. His eyes pinned mine, unblinking. I swallowed hard, lifting my gaze to meet his. "You're my boy. Okay?" I nodded, a single, jerky movement. His face broke into a smile then.

His hand dropped, and our eyes drifted back up to the sign gleaming in the dark. I thought about what life might look like in ten years—me in expensive suits, heavy watches on my wrist, sliding behind the wheel of cars most people only saw in magazines. Running this place with him. A grin tugged at my lips. "So," I said, breaking the quiet, "does that mean I get a luxury car when I'm old enough to drive?"

Joey's eyes flickered toward me, a smile tugging at the corner of his mouth. "You get whatever you want. Name it. It's yours, kid."

"Could I have your Ferrari if I wanted it?" I teased, lifting another scoop of gelato to my mouth.

He let out a low chuckle, shaking his head. "You think I'd let you get behind the wheel of my Ferrari—" his hands brushed the wheel "—before you learn how to keep both hands on the wheel?"

I smirked, glancing down at the almost empty cup of gelato. "So...a Maserati, then?"

His chuckle turned into a full-blown laugh, his hand reaching over to muss my hair. "Smart mouth. Keep it up, and I'll get a Vespa imported in for you instead."

I pushed his hand away, laughing as I smoothed my hair back down, but a curl had sprung free and landed on my forehead. "Come on, ma wouldn't let you put me on a scooter. I'm lucky she lets me ride my bike without a helmet."

"Your mother doesn't get a vote on this one," he said, his tone playful. "But the truth is...you'll never have to ask me twice. If you want it, it's yours. That's how it works in this family. Capisce, kid?"

My jaw ached from how wide I was grinning, "Capisce."

"You know," Joey said, his smile faltering, replaced by something heavier. His fingers drummed against the steering wheel before going still. I frowned, waiting for him to continue. He exhaled slowly, as if he'd been holding it for days. "I want you to hear this from me. Not the neighbors. Not your friends. Not the news. Not the papers. *Me*. Because it's gonna come up. People are gonna talk. And if anyone—*and I mean anyone*—tries to mess with you about it, you come straight to me. Understand?"

My chest tightened. "Okay..." I muttered, though I wasn't sure what I was agreeing to.

Joey's eyes stayed fixed on the windshield. "Vincent was killed today."

The words slammed into me. "What?" My voice cracked, my throat burning. "Killed?" I echoed. "Who would even—" I stopped myself, because the list of who would want Vincent dead was too long.

Joey turned, his eyes locking with mine. Full of desperation to believe him. "It wasn't me. Do you hear me? People will say it was. They always do. They'll point fingers because I'm the scapegoat for half the sins in this town. But I want you to know, I'll clear my name. I'll fix this. Don't let anyone put doubt in your head about me again."

This drive wasn't about gelato. It wasn't about cars. It was about handing me the keys before anyone else could take them from him. He was preparing me for something worse. He was naming me as his heir of the shop, of his dreams, of his legacy. The worst part, the part that curdled in my gut, was knowing it all circled back to me. The longer I sat there, the more the truth hardened like cement in my chest.

"Vincent was a fucking monster," Joey continued, a muscle ticked in his jaw. "He deserved everything he got...and then some. But I want you to hear this from me, straight from me. I love you. You're my son. No one touches you or your mother and gets away with it. So, he's only lucky it wasn't me who got to him first after what he did to you."

No matter what happened, Joey was my father, and I'd protect him at all costs.

Chapter Eight

Adriana
One day after Vincent's murder

Behind the wheel of my cherry-red '59 Chevy Impala, the last notes of *Save the Last Dance for Me* by The Drifters faded into static and then silence. The big V8 purred beneath me, smooth as velvet, while the polished chrome dash gleamed in the late-morning sun. I sat low against the wide bench seat, one gloved hand on the wheel, the other tapping idly on the thin steering column.

The stoplight ahead held me just before *Pat's Bakery*, and the radio announcer's voice crackled back to life: "Breaking news last night—alleged Giordano crime family underboss Vincent 'Lucky' Accetta was gunned down in his Staten Island home. His housekeeper, María Venezuela, discovered the body hours later and alerted police. NYPD's lead investigator, Detective Benjamin Hudson, stated, and I quote, 'If there's a mafia—which we haven't proven—I'd suppose this was related. In all my years on the field, he's been known to stir the pot.'"

My stomach knotted as the announcer continued.

"Meanwhile, an NBC photographer captured an image of reputed capo Joseph 'Joey the Shark' Romano surveying the crime scene. With the two men long rumored to be rivals, speculation now swirls...was it the Shark who finally pulled the trigger? For legal purposes, we can only—"

I slapped the radio off before the man's voice could finish. My pulse twitched in my neck, and I gripped the wheel hard enough to feel the grooves of the leather against my palm.

The light turned green, and I eased the Chevy into Pat's crowded parking lot. The whitewall tires crunching softly over the asphalt. I slid out, smoothed my skirt, and removed my black cat-eyed sunglasses. The sharp tap of my summer heels echoed off the pavement as I walked toward the bakery doors, trying to shake the chill that had settled over me with that broadcast.

I wore a red-and-white polka dot square-neck dress; a slim red belt cinched tight at my waist so the skirt could flare out toward my knees. The shoulders were wide and cut off, leaving my arms bare, and white lace gloves trimmed neatly at my wrists. On my arm hung the Louis Vuitton Speedy 25 Joey had given me as a wedding gift, one of many, but the only one I truly adored.

The glass door to *Pat's Bakery* jingled with its hanging sign as I stepped inside. I smiled at the sight of Pat behind the counter, an espresso cup poised at her lips. The shop was packed, the line nearly spilling out the door, and I found myself behind three others. Every head turned at once to look at me. I offered my brightest smile in return. But no one smiled back. Instead, they twisted forward again, murmured their orders, paid, and hurried out.

When it was my turn, Pat's warm voice rang out, thick with her accent. "Adriana! You're a dream in that dress, my God!"

I smoothed a hand over the fabric, my cheeks warming at the compliment. "Thank you."

"Did Joey praise you when he saw you in it?" she teased, arching a brow.

I laughed softly, waving her off. "No. He was out the door before I'd even finished dressing."

Pat shook her head with a sigh. "Then I suspect he'll lose his mind when he comes home. What can I get you this morning?"

"Three cannolis, please."

She fetched a small white box, filled it, and set it in front of me. I opened my wallet, but she pressed her palms to the counter. "On the house. Joey and Antonio came by last night, and he overpaid me three times what I asked."

"Oh, I couldn't—"

She slid the box closer. "Have a great day, Adriana."

I smiled, nodding as I gathered the package and spun on my heels. Behind me stood Cynthia from the diner, who always carried a kind word or a wave for me. Today her gaze slid past me, eyes fastening on Pat instead. Not even a flicker of acknowledgment.

The frown touched my lips before I cast my eyes down and hurried out, the furious click of my heels echoing against the pavement. I slipped back into the Impala, set the box on the seat beside me, and gripped the wheel.

This was all because of Joey. Or what they thought was Joey.

* * *

I parked in front of what had once been Rosa's flower shop, *La Rosa d'Italia*. Joey had coaxed her into selling it to Lucy so she could move in with us. Rosa never would see a doctor, but each day it became harder to ignore her slipping mind. Joey, blind with love for the only mother he'd ever known, refused to call it what it was: senility.

Lucy's pride and joy, a bubblegum-pink 1960 Chrysler 300F Convertible, gleamed beside me in the sun. Angela teased her by calling it a "banker's hot rod," but Lucy adored the car. Next to it sat Angela's sleek and serious in black, the hardtop twin to Lucy's droptop. I slipped out of the Impala, balancing my purse and the white box of cannoli, and pushed through the front door.

The shop no longer smelled of roses. A faint trace of soil and old stems lingered, but it was buried under the stench of hair dye and chemical cleaners. Half the space had been stripped to its bones, drywall raw and spotted where wallpaper once clung. The other half was slowly being reborn, crowded with salon chairs still wrapped in crinkling pink plastic, their chrome arms catching the light that came through from the windows. A row of mirrors leaned against one wall, waiting to be hung.

In the far corner, a lone hair-dryer chair sat tilted on uneven legs, abandoned mid-assembly, as though someone had gotten halfway through and thrown up their hands. Knowing Lucy, that was exactly what had happened, her patience never outlasted her ambition. She loved to command, but hated to follow instructions.

"Who's there?" Lucy's voice floated from the back.

"Me!" I called back.

"Oh, Adriana! We're back here! Just watch your step!" Lucy's voice rang out.

I dropped my gaze, careful where I placed my feet. The floor looked like a battlefield—paint cans streaked with dried drips, a hammer abandoned in the middle of the walkway, torn rolls of wallpaper, an overturned stool, and a tangle of electrical cords snaking across the room. I picked my way through the chaos until I reached the far back, where Lucy had buried herself in the utility closet.

Angela was perched atop a black milk crate. She wore a skintight leopard-print dress with a heart-shaped cutout bearing the swell of her chest, a Lucky Strike poised between her fingers, and a white paper cup of black coffee balanced in the other. An empty flowerpot sat beside her, doubling as an ashtray. She drew in a breath of smoke and exhaled with a smirk. "You're precious in that dress, Adriana," she purred, lashes so long they nearly brushed her brows.

I smiled at the compliment.

"Oh! Wait! I'm almost done! I want to see the dress!" Lucy's voice floated out from inside the closet.

Angela rolled her eyes. "Well, I don't think she's about to strip butt-naked for us before you come out of there."

I laughed under my breath at Angela's dry humor. "I brought cannoli's from Pat's," I said loud enough for Lucy to hear.

Angela stubbed out her cigarette in the flowerpot and groaned. "Bless you, Adriana. I didn't eat breakfast on purpose, thought maybe Lucy would offer something when she begged me to come help. Should've known she was on another one of her diets."

"Because you're a giant!" Lucy's muffled voice shot back. "I don't want a man in here helping me. This is for us! They've pissed on every building in this neighborhood, claimed it all, but this one is ours!"

Angela and I traded glances, biting back our laughter as the sound of something toppling over clattered from inside the closet. A moment later, Lucy emerged in an orange-and-pink floral minidress, white thigh-high boots, and a random paintbrush clutched in one hand. Her cheeks were flushed from the effort, strands of hair clinging to her forehead.

"And I'm redecorating, not running a bakery," she sniffed, though her paintbrush gestured toward the counter by the cash register. "If either of you wants more lukewarm coffee, help yourselves."

Angela rose from the crate, towering as always in her impossibly high heels. Lucy was right, her height could make even a man shrink. She gave a dramatic sigh. "To think, I always thought you were the classy one of the three of us. I'll take one of Pat's cannolis, though. Even if eating it with lukewarm coffee should be a crime."

Lucy grumbled as she brushed past us, leading the way down the narrow hallway to the counter where the old cash register sat. A French press half-filled with coffee waited there, along with a stack of flimsy plastic to-go cups. I set the white bakery box beside it, and Lucy poured herself a cup, Angela grabbed a cannoli, and I reached for another.

Lucy held the French press up toward me. "Adriana?"

I shook my head, a hand covering my mouth as I took my first bite. "Oh no, thank you."

"Oh, don't listen to Angela," Lucy insisted. "It's not *that* bad. I'm drinking it." She winced mid-sip, proving herself a liar.

I lifted my brows. "That wince is all the answer I need."

Lucy huffed, one hand propped on her hip. "Goodness, what's Joey turning you into?"

"Turned her into the classy one," Angela said through a mouthful of pastry before chasing it with a sip of the cold coffee.

Lucy waved her off. "So...on a scale of one to full-blown funeral, how bad is it out there? I woke up and decided to hide in here before I could hear the accusations and allegations from everyone."

Angela clapped her hands free of powdered sugar, leaning on the counter across from Lucy. "You mean the fact that

Vincent got gunned down in his own house? In broad daylight? And everyone's already alleging it was Joey because he was the only one spotted at the scene?"

Lucy blinked at Angela's bluntness. "Yeah, *that*, Angela."

"Jesus," Angela muttered, shaking her head. "I nearly dropped my ashtray when Marco came barging into my place with the news."

I took another bite of cannoli before speaking. "When I walked into Pat's, it felt as though I were the biggest attraction at the zoo. Cynthia wouldn't even look me in the eye. If I'd wanted to embarrass myself further, I would've ordered an espresso just to spill it on her."

Lucy snorted, shaking her head. "You've been hanging around Angela too much with that comment."

"If by that you mean she's become bold enough to wear her best dress and walk through this town with her head held high, despite what people say about her or Joey...then yes," Angela said, smirking my way.

I mirrored her expression.

Angela stood up again, her palms pressed into the counter-top. "Because for a second, even I thought Joey might've done it. The way he hated Vincent. But not enough to cross that line. Granted, Vincent was a snake in the grass, sure, but I never thought anyone would actually kill the man. Much less, jump ship and get away with it." She shrugged. "Then again, anything's possible in this town."

"Not to speak ill of the recently deceased," Lucy added, "but Vincent was bound to get his number called. The man-made enemies as if it were some hobby. Unfortunately, I'm just a woman, so my opinion never matters in these situations, but I told my father to keep an eye on Vincent *years* ago. I always had a gut feeling about him, but you know—" she huffed, mumbling into her coffee, "—nobody cares about a woman's gut intuition."

"You're just not loud enough," Angela said to Lucy. "Nonetheless, this was a bold move. And now we've got a killer on the loose. So naturally, it's all anyone is going to be talking about for who knows how long. It's not that surprising, considering the streets are full of paid hitmen."

"These men do nothing besides kill each other. The only reason this is shocking is because of who he was," Lucy said, sighing. "The man had it coming. I mean, who walks around calling themselves 'Lucky' because they've managed not to be assassinated yet? He nicknamed himself Lucky, for crying out loud. I'm telling you one thing, only a man has an ego big enough to do something like that."

"Perhaps *you've* been hanging around me too long," Angela smirked, leaning her body back against the countertop. "For a second, I thought I was the one making that speech."

I nodded. I was sure this had to do with either Hector or Ben. "Angela's right, when did you become so defiant against men?"

"Since I had to be surrounded by them and finally see them for who they actually are," Lucy said. Angela and I exchanged a glance. "Idiots!" she declared.

"Speaking of killers, do you need me to kill a man for you? Because I don't mind," Angela said in a teasing tone. Lucy bit back her grin as she rolled her eyes.

"Not yet, you little psycho," Lucy purred. "I've made up my mind, I'm going to focus on turning this into the place of my dreams. This and Michael, the only man in my life. Well, he's not a man yet. Even if he were, he'd still be *my* baby. You know, I walked into his bedroom this morning, and I noticed he had a beard growing over his top lip. Hector's such an idiot, he doesn't even tell him how to shave it. Good thing he's going to my father's, so I asked him to talk to him about it."

"That's nothing," Angela waved her off. "You should see

Enzo. I'm half convinced he's part-werewolf with the amount of hair growing on his chest. But then I remember he's my son, so—" Her voice trailed off.

Lucy walked past us, navigating the landmine that was the beauty salon. She spun in a circle, gesturing dramatically at the space. "I've got three names, and I need you two to come to an agreement because I'm far too indecisive to choose between them," she said, holding up one manicured French-tip nail. "Cosa Bella," she rolled her tongue, then lifted her second finger. "The Powder Room," she added, raising the next finger, "or Lucy's Boudoir?" Her hand dropped to her side. "I need signage. The window painter is coming next week—the same guy Joey used for the wholesale remodel. I want something as luxurious as that sign he has hanging at the shop."

"Cosa Bella is elegant. It fits you," I said softly.

"Thank you!" Lucy threw her hands in the air. "Adriana, you're such a help!"

"Oh, I'm sorry," Angela stood up, her hand over her nearly exposed chest. "You called me over here to help and won't let me do anything. You serve me cold coffee and give me a flowerpot to drop my ashes in, and now you're asking me to help name your beauty shop while we're sitting here talking about a murder and men who are clearly involved in it. Excuse me for not being sharp on my feet."

Lucy rolled her eyes, sighing before plopping down on the bench near the door. "You know..." Her body leaned forward, elbows digging into her thighs as her face fell into her palms. "Hector asked me if Ben killed Vincent. We had a huge fight over it." She sat back, her shoulders slumped. "But he didn't, because I was with him in his apartment. That's why I was late picking out dresses yesterday."

She shook her head, letting it fall against the wall, eyes drifting up toward the ceiling. "He had to go back to Boston, where his wife is, and we fought over it. I stormed out, met up with you two, and then, hours later, he's outside my house begging for forgiveness. You'll be pleased to know I told him to fuck off."

Angela's eyebrows shot up, her head jerking in surprise. Lucy's eyes met ours, the usual carefree sparkle replaced by a quiet sadness. Angela moved over and took the other half of the bench, and as soon as she sat down, one of the legs creaked ominously, like it might give way.

"Oh my God, this is vintage Angela! Both of us can't sit on this thing," Lucy laughed. Angela helped Lucy up, slipping an arm around her shoulders. I stepped closer, wrapping a hand around her small frame.

"Cosa Bella," Angela muttered. "You should name it Cosa Bella. Adriana's right, it's elegant and fits you."

Lucy nodded, forcing a smile, though I could see tears gathering at the edges of her eyes. "Perfect. Thank you. I know I said I'm trying to quit smoking, but...I'd really appreciate it if you could pretend I never said that and hand me a cigarette."

Angela dropped her arm from Lucy's shoulders, and I eased mine from her waist. Angela handed over the gold cigarette case, letting Lucy help herself to a cigarette and a lighter. "I'll just go get the flowerpot."

"Christ," Lucy muttered, exhaling smoke into the air. "She's right." Her head turned toward me. "What has it come to? Using a flowerpot as an ashtray?"

"Nobody will see this moment besides Angela and me," I said with a smile. She returned with the flowerpot and set it on the countertop.

"You know," Lucy said, glancing toward the door, "maybe I should put up a 'No Men Allowed' sign." Angela and I laughed, and Lucy spun around, joining in.

"Perhaps you should have put it up sooner," Angela

muttered, her eyes flicking past Lucy to the door. Ben stood there in full NYPD uniform, his hand gripping the door, eyes taking us all in before he pushed it open and stepped inside.

"Good morning, ladies," he said with a smile, shoving his hands into his pockets.

"I'm calling the police if you don't leave," Lucy shot back.

"I don't think that's going to go in your favor," Angela replied with a smirk. "I'm afraid they're already in the building."

Lucy sighed, rolling her eyes, and planted herself between Angela and me with one arm wrapped across her chest, the other holding a cigarette up to her mouth. "What do you want?"

"I was hoping I could speak with you in the back," Ben said, his tone pleading.

"Adriana and I were just leaving," Angela announced, locking eyes with me. I grabbed my purse, following her lead.

"No," Lucy exclaimed. "*He* was just leaving. There are *no* men allowed in here."

Ben smiled as Angela and I passed, but Angela met his height, brushing his shoulder, forcing him to step aside. She gave him a dangerous look before following me outside.

"Princess, you know—" Ben started as I held the door open for Angela.

"Don't you *fucking* princess me," Lucy spat, the door slamming behind us.

Angela and I hugged, standing there for a moment, taking in the scene behind us. Lucy's flailing arm, Ben's apologetic eyes, the screech of her voice, and the lingering hint of his Boston accent begging for forgiveness.

Chapter Nine

Antonio
One day after Vincent's murder

I was bent over my vanity, smearing Brylcreem into my curls and smoothing them back with a comb and my palm, when I heard the front door slam, footsteps across the floor, and then what sounded like a herd of elephants charging up the staircase. When my bedroom door swung open, it was Enzo, with Michael peering over his shoulder.

I dropped the comb onto the vanity and straightened up. They barreled in like they owned the place—Enzo tossing himself onto my bed, propping his head up on one hand, while Michael slid into the chair by the record player and shut the door behind him.

"Ever heard of knocking?" I asked, pressing my back against the vanity.

Michael shrugged. "It was him," he said, pointing at Enzo.

Enzo shot him a look over his shoulder before turning back to me. "Actually, Rosa was in the yard near mine. Sal told me to bring her home, said she'd wandered too far and he was worried. Which, by the way, was *not* easy. She insisted on picking dandelions the whole way."

I smirked. "She's just trying to eavesdrop on Sal's conversations."

Enzo deepened his voice into a gruff dad impression. "That's no way to talk about your grandmother, young man. She's nearly senile."

I snickered, and Michael joined in. "She's not senile, she's conning you. She's a little crazy and a lot nosy, always trying to get the inside scoop straight from the source."

"Well, Sal's dumb enough to serve it up on a silver platter," Enzo muttered. That set Michael and me laughing again.

"But that's not why I came over," Enzo continued, sitting up now. "I might've pulled a Rosa myself. I heard Val whisper-shouting at Sal, asking if he killed Vincent for Joey. At first I thought, no way I heard that right. But I listened harder, and I didn't hear wrong." He leaned forward, his forearms pressing into his thighs. "So what the fuck is going on? Nobody in my house will tell me anything. And if I try, they practically serve my head on a platter for Rosa."

I had to collect myself before answering, which wasn't easy, not with something this serious.

"My mom told me this morning," Michael cut in. Enzo snapped his attention to him. "She was vague," Michael went on, brushing a fingertip over the faint mustache on his lip. "More worried about this than anything else." He slicked the few hairs down over his upper lip. "But she said it can't be anyone we know. I don't know, I only half listened."

"Hmmph," Enzo blew out. "I live with two PMSing women who joke about killing men in their free time. Mom says I'm the exception, of course. While Val disagrees. So nobody tells me anything. Which brings me to this..." His eyes locked on mine. "Did Joey kill Vincent?"

"No," I said, folding my arms across my chest. "He was here with me."

"Well, excuse me for getting suspicious. I saw him arguing with Paul and thought maybe it was about Vincent."

"You know," Michael said with a shrug, "now that Enzo mentions it, it does kinda look like he did it."

"Especially after everything Vincent did to you," Enzo added.

"Yeah," I admitted, my head dipping, fingers dragging through the freshly dried Brylcreem. "It might look that way. But Joey didn't do it. He was with me when it happened. He told me last night he knows people will accuse him, and clearly —" I huffed, gesturing at the two of them. "But he's going to clear his name. Prove he didn't do it. Which is fucked up, because he's only in this position because of me."

"Because of you?" Enzo choked out, his bushy eyebrows climbing.

I shot him a glare, arms tightening across my chest.

"Alright," Michael cut in, springing up from the chair. "My mom quit smoking, so she tossed these babies out—" He whipped a fresh pack of Lucky Strikes from his back pocket and waved them like treasure. Enzo's jaw dropped. He shot off the bed, rushing to Michael's side as Michael laughed. "Let's go enjoy the first day of summer," Michael declared.

Enzo slung an arm around his shoulders, grinning ear to ear. "Man, the women in your house are way better than the ones I live with. Do you know how hard I work—like actual sleuthing levels—just to secure a pack of Luckies for us? And yours just throws them in the trash?"

Michael snickered, and I couldn't help but laugh too.

* * *

We'd managed to convince Rosa we were headed to the park to practice baseball. When she asked why not just use the backyard, Enzo told her he needed the walk and said he was putting on too much weight. Which wasn't unbelievable, considering he was wheezing by the time we reached the end of the street.

"It's probably from all the cigarettes you keep stealing," I teased.

"No, it isn't," he huffed, slinging an arm onto my shoulder for support and dragging his feet. "You're supposed to be on my side, by the way." I snickered.

"He's right," Michael said. "It's not the Luckies. It's all the junk you eat." I burst out laughing as Enzo snapped upright, glaring at Michael's smirking side profile.

When we passed the park sign, we climbed midway up the bleachers and settled in. I ended up sandwiched between Michael and Enzo. Michael lit his first, took a drag, then flicked the lighter toward me. I sparked mine, inhaled, and passed the lighter to Enzo. A moment later, all three of us were leaning back with cigarettes in hand, smoke curling up into the summer air.

"This is the life," Enzo declared, leaning back on his elbows, balancing them on the bleacher row behind us with the cigarette dangling from his lips.

I hunched forward, my elbows digging into the skin above my thighs, the cigarette loose between my fingers as I stared down at my loafers.

"Hey." The soft coo pulled all our heads up at once. Even Enzo sat upright. Mia Garcia stood at the base of the bleachers, swaying side to side with her hands clasped behind her back. Behind her was her twin, Maria, and beside Maria was their best friend Alessia, who happened to be Paul's daughter.

"Hello," Enzo rumbled from over my shoulder. I forced a smile and gave a weak little wave with the hand holding my cigarette.

"Would you mind if we joined?" Mia asked.

"We're smoking," I said, lifting the cigarette like proof.

Enzo smacked the back of my head. I spun toward him as he muttered something I couldn't make out. "Don't listen to him. He's not as misogynistic as he sounds." I shot him a glare. "You can join us," Enzo went on, "Michael's got more cigarettes if you want one." Michael's glare cut into him this time.

"Sure," Mia chirped, climbing into the row across from me. Maria sat across from Enzo, Alessia across from Michael. Michael offered them the pack, but only Mia took one.

Alessia had climbed up beside Michael, whispering to him about the summer book assignment, the one I'd barely started. Enzo was laying it on thick with Maria, who gave him big puppy-dog eyes and soaked up every compliment. I had to bite down on my lip to keep from laughing.

"Do you want to go for a walk?" Mia asked.

My eyes met hers. Part of me wanted to say no, but guilt tugged too hard within. "Sure," I said, pushing myself off the bleachers. Michael and Enzo both glanced up. "We'll be back," I told them. Michael turned back to Alessia, and Enzo raised his brows, tilting his head with a smug smile. I bit back my own and shook my head.

Mia and I stepped down from the bleachers onto the paved path looping around the park. Boys tossed baseballs across the grass, little girls shrieked on the playground, and a few older women marched by on their morning powerwalks.

We walked in silence. My head stayed dipped, eyes on my loafers, until I scratched the back of my neck and forced myself to look at her. "I don't think Giovanni would be happy seeing you take a walk with me right now."

She smiled, her eyes forward on the path ahead. "Probably not. But he's not my boyfriend."

"Does he know that?"

Her head turned, breaking into a wide smile that pulled one out of me, too. "I don't think so," she hummed.

"What are your plans for the summer, besides this stupid book report?" I asked, glancing between her and the path. She wore a sleeveless white cotton blouse with tiny embroidered flowers at the collar, pastel pink high-waisted capris, and scuffed white Keds. Her thick dark hair was pulled into a high ponytail, tied with a red ribbon bow, baby hairs curling along her forehead.

She shrugged, toying with the hem of her blouse. "Hopefully, walking in the park with you."

I smiled, my eyes lingering on her warm, golden-brown complexion glowing in the sun. "And why would you want to do that?"

Her eyes dropped, a shy smile tugging at her lips. "Maybe so I can get to know who you are outside of school, and away from Giovanni."

"And then when we go back to school, you'll pretend I don't exist?"

Her gaze lifted, meeting mine. "No, *you'll* pretend I don't exist."

I let out a soft chuckle. "What are you talking about? I don't do that."

"Yes, you do," she said, nodding.

"You sure about that?" I asked, a smirk riding on my lips as I shoved my hands into my pockets. "Maybe you just don't notice when I *am* paying attention."

Her soft laugh spilled into the space between us, making my chest feel a little mushy. She folded her arms across her chest, her hip jutting to the side as she tilted her head at me. "Oh, so you're secretly obsessed with me? That's good to know."

"I do recall fighting Giovanni last year over that school

dance you didn't even follow through with after you asked me to take you," I said, kicking at a rock on the pavement.

The smile slipped from her face. She slowed her steps, her gaze dropping to the path. "I didn't want to be the cause of any more problems between you two."

I ran a hand through my hair, shaking my head. "You have nothing to do with Giovanni and me. That's a lifelong hatred that will never go away."

Her eyes flicked to mine, again. She brushed a strand of hair off her cheek, fingers lingering near the ribbon in her ponytail. "Why do you two hate each other so much?"

I shrugged, rolling my shoulders and glancing away toward the baseball field. "He's jealous of me, and I hate his attitude." My jaw tightened, and I shoved my hands deeper into my pockets.

"So...you're saying Giovanni's the only reason you didn't ask me out last year?" Mia smirked, glancing at me sideways.

I wet my lips with my tongue and returned her smirk. "Part of it, yeah."

"I would have asked you, but I didn't want you to think I was...messing anything up for you."

I stopped walking and turned to face her, my eyebrow raised. "Messing things up for me? I don't think that's possible. You shouldn't think that way."

Her smile softened, head dipping slightly, before her dark eyes met mine again. "Really?"

I squinted at her, smirking as I pretended to study her. "You know what I think? You've got that look in your eye," I said, letting my gaze linger. "That look that says trouble's coming. Maybe I got a little nervous by it."

She shook her head, smiling. "That's what you look like."

"Me?" I pressed my fingers to my chest. She nodded. "I'm not trouble."

"I think you will be someday," she mumbled, her voice soft.

"Why do you say that?"

Her eyes locked on mine. "Because you're really cute, and it's always the cute guys who end up breaking the most hearts and causing the most trouble."

I tilted my chin up, smirking. "You know, I think I'm going to clear my whole schedule for these walks with you."

She giggled softly, pressing her hand into my arm. "You see what I mean," she teased. "Does that mean you'll start talking to me inside *and* outside of school?"

"I already am talking to you outside of school," I said, "and if I have to knock Giovanni out again to talk to you when it starts back, I will."

We looped back around to where Michael, Enzo, Alessia, and Maria were waiting at the end of the bleachers. "We were talking about meeting up for a movie tomorrow night," Enzo said, pointing a finger at Mia and me. "You two in?"

"Yeah, sure," I said, smiling at Mia. She returned the smile before walking over to Maria and Alessia. The three waved goodbye as they headed the other way, and we retraced our steps past the park and toward Davidson's. We paused at the sidewalk, waiting for traffic to clear before sprinting across.

A baby-blue 1960 Ford Thunderbird Convertible rolled up beside us, coming to a smooth stop. Sal had the top down, some doo-wop blaring from the speakers before he turned it off. He wore a short-sleeve silk shirt with stripes running down it, cream slacks, and one hand on the steering wheel, showing off his flashy silver watch. Aviators covered his eyes, and with the other hand, he let out a whistle, thumb and pointer finger framing his mouth. "If you're looking for trouble, you came to the right place," he sang in his best Elvis accent. "If you're looking for trouble, just look dead in these kids' faces."

The three of us grinned wide, letting his showmanship wash over us.

"What do we have here? A bunch of rascals walking in my territory?" Sal teased.

"You don't have any territory," Enzo folded his arms over his chest, smirking. "You're not cool enough to claim one."

"Not cool enough?" Sal repeated in mock shock. "I may not be as cool as you three, but I *do* offer rides...if anyone's brave enough to jump in."

"Oh, I'm brave enough," Enzo huffed, though it was probably just because he didn't feel like walking the distance back home.

"You know my mom says I'm not allowed to take rides with weird men who impersonate the King of Rock 'n' Roll," Michael teased as Enzo hopped into the front seat and Michael and I climbed in the back.

Sal's booming laugh rang out as he merged onto the street. "That's a damn good impersonation, and you *know* it," he said, glancing at Michael over his shoulder.

"You better be careful with that corny stuff," Enzo pretended to be serious as he glanced over at Sal. "Or you'll lose your street cred before the week even starts."

Sal feigned offense. "I've got plenty of street cred, thank you very much!" he said, fluffing up Enzo's shaggy hair. Enzo ducked his head down, laughing. "Alright, you little filthy-mouthed rascals," Sal said in a fake broadcast announcer voice, slamming his foot on the gas. "This Thunderbird waits for no one!"

The car shot forward, wind whipping through our hair. I let my head fall back, eyes tracing the bright blue sky, and laughter flowing freely from my throat, the roar of the engine mixing perfectly.

Chapter Ten

Joey
One day after Vincent's murder

I shoved open the heavy double doors of *The Wise Guy*. The place was packed wall-to-wall, bodies pressed in tighter than the room was ever meant to hold, but the laughter and the haze of cigarette smoke made it clear nobody minded.

I paused at the bar before heading toward the booth where Paul and Ben sat. Leaning forward on the counter, I drummed my fingers against the top, my arms stretched out as I craned my head back, watching Angela work. She moved quick, her smile never leaving her face as she poured drinks and slid them across the bar like it was second nature.

Marco stood across from her. "All I'm saying is cheetah print suits you," he said, flashing that lazy grin of his. "And if you need a victim for the night, I volunteer."

Marco's thick jet-black pompadour was styled to perfection, not a strand out of place. The scent of Tabac Original clung to him—a heady mix of tobacco, spice, musk, and a trace of florals. A tailored charcoal suit, Italian cut, with a deep-red silk pocket square tucked neatly at his chest.

Marco was doing what he did best, chasing a woman who barely looked his way. Angela wiped down a glass without so much as a grin in his direction now. I had to admire the guy's commitment. He was all in when it came to melting her ice-cold heart. No other woman ever stood a chance, and it'd been this way from the very beginning. Though every woman in a 100-mile radius had their hearts set on Marco. He was long taken by Angela.

"Give her a break, huh?" I called from the other side of the bar, smirking.

"Oh, Joey! My saving grace!" Angela said with a dramatic hand over her chest.

"You don't mean that, do ya?" Marco frowned, then turned to me. "She's just playing hard to get in front of everyone. Deep down, she's got a soft spot for me."

"Angela? With a soft spot?" I raised an eyebrow. "Those two words don't belong in the same sentence."

Angela smirked, leaning across the bar so she could torture Marco more by pressing her chest together and nearly shoving it at his face. "That's what I was thinking," she smiled, her eyes bouncing off me to Marco, who had to peel his eyes off her chest. "You should be more careful, because one more cheesy line and I'll have to start charging *you* for entertainment."

His lips tugged into a half-smile, dark eyes locked on hers, though I knew the fight to keep them from drifting south must be difficult for him. "I can provide whatever kind of entertainment you're in the mood for."

I pushed myself off the counter and stepped over to Marco, resting a hand on his shoulder and curling my fingers around it as I pulled him off the counter too. "I've got the deal of a lifetime for you," I said to Angela, who smiled, waiting for me to continue. "You bring me a Manhattan, and I'll get this guy off your hands."

"She doesn't—" Marco started, but Angela cut him off with a nod. "You got it, thanks, Joey!" Marco's eyes widened, lips parting in shock as I tugged him further away from the bar.

"Pull it together," I said, leaning closer to him. "What kind of self-respecting man lets himself get flustered by a pretty woman in a cheetah-print dress who's clearly emotionally unavailable?" Marco and I hadn't moved far, our eyes still locked on Angela as the three of us smiled. She gave a subtle nod of approval at my comment.

"Who said I had any self-respect?" Marco muttered.

I laughed, draping an arm over his shoulders as we headed toward the booth where Ben and Paul were sitting. "Well," I said in a low tone, "get some. Free of charge, because she's got you by the collar, my friend."

"That'd be *exactly* where I want her to grab me, anyway," he smirked as we slid into the booth.

Marco sat across from me, Paul next to him, and Ben across from Paul and beside me in the booth. Marco and I were still trying to get the happy-go-lucky smile off our faces, while Paul and Ben wore serious scowling expressions. "How's it going over here?" I asked, leaning back against the back of the booth.

"Oh, you know," Paul said with a shrug, swirling the whiskey in his glass. "Just drinking away the stress of the past few days, while the one person who should be the *most* stressed of us all,"—he gestured toward my chest—"is walking around laughing and joking like nothing happened."

"It's hardly been twenty-four hours since everything happened—"

"The news has reached California by now," Ben muttered into his drink.

"And it's always the same shit," Paul growled, slamming his glass down. "Joseph 'Joey the Shark' Romano...Joey the Shark Romano," he mimicked in a mock announcer's voice, making

Marco and me grin. "Always at the forefront of all this bullshit. It's just a matter of time before Christopher whips out his butcher knife and starts hacking away."

Angela sauntered over, a Manhattan in each hand, and set them down in front of Marco and me. I smiled up at her, then watched as Marco couldn't seem to tear his eyes away, practically drooling into his glass as he drank in every curve she flaunted so confidently. "Refills?" she asked, tilting her head toward Paul and Ben, a teasing smile tugging at her lips.

"Please," Paul said, handing over his empty glass. Ben followed suit, sliding his glass toward her.

Angela took both glasses, but then her smoldering gaze landed on Ben, who stiffened next to me. I couldn't blame him, that look was cold enough it could freeze fire. "By the way... how's your wife, Ben?" she asked.

Ben dropped his head, looking at his fingers as they toyed with the coaster his drink was once on. Angela wasn't afraid of much, least of all a man. If I'm honest, she had more grit than most of us combined, and she carried herself with a kind of authority that didn't ask for respect, it demanded it. Even Ben knew that. He cleared his throat, forcing his eyes up to meet hers. She hadn't blinked once. "She's...fine," he murmured.

I took a long sip of my Manhattan, already knowing that was the *wrong* answer. There wasn't really a right one, but that was the *worst* he could've picked.

Angela's voice dropped to a hiss. "Be careful, Detective. You break hearts. I poison men. Slowly...or quickly. Depends on the mood I'm in. How many tears get shed. How deep the damage goes."

Ben swallowed, his Adam's apple bobbing in his throat. He knew Angela wasn't bluffing. She didn't operate on empty threats. The four of us watched as she spun on her heels and walked back toward the bar, her heels tapping out her warning with every step. Once she was out of earshot, I finally spoke. "What in the fuck have you done to Lucy?"

Ben looked at me, his mouth opening and closing like he was trying to find the right words. Finally, the words spilled out in one swift sentence. "What...What makes you think *I've* done anything to Lucy?"

I gestured toward the bar, where Angela was pouring refills like she was loading a weapon. Her eyes hadn't left Ben once since she'd gotten behind that bar. "What the hell is she talking about?"

Ben shook his head, stammering. "Lucy's upset with me, that's all. I mean...come on. I'm married. She's married. We knew this wasn't simple. And now, with everything going on after Vincent, she thinks it's smart to leave Hector right in the middle of the storm. I told her I was going back to my wife in Boston, and she needed to stay put with Hector. So...you can imagine how that turned out for me."

"You know," Marco began, holding his Manhattan in one hand and using it to jab toward Ben, an ice cube rattling against his teeth, "all those times she threw a high heel at you? You could probably get it tattooed as a trophy. That's what I'd do." Ben blew Marco off, and Marco shrugged. There was no doubt in my mind that was *exactly* what Marco would do.

"Don't you have any idea how women operate?" I said, running my finger around the rim of the glass, my eyes narrowing on Ben's. "You keep getting shoes thrown at you because it's something *you* keep doing wrong. Now, don't make this worse. The last thing anyone needs is for another woman to be pissed off. If Lucy's upset, Angela's going to be seeking revenge, and I don't imagine my home life will be much better for it either."

"Well, that's easy for you to say," Ben huffed, his brow quirking. "Because you don't know Lucy like I do."

"*Nobody* knows Lucy like you do, Benny Boy," Marco teased, taking another sip of his drink. I fought back a smirk.

"Oh, Adriana goes along with whatever the hell Joey says," Paul chimed in, smacking his lips. "He doesn't know what it's like being with a headstrong woman who won't back down from a fight. She should have fought him tooth and nail when he tried to leave that day, but we all saw his picture in the papers, didn't we?"

"She doesn't just 'go along with whatever the hell I say,'" I shot back, swirling ice around in my glass. "She respects me. I respect her. It's mutual. That's called a healthy marriage, by the way, in case anyone at this table was curious."

Marco snickered like a mischievous kid into his glass, shaking his head as if he couldn't believe my audacity.

Angela reappeared with fresh drinks in each hand. She set them down on the table, her eyes lingering on Ben for a moment before she turned and walked away, leaving the faint scent of perfume and a trace of fury in her wake.

"Switch drinks with me," Ben hissed at Paul, his voice low and laced with urgency.

"What? No way!"

"Come on, man," Ben pressed, his hazel eyes flicking toward the bar where Angela had disappeared to.

Paul rolled his eyes, yanking the glass from Ben's hands. "You know what? Might be a blessing to get poisoned," he muttered, taking a long, exaggerated sip. We all went quiet, watching him like something catastrophic might happen at any second. It didn't.

I pressed farther into the depths of the back of the booth, studying Paul. "Care to share what else is going on with you?"

He sighed, shaking his head, but he told us anyway. "My wife's been on edge for the last twenty-four hours. Paranoid. Jumping to conclusions. I'm lucky she didn't tie me to the bedpost this morning, the way she was arguing with me to stay home."

"Don't count it out yet," Marco said, tilting his head. "By the sound of it, she didn't catch you sleeping in order to pull it off."

"How was Angela when you told her?" I asked Marco.

"Well...I did barge into her house without knocking, so that startled her. Then I told her, and she was shocked. But, you know, nothing gets past that woman," he said, shaking his head with a grin.

My gaze bounced back to Ben. "And Lucy? What'd she say?"

He shrugged, running a hand through his hair. "It's been hard to talk about Vincent, between dodging high heels and verbal lashes, but she said he had it coming. And she wouldn't be wrong."

"I think that's code for your next," Marco said with a sly grin.

My brows knitted together. That didn't settle right in my chest. Lucy, of all people, dramatic as she was, didn't care...that wasn't a typical reaction. The thought crept in before I could stop it. *Could Lucy have done it? Could she have pulled the trigger?*

I imagined it...Lucy standing there with a gun in her manicured hands, facing Vincent as she fired into his skull. Lucy might've been born into this life, a mafia princess through and through, but she didn't have the stomach for that kind of blood. Vincent's blood would've splattered all over her, and there's no universe where Lucy could've handled something like that without screaming, fainting, or ruining her dress and giving herself away.

But maybe that's exactly what happened.

Maybe Lucy gave herself away.

Maybe Ben had to step in, play the hero, and clean up a mess he never saw coming.

Now that I think about it, Ben was the first one to the crime scene.

What if that wasn't a coincidence? What if Ben came to Lucy's call as she was panicked, covered in blood, realizing too late what she'd done? What if he showed up to clean her up, get her out before anyone saw? What if all the tension between them wasn't about their separate marriages? What if it was about what they were hiding? They were notorious for keeping secrets, and this could be one of many they harbored.

* * *

I twisted the front door open and stepped inside. The hum of the evening news filled the house, the flicker of the TV casting pale light across the living room walls. Adriana stood at the threshold between the dining room and the living room, a kitchen towel clenched in her hands. My eyes trailed up the length of her toned calves, the red-and-white dress hugging every line of her frame, up to the cascade of victory curls that framed her face. I couldn't get to her fast enough. She glanced at me, one quick flick of her eyes before turning back to the television.

I slid in behind her, my arms snaking around her waist as I pulled her against me. "You look beautiful, sweetheart," I murmured against the shell of her ear, brushing a kiss to her cheek. She didn't move. Didn't smile. Didn't even acknowledge I had come inside the house. Her eyes stayed locked on the screen. My gaze followed hers. The six o'clock anchor sat behind his desk, a tiny inset box in the corner of the screen showing my face—the one that the NBC reporter had snapped yesterday.

"That's a good-looking guy, don't you think?" I whispered against her ear again. "Go on, you can compliment him. I won't get mad."

Her hands pushed mine off her waist. My frown pulled tight as she crossed the room, grabbed the remote off the coffee table, and turned the volume up.

"Alleged mob boss Vincent 'Lucky' Accetta will be laid to rest in a private ceremony this Saturday morning in his home-town of Staten Island, New York," the news anchor announced. "The funeral will be held at *St. Augustine of the Sacred Heart,* a church he was said to attend on occasion. No arrests have been made in connection with his violent murder, but NYPD Detective Benjamin Hudson assures residents there is no reason to fear as the investigation continues. Sources suspect an inside job, pointing to none other than his former son-in-law, Joey Romano, known to federal agents as 'The Shark' for his alleged loan-sharking operations—"

Adriana flipped the TV off, placed the remote back on the coffee table before she walked past me to the kitchen, but I heard her scuff under her breath, "*Ex* son-in-law? You've got to be kidding me."

My fingers wrapped around her small wrist, both of our heads turning to face the other. I was sure I had a pleading look in my eyes as I said, "You know better than to listen to that garbage, sweetheart."

Her chin tilted up, those deep brown eyes flashing at me. "Garbage or not, Joey, it's your face plastered across the damn screen." She yanked her wrist free, taking a step back, still clutching the dish towel.

"Would it be the first time my face was on the TV screen?" I lifted a hand, gesturing toward the darkened TV screen.

"No," she said, her arms crossing over her chest. "But this

isn't the usual stuff they say about you. This is bad, Joey. And you know it."

I stepped closer, cupping her face in my palms, my gaze locking on hers. "Then here's an idea, don't watch until that idiot on the six o'clock news is done with his nightly circus act." Her eyes darted away for a second, the corner of her mouth twitching like she was fighting back a grin.

I dipped down, brushed her lips with mine, smiling against them. "You heard the man...Detective Hudson's on the case. But we both know the joke's on them, don't we, sweetheart?"

That earned me her smile, the one that undid me every time. Her arms fell to her sides, surrender written all over her. "He called you Vincent's son-in-law."

"Oh, no, no, no," I muttered, shaking my head, my forehead pressed against hers. "That won't do. If they're going to report on Joey Romano, they'd better get it right, shouldn't they?" Her eyes sparkled with mischief as she tugged her bottom lip between her teeth and nodded. "They should know Joey Romano's heart has, and will *always*, belong to one woman. Do you happen to know who she is?"

Her smile widened. "Who?" she murmured.

I chuckled, heat rushing through me as I bent and hooked my arms around the backs of her legs, lifting her clean off the floor. She squealed, laughter spilling from her lips as I tossed her over my shoulder. Every sound stripped away the tension in my chest.

"Joey! Put me down!" she cried between laughs, her hands gripping at my waist.

I carried her to the couch, tossed her down, dropped to my knees, and caged her in with both arms. My voice dropped low, rough against her lips as I leaned in. "What kind of reporter thinks he can upset Joey Romano's wife and get away with it? He should look over his shoulder for that act."

She smiled up at me, her fingers gliding up the back of my neck and head, pulling me closer.

"My heart belongs to you, sweetheart," I whispered against her mouth before kissing her again. My forehead rested against hers, her hands on either side of my neck, her red lipstick completely gone from the bruising kiss we'd just shared.

"You drive me crazy sometimes," she whispered, her lips brushing mine.

"Yeah?" I grinned. "That's exactly how I want you...crazy about me, crazy for me."

She rolled her eyes, though the sparkle in them betrayed her. "Will you promise me something?"

"I'll promise you anything. Name the price, sweetheart."

"Promise me you'll come home," her minty breath fanned my lips as she confessed, "I can't be without you, Joey."

I cupped her face, pressing my lips against her forehead. "Oh, sweetheart...there isn't a force on this earth that could keep me from you."

I was up against more than I could handle with no moves left to play, just bluffing through each day from here until who knew when, hoping the stakes didn't kill me. A bloody war was coming, and clearing my name would be the hardest task I'd ever had to do.

Chapter Eleven

Antonio
Two days after Vincent's murder

I jerked awake in the dark, hand clamped over my pounding chest, sweat soaking the ivory sheets striped in burgundy beneath me. My ears rang like a gun had just gone off at my temple. "No," I rasped, dragging both hands down my face, trying to catch my breath. "It was just a dream."

I reached over, tugging the string of the bedside lamp. A warm glow filled the room, too soft for the chaos inside my mind. I sat up, yanking my damp white ribbed tank top over my head and let it drop to the floor. The sheets clung to my legs, heavy with sweat, so I kicked them off and sat there, my breath stuttering.

From the vanity mirror across the room, my reflection stared back—curls wild, sticking up like I'd shoved my fingers in a wet socket. I pushed my hands through them, but it was useless. None of it mattered until I got my breathing under control anyway.

The dream lingered like smoke. The gun in my hand. Joey's body collapsing against the brick wall of *Davidson's Corner Store*. Blood blooming across the white of his shirt like spilled ink. Ma's scream splitting the night in half. My finger locked around the trigger. I grabbed the pillow behind me, giving it a squeeze as I buried my face in it, and mouthed the only words I had left. "Stop it. Just stop."

I sat there for a long moment, eyes fixed on my reflection, coming to terms with the fact that sleep had abandoned me again. I pushed myself out of bed, rounded the edge of the bed, and plopped down in the office chair.

Might as well get that stupid book report done, I thought. At least if I tackled it now, I wouldn't have to think about it or the nightmare for the rest of the summer. The soft glow of the lamp and the scratch of pen on paper were almost comforting, though my mind kept straying back to the dream, to Joey, to the gun, to everything I couldn't unsee.

Outside my window, I heard a car pulling into Enzo's driveway, the low whisper of doo-wop drifting through the warm night air, and I knew it had to be Sal. I pushed myself out of the chair, leaning over the blinds to watch. Sal stood on Enzo's lawn, his neck craning back to catch the glow of the upstairs window. My eyes followed his, and *God*, the lack of sleep barely registered when I saw Val, her blinds pulled up, her body on full display in a nightgown that hugged every curve— Mid-thigh, blush pink, with a delicate cream lace V-neck tracing her chest. Thin spaghetti straps, lace-trimmed hem that fluttered as she shifted.

"Oh, fuck," I hissed under my breath.

Sal lifted his shirt like an idiot, hoping to coax her into doing the same, but she blew him a kiss instead. He caught it with a hand to his pocket, grinning like a fool. I rolled my eyes at him, but then his lips parted, and I knew *exactly* why. My gaze snapped back to Val. The nightgown was gone. In its place, the sight of her perfect hourglass frame, the swell of her breasts, and pink panties peeking from her hips. Her finger curled, beckoning him closer.

What a lucky idiot.

Damn...this might just be all I need to finally fall back asleep.

Best. Damn. Dream. Ever.

* * *

I stood in front of my bedroom vanity, checking the last few touches of my slicked-back hair. My short-sleeve button-up in light sky blue with crisp white stripes was perfectly pressed, the top buttons left undone. Slim-fit beige chinos hugged my legs, and my white leather penny loafers gleamed under the bedside lamp.

A soft tap at the door made me turn, and Joey's head peeked through. He pushed the door open, his hand resting on the doorknob, his full frame now filling the doorway. His eyebrows lifted, a smirk tugging at the corner of his lips. "Well, well...look at my son," he drawled, eyes scanning me from head to toe.

I chuckled, turning back to the mirror to smooth my hair one last time. Joey stepped in and perched on the edge of my bed near the lamp. I turned to face him, pressing my lower back into the vanity, and my palms resting on the edges.

"Whose girl's heart are you breaking?" he asked, eyebrows raised, a smirk tugging at his lips.

"I'm not breaking anyone's heart," I laughed.

"No," he said, letting the word drag out. "Of course not. Romano men don't do that." He winked. "But I do suspect whoever she is, she'll be very infatuated with you after tonight, dressed like that." I laughed, shaking my head. "Who is she anyway?" Joey asked. "Your Ma said it was a bunch of you going down to the cinema. What are you seeing?"

I shrugged. "Michael and I want to see Dean Martin and Sinatra in *Ocean's 11*, but Enzo's pouting because he wants to see *Psycho*."

"Go with *Psycho* if you want her to lean up against you." He smirked. "Speaking of which, have we spoken about the birds and the—"

"Oh, please, stop," I interrupted, pressing my palms over my ears. Joey's laugh filled the room, and Ma appeared in the doorway, a smile playing on her lips. Her eyes bounced between the two of us.

"What's going on?" she asked.

"Oh, just talking about the—"

"Nothing!" I chirped, cutting him off, and he dissolved into another fit of laughter.

Ma strolled over, cupping my face in her hands before letting them rest on my shoulders. "You're so handsome, Antonio."

"Don't get your lipstick on him, sweetheart," Joey teased, a hand patting his knee. Ma glanced over her shoulder at him, and with a smile, she moved between Joey's parted legs, his hands circling to pull her down. Her arms draped over his shoulders, leaning into his chest.

"She's just a friend, I promise," I said, gesturing in a wide circle. "It's *nothing* like that. And I already know about all of *that*, so I don't need you two explaining it to me. I'd rather face-plant out my bedroom window than have this conversation with either one of you."

Joey laughed into the crook of Ma's neck, her hands cradling his face. My eyes drifted toward the window, and I remembered Val just hours ago, standing in her bedroom window, clad only in her panties.

"Antonio!" Rosa's voice rang out from the bottom of the staircase. "Zeno and Mike are here!"

"You see what I mean?" Ma whispered to Joey. He tilted his head and tapped her hip as she started moving off his lap. "Thank you, Rosa!" Ma called back as she walked toward my bedroom door. Joey and I followed close behind, his arm draped over my shoulders as we made our way down the stairs.

"It's Enzo and Michael, Rosa," Ma said as she reached the last step.

"That's what I said," Rosa huffed.

Ma sighed under her breath, then lifted her face into a warm smile for Michael and Enzo.

"You two look handsome! All three of you!" she proclaimed.

"Thank you," Michael and Enzo said in unison.

Michael wore a short-sleeve Cuban-collar shirt in pale mint green with thin white vertical stripes, white trousers, and brown leather loafers. His hair was neatly styled in a side-parted comb-over. Enzo, by contrast, always went darker—a fitted black button-up, slim trousers, black leather loafers, and a gold cross necklace glinting against his chest. His pompadour was overgrown, a few rebellious strands falling across his forehead.

"Goddamn, the three of you are about to wreak havoc on this town," Joey declared, squeezing me into his side, and I grinned.

Ma laughed, pressing her palm to the back of his shoulder. "Stop it and let them go."

"My apologies," he muttered, dropping his arm. He pulled out his wallet and handed us each a twenty-dollar bill. "Treat the ladies right," he said, wagging a finger at us with a sly grin.

"The only one wreaking havoc in this town is you," Ma teased, smirking up at him.

"Enough outta you," Joey said, slipping his hand around her waist and tugging her close. I opened the front door before I had to see them kiss, and the three of us headed out, down the entryway, past the driveway, and onto the sidewalk in front of Enzo's house.

Sal leaned against his baby-blue Thunderbird, a Lucky Strike burning between his fingers. Val was pressed against him, her back to us, her nightgown replaced with a fitted dress that clung in all the right places. My eyes trailed up the curve of her legs, over her hips, along her back. Her arms were looped around Sal's neck, his hand gripping her waist as they whispered and giggled like two lovebirds.

"Can we go?" Enzo's voice cut through the night as we all stopped, watching Sal mumble against her lips, and she kissed him in return. I could only imagine the filthy garbage he was feeding her, and it made my eyes roll. "All you two ever do is stick your tongues down each other's throats," Enzo groaned.

"That's not true," Sal shot back, smugness playing across his features. "That's not *all* we do. We do plenty of other things too." He smirked, Enzo recoiled, and I nearly gagged.

"Sal!" Val's giggle carried through the air as she smacked his chest. He only grinned and pressed a kiss to the top of her head.

"Alright, alright," Sal drawled. "Get inside the Thunderbird!" Michael and I darted around the back, sliding into the rear seat. Enzo strolled around to the front and dropped into the passenger side, twisting in his seat to face me.

"I told you Rosa's losing her mind," he said. "She called me *Zeno*."

"She called me *Mike*," Michael added beside me.

Sal slid into the driver's seat, flashing Val one last grin. "Be right back, baby!" he called. Val stood on the lawn, her arms crossed, watching him start up the car.

"She's not senile. She does it on purpose. I'm telling you."

"Who isn't senile?" Sal asked, pulling onto the road.

"Rosa," I replied.

"She called me *Zeno*," Enzo huffed again, slumping against the door.

Sal shot me a glance over his shoulder. "Hate to break it to you, kid, but she's as senile as they come. You know how many times I catch her hovering by my car—" he lifted one hand to make air quotes, the other steady on the wheel—"just *clearing out the weeds*."

Of course, she wasn't clearing out weeds. She was eavesdropping. And Sal was dumb enough to keep falling for it.

* * *

The smell of buttery popcorn drifted through the air, clinging to the coolness of the auditorium. The hum of the air-conditioning mingled with the low murmur of voices, fading as the velvet curtains framed the glowing white screen. Trailers flickered and vanished, swallowed by black.

A couple of giggles slipped from Enzo and Maria, but Bernard Herrmann's first jagged violin notes cut them short. Shadows slashed across our faces as the opening credits blazed onto the screen. We sat dead-center in the middle rows—the *perfect vantage point,* according to Michael.

It didn't take long before Mia's hand clutched my arm, her knuckles whitening against my bicep. I glanced down at the grip, then up to her wide, frightened eyes. "I'm sorry," she whispered. "That scene...it really startled me."

"It's okay," I said softly, shifting my arm closer.

Her smile was soft, but the squeeze of her fingers lingered against my skin. Suddenly, every sound around me sharpened —the crackle of candy wrappers, the hiss of a soda cap twisting free, the whisper of a skirt brushing down the aisle. Then the shower scene struck. Steam, porcelain, and shrieking strings. Herrmann's violins knifed through the silence, stabbing until the whole auditorium gasped in horror. A few screamed outright; Michael gave a nervous whistle from a few chairs down.

Mia buried her face into my shoulder, trembling. My heart fluttered under her touch. Onscreen, the curtain ripped back in a flash. In the seats, no one moved, no one breathed. Even the popcorn stopped. I dipped my head, brushing my lips to the crown of her hair. "It's over now," I murmured.

She exhaled, lifted her face, but kept hold of my arm. Her hand drew it into her lap, pulling me closer until our bodies were flush. The movie blurred into nothing now. All I could feel was the fire in my hand, trapped against the smooth fabric of her skirt, my knuckles brushing the warm shift of her thighs each time she shifted. Every breath she took rose and fell against my arm, searing straight through my shirt.

Hitchcock wasn't the one killing me. Mia was.

"Goodness." Her whisper barely rose above the swell of violins on the screen. "That...that was just awful."

I turned my head, catching the faint tickle of her lilac perfume. Even in the glow of the film, her face looked pale, her wide eyes shining like dark glass marbles. "It's only a picture. It's not real. Hitchcock just likes spookin' folks," I murmured, careful to keep my voice low so Enzo—glued to the movie— wouldn't shush me.

"I know..." Her grip on my arm tightened. "But the way she screamed—" She shivered, pressing in until she was practically molded to my side, all nerves and perfume and trembling curves. I swallowed, trying to focus on the film instead of the heat building in my body from how close she was. My hand twitched in her lap, and I prayed she didn't notice.

"You're safe," I said, steadying my tone. "I'm right here. Nobody's gonna hurt you."

Her head tipped toward me, lashes fluttering. The flicker of the screen skimmed across her lips, drawing my eyes down to their soft pink curve. "Do you promise?" she breathed, her words brushing warm against my mouth.

My throat went dry as I nodded. "Cross my heart."

Another scream tore through the theater. She breathed a tiny gasp, burrowing even deeper into my chest. My pulse thundered in my ears. I tried to keep my eyes on the screen, but all I could feel was the burn of her thigh under my palm and the brush of her hair against my jaw each time she inched closer.

Chapter Twelve

Adriana
Two days after Vincent's murder

The house was quiet except for my own movement as I crept slowly throughout the house, one hand smoothing over the silk tie of my robe. It matched the nightgown underneath—pale blue, delicate lace along the hem and collar. My hair was still damp beneath the curlers I'd twisted in after my bath. The scent of lavender lingered on my skin. It was nearing midnight and Joey still hadn't come upstairs for the night so I went to him.

I padded down the hallway, the soft soles of my slippers muffled against the hardwood. His office door was cracked open, light spilling out in a warm stripe across the floor. I paused there, just watching him. He was perched on the edge of his desk, one leg crossed over the other, a half-full glass of whiskey raised near his mouth. His other arm was folded beneath it, tucked tight against his ribs. His eyes weren't on anything, but his stare was intense, brow furrowed. Jaw locked so tight I could see the muscle twitch.

I nudged the door open and slipped inside. His gaze tore away from the wall across the room and landed on my eyes. "I couldn't sleep without you," I said. I stepped closer to him, the silk of my robe swishing around my ankles. "You're gonna burn a hole through the wall if you keep staring at it like that."

That earned a twitch of his mouth, not quite a smile, but close enough. I stopped a foot in front of him. "Come to bed with me."

He stood up a little straighter, taking a slow sip from his whiskey before setting the glass down on the desk. The amber liquid caught the light overhead, but it was him I couldn't look away from. The way his suspenders pulled snug over his broad shoulders, his sleeves rolled up just enough to show the tension in his forearms, the top button of his shirt undone, he looked like a man who carried too much, too often, and made it look effortless. Charming, even. I hadn't even realized I was smiling until I caught myself doing it, as though my body recognized him before my mind did.

I walked toward him, closing the space between us, and brought both hands up to his face. My palms cupped his cheeks, my thumbs brushing over the stubble he hadn't bothered to shave. I knew it'd be gone by morning, but tonight it was there. He exhaled, the tension in his shoulders giving way as his arms came around me, pulling me close. The front of my body pressed against him, and his head dipped low. Our lips met in a slow, tender kiss. I could still taste the whiskey on his breath when we parted.

"I'll be there soon," he murmured against my lips.

I tilted my head, searching his face. We both knew that was a lie. "You need rest, Joey," I pleaded. "You keep pacing this room like it's gonna hand you answers. You're going to drive yourself crazy down here."

"Sweetheart, I promise ya, I'll be up there soon. Don't worry about me," he said, his voice soft and coaxing. "You need the rest more than I do."

The sound of my sigh filled the room as I studied him. Joey was a smooth talker, always turning things back on me, hiding behind his charm so I wouldn't notice the weight he carried. But we were one, and no matter how much he tried to shield me, his burdens lived in my bones too, and I was okay with that. "What are you down here thinking about? Is everything happening with Vincent?"

His eyes lifted to meet mine before he shook his head. "It's nothing, sweetheart." His lips pressed a kiss to my forehead, lingering afterwards. I pressed my face into his chest, breathing in the mix of cigarettes and Old Spice.

I lifted my chin, pressing it into his chest, as his arms wrapped around me, and he looked down with a tender smile that made my heart ache with happiness. "I'm not falling for that, and you know it, Joseph Romano. It's always something when you say it's nothing."

A smile broke out along his face before I felt his chest shake from the rumble of his laughter. "Well, it's nothing I care to discuss with my wife. How does that sound?" His eyes met mine again.

I tried to force the smile off my face but it was no use. "Well, I'm not going upstairs until you tell me what it is that has you so spent. I think I should know what has my husband from coming to bed with me."

He chuckled against my lips before he kissed them softly. "Come on, sweetheart," he breathed against my mouth, forehead pressed against mine, and his hands running up and down the length of my back in a soothing rhythm. "You shouldn't lose sleep over what I've got going on. And it's nothing really, I promise you. I'm hardly thinking about the Vincent situation. You know, I have difficulty sleeping sometimes."

My arms left his body, traveled up to the sides of his face, and my eyes drilled into him. "We're husband and wife. We took vows, Joey. We made an oath—a pact. We're not supposed to be living two separate lives under the same roof. I know who you are, *every* side of you. You can't ask me to pretend I don't."

His lips curved into a mischievous smirk. "So what? You think we're the new Bonnie and Clyde?"

I let a small grin play at the corner of my mouth. "Yeah. Perhaps, more subtle...smarter...and far more strategic."

He curled a brow, amusement playing across his features. "You should be careful, sweetheart. You're gonna get me real excited talkin' like that."

I hummed. "Good. Maybe that'll finally get you upstairs."

His fingers pressed into my lower back, drawing me close enough that I could feel the bulge concealed by his trousers press against me. "I'm sorry, but are you trying to seduce me?"

My heart pounded in my chest. My hands slid from the sides of his face to his shoulders, fingers tracing the straps of his suspenders as I eased them down, watching them fall along the length of his arms. "I don't know. Are you trying to corrupt me, Mr. Romano?"

His gaze darken, like a man starved of something only I could give him. His breath came shorter, chest rising with each inhale. "Oh, I'm going to corrupt you, alright," he murmured.

His hands slipped beneath the collar of my robe, easing it off my shoulders. The silk fell in a soft rustle to my elbows, leaving my skin bare to the warmth of his mouth. He dipped his head, placing slow, measured kisses along the curve of my neck, down to the place where my collarbone met my shoulder. One of my arms curled around his back, the other wrapped around his neck, drawing him closer.

"Joey," his name came out as a sigh. His mouth trailed fire across my clavicle, his tongue drawing slow, teasing circles. His fingertips dug into my hips, anchoring me, while my head fell back, giving him access to every inch of me.

"Joey, you didn't tell me what it was you were thinking about."

"Later," he grumbled against my skin. His hands tugged the robe from the crease of my elbow where it had landed, letting it pool behind me. They traveled up the backs of my thighs, sending heat pooling between them, aching for his touch. But before that could happen, questions formed in my mind. My palms pressed against his chest, forcing a small distance between us. A frown tugged at his brow, lips parting in protest.

"Tell me what's wrong. No more stalling. No more keeping it to yourself."

He blew out a breath through parted lips, his eyes shutting for just a split second as his chest rose and fell. Both hands cupped his face, dragging down over his cheeks and the sides of his head. "Was Lucy with you shopping the other day?" he asked, his gaze fixed somewhere over my shoulder instead of meeting my eyes.

My heart lurched into my throat. I recoiled, scanning his face as the weight of his implication sank in. "Yes," I stammered. "Why are you asking?"

"That's all I wanted to know."

I shook my head. "No it's not. Why was that what you were thinking about?" I asked, stepping toward him. "Are you trying to rule her out or something?"

His lips parted and then closed.

"Lucy would *never* kill anyone. I mean...well, she talks about killing Hector all the time, but that's different. And if she ever did it, she'd probably hire someone." *Like Angela.* I caught myself and looked away, suddenly aware I'd said too much.

His eyes flared in shock. "Jesus, sweetheart, why the hell do the three of you talk about killing Hector?" He ran a hand over his face, shaking his head.

My hand rested against his chest, feeling it rise and fall.

"What I mean is that I don't think she'd do something like that. In fact, I know she wouldn't. I know she didn't."

His soft blue eyes poured into mine, and he gave a small nod before reaching for the watered-down whiskey on his desk, draining the last of it in one go. "Please," I begged, my fingers curling around the fabric of his shirt. "Tell me you don't really think Lucy would do this."

His eyes searched mine before his hands scooped my face up and tilted my chin up, "I thought it for a second," he confessed. "But I realize now it was far-fetched."

Chapter Thirteen

Joey
Three days after Vincent's murder

Adriana lingered in the doorway of our master bathroom, arms crossed over the front of her black silk-crepe sheath dress. Black patent stilettos, a pillbox hat with its birdcage veil dipping slightly below her eyes, and satin gloves at her wrists. Pearls kissed her throat, victory curls perfectly lacquered beneath the hat, winged liner framing eyes that burned straight through me. Even without turning, I felt the weight of her—her flowery perfume, her silent sighs of pleading, the disappointment in her along her crimson-stained lips that were drawn in a straight line. I dragged the razor along my jaw, pretending not to notice, when all I wanted was to drown in her reflection.

"I don't think we should go to this, Joey," she sighed. She had been saying that for hours now. Nobody wanted to go to Vincent's funeral, but it was an unspoken rule. I rinsed the blade, flicked off the excess water, and went back to my face.

She crossed the threshold of the backroom, her heels clicking as she pressed one of her hands against the counter, her voice more urgent now. *"Please."* I could see her reflection next to mine in the mirror. Her face was turned toward me, eyes wide with worry. "Just this once...don't do what they expect of you. This is dangerous."

It was more dangerous *not* to go.

I finished the shave in silence, patting my skin dry with a towel before splashing on aftershave. The sting grounded me, the scent of Old Spice cutting through the bathroom. My black lightweight wool, single-breasted, two-button suit settled on my shoulders, heavy with what was to come. A black silk tie, knotted perfectly in a Windsor, glinted faintly under the discreet gold tie bar pinned to my white button-down. Polished black leather oxfords graced my feet. I adjusted the black fedora on my head before finally turning to face Adriana. Her eyes—big, brown, pleading—locked on mine. I could feel the weight of what she wanted, the unspoken need in her gaze, and the ache that I couldn't give it to her.

"Sweetheart, do you think I want to go? No, of course not. If it were up to me, I'd have him at the bottom of the bay. But it's not up to me," I relented, placing my hands on her shoulders, gripping gently. "There are rules. And there are some rules I can't break. There's some I have to follow. If I don't show up, it looks like I got something to hide, and I don't."

"Renee's going to be there. And you know she's going to cause a scene."

"Don't worry about her. It's a funeral. We're not going to make a spectacle. We'll pay our respects, then we'll leave. In and out, sweetheart."

But even as I said it, I didn't believe it. And by the look on her face, neither did she.

"Pay our respects?" she scoffed, face scrunched. "To Vincent? He was a terrible person, Joey. A monster."

"But he was my boss." I leaned forward, pressing a kiss to

her forehead. My lips lingered for a moment before I whispered against her skin, "Come on...let's leave before we're late."

* * *

The sky was overcast, heavy with gray clouds that looked as if they were holding back something worse than rain. The forecast said we were expecting a heavy thunderstorm, and that was my sign from the universe that a storm was brewing on the streets and about to come raining down. I tightened my grip on the steering wheel as the car rolled down the road. It felt like the whole world was holding its breath today. Probably because it was.

Adriana sat beside me in the front seat, staring out the window, her hands resting in her lap, gripping the straps of her black clutch purse. Rosa and Antonio were in the backseat. Rosa whistled to Sinatra on the radio, and Antonio fiddled with the edge of his sleeve. Out of my periphery, Adriana's eyes flick toward me every few seconds.

I slowed the car as we approached *St. Augustine of the Sacred Hearts*. Black Cadillacs were lined up along the curb. Men in black tailored suits stood outside smoking. Everyone pretending this was grief when really, it was a headcount. I pulled into a parking space and turned off the engine.

I stepped out of the car, adjusted my cufflinks, then opened the back door to help Rosa out. She patted my back as she placed her black purse over her shoulder and began walking towards the church with Antonio next to her. Adriana's hand slid into mine as we walked toward the church—the four of us dressed in all black, walking into the lion's den.

Chapter Fourteen

Joey
Three days after Vincent's murder

Vincent's closed casket rested at the front, polished wood under soft light filtering through the stained-glass windows. Every head turned our way the moment we stepped inside, the hush of whispered prayers and soft sniffles filling the air. The scent of incense clung to the rafters, mingling with the faint metallic tang of polished brass and the faint floral perfume of lilies and roses arranged around the altar.

Candles flickered, their flames dancing against the dark oak pews, casting shadows across the polished tile floor. Father Delgato stood near the pulpit, robe heavy and dark against the soft, golden glow of the sanctuary, while mourners in black held their hands folded, eyes glistening with fake tears, faces pretending to be etched with grief.

I tightened my grip on Adriana's hand, our fingers intertwined. I was used to all eyes on me, but for different reasons. *Fear. Respect. Admiration.* Today was different. My eyes met Adriana's, and she forced a practiced smile onto her lips. Her other hand crossed her body, gripping my forearm with a squeeze. I returned it, letting my fingers press around hers.

Rosa drifted ahead to speak with Pat, who stood near the altar. Antonio stood on my other side, and the three of us slipped into a pew halfway down the aisle. From there, I could see the casket, closed tight beneath the crucifix. A dozen floral arrangements surrounded it, but nothing could soften the heaviness pressing down on the room. Vincent might've been laid out in polished wood, but every man here knew the truth... he hadn't gone peacefully. His real cause of death was sitting in one of these pews, pretending. Playing the act of their lifetime.

Father Delgato's voice echoed through the space, but it barely registered to me. My eyes swept the room instead, catching nods from men I'd done business with over the years. A well-orchestrated show where everyone played their part perfectly.

Paul approached from behind, his hands resting on my shoulders, Florence and Alessia trailing quietly at his side. I turned to face him, ready to say something, but then my eyes landed on her.

Renee.

And her hazel eyes landed on me.

She marched straight down the center aisle, the clap of her heels echoing off the floor. She stopped at the aisle I was seated in, eyes wide with fury, finger pointed at the three of us. "*You!*" she screeched. "What are you doing here?" Her head whipped around to the congregation. "What is he doing here? Who let him in? I want him removed!"

Adriana tensed against my side, her fingers digging into my hand. The flutter of her lashes as she turned toward me. I pushed myself up, freeing her hand, and stepped past her, the fabric of her dress whispering against my fingertips, until I stood across from Renee. "Renee," I pleaded. "Let's not do this. I'm here to pay my respect, and then I'll leave."

She scoffed, her arms crossing over her chest. "You think I give a damn about you putting on an act in front of everyone?" Her voice cracked as it rose. "You show up here like you're innocent, parading your wife and child around like it's just another Sunday? Have you no shame? You're the reason we're all here!" Her finger jabbed into my chest at the final statement.

"That's not true—"

"You killed him! I know you did. You *always* hated him. You wanted him dead and now look at him!" Her hand gestured towards the casket just a few rows away.

"I didn't kill Vincent."

Her glare shifted over my shoulder. "And *her*? You brought *her* here?"

"She's my wife," I gritted out through a jaw so tense I thought I'd have to pry it open once I left.

"She's a homewrecker. And you're a murderer. Though I suppose that makes you two the perfect pair...a match made in *fucking* heaven," Renee spat.

Adriana tugged at my hand, her fingers warm against mine. Her soft voice cut through Renee's fury. "Joey," she whispered, an edge of worry in her tone. "Let's just leave."

I closed the gap between Renee, finger pointed directly toward her chest. "Watch how you speak to *my* wife."

Frank Costa, a made man in the Moretti family, strode down the aisle. One hand pressed against my chest, the other draped around Renee's back. My gaze dropped as his hand flicked me backward, an unspoken warning. Adriana rose beside me, her hands clutching my arm. "Joey, please," she whispered, her voice trembling.

"Joey," Frank warned. "Why don't you put your finger down and back up?"

One corner of my mouth twitched upward as my eyes bored into him. I stepped closer, looming just a few inches over his frame. "Why don't you talk some sense into your woman? She's not going to come at my wife and think I'm going to sit back and let it happen."

"You're skating on thin ice," Frank growled, stepping closer until we were nearly chest to chest. "It might be wise, for a man like yourself, to watch his back in time like this."

"You should know better than to come to my territory and speak to me like that. If anyone should watch their back, it should be you," My nostrils flared, chest heaving as the image of Frank on his knees, begging for forgiveness while I loomed over him, flashed through my mind.

"Joey." Adriana's voice broke through the tension again. Her hand tugged harder on my arm. "Please just sit down."

We stood like that for another second—eyes locked, as if one wrong move could detonate the whole church. Renee grabbed his arm and pulled him back. Adriana pulled me with her the same way. Two women saving us from each other.

I dropped into the pew between Antonio and Adriana, jaw clenched, nostrils flaring, leg bouncing with barely contained fury. Father Delgado's voice droned in the background, a dull hum against my seething thoughts. Adriana's hand tightened around mine, her fingers gripping my thigh, forcing my leg still, and I could practically feel her glare searing into me. "You said we wouldn't make a scene," she whispered against my ear.

Chapter Fifteen

Antonio
Three days after Vincent's murder

Vincent's headstone read: "Vincent *'Lucky'* Accetta. Husband. Father. Luckiest man to live."

I stared at it, fighting the laugh crawling up my throat. To see that carved into marble—*Luckiest man to live*—was almost comical. Because Vincent Accetta *wasn't* lucky. He had a closed casket because he was *that* unlucky.

All around me stood men in tailored suits and shiny shoes, reeking of cigarettes and expensive cologne. Most of them wore the same slicked-back hair, same gold watches. A whole crowd of Joey knockoffs. I was pretty sure he'd started the trend. That's the thing about Joey, he was bold, one of a kind and everyone wanted to be him.

They all kept their faces blank. A few women dabbed their eyes with tissues, but I couldn't tell if the tears were real or just part of the performance. The women behind men like these were no different. I watched Ma stand beside Joey, the two of them with sorrow written all over their faces but I knew it wasn't real sadness. Everyone in this cemetery was placing their bets that Joey was the one who pulled the trigger. I knew, even if he had, Ma would stand by his side and say he hadn't. Rosa stood near the entrance of the church with Pat, both of them dabbing at their eyes every few seconds. I was almost certain they were faking it too.

Pat kept sneaking sips from her flask hidden inside her purse but I stopped counting after the fifth time I'd seen her do it. Ma and Joey stood next to Angela and Marco a foot away, talking quietly with Paul and Florence. Michael stood with Lucy, Hector, and Christopher, but he kept looking at me like I was his escape route. I gave him a look back that said you're on your own, and he must've gotten the message, because he sighed and resigned himself to his fate.

I slipped back into the quiet church, the faint echo of my footsteps bouncing off the polished pews. The smallest form of light flowed through the stained-glass windows, splashing colored patterns across the floor, painting the aisle in reds, blues, and golds. I thought I might find solace with Father Delgato, the soft murmur of his prayers drifting from the altar. Then I saw the back of Giovanni's head slipping into the restroom. My mind hesitated, weighing whether I should confront him, but my body had already made the choice. Long, purposeful strides carried me down the aisle until I reached the heavy oak door marked in bold letters: **"MENS."**

The door shut behind me and I stepped forward. Giovanni's eyes locked onto mine as he slapped the bathroom facet down and grabbed a paper towel drying his hands. "I just came to tell you. I don't know who killed Vincent. But it wasn't me. And it wasn't Joey. The day he died, I was at home with Joey. I told him everything we did. I wouldn't lie about this."

Giovanni's eyes narrowed, a smirk creeping onto his face as he tossed the paper towel into the trash can. "Save your soap opera. I don't believe a word that leaves your mouth. You've already shown what kind of traitor you are, trying to kill the man you call your father. The only thing I see is that you and Joey are cut from the same fucked-up cloth. Maybe you two even teamed up to kill my grandfather, for all I know. And when Joey found out what you did you probably blamed it all on my grandfather."

"That's not true," I shook my head, my throat tightening. "That's not true at all."

He stormed forward, standing nose to nose with me. His hand gripped my suit, and I searched his eyes. "Stay the fuck away from me, you creep." He let go of my suit and shoved me hard, forcing me to hit the floor with a thud. He loomed over me. "Mark my fucking words, Romano," He bent at the waist, his finger dangling in my face. "First, Joey will pay for this. And someday...when we're older...you'll pay too. Enjoy your youth while it lasts because your days are numbered."

He straightened, kicked his shoe against my shin and then he was gone, leaving me sitting against the cold bathroom wall.

I forced myself off the floor, my shin aching as I pulled the bathroom door open and walked back into the main area of the church. Enzo strolled up, chewing on a toothpick leftover from the antipasto platter. "I stole a cigarette from Val's coat pocket," he said, smirking. "Wanna sneak a drag behind the church?"

We both started walking back down the church aisle, nodding and smiling at the mourners we passed like we were two altar boys just heading back from confession. When we were clear, we threw one last glance over our shoulders and bolted toward the side of the building farthest from the graveyard. Laughter broke out of us the second we were hidden.

Enzo stuck the cigarette between his lips and lit it, taking a long drag before handing it over to me. I leaned back against the brick wall, inhaled, and exhaled slowly. "They've got some hot chicks here," Enzo said, looking out toward the parking lot.

"Didn't know half these short, ugly fuckers could pull women like that."

I choked mid-inhale, coughing smoke as I laughed. Enzo slapped my back, laughing too.

"What is it with pretty girls liking ugly gangsters?" I said, wiping my eyes. He didn't need to know I was referring to Val.

"Well, for starters...they're *loaded*," he said, shrugging. He took another drag and passed the cigarette back. "And they're powerful. Rich, powerful gangsters aren't that different from rich, powerful politicians and women lap that up on a spoon so I suppose I'm going to have to pick which one I want to be."

The mayor was short, balding, and looked like he hadn't seen a gym since Prohibition, but his wife was something straight out of a movie.

"You think there's a sign-up sheet around here some-where?" Enzo asked, grinning.

"They'd probably let you in. Because you are pretty damn ugly. Kind of short, too."

"I think I walked myself into that one." We both burst out laughing again, the sound echoing off the bricks.

"You know," Enzo said, slinging an arm over my shoulders, "this is a long way from the days we used to stalk Joey, trying to prove the mafia was real. Now look at us." He paused, grinning. "You don't think all this is giving us a trauma bond, do you?"

I would've laughed—*should've*—but the moment he said it, my face dropped. Enzo was a jokester. As much as I wanted it to be a joke, it wasn't. He looked at me, studying my expression. We didn't say it out loud, but we both knew.

"You okay?" he asked. "I mean...with everything that's happened?"

I shrugged, letting the back of my head thud softly against the brick wall behind me. I looked up at the gray sky. "No one's ever *really* okay. Are they?"

"What kind of depressing, morbid shit is that? I figured you'd be relieved that he's dead. I know I am."

"I am glad," I admitted. "But it doesn't fix anything. It just creates a whole new set of problems."

A raindrop hit the bridge of my nose. I wiped it away as Enzo shifted beside me.

"Hey, everyone knows Joey didn't do it. Give it some time. Things'll settle. They'll find the real killer. Renee's crazy and everyone knows that so don't let that little thing she pulled inside get you worked up."

My eyes met his. "They don't want the real killer. They want a scapegoat. And Joey's the perfect choice. If I hadn't done what I did, he wouldn't be in this mess." Enzo went quiet. He didn't know what to say, and honestly, I didn't know what I needed to hear. Nothing could make this feel any less heavy in my chest.

He sighed, "I don't think that's true. Even if it is, you need to let it go. Michael's right for once in his life." Enzo smiled, nudging his elbow into my ribs and I let out a laugh despite the sadness I could feel creeping into every crevice of my soul. "Want to know something else?" He blew out smoke before passing the cigarette over to me. "I made out with Marie this morning at the park and I sneezed and head-butted her."

Chapter Sixteen

Joey
Three days after Vincent's murder

The funny thing about Mother Nature—she's a force to be reckoned with. The moment the first drops of rain started to fall, the funeral began to unravel. People gathered their families and hurried out as if the storm itself was chasing them away.

Rosa and Antonio were already walking toward us as the rain picked up. I took Adriana's hand, and we waved goodbye to Paul and Florence. The second we were out of earshot, Adriana leaned in, her lips curled in a polite smile for anyone watching. "What did I tell you in the bathroom, Joey? I warned you she'd cause a scene."

"And I told you we still had to go," I said through gritted teeth, a smile plastered on my face for everyone passing by.

Antonio jogged past us toward the car, hands shielding his slicked-back hair. "Hurry! My hair's getting wet!" he muttered. Rosa wasn't far behind, using her purse as a makeshift umbrella while she hustled after him.

Sal's voice came from behind me out of nowhere. "Hey, Joey. You got a second?" I peered over my shoulder to find Sal standing beneath a massive oak, the branches offering him just enough cover from the downpour. I slipped the car keys into Adriana's hand. She looked like she wanted to protest, but she knew this wasn't the time. So she pressed her lips together and marched toward the car.

I met Sal under the oak, slicking my hair back and shaking the rain off my fingers. "Make it quick."

"Meet at the warehouse. Ten tonight."

"Who called the meeting?"

"Christopher. Hector told me to pass it along."

Hector.

That name sent a cold ripple through me, harsher than the rain gliding down my back. *A traitor.* I could feel it in my bones. If someone was trying to pin this murder on me, I'd bet my life *Hector* was behind it.

Chapter Seventeen

Adriana

Three days after Vincent's murder

The rain came down in sheets, blurring the stained-glass windows of the church until they looked like watercolors bleeding together. I sat stiff in the passenger seat of the Ferrari, the cream leather cool against the back of my legs. The windshield wipers swung back and forth, but were useless against the storm.

Through the glass, I watched Joey jog down the slick sidewalk, his dark suit plastered to him, the perfect slick of his hair ruined by the downpour. Strands fell loose across his forehead, and he shoved them back with one sweep of his hand. He was a sight to behold, even soaked to the bone, even when I was furious with him. My chest ached with the contradiction: wanting to stay mad, but unable to stop seeing him as the most handsome man alive.

He yanked open the driver's side door, sliding in. The rich scent of rain and Old Spice clung to him as he settled into the seat. Joey turned his head, water still dripping from the ends of his hair, and smiled at me. I forced my eyes off him, sitting stiff against the seat, hands tucked into my lap.

Joey reached for my hand, but I pulled it away. At every stoplight and stop sign, I saw from my peripheral that his gaze was on me, but I kept my eyes fixed ahead, watching the windshield wipers battle the rain.

"This is the devil at work," Rosa declared as we pulled into the driveway. "Vincent was the devil. It says something that at his funeral, we have a thunderstorm like this."

Joey turned his head, draping one arm across the back of my headrest as he glanced into the backseat. His blue eyes flicked to Antonio. "You think you could help Rosa inside for me?"

Antonio's sigh filled the heaviness in the car. "How fast can you run?"

"I'm an older woman, Antonio," Rosa huffed out a breath.

"Fine. How fast can you walk?"

Rosa muttered something under her breath as Antonio shoved the door open and bolted up the entryway. She hustled after him, heels clicking against the wet pavement. Antonio held the door wide, ushering her in with an exaggerated sweep of his arm. Rosa shot a finger up at him, saying something that made his eyes roll. A second later, the front door banged shut behind them.

Joey's hand slid onto my thigh, his thumb grazing across my kneecap. The chill of his rain-damp watch clashed with the heat of his touch, sending tingles racing upward, unwanted and traitorous because the last thing I wanted was to feel anything like this for him right now. "Adriana," he hummed. "Sweetheart. Talk to me. I know you're mad, and you have every right to be mad. I have no control over Renee—"

I sighed, shaking my head, trying to push the heat from his touch out of my mind. "What did Sal want from you?"

"Oh...he's just letting me know there's a meeting tonight in the city."

My eyes snapped to his, dark and burning with the kind of fire Joey Romano should know better than to play with. "A meeting? Are you sure it's a meeting? Or a setup, Joey?"

His shoulders squared, chest still, hand now resting on the steering wheel. "It's just a meeting, sweetheart."

"I know you're lying."

"I wouldn't lie to you, sweetheart." *I knew that was a lie.*

"How do you know it's not a setup? After what Renee pulled in there, how can you be so sure?"

"Renee's got nothing to do with anything anymore. Her only link to the family was Vincent, and he's gone."

"Who was that man with her? The one you almost caused a scene for?"

Joey let his head fall back against the seat, closing his eyes. "Some loser, sweetheart. Her next victim. Nobody that matters to me. Nobody that matters to you either."

I narrowed my eyes as his gaze locked on mine. "That's not what I asked, and you know it. Who is he? You know him. You don't like him. He doesn't like you either. How do you know him?"

"Frank Costa. He's a made man in the Moretti family," Joey said.

I waited, my patience thinning.

"I knew him," he continued, his voice low. "Back in the day. We've never been friends, never gotten along... and we never will. But like I said, Frank and Renee? They're nothing. Today was the last day either of them will matter to the Giordano family. She's with him because of his status. From here on, they're the Morettis' problem. And it's the best thing that could've happened for anyone involved."

My shoulders settled a fraction. "I told you she'd cause a scene. And I was right. She called you a murderer in front of everyone who matters, in the middle of the damn church."

"Yeah... you were right. And I'm sorry. I'm sorry that happened. But no one takes her seriously. It's over now. So let's not let her come between us." His hand reached over, covering mine in my lap, fingers intertwining with mine. The side of his face pressed into the back of the headrest, eyes searching mine, pleading.

"How can she get away with this? You say she has no status. No power anymore. But she stood there and said those terrible things, to you and to me, and no one stopped her. People are going to talk about that, Joey. They're going to say you killed Vincent because of her. I know it."

His hand rose, cupping the side of my face, and pulled me closer. I could feel the warmth of his palm, and his breath fanning across my cheek, making my pulse spike. "It's over, sweetheart. We showed up. We played our part. We did what we were supposed to do. That's what matters. We played by the rules. I know you're upset, but wasting your energy on someone like her—"

"No, Joey. That's *not* all that matters. She painted a target on *our* backs, and everyone in that church saw it. You can't just stand there and do nothing. You have to do *something*." My eyes blazed as I searched his, daring him to respond.

"What do you want me to do?" he asked, pressing a kiss to my forehead as he whispered against it, "Tell me what you want. Tell me what will make you happy, and I'll do it."

Kill her. The words rang loud in my mind. But I'd take a good threat, too. "She's coming after you. She always has been after you. Now she's partnered with this man...this Frank, who is also after you. Because if Vincent couldn't get to you. She will. She's going to turn this whole town against you. I can see it happening already."

"People will never stop trying to take me down. It comes with the territory. But that's who I am, sweetheart. I'm a man who gets thrown to the wolves and comes back leading the pack."

The thought alone made my chest cave in. The idea of losing Joey—it was enough to shatter me. "I just want it to be over," I whispered. "All of it."

Joey cupped the base of my neck, his forehead resting against mine. "I swear to you," he murmured, his eyes burning into mine, "this will pass. I'll come out on top. And when everyone who's tried to smear my name pays, when the dust finally settles, we'll be untouchable. We'll never have to worry about a damn thing again because we"—his grip tightened, making me shiver—"we make our own damn rules." A slow smile tugged at the corners of his lips. I felt the corners of my mouth lift in response. "Clyde's nothing without Bonnie. Isn't that right, sweetheart?"

I nodded. "That's right."

His thumb skimmed my bottom lip, his lips inches from mine. I melted under him, powerless to resist Joey Romano.

Chapter Eighteen

Joey
Three days after Vincent's murder

I hadn't bothered changing out of my clothes from Vincent's funeral. There was no point, chances were, I could be attending my own next. Telling Adriana the truth in the car was out of the question. In the underworld, you could walk through a door and never walk back out. Only an amateur thought otherwise.

Gravel crunched underfoot as I slipped out of the driver seat. The warehouse loomed ahead, steel double doors, streaked with rust and scratched from decades of use, blocked the entrance. To the left, a narrow dock stretched toward the NY Bay, trees lining the edge, their leaves whispering in the summer breeze. Across the water, Staten Island's outline shimmered faintly, the city skyline a distant, jagged backdrop.

Sal stood at the door, shifting his weight from foot to foot, hands tugging at his cuffs. Young, flashy, eager to impress, every inch the rookie trying to look like he belonged. He wore a short-sleeve white linen shirt, unbuttoned at the top to show a hint of the gold chain I'd gifted him, shirt tucked into pale tan trousers with a slim crease down the front. It used to be Hector guarding the entrance to meetings. Seeing Sal take his place told me everything I needed to know.

A smile flickered across my face, breaking the tension I'd been holding. His expression shifted, gone was the usual easy-going, happy-go-lucky vibe. "Joey...I'll need your gun," he mumbled. I reached under my suit coat and pulled the revolver from my waistband. He held his hand out, waiting. I laid the grip in his palm, barrel pointed toward me.

His hand curled around the steel door handles, swinging the warehouse doors open. A sudden chill hit me, harsh against the lingering summer heat outside. Dim overhead lights cast long, jagged shadows across the concrete floor. Every top-ranking member of the Giordano crime family was already seated, their eyes tracking the entrance. Two chairs remained empty. One beside Paul, the other at the center of the room. Sal slipped in behind me, the door locking with a loud click, and moved past me to slide into the chair next to Paul. That told me exactly where I stood tonight. I took the seat in the center of the room. Forced myself to sit tall and straight. If there was one thing I'd mastered over the years, it was pretending I didn't smell the blood in the water.

Christopher leaned forward from his chair, the dim light catching the lines of his face. Broad-shouldered and solidly built, with a square jaw and deep-set eyes, he carried authority in every movement. His slicked-back dark hair gleamed under the overhead lights, and a faint shadow traced his chin. Even seated, there was an air of menace and control. "Joey, I think we all know why you're sitting there. I want you to tell me where you were the day Vincent was killed."

"Home. I was home with my son."

"That's convenient. Isn't it? He just happened to be with the one person we can't question...a child," Hector leaned back in his chair. Broad-shouldered with a smooth jawline and piercing dark eyes. His dark hair was neatly combed, a faint shadow of stubble tracing his chin.

Christopher shook his head. "We don't bring kids into this."

"I can vouch for him," Paul said. Every head in the room turned, first to Paul, then back to me. "He was home. Just like he said. I stopped by that day when I heard what happened."

"I saw him too," Marco said, on the other side of the table. "I was next door with Angela and the kids."

"Is that true?" Christopher's eyes pierced into me.

"That's the truth. That's what happened."

"Then explain how you were photographed outside of Vincent's house," Christopher said, his sausage-like fingers folded together, but the weight behind them promised trouble.

"After Paul came to the house and told me what happened, I was shocked." I shook my head slowly, letting the disbelief linger in my tone. It wasn't entirely a lie, but I had to play the part of a man blindsided by Vincent's death. "So I drove over. I had to see it with my own eyes."

"Why would you want to see a dead man bleeding out in his own home?" Hector snarled.

One more comment from this bastard and I'm slitting his jugular with a box cutter.

I locked eyes with Hector, refusing to blink. "Because Vincent wasn't just the underboss of this family, Hector. He was nearly my father-in-law." The bile rose in my throat the second I said it, but I had to play the hand before Hector played it for me.

The lines of his jaw spasmed, his lips pressed so tight they turned white. His eyes burned black with hatred. It felt less like Hector sitting across from me, and more like the devil himself had pulled up a chair.

"Joey, pull up your chair." Christopher leaned back, settling into his seat. I pushed to my feet, the scrape of the chair legs screeching across the concrete as I dragged it up to the long table. The sound echoed in the cavernous warehouse. "Now that we're all in attendance..." Christopher's thick lips curved into a smile. "Let's get to the real reason we're gathered here tonight."

So this wasn't the reason we'd all been called tonight.

Christopher pushed back from the table and rose to his feet, smoothing the front of his cream-and-maroon polo over the swell of his stomach. His thick fingers came to rest on Hector's shoulder. "We're the strongest family in this city," he declared, his voice rolling through the warehouse. "And we can't afford to look weak. Vincent's seat needs to be filled. So, naturally... there's no one I'd rather see take that spot than my son-in-law—Hector Russo."

The room erupted in applause. I forced my palms together, the hollow sound of my clapping masking the bile rising in my throat. My gaze stayed fixed on Hector, his smug grin spreading wider as Christopher hauled him up and wrapped him in a proud embrace.

If only Christopher knew. Hector wasn't the future of this family, he was its disease. A traitor. A liability. If he held that seat for long, the Giordano's wouldn't rise. They'd rot from the inside out.

Chapter Nineteen

Joey
Three days after Vincent's murder

It was past midnight when I slipped through the front door. The house was dark and silent. I stepped past the foyer to find Adriana sitting on one end of the leather couch, legs crossed, a floral teacup in one hand. Her hair was wrapped in rollers beneath a pink pastel silk scarf, a white silk robe cinched tight around her waist. I smiled, relieved to see her. She didn't smile back. Her eyes followed me as I walked toward her. I leaned down and kissed her cheek before sinking into the cushion beside her.

"What are you doing up?"

"What do you think I'm doing up?"

I rested a hand on her thigh, giving it a light squeeze. "I'm alive, sweetheart," I chuckled, my head tilting to take in her stern expression. "Come on, let's get some sleep."

"That's not funny," she hissed, setting the teacup down on the table with a *clink.*

"I'm sorry. I was trying to lighten the mood, sweetheart. There's no need to be upset when everything is fine."

"I was worried."

"I know you were. But I've told you, sweetheart, I'm not going anywhere. Other than upstairs with you," I said, a devious smirk sliding across my lips.

"You can't promise you're not going anywhere."

"But I just did. I promise, I'm not going anywhere. I promise nothing is going to happen to me. Unless there's something you have planned to do to me, in which case, I'll let you."

"Stop saying that. Stop promising stuff you can't promise. Every time you say things like this, I feel like you're daring the world to prove you wrong. You don't get to play God, Joey," she said, her eyes blazing with fury.

I sat up straighter. "Okay, I'm sorry, sweetheart—"

"Sorry doesn't fix everything."

"Tell me how to fix it then."

"Don't give me a reason to sit here alone in the middle of the night again."

"I'll try my best."

She shook her head, and her lips drawn in a line. "See! See what I mean! You can't even promise you won't keep me sitting here all night worrying if you'll return or not."

I stutter, unable to find the words because she's right. I can't promise her this, and she knows it. She's trying to prove her point.

"I can't lose you. Do you hear me? I *can't*." Her voice cracked, edged with panic.

I pushed myself off the couch and stood in front of her, taking her arms in mine before pulling her up. My hands cupped her pouting face, tilting it toward me. "I know, I know," I murmured. "But you won't lose me. I don't want to lose you either. Right now, I need you to come upstairs with me. I need you. I need my wife, the one person who makes everything better."

She pulled back, wrapping her arms tightly around herself

as a few tears fell. "I didn't want to fall for another man," she said, jabbing her finger into my chest. "But *you* came into *my* life, fixing every little problem, making everything feel so easy. And I fell for you. I thought we were going to be untouchable. That the deal was: we made our own rules. That we didn't answer to anyone. That we were powerful."

"We are. We still are. But power like this...sweetheart, it draws enemies. People want to take it from us. I can't promise everything to you, but I can promise nobody will take this from me. They will not win. It'll be over my dead body that I allow Hector Russo to take me out."

She exhaled, her mouth slightly open, wiping the tears from her face. "Yeah, well...let's hope it doesn't come to that," she muttered, turning on her heel and heading for the stairs.

"*Sweetheart—*" I called after her, chasing a few steps behind. "I didn't mean it like that. Not literally. It was a figure of speech."

I reached for her wrist, trying to turn her back to me, but she yanked it away like my touch seared her. She didn't look back. She kept walking, her bare feet silent on the stairs. She opened the bedroom door, and before I could say another word—

SLAM.

"Adriana!" I shouted up the staircase. "I'm not going to die! I didn't mean it like that!"

But the only response was silence behind the closed door. *Fuck.* I guess the couch is my companion tonight.

Chapter Twenty

Antonio
Three days after Vincent's murder

The palms of my hands stretched out in front of me, my eyes drifting down the length of the black suit I'd worn earlier that day. My head whipped side to side, searching frantically, but the pull dragged me forward, summoning me down the slick sidewalk and up to the looming entrance of *St. Augustine of the Sacred Heart*. Father Delgado stood waiting, the entrance cracked open. His smile was too wide, too knowing, as he lifted a hand and ushered me inside.

"Hurry, Antonio. You don't want to be late."

Every head in the pews turned at once, their gazes pinning me in place as I made my way down an aisle that stretched longer with every step. Vincent's casket rested beneath the crucifix. Something icy pressed into my palm. I glanced down and stuttered. A revolver. My hand slick with blood, crimson dripping steadily to the floor, spattering in perfect rhythm with my heartbeat. I shook my hand, tried to fling the weapon away, scrub the blood off my skin, but the gun clung to me, fused to my grip, the blood multiplying no matter how hard I fought it. When I finally forced my eyes up, the casket wasn't closed anymore. The lid had creaked open, and it was now empty when I peered inside.

A hand tapped my shoulder. I spun around, the revolver jerking upward on its own, my finger tightening against the trigger, though I begged my body to stop. Vincent stood before me. Not dead. Not alive either. His suit was damp with soil, his skin waxy and gray. His lips peeled back into a smirk that didn't reach his hollow eyes. "I always knew you had fire in you," he drawled, his voice dripping with mockery.

"No," I whispered, shaking my head, trying to force my arm down, but it refused, locked, trembling in midair.

He stepped closer, the scent of rot crawling up my throat. "Our time together was just the beginning."

"No," I rasped.

"Go on," he urged, his grin splitting wider. "Show them what you're really capable of."

I whipped toward the front pew. Ma sat there, rigid as marble. Beside her, Rosa. Then Lucy. Michael. Angela. Enzo. All of them staring at me, wide-eyed and silent. But Joey wasn't there.

"Pull the trigger," a voice hissed from behind me, so close it brushed the back of my neck. "One chance, kid. That's all you've got. Make it count. Take this motherfucker out."

When I twisted my body toward the voice, it was Joey standing in front of the casket now. Pale, his eyes on mine. My hand jerked higher, revolver fixed on his chest. My other arm rose on its own, the barrel leveled at Vincent.

Tears burned my eyes. "No," I choked. "I didn't mean to. You know I didn't mean this, Joey."

"Do it!" Vincent's voice cracked through the air. "Show them what you did!"

A gunshot cracked through the air. My whole body jolted as tears streamed hot down my face. Joey staggered back into the casket, his eyes blown wide with disbelief as crimson spread across his black suit. He gasped for air, voice breaking. "How could you do this to me?"

"I didn't!" I screamed, my throat raw. "I didn't mean to—"

A chill slithered down my neck. Vincent's breath, cold and foul, brushed against my ear. "What are you going to do now? Hm? Show them."

Another shot exploded. Vincent's body snapped backward, crumbling to the floor.

I shot upright in bed. My chest heaving, sweat soaked through my white ribbed tank top, the sheets twisted tight around me like restraints. My cheeks were wet, and when my trembling fingers touched them, I realized I'd been crying— both in my dream and in my sleep.

Chapter Twenty-One

Antonio
Four days after Vincent's murder

I didn't sleep much that night. Not after the nightmare, not after the sound of Joey and Ma arguing on the staircase. "I'm not gonna die!" Joey bellowed after her, but the slam of the bedroom door swallowed his voice. The echo lingered long after. So did the ache it left in me. Joey was all we had. If we lost him...we'd lose everything.

I stood at my vanity mirror, giving myself one last look. Cream slacks with a crisp crease down the front, a pale yellow button-down tucked into a leather belt, and brown loafers to finish the part. I stepped into the hall. The scent of fresh bread and coffee rose to meet me as I descended the stairs. In the kitchen, Rosa stood at the stove, pouring steaming water through the percolator while a loaf rested warm on top of the counter. Joey's lanky frame took up every inch of the couch, legs bent where it was too short to hold him. His trousers clung loosely to his hips, his chest bare, the shadows from the window cutting across it. One arm dangled over the side, the other flung over his eyes.

"Where's Ma?"

Rosa handed me a small cup of coffee with milk and sugar. "She's still asleep."

Rosa always knew everything but acted like she didn't. People around here said she had gone senile, but I knew better. Rosa was far more clever than any of us. She just let folks think what they wanted.

Joey's blanket crumpled on the floor, sandwiched between the couch and the coffee table. I picked it up and draped it over him. He was a man of dignity, he'd lose his mind if he knew he'd spent the night half-naked, passed out on the couch like that. So really, I was doing him a favor.

As I turned to walk back into the kitchen, he stirred, his eyes fluttering open. I guess I should have known men like him sleep with one eye open. He blinked against the sunlight pouring through the windows behind the couch, squinting up at me. I gave him a small, awkward smile. "What time is it, kid?" Joey asked, his New Yorker rasp still thick with sleep.

"Close to eight."

"Where are you heading off to?" He rubbed his face with one hand, then ran his fingers through his messy half-slicked-back hair. His hair stuck up in every direction. If he could see himself right now, he'd probably pass out.

"I'm meeting friends at the diner for breakfast."

He yawned and pushed himself off the couch, reaching behind it for his white button-down shirt. "Friends? Something tells me it's not just Michael and Enzo."

"The girls will be there."

"Ahh, girls," he smirked, buttoning his shirt and tucking it into his black trousers. "Well, let me drive you. I'm going to the shop anyway."

"You sure? I was going to take my bike." I asked, guilt creeping in. A man like Joey probably never slept more than a few hours a night. Not because he couldn't, but because sleep was more of a luxury.

He sighed, tossing his arm over my shoulders and pulling me into his chest. I wrapped my arm around his waist, and a soft, tired laugh slipped free. "I'm more than sure."

"Good morning," Rosa said, smiling as she handed Joey a cup of black coffee.

"Morning, Rosa," he hummed into his coffee cup. "When Adriana wakes up, let her know I'm out for the day," he said, slipping on his shoes and reaching for his car keys.

"I will," Rosa nodded.

"And tell her I love her. If she wants to stop by the shop, she can."

"Of course, I will let her know."

I downed the last of my coffee and followed Joey out the front door. He looked nothing like himself, still in the day-old suit he'd worn to Vincent's funeral, hair sticking up every which way, and carrying one of Ma's good coffee cups with him to the car. The summer heat clung to us the second we stepped outside, the cicadas buzzing in the trees while the smell of cut grass carried down the block. Joey's Ferrari sat in the driveway, the chrome catching every beam, the cream leather seats glowing a shade of ivory.

I slipped into the passenger side, and Joey slid behind the wheel, dropping the roof before he backed out. The warm air poured, carrying the briny tang of the bay. The radio hummed so low it was barely there, enough for him to whistle along, tapping the wheel in rhythm. Fifty miles an hour might've been the fastest anyone was allowed to go here, but Joey never got close. He coasted down the street as if time were his to waste. I knew for certain, he'd never been anyone's hired getaway driver. He was the brains, not the wheelman.

"Did you hear anything last night?" He drummed his

fingers against the wheel, glancing sideways at me when the car rolled to a halt.

I stared straight ahead at the red light. I didn't want to admit I'd heard everything. So I lied. "No."

Joey let out a breath and nodded, tapping the gas when the light turned green. "Sorry if we woke you."

"You didn't," I said. Technically true, I'd already been awake from my nightmare.

"Marriage is hard. Life's hard. But I love your mother. And she loves me. It's normal for married couples to bicker. It's just...it's just a rough chapter right now for us. But that's all it is, just a chapter in the long novel life is. Things will turn around." The words were meant for me, but his voice carried the weight of someone trying to believe them for himself.

"Okay," I nodded.

The Ferrari glided into the empty stretch of asphalt in front of *Cynthia's Diner*. Neon letters shone above the entrance, casting a warm pink and turquoise glow onto the pavement. The breeze carried the scent of sizzling bacon and freshly brewed coffee from the diner's open front door. The faint sea breeze drifting in from the harbor right next to the building. New York City in the backdrop.

A lone metal bench sat near the door, where an elderly man gripped a worn leather briefcase and puffed on a cigar, the smoke curling into the humidity. The parking lot was full, a mix of rattling sedans, gleaming coupes, and a couple of beat-up station wagons. The clink of heels on the asphalt echoed as a waitress from inside darted out to wipe down the glass entrance door. Horns honked in the distance as a delivery truck rumbled past, the low growl of its engine vibrating.

Joey turned toward me, one hand still resting on the steering wheel. "You like this, Mia girl?"

I shrugged. "I don't really know her well enough to say if I like her or not."

"How was the cinema? Did you see *Psycho*?"

I nodded.

He smirked, the back of his hand tapping my chest. "That's my boy. Did she get real close?"

I huffed out a laugh.

He hummed, nodding in approval. "Did you kiss her?"

"What? No. I didn't kiss her. I told you we're just friends."

Joey's eyebrows rose. "Just friends, huh?"

"Don't be ridiculous," I laughed, my cheeks heating as I darted my eyes toward my lap. I could still feel Mia's hand in mine, her body pressed against me, her breath fanning my neck.

"Ridiculous?" he echoed with a chuckle. "Come on, kid, you can't hide it from me. I know my boy."

I rolled my eyes, trying to ignore the grin tugging at the corners of my lips. " She's cute, but we're just friends."

"Just wait," he said, wagging a finger in the air between us. "One day, someone's gonna knock you off your feet, and you're not gonna know what hit you. You've got to learn from the master. You know how many times your mother knocks me on my ass when I see her."

"Is that because she gives you a hard time?" I smirked.

"Ohhh," he barked out a laugh.

Over Joey's shoulder, Mia stood by the entrance of the diner, sunlight catching her dark brown curls that framed her face. Her warm, golden-brown skin glowed against the cream sundress she wore, dotted with tiny red flowers and a belt cinched at her waist. Barefoot in white sandals, she hugged a small leather satchel against her chest. Her big, almond-shaped eyes met mine for a moment before she dropped her head, cheeks flushed like ripened peaches, a shy smile tugging at her lips.

Joey peered over his shoulder at her before turning back to me. "Don't let me hold you up. It's summertime. Go have some fun. I love you, kid."

"I love you too, Dad," I breathed out in one word before I could stop myself.

His smile froze. My stomach dropped.

Did I really just say that?

"Dad?" he repeated, eyebrows raised.

"Yeah, is that okay with you?"

"Is that okay with me?" He smiled, his eyes softening at the edges. The corner of his mouth twitched as he tried not to grin. "Yeah, that's okay with me, kid."

He reached over and gripped the back of my neck, pulling me in. A muffled laugh filled the air as I wrapped my arms around him and he pressed my head to his chest. I could feel the steady thump of his heart against my ear, grounding me as I hugged him back as tight as I could, given the awkward position and the fact that Mia was in the background.

"Okay, okay," I said, pushing away from his grasp. "You're gonna mess up my hair and embarrass me."

His face twisted into mock seriousness. "You're right, I'm sorry. I should be more composed than this." I laughed, rolling my eyes as I slid out of the passenger seat of his Ferrari and walked around to the front. "Have a good day, son!"

"You too, Dad!"

A grin wider than I'd ever seen splashed across his lips, the sunlight catching his disheveled hair as we parted ways.

I stopped in front of Mia, a gentle smile tugging at my lips. "Hi."

"Hi," she whispered, her voice soft.

"You look beautiful in that dress," I said, my eyes taking in every detail.

Her eyes widened, scanning the length of her dress before

flicking back to me, cheeks flushing a soft pink. "Oh...wow. Thank you. You—you look really handsome, too."

"Thank you." I stepped to the side and opened the door for her, lowering my hand in a small, practiced bow. "Ladies first."

Stepping inside, the summer heat gave way to the coolness of the diner's air-conditioning. The walls painted a cheerful shade of pink and turquoise, sunlight streaming through the wide windows and casting soft reflections across the black-and-white checkered floor. Leather booths lined the windows, while tables with chairs ran down the middle of the room. The long bar, lined with polished stools, offered a clear view into the kitchen where the clatter of dishes and the hiss of the grill played a comforting background rhythm. A jukebox stood in the far corner, ready for someone to drop a coin and fill the air with the hits of the summer.

Enzo, Michael, Alessia, and Maria had pushed together two 4-seater tables. Alessia and Michael exchanged shy smiles and hushed words, while Enzo, his arm stretched behind Maria's chair, bit into a piece of bacon with a sly grin. Maria watched him, wide-eyed and enamored.

Mia and I slid into the two seats next to Michael and Alessia. The table was already crowded with plates of food. Enzo was digging into the breakfast sampler—bacon, two scrambled eggs, and pancakes drowned in syrup—while Maria nibbled at a single waffle, eyes drifting toward Enzo with a starry look. Michael and Alessia were sharing a breakfast platter, leaning in close as they whispered. The waitress approached, notepad in hand, her pencil tapping against the paper. "What can I get for the two of you?"

"Oatmeal," Mia said, brushing one of her dark curls behind her ear.

"Chocolate chip muffin."

The waitress nodded and gathered up our menus, scribbling down our orders before moving on to the next table.

"So...do you eat here a lot?" I asked, the words tumbling out before I could stop myself. As soon as they did, I winced inwardly. *Smooth, Antonio. Real smooth.*

"Not really," Mia said, tilting her head toward me. "But sometimes. I like the fries with gravy. And their cherry pie is great. What about you?"

I shrugged, glancing at her before looking down at the table. "We used to come here all the time, but not so much lately. I'm a sucker for the chocolate milkshakes."

The waitress slid by, placing Mia's steaming bowl of oatmeal in front of her and my chocolate chip muffin in front of me before drifting off again. Mia stirred her oatmeal slowly, her spoon circling the bowl as if she were buying time. Her lips parted, then pressed shut, like she was working up the courage to say something but couldn't. Finally, she glanced at me through her long lashes. "I...I had a good time at the cinema with you the other night."

My eyebrows shot up before I could stop them. "Really? You seemed terrified."

Her blush deepened as she ducked her head. "Well, yeah. But...it was a good kind of terrified. Plus, you made it a little less terrifying."

"How so?"

"Because you weren't terrified...and you let me cling to you, which—"

"—is making you blush," I cut in with a grin, studying the soft pink blooming across her cheeks.

Her elbow brushed against my arm as she giggled. "Stop it. I'm hardly blushing."

"Yeah, you're blushing," I laughed.

"You're terrible." She tilted her head, lashes fluttering upward enough for her gaze to brush mine.

"Terribly charming," I teased. "And happy I get to see you again."

"Me too." Her smile softened, her gaze holding mine. My eyes flickered to her lips before darting back up.

"I've been thinking about you since the cinema date. A lot, actually."

My heart kicked up a notch. Wait. What did she just say?

"Date?" I echoed, surprised.

Her smile faltered. "It...wasn't a date?"

"I mean, it kind of was. I just hadn't thought of it that way until now."

"Oh." She let out a quiet breath, eyes dropping to her oatmeal as she stirred it, the disappointment clear in the small downturn of her mouth.

"I didn't mean it like that," I said, my hand brushing her knee before I even thought about it. Her eyes shot up to mine, wide and startled.

"No, it's okay," she whispered.

"I just...I meant I've never been on a date before, so I didn't think about it as a date, but I do suppose it was. And now I'm making this way more awkward than it has to be." I exhaled, shaking my head with a crooked smile. "How about this...we ditch sitting here listening to Michael whisper in Alessia's ear and Enzo try to set a world record for bacon, and instead...walk over to the record shop? Make it feel like a *real* date."

Her lips parted, a small smile tugging at the corners. "I'd like that."

* * *

The record store sat snugly next to Cynthia's Diner, colorful paper signs advertising the latest hits—Elvis, Ricky Nelson, and the Everly Brothers in the glass windows. Inside, rows of wooden bins stretched in neat lines, each packed with LPs in paper sleeves, their spines labeled with scribbled chalk in a faded hand. A small turntable in the corner played soft, scratchy rock 'n' roll and doo-wop from a record spinning for listening customers. A low ceiling fan stirred the warm air, making the store feel alive with the hum of summer energy, the occasional click of records sliding in and out of their bins, and the muffled laughter of other teenagers discovering their favorite records.

The narrow aisles were just wide enough for two to walk side by side, the floor worn smooth from years of sneakers sliding over the scuffed linoleum. A counter near the back held a cash register, stacks of 45s ready for purchase, and a small bell that rang whenever the owner or clerk wasn't behind it.

I held up the vinyl, Buddy Holly's *"That'll Be the Day."*

"You ever heard this one? Rosa says he was the best there ever was." My fingers traced the edges of the record.

Mia stood a few steps ahead of me, her head tilted, dark curls brushing against her shoulders as her big brown eyes studied the cover. "I think I heard 'Peggy Sue' on the jukebox at the diner once. Is Rosa your grandma?"

"Yeah, I suppose the closest thing I've got to a grandma."

"She used to have a really beautiful flower shop."

"Yeah," I said, passing the vinyl to Mia, "she planted a nice flower garden in our front yard, and an even better one in the backyard, full of fruits and vegetables. Smells amazing in the summer."

Mia's eyes lit up at the image. "You know, I recall when I heard 'Peggy Sue' playing, I thought I wanted to get up and dance. But I'm not too good at dancing."

"Me either," I said, a faint grin tugging at my lips. "Maybe we'd look less ridiculous if we danced together."

She laughed softly, brushing a curl behind her ear. "Yeah, maybe." Her gaze returned to the vinyl. "Don't you think Buddy Holly and Michael look the same? If Michael had glasses, I think he'd look just like him."

I snorted. "And that weird peach fuzz Michael's got growing above his lip that he's become so fond of. He'd pass for a teen idol, Buddy Hall, if he shaved it and put on some glasses."

We kept flipping through the vinyls when Mia pulled out an Elvis Presley album. "Maria's obsessed with him. She says he looks kind of like Enzo, but I don't see it."

I shrugged, leaning against the record rack. "I don't know if he looks like Enzo, but I don't get why everyone's crazy about Presley. My ma included. All he does is sing and wiggle on stage, and somehow everyone loses their minds."

Mia tilted her head, studying the cover. "His music's good, though, don't you think?"

I shook my head, a small grin tugging at my lips. "Not really my style."

"Oh? So, what's your style?"

"I like the blues," I said, fingers brushing over the edge of a vinyl.

Mia's eyes lit up. "Blues? Like...B.B. King?"

I nodded, pulling a record off the shelf and flipping it over. "Yeah. He's the king of blues, like his name applies. I like the stuff with real guitars. Something that makes you feel like the music's alive."

"I've never really listened to blues. Do you think I'd like it?"

"I suppose there's really only one way to find out," I grinned, snatching the first B.B. King album I could find, and took her hand, leading her toward the turntable tucked on a corner shelf. I slid the record into place, and as the needle dropped, the first slow, wailing notes filled the small shop, reverberating through the floorboards.

"Oh...wow," she breathed. "That's...different. But it's a good kind of different. I like it. It's kind of...sad but good-sad. I see what you mean about the guitar and music that feels alive."

I grinned, pleased she liked it. "That's the blues for you. It makes you feel things. That's why I like it so much. The way he plays that guitar...You don't even need the lyrics because you feel everything through the guitar, so his vocals are just an added bonus."

"What's this song called?"

"'3 O'Clock Blues'. It's probably one of my favorites."

"Do you always pick the sad songs? You don't strike me as someone who would listen to this kind of music."

"He's got some other ones that aren't sad, but this just happened to be my favorite. Sometimes I listen to it at night when I can't sleep. The thing about Blues and B.B. King is he's not Presley, you feel his music under your skin."

Mia smiled softly, turning back to the spinning record. "I think I get it. It makes everything feel...bigger. Like you said, you can feel it under your skin. Like, even a small place like some record shop in Staten Island can suddenly feel bigger. Better than what it actually is."

A smile tugged at the corners of my mouth. "Yeah...see you get it."

I watched her eyes, the soft light of the shop catching the warmth in them. B.B. King's music wrapping around us and filling every corner of the tiny room.

"You've made me see something...magical," she whispered, her voice barely above the hum of the record.

I took a step closer, my hand brushing against hers, still resting on the turntable. "It's not just the music that's magical.

The music makes you feel things. But," I said, my voice low. "It's...everything else that's magical." Her cheeks flushed pink. My thumb traced the back of her hand.

"What do you mean by that? Everything else is magical?"

"Being here with you right now as you discover B.B. King seems pretty magical to me."

I closed what distance was left between us, my lips hovering over hers. I was both eager and terrified to kiss someone for the first time. When she didn't pull away, I brushed my lips against hers. Her hand moved to my shoulder, and I pressed my lips harder against hers. The music swirled around us, the wailing guitar a perfect soundtrack to our first kiss, the tiny record shop suddenly feeling bigger than the whole world.

Chapter Twenty-Two

Joey
Four days after Vincent's murder

I pushed open the office door, the scent of fresh coffee hit me before I even stepped inside. A few of the guys were huddled around the coffee maker in the hallway, cradling steaming mugs. The moment they spotted me, every head turned, eyes widening enough to betray surprise. A wide lopsided grin broke out across my face. I was still riding the high from Antonio calling me "Dad," a simple word that sent warmth flooding in every part of my soul. Paul froze mid-sip, his coffee cup hovering near his mouth. He looked like he'd just seen a ghost. I glanced over my shoulder to see what he was staring at.

There was no ghost. Just me.

He exchanged a quick look with Marco, then both of them walked over.

"What the fuck happened to you?" Paul asked in a low voice as we made our way toward my office. "Why do you look like that?"

"Nothing's wrong. I don't look like anything," I said, tossing my keys on the desk and dropping into my chair with a groan.

My back still aching from sleeping on the couch. "It's been one of the best mornings I've had in a long time."

"Sal!" Paul called down the hallway. "Get him a coffee!"

"I told you he was gonna spiral," Marco muttered, mostly to Paul.

"I'm not spiraling."

Paul stepped in front of my desk. "I just want you to know, we've got this. If you go down, we all go down. So whatever's happening, we'll handle it. You don't have to carry it alone. We've got your back. Just because Hector is the underboss doesn't mean we won't do everything we can to prove he was the one who killed Vincent and that he has been after you since the very beginning."

"I know," I said as Sal slipped in and placed a fresh coffee in front of me. "Thanks," I mumbled, bringing the cup to my lips. The steam hit my face, and I reveled in the second cup of coffee.

"With that being said, you look like shit. You can't have people seeing you like this." Marco waved his hands animatedly toward me, eyes wide.

"What's wrong with how I look?" I asked, taking another sip of coffee.

"You look like someone who lost a fight with life. And that's not the Joey Romano I know. The Joey Romano I know," Marco jabbed a thumb into his chest, "he's the best-dressed man to grace the streets of Staten Island. The poster boy of Brylcreem. And yet here you are, hair a mess, still wearing that funeral suit from yesterday."

"The only fight I lost was with Adriana last night," I replied, rubbing at my shoulder, "which landed me on the couch, and now I'll probably need a skilled chiropractor before my back ever feels normal again."

Paul crossed his arms over his chest, the smirk tugging at

the corner of his mouth as if he'd already won some invisible argument. "I suppose you should've listened to me whenever I told you not to go over there."

I leaned back in my chair, letting out a low groan, and muttered, "You think I'm gonna tell you that you're right? Unfortunately, you're real wrong...because that's *never* gonna happen."

He chuckled under his breath, shaking his head, eyes twinkling with mischief. "I don't expect you to say I'm right. I already know I am."

He was, of course, but I would never, *ever* admit that aloud.

"Didn't you say y'all had a healthy marriage?" Marco piped up. "You told us all the other night at *The Wise Guy*, and then you go home and sleep on the couch?" He let out a childish snicker.

I stared blankly at the two of them, as their grinning, smirking faces dared me to crack. "We had a disagreement," I muttered, taking a slow sip of coffee as if it would shield me from the teasing.

"Man," Marco exclaimed, throwing his hands up in exaggerated triumph, "it feels good to be the only one not married in this group." He shook his head and laughed, a sound full of both amusement and relief.

"Yeah, right. You're not married because Angela won't say yes. It's not because you chose it." Paul punctuated the jab with a teasing tap on Marco's shoulder, grinning.

I set the coffee cup down, letting out a small laugh that was equal parts exasperation and fondness. "Keep talking, and I might just start charging rent for all this advice I give you two. Sure, I slept on the couch but that doesn't mean our marriage isn't the healthiest out of everyone else's."

"Advice?" Marco repeated. "Nah, this is called witnessing a marital dispute between one of the most feared men in the city and his meek wife who strips his dignity away, my friend. You squabble with Adriana, and Paulie and I get front-row seats to whatever this—" He waved his hand at me again. "—is."

"Yeah." Paul smirked. "And trust me, you don't even realize how much we enjoy seeing you like this."

I bit back the smirk trying to break free. "I thought you were worried about me."

"That was when we thought you were going senile. Now that we know, quiet, sweet Adriana forced you, of all people, to sleep on a couch and wear the same suit the next day," Marco said, breathless as he laughed so hard he was wheezing, while Paul did the same, resting an arm on Marco's shoulder. "Now it's just the funniest thing I've ever seen."

"With all the joking aside," Paul huffed out through his laughter, "how are you feeling after yesterday?"

"Which part?" I asked.

"Yeah," Marco nudged him. "Which part? The funeral? The meeting? Or the fight with his wife?"

Paul snickered. "You know we didn't know anything until we got to the meeting and were told to take our seats. And then, as everyone began to fill the warehouse, I realized they had told you to come at ten, which meant you were the last one in the building and that your seat wasn't at the table."

"I know you didn't know. I know how it works, Paul."

"What are we going to do about Hector becoming the underboss?" Marco asked.

I shrugged. "I don't know yet. We need to wait on Ben to clear a few things up in the city so we can figure out if Hector killed Vincent or had someone else do it. Either way, we need proof to bring to Christopher. In the meantime, we have to play our cards right."

"Yeah, we play our cards right," Paul said, nodding, a serious edge creeping into his voice.

"Let's get this day started," Marco exclaimed, clasping a hand on Paul's shoulder. "And hey"—he paused at the door of my office—"if Adriana puts you on the couch again, I'll show up with backup."

"Backup?"

"Yeah," Marco said, smirking. "Paul and I will form a couch patrol for you, make sure you get proper sleep and don't come in looking like this." He gestured toward me again.

"Patrol?" I groaned, shaking my head. "You're unbelievable. Get out of here."

"Unbelievable is my specialty," Marco grinned. I heard Paul laughing from outside of the office.

"We've got your *back* no matter what," Marco smirked. "See what I did there? We've got your back literally and figuratively."

Chapter Twenty-Three

Adriana
Four days after Vincent's murder

Waking up in an empty bed was one thing, but knowing it was because I'd stormed up here after our fight last night felt like a punch straight to the gut. As my hand reached across the sheets and found only cold linen, my heart sank.

I forced myself out of bed and into the closet to choose a dress for the day. At the vanity, I brushed out my victory curls and gave myself a once-over. The pale blue bodice buttoned neatly down the front, the short flutter sleeves brushing against my arms. A navy collar framed my throat, and the skirt fell in a deep, flowing sweep of the same shade, whispering around my legs as I moved. I liked the contrast—the light against the dark, the structure against the sway. It made me feel put-together, elegant, as though I belonged at a summer garden party or in some polished photograph, even if my nerves told me otherwise.

On my way out of the bedroom, Rosa stopped me in the hallway, clutching a stack of neatly folded linen. "Joey's gone for the day," she said. "He asked me to tell you that he loves you, and he'll be at the office all day if you need him...or perhaps, want to stop by."

I should rush to him. I should forgive him. But anger still coiled in my chest, and stubbornness flooded my veins. "Thank you, Rosa." Instead of heading toward Joey's office, I drove to Lucy's beauty salon. Rosa's freshly baked bread and a block of Beurre d'Isigny, in its parchment wrap, sat in the passenger seat.

I pushed open the glass door to Lucy's salon. She stood behind the counter in a scarlet halter-bodycon dress that plunged daringly at the chest. "Good morning," she greeted, tilting her head to admire my freshly curled hair. "Those are fresh curls, aren't they? Stunning, Adriana. I don't think there's anyone who can wear them as well as you."

"Thank you, I don't think anyone has a better fashion sense than you," I smiled, placing the loaf of bread and the butter on the counter. "Rosa made some fresh bread, so I thought I'd bring it over for us. Plus, I don't think I can face Pat and everyone inside Pat's for cannolis after that funeral."

Lucy's eyes softened. She stepped around the counter and pulled me into a tight hug. "I'm so sorry about what Renee did," she murmured into my hair. She pulled away, her arms gripping my shoulders, "She's a real bitch for that. She's psychotic, and anyone who trusts or believes her has more screws loose than they'll ever get back."

I sighed at the relief of her embrace. "She humiliated us, Lucy."

Lucy's grip on my shoulders tightened. "No, she *tried* to humiliate you. There's a difference. She tried, and you will not let her succeed. Anyone who matters saw right through her."

"Every eye in that church was on us, Lucy. I wanted to crawl out of my own skin."

"She thrives on that. She thrives on making people feel

small so she can feel bigger. Don't give her that power," Lucy urged, her eyes narrowing with fierce protectiveness.

I blinked back the sting in my eyes. "You make it sound so easy. But I'm terrified she's going to plant seeds in the minds of everyone in this town and paint a target on Joey's back."

"It's not easy. But it's possible. And until you believe it, I'll believe it for you. Because I won't let anything happen to Joey."

My entire body sagged. "How could you be so sure? I think she's got the entire town's mind convinced. She got the final word in that church, and it was the worst thing to happen to Joey."

"Then it's up to us to remind her she doesn't get the final word. Joey's been unstoppable for as long as I've known him. She can't take that away from him, no matter what poison she spits."

Lucy and I both turned our heads as the front door opened and Angela breezed inside. "What's happened?" she asked, slipping her black-and-white cat-eyed sunglasses up to rest on her glossy dark hair. Her dress was a curve-hugging sheath in bold cherry red, cinched at the waist with a slim patent belt. The wide scoop neckline showed enough collarbone to make you do a double-take, while the hem flirted just above her knees, perhaps shorter than most women would dare, but Angela wore it like it was made for her. A pair of strappy white slingbacks clicked against the floor, and pearl drop earrings swayed at her ears every time she moved.

"Renee," Lucy replied. "She's upset, Adriana."

"I swear, I wanted to sneak up behind her with the church's brass crucifix and bonk her right on the skull." Angela huffed, her lips curling into a wicked grin.

I snickered despite myself at the mental image of Angela's furious swing. Some of the tightness in my chest loosened.

Lucy huffed, rolling her eyes, but her smirk said she was enjoying it just as much as I was.

"What she did was terrible, and karma will come back to bite her in the ass someday," Lucy began, peeling the wax paper off the butter. Then she reached into her designer purse —a soft, structured leather bag in a pale cream shade. I watched, barely blinking, as her fingers fished past a compact, a tube of lipstick, and a folded handkerchief before closing around the slender handle of a knife. She drew it out as if it were the most normal thing in the world. I didn't ask. With Lucy, it was better not to.

Angela's eyes went wide. "Uh...did that just come out of your purse?" she asked, one brow raised. "Because, Lucy...I don't believe that's in the summer accessories catalog."

Lucy shrugged, butter knife in hand, scooping a generous slab of butter onto the top of her blade. "Well, it should be. Don't you think?"

Angela tilted and shrugged in agreement, "Perhaps, I'm only jealous I didn't consider it sooner."

"You know, speaking of that psychotic bitch, Renee," Lucy began. "I had to listen to her fake cry for hours like she was auditioning for a daytime soap. It was enough to have me committed. I drank myself stupid trying to survive her wailing, as I stood next to that dirtbag, Hector, while he reeked of cheap perfume, and pretended as though I was okay with my father naming him underboss of this family." She stabbed the air with the knife for emphasis. "Because clearly, my opinion counts for nothing."

Angela and I watched, stunned, as Lucy—in her firetruck-red halter dress—ranted and licked butter off a pocketknife.

"I have so many questions," Angela mouthed to me. "Starting with why the hell are you eating butter like that?"

Lucy froze mid-lick, her eyes wide and unbothered. "I

binge-ate half a bakery trying to cure my hangover the next day. I've decided to cut carbs now, cold turkey, because if my hips get any wider, I won't fit into my wardrobe. And that would be the real end to Lucille Giordano."

"Right," Angela nodded. "And I suppose a pound of butter is the healthy choice here?" she laughed softly, raising one perfectly shaped eyebrow.

"It has no carbs, Angela," Lucy said matter-of-factly, licking another swipe of butter off the blade before flopping dramatically into one of the blow-dryer chairs.

Angela chuckled, grabbing a piece of the fresh bread and slathering it with butter. "Well, thank God, I'm not low-carb. I'd be dead by now."

Everyone in town knew Lucy and Hector had a...*peculiar* marriage. A union arranged by her father—one that came with affairs on both sides, secrets swept under the rug, and power plays Lucy could *never* escape. Hector would never *willingly* give up his status, even if it meant setting her free. If he ever did agree to a divorce, and Lucy ran off with the one man who had always had her heart, Ben, that would only end in one way: Ben in a body bag before Lucy's heels even touched the pavement. Mafia royalty and a rogue cop could never be a thing in their world.

"You look hot today," Angela said, chewing around her mouthful of bread. She glanced at herself in the reflective glass windows facing the street. "Maybe I should lay off the bread, too."

"You're tall," Lucy said, waving her off. "You'll be fine. But if I die before Ben leaves his wife, bury me in this dress. Let the world know I went out glamorous."

"You'll outlive us all, just to keep stirring up trouble," I smirked at Lucy, nibbling the edge of my bread. No butter. I was trying to lay off fats.

Angela scoffed playfully. "Honey, if there's a heaven, I'm convinced God would stop you at the gates just for showing up in a dress with that much cleavage."

I laughed, and Angela joined in, but Lucy didn't. Her eyes had drifted, her smile faded.

She lurched forward, voice cracking slightly. "You wanna know what kills me?" Her eyes shimmered. "He looks at me like I'm his whole world. He says it too, tells me I'm his *every-thing*. And then he still goes home to *her*. Whoever she is. I bet she's some beautiful blonde with a Boston accent who makes him dinner every night." *So, the exact opposite of Lucy.*

I rose and sat beside her, slipping my hand into hers. I gave it a gentle squeeze, waiting until her eyes found mine. "Hey... You know what she's not? She's *not* Lucille Giordano."

Lucy's lips curled into a soft smile. She pulled me into a side hug, holding on tight. "I love him, Adriana," she whispered into my hair. "Perhaps too much for my own sanity."

Love did that. It unhinged you, broke all your rules. It made you someone you didn't recognize. It made you do things you didn't know you were even capable of.

"You know," Angela said, leaning against the countertop. "I have to admit, when Marco touches me...it feels like the world stops for a little bit." She looked down at her fresh red mani-cure, her thumb grazing over one polished nail as if it held answers. She wasn't one to show emotion, least of all tender-ness. Though when it came to Marco, even Angela had her soft spots.

"So," I said, more to the air than to either of them, "I guess we all love men who are...*questionable* at best. And the truth is, perhaps, we'd rather have part of them than nothing at all." I paused, unsure if I'd meant to say it out loud. "Maybe that's what will be our downfall."

Lucy chuckled. "God, we're tragic."

"And terrifying," Angela added with a wicked grin, wagging a finger toward us. "Don't forget that part. I might like Marco some nights, but I'm not falling victim to another man for as long as I shall live. He should fear me if he values his life. And that's how you should treat Ben. And Joey, too, while you're at it."

Chapter Twenty-Four

Joey
Four days after Vincent's murder

Later that day, the guys tried to drag me out to *The Wise Guy* for a drink. I almost gave in. Though if I avoided Adriana any longer, I'd be sleeping on the couch another night and there was no way in hell I was letting that happen. So around nine, I walked through the front door. Rosa was on one couch watching an episode of *The Jack Benny Program*. Adriana sat across from her, arms folded, eyes locked on the screen, until they shifted to me. The look she gave me was straight up déjà vu from the previous night. I forced a smile, hoping she'd crack.

She didn't.

"How was your day, Joey?" Rosa asked, as I stepped into the living room.

"Not too bad," I said, my eyes fixed on Adriana. "My back's a little sore, but I managed to get through the day just fine."

"You want me to make an appointment with that chiropractor over on Mulberry?" she offered.

"Nah, I'll live."

"Are you hungry?" she tilted her chin up toward me, forcing her eyes off the tv screen.

"You sit tight," I smiled down at her before my eyes bounced back to Adriana's hardened expression. "I can reheat dinner myself, unless, of course, my beautiful, loving wife wants to help out her poor husband, who's still in yesterday's suit and walking around with a back that's barely holding up." I smiled wide at Adriana, trying one last time. Pleading, really.

Adriana's eyes slid up the length of my body until they landed on my eyes. "I think you can manage warming your plate, honey." She flashed a smile that was all gritted teeth, while Rosa pretended not to notice the tension in the room.

I made my way into the kitchen. A plate was waiting on the counter, wrapped neatly in tinfoil. I peeled it back and inhaled as if I hadn't eaten in days. Adriana's meatballs and red sauce. Was she trying to torture me? She knew exactly how much I enjoyed this meal. I wandered back into the living room to find only Rosa sitting on the couch. My eyes scanned the room as I asked, "Where's Adriana?"

Rosa looked up from the TV. "She said she was going up to bed."

Bed? Hell, no.

I took the stairs two at a time and reached our bedroom door. Closed, but not locked. Thank God. I turned the doorknob and slipped inside. She was at her vanity, dabbing cream onto her cheeks, moving with the same graceful routine I'd seen a thousand times. She looked over, met my gaze for a second, then turned back to the mirror as if I wasn't even standing a few feet away from her.

"Dinner was good," I said, still standing at the door, one hand resting on the knob.

She nodded.

I exhaled, pushing off the door and closer toward her. "Alright, sweetheart," I stood behind her. She met my eyes in the mirror, her glare steady and unblinking as her lashes batted up toward me. "You can be mad at me...I get it...If I were you, I'd be mad too. But here's the thing, you're my wife. I love you. And I'm not spending another damn night on that couch. You want to give me the silent treatment? Fine. Slam doors? Go for it. But I'm not sleeping downstairs like some dog."

When I was finished, the room filled with more silence.

"Fine," she said at last, as she stood from the vanity.

"Fine?" I repeated, rubbing the back of my neck. *Wait. Was this the reverse psychology the guys had warned me about?*

"Yeah," she said, slipping off her pink lace robe and hanging it over the chair of her vanity.

Oh, what the hell. Her nightgown was so sheer it barely covered her. The neckline dipped dangerously low, and her breasts—full and soft—threatened to spill out. My entire body tensed, my cock pressing tight against the zipper of my trousers. I ached just looking at her.

"So just like that? You're over it?" I asked, my eyes locked on her body. Though I tried desperately to keep my gaze fixed on those brown eyes I loved so much. She stood a few feet away, letting me drink her in.

"I'm getting over it," she said with a shrug, as if she wasn't currently undoing me without lifting a finger.

That was enough for me. "Is Antonio in bed?"

"He's staying at Enzo's for the night. Michael's over there, too."

Perfect. I closed the distance in two strides, one arm tightening around her waist while the other slid up the curve of her neck, drawing her mouth to mine. I kissed her as though I'd been starved, and thank God, she met me with the same hunger.

Her fingers fumbled slowly with the buttons of my shirt, but I had no patience for slowness. I tugged open the fastening at my trousers in haste, even as she tipped her head back and let out a low laugh. That sound made my knees weak. Before I could reach for the hem of her nightgown, she pressed her palms against my chest and pushed me back onto the bed.

I went willingly, eager for her.

She sank gracefully to her knees between my legs, her eyes dark with heat as her hands smoothed along my thighs. When her fingers reached my waistband, she drew the fabric down slowly, and I groaned as the tension between us shattered. Her hand closed around the base of my cock, and the sound that left my throat filled the space between us. My body arched into the mattress as she stroked me with a slow rhythm that would soon drive me insane.

The moment her mouth closed over the tip of my shaft, my entire body jolted upright. My fists knotted in the sheets, breath catching hard in my chest. I forced myself to think of anything but the sight of her lips and hands working in perfect rhythm now, the way she looked in that moment threatened to undo me far too quickly.

"Sweetheart, come on," I practically begged, my voice rough, breath catching between words. I lifted my head, and her eyes were dark and dangerous, smoldering with lust. Her cheeks were hollow from the way she was working me, and I was three seconds from losing it. She knew. She could see it written all over my face.

Mercifully, she relented, rising slowly. The nightgown slipped from her shoulders and pooled at her feet, revealing the perfection beneath. For a moment, I could only stare, scarcely believing my fortune—that this woman belonged to me, that I had the right to call her my wife.

She climbed onto the bed, crawling up the length of my

body as though every inch were already hers. Because it was. Her palms pressed firmly to my chest, pinning me against the mattress, and I surrendered without a single thought. My fingers raked through my mussed hair, a futile attempt at composure, though I was clinging to it by a single, fraying thread.

Her hand reached down, closing around the base of my cock as she lifted her hips. My eyes dropped, helpless to do anything but follow the sight of her body as she lowered herself. I blew out a strangled breath as soon as she took me in. My head fell back, eyes rolling shut as the sensation consumed me.

When I managed to open them again, she was a vision—head tilted back, lips parted, hips moving in a slow, steady rhythm that felt nothing short of divine. I reached for her, desperate for some anchor. One hand clutched at her thigh, holding her close, while the other slid upward to cup her breast —full, perfect, and wholly mine.

Her rhythm quickened, and the sound she made—half-moan, half-sigh—nearly undid me. My thumb brushed across her nipple, earning another sharp intake of breath from her lips. I groaned low in my throat, the sound guttural, torn from some-where deep as her body clenched around me.

I shifted my grip, sliding one hand to her hip, guiding her as she rode me with a confidence that made my pulse pound in my ears. Every rise and fall, every rolling sway of her hips pulled me deeper into ecstasy, until the line between her plea-sure and mine blurred into one unbearable ache.

"God, you feel..." I couldn't finish the thought, the words breaking apart as my head pressed back into the mattress. She leaned forward, bracing her hands on my chest, her eyes burning into mine. The sight of her, flushed, trembling, robbed me of what little composure I had left.

I thrust up to meet her, unable to hold back, and the cry that broke from her lips made my entire body tighten in response. My hands roamed her back, her waist, needing to touch every part of her, to remind myself this wasn't a dream, that this fierce, beautiful woman was mine and she always would be.

Her pace grew wilder. My grip on her hips tightened, meeting each descent with a desperate thrust of my own, the rhythm between us spiraling faster and harder. The sound of our bodies joined with her cries, each one more breathless, until I could scarcely tell where she ended and I began.

Her nails dug into my chest, her head thrown back as a shudder rippled through her. The cry that tore from her lips was raw and unrestrained, and the moment I felt her clench around me, I lost the battle entirely. A strangled groan wrenched from my throat as I surged deep, my own release crashing over me in violent waves. She collapsed onto my chest, her breath hot and uneven against my bare skin. My arms wrapped around her, pulling her close as though I might never let go. I kissed the top of her head, murmuring against her hair, "I love you, sweetheart. I hope you never forget that."

She glanced up, her chin resting against my chest, a soft smile playing on her lips. "I love you too. And I hope you never forget it either."

"Oh, I won't, sweetheart," I said, smiling down at her.

Her hand came up against my face, guiding me into a soft kiss. When we pulled apart, I gave her the one piece of news that had carried me through the day. "Antonio called me Dad today."

Her eyes widened. "What?"

I nodded, still grinning. "Yeah. He called me Dad."

"He didn't tell me that. But that's...that's incredible news. That makes me *so* happy."

She kissed me again, and shortly after that, the two of us drifted off—naked, tangled together, hearts full. Despite what awaited us outside this bedroom, we had everything we needed in that moment.

Chapter Twenty-Five

Antonio
Five days after Vincent's murder

Enzo's room smelled of leather, hair tonic, and cigarette smoke. Posters of Elvis and Chuck Berry were plastered unevenly across his bedroom walls, some curling at the corners, others practically peeling right off, but all proudly proclaiming allegiance to the music that made Enzo who he was. A black guitar case leaned on the corners. He never took it out of the case because it was the last gift his father had given him.

His bed was haphazardly made, a dark quilt thrown over rumpled sheets, even the dresser was a mess with stacks of vinyl records, empty soda bottles, and a half-eaten pack of bubble gum balanced against a transistor radio. Enzo had an entire collection of black leather jackets that he took great care of, one of them was neatly draped behind the chair I was sitting in. A single lamp sat beside me on the nightstand.

The small fan wheezed in the summer heat, sending the midnight breeze through the room, making the edges of a "Black Sabbath" sticker he had seen in a magazine flicker with movement. On the floor next to Michael, a pair of scuffed black boots sat under the bed. Michael was slouched against the bed with a cigarette dangling between his lips as he laughed at one of Enzo's comic books.

Enzo was laid back toward the end of his bed, one leg dangling off the other propped up as he blew smoke into the air. Angela was still working her nightshift at *The Wise Guy*. Val was supposed to be watching us but she had yet to come check on us. We'd swiped her pack of cigarettes when she wasn't looking.

In the same second, we heard Val's footsteps marching up the stairs. "I know they took it!" she screamed at Sal, who was trying to shush her. Michael dropped the comic book. Enzo shot up from the bed. And I pushed myself out of the chair. The three of us stubbed out our cigarettes in the ashtray, and Michael shoved it under the bed as she threw open Enzo's bedroom door.

I don't know what's come over me lately, but I can't seem to ignore Val—Enzo's older sister, Sal's girlfriend, and *completely* off-limits. Maybe that's exactly what makes her irresistible. My eyes followed the curve of her legs, the purple cotton shorts hugging her hips, the white satin ribbon at the waistband hung loose. Her short-sleeved blouse, striped in white and purple, was undone enough at the top to tease, showing the slightest hint of skin. I had to look away before I betrayed my best friend.

"I know you little shits took them!" she shouted, eyes scanning the room. "I can smell them on you!"

Enzo fought to hold back a grin but failed miserably. "I didn't take your cigarettes," he said, holding his hands up in mock innocence. "Could it be that you smell them on yourself? That you smoked the entire pack and forgot you did so?"

Sal trailed in behind her, hands on her hips. "Let it go,

baby," he murmured. "You can have mine. I already told you that."

My eyes drifted to the curve of her hips, and boy they were perfect.

"That's not the point, Sal!" she snapped, shrugging him off. "They're just kids smoking like a bunch of damn heathens!"

She stormed into the bedroom, arms crossed over her chest. "I didn't smoke the pack. I know you did it!" Her finger jabbed toward Enzo, whose eyebrows shot up as he shrugged.

"Heathens?" Enzo barked out a laugh, making me scarf down the snort trying to travel up my throat. "You're two years older than us, Val. And last I checked, you're not even supposed to be smoking either. So really, what are you going to do? Tell mom?"

Val's glare could've cut through glass, but Sal's arms wrapped around her waist from behind, his head leaning on her shoulder. She was smoking hot, and I hated how much I noticed it. "Ughhhh!" she groaned dramatically, throwing her hands in the air before storming out and slamming the door behind her.

Enzo tossed himself back onto the bed. The back of Michael's head pressing against the mattress. I sank further into the cushion of the chair. The three of us let the laughter leave our chests. Enzo pulled the brown paper bag off the floor and let the contents of it empty onto his bed. Inside the bag was a treasure trove of delicacies. Necco Wafers, Charleston Chews, Red Hots, Tootsie Rolls, Milk Duds, Pixy Stix, and a couple of glass bottles of Coca-Cola and Orange Crush. The three of us flipped through Look Magazine as we sat on the floor of Enzo's bedroom eating junk. The three of us gawking at Marilyn Monroe on the cover and reading the article inside.

"Jesus," Enzo muttered, mouth full of red hots. "I didn't know it was possible to look that hot."

"What a moron DiMaggio has to be," I said, popping a Milk Dud into my mouth. "Letting her slip through his fingers like that? Guy must be brain-dead."

"I thought DiMaggio was the best baseball player to ever live," Michael snickered as he emptied a pixie stick into his mouth.

"Well he is," I admitted. "But he's stupid if he let someone like Marilyn Monroe slip through his fingers."

"I heard she's having an affair with her co-star in that new picture she's filming," Michael added, opening an Orange Crush.

"Wish she was having an affair with me," Enzo muttered.

I smacked him in the chest. "No shot. I call first dibs."

He clutched his heart dramatically and gasped. "So this is how our friendship ends?"

* * *

The clock read two a.m. Michael was passed out on Enzo's bed, sprawled out. Enzo was face down on the floor, snoring, an empty Coke bottle still loosely clutched in his hand. I stared at the ceiling, willing my mind to latch onto anything that might keep me awake. I didn't want to drift off, not with the thought of a nightmare sneaking in and scaring me in front of the two of them.

I sat up, my mouth dry, eyes scanning the room for something to drink. But we'd already devoured everything. I debated lying back down, but I decided against it. I was going stir crazy, trapped inside my own thoughts. The house was quiet. Angela still hadn't come home.

I pushed myself off the floor, twisted the doorknob, and crept out of Enzo's bedroom, down the hallway, and into the kitchen. I swung open the fridge, and a wave of cool air hit my face. On the top shelf sat a carton of milk and a small bottle of cream, along with the same French butter Ma loves, wrapped neatly in parchment. A couple of glass jars of preserves sat beside it. Rosa must have given them to Angela.

Inside the fridge door were bottles of condiments. Tucked among them, I spotted a small row of Anheuser-Busch beers. My hand reached past the ketchup and mustard, curling around the cold glass bottle, and I pulled one out, feeling the condensation bead against my fingers.

I had just cracked it open when I heard a door upstairs creak open and then shut. Footsteps followed it down the staircase. "Shit," I muttered, glancing around for a place to hide the bottle.

It was Sal, sneaking down the stairs, shirt half-untucked, hair messy from whatever he and Val had been doing. I rolled my eyes as his gaze landed on me, and he flashed that cocky grin my way. "What you doing down here? Got the munchies?" He chuckled, pausing in front of the hallway mirror to slick his hair back.

"I couldn't sleep."

Sal strolled into the kitchen, his eyes catching the open beer in my hand. He let out a low laugh. "Damn. Is there any more of those?"

I nodded and took a swig. It tasted like absolute piss, but it was something to help drown out the noise in my head. He pulled a beer from the fridge and twisted the cap off, taking a long drink.

"I need something to hydrate after Val tossed me out," he said, nudging my arm with a grin. "She's feisty tonight, if you couldn't tell after you three rascals stole the whole damn pack of cigarettes. You know, cigarettes and alcohol are bad for you. And not recommended for kids your age."

It took everything in me not to roll my eyes again. "You sound like a bad public announcement campaign."

Sal snickered. "Why aren't you asleep? Is everything okay with you?"

"I'm fine," I lied, not even bothering to sound convincing. "Could I ask you something?"

"Yeah, of course," he said, leaning against the counter, bottle in hand.

"When will you find out who killed Vincent?"

He shrugged. "I hope, soon."

"What happens if you don't find out soon? Will Joey take the rap for it?"

"I'd hope not."

"You're doing a lot of hoping, and that's not very reassuring."

"I'm a hopeful person, what can I say?"

"Something other than a load of bullshit."

Sal's eyes popped open like saucers. "What is happening with the kids these days? They steal cigarettes. Drink beer. Stay up all night. And curse like sailors." He barked out a laugh at his own joke, and I stood there watching him until he told me something worthy of listening to. "Whoever did it knew what they were doing. But we're working on it. We'll get 'em."

I stared at the label on my bottle, then looked at him. "I swear he didn't do this. We were home. *Together*. When it happened."

"I believe you. But this thing...it's messy. It's not simple. And not everyone cares about the truth. Some people just want blood." Sal let out a sigh. "Joey's under a microscope right now. I know that sounds scary, but you don't need to worry. I've been working around the clock to keep the heat off him. So has Paul. Marco. Lee. Tommy. Everyone knows Joey hated Vincent, but not enough to kill him. The people that matter know that."

I swallowed a long gulp of beer, letting it burn down my throat before I said the craziest thing that had possibly ever formed in my mind. "Can I help you?"

Sal's eyebrows shot up. He straightened off the counter. "Come again? I don't think I heard that right."

"I want to help you. He's the only dad I've ever had, and I want to help clear his name. I need to help you do this." I couldn't tell him it was because I felt like this was all somehow my fault.

Sal stared at me like I'd grown two heads. "Joey would skin me alive if I let you anywhere near this mess."

"He won't find out. I'll use a code name, like you guys do. I'll work through you. Just you. No one else has to know. Please, Sal. He's all I've got. And I love him. I owe him this."

"I appreciate the dedication, and I'm sure Joey would too," Sal slapped his hand against my shoulder. "But you can't help with this. If you want to get involved in this business, you've got five years left."

"Four and a half years left."

Sal snickered, shaking his head as he brought the beer bottle up to his mouth and took a swig. "My bad. Four and a half years."

"I'm serious—"

"Oh, I know. But the answer is no."

"Sal, he's my father. I can help you. You need more people helping you clear his name. I can do that. I have the whole summer to do nothing. I can do this. I want to do this. I'm begging you. What would you do if your own father had a target painted on his back and everyone had arrows just waiting to take a shot at him?"

Sal sighed, shaking his head. "This ain't a schoolyard scrap. You step into this world, you're in with the big dogs. There's no un-ringing that bell."

"I'm already in this. I'm Joey Romano's son."

A crooked grin tugged at his mouth as he shook his head slowly. "You've got some balls for a thirteen-year-old, I'll give you that." He raised the bottle and pointed it at me. "If I let you do this, you have to promise to keep your mouth shut. Don't get excited and start telling your little friends shit to sound cool. You do exactly what I tell you to do. And if Joey finds out, this was your idea. Not mine. I had nothing to do with any of it. Is that understood?"

I nodded, my heart pounding. "Understood."

"Good," Sal said, tossing his empty beer into the kitchen trash. "I've got to figure out the logistics of how to bring you in. But before I can do that, I've got to meet the crew downtown. So I'll catch up with you later." He started toward the door, then peered over his shoulder with a smirk. "Now get some damn sleep, because you're gonna need it."

He slipped out the front door. Sleep didn't come any easier for me. My heart was still pounding. A smile wouldn't leave my face. I wasn't waiting around hoping things would work out. I was going to do something about it. I was going to make this right, once and for all.

Now I was finally going to pay Joey back for all he'd done for me.

Chapter Twenty-Six

Adriana
Five days after Vincent's murder

I sat beside Angela on a tufted velvet bench in the middle of Mariani's, the most glamorous department store in the city. Expensive perfume and freshly pressed fabric filled the air, while the floor around us gleamed as though it had been polished just for our arrival. On either side, tall racks displayed rows of designer gowns.

My own choice already hung on the hook beside me: a striped dress in black and deep green. Angela had hers too—something black, sleek, and daringly backless, as if she were born to stop men in their tracks. Because let's face it, she was. As usual, we were waiting for Lucy, who was still behind the curtain, taking her time to make a dramatic entrance.

Angela lit a cigarette with the flame of her gold lighter. She exhaled smoke as if it were part of her very breath. "How's Joey doing?"

I smirked, remembering the night before. "He's doing good."

Angela's eyes narrowed slightly, the corner of her mouth twitching as she blew a slow trail of smoke upward toward the crystal chandelier that glittered above us. "Mhm. Heard from someone that he showed up to the office in yesterday's suit. Hair a mess, whining about his back hurting. Said he got put out like a dog. He didn't say the last part, I added it in when Marco told me you'd forced him to sleep on the couch."

A laugh burst out of me before I could stop it, the sound bouncing off the marble floor. Angela shook her head, grinning, her red lipstick still flawless against the cigarette filter. "I always knew you had it in you. Give that man hell. These men get their egos fed all day long out there, not in the house. So... good for you."

I leaned my head against her shoulder, still thinking about last night. Joey, pleading for my forgiveness...and then pleading for something else entirely. I had taken back my power when I pushed him down on that bed. I had taken what *I* wanted, on *my* terms.

"How's Marco?" I asked, lifting my head.

"He's Marco. Nothing to report." She took another long drag, smoke curling from her lips in ribbons.

The curtain swished aside, and Lucy emerged in a deep wine-colored velvet dress—off the shoulder, hugging every curve she possessed as though it had been sewn onto her body. Her chin tilted high, her expression regal, though the sight of Angela smoking made her eyes flash. "Angela! Put that cigarette out, some of us would like to breathe, for heaven's sake."

Angela rolled her eyes, waving the cigarette. "Oh, spare me. You're the one who's miserable without carbs and cigarettes. That's nobody's fault besides your own."

I sat up straighter, unable to keep the smile from tugging at my lips as I admired Lucy. "You look beautiful in that dress, Lucy. I hope that's the one you're going to purchase because it's certainly been made for you."

She twirled, velvet sweeping around her legs like a curtain on stage, her face lit with genuine delight. Beaming, she stopped in front of the full-length mirror, smoothing her hands down her hips as though savoring every detail of the fit. With a satisfied nod, she spun back toward us, hands settling on her waist. "Be honest," she said, her eyes gleaming with mischief. "Do I look like a woman who'd ruin a man's life?"

Angela lifted her cigarette for one last drag. She pressed it into the glass ashtray, smoke curling between us. "You look like you already did."

Lucy grinned, turning back to the mirror with a flash of teeth. "That would be true. I suppose I did. Twice. Just this week, actually."

Angela chuckled, low and throaty, shaking her head. "Like I told Adriana...give these men hell."

Lucy's eyes caught mine in the reflection. "Is everything okay between you and Joey?"

I nodded quickly. "Yeah. Everything's good."

Her brow arched, unconvinced by my reply. "You'd tell me if it wasn't, wouldn't you? I know you like to keep things close to the chest, but I swear to God, Adriana, I'll kill a man for you. I wouldn't give it a second thought."

"And I'll bury the body," Angela added, slipping an arm around my shoulders, her perfume filling my nostrils. "I don't care if he's the president or the pope. The three of us stick together."

"She's right." Lucy gave a solemn nod, her reflection in the mirror looking less like a woman in a velvet gown and more like a queen with her court.

"Let's not get ahead of ourselves. I can handle Joey Romano just fine. But if I ever need backup, you'll be the first people to know," I said with a smile.

Lucy's eyes glittered with mischief, her grin wide enough to light the whole department store. "What did you do to him? Tie him to the bed and torture him?" Heat flooded my cheeks, and a laugh slipped out before I could catch it. Lucy's hand flew to her mouth before she gasped, then dramatically pointed at me like she'd caught me red-handed. "Angela! She did!"

"No," I said quickly, still laughing, my face warm. "I didn't tie him to a bed. Thought perhaps I should next time."

Angela smirked, her voice dry as smoke as she muttered toward Lucy, "Only you've ever done that."

My head snapped toward Lucy, eyes wide. "What? When?"

Lucy flicked her hand dismissively, her Chanel bracelet jingling with the motion. "It was a long time ago. And it's not what you're thinking. It's a memory I wish to forget."

Angela exhaled as if she'd been waiting for this moment. "She tied Ben to the bed with his own handcuffs when she found out who he really was—"

"Angela, please say no more," Lucy pleaded, clasping her hands against her chest, her face flushed slightly.

"Well, in any case, Joey's finally met his match, and I hate it for him, but I love it for me."

"You know what I think it is?" Lucy said, tilting her chin and admiring her reflection in the tall, gilded mirror. Her fingers traced down to a glittering brooch nestled at the base of her scandalously low neckline, the rhinestones sparkling. "It's this little pin right here. Distracts a man just long enough for me to do irreversible damage. What do you think?"

"Or maybe," Angela replied, one brow arched, "it's the way your neckline's playing peek-a-boo."

Lucy smirked, clearly pleased with herself. "That too." Then she spun around, her eyes wide as if inspiration had struck. "Wait! I've got it. Adriana needs to wear the navy one! Navy is her color!"

"Oh no," I said, shaking my head quickly. "You'd have better luck dressing a brick wall. Besides, I'm not so sure we share the same fashion sense. You're far more glamorous and fashionable than I. I'm rather simple."

Angela pressed a palm to the small of my back as she nudged me to my feet. "Men don't care about a little belly, if that's what you're worrying about. I'm far curvier than you. And I've had a man tell me no—"

"Perhaps because you terrify them," Lucy chimed in, her grin flashing in the mirror.

"They won't see past the neckline. And once that dress hits the floor, their brains melt. All they can think about is...well, you know." Angela's red-painted smile curled, wicked and knowing.

"Of course she knows! It's their own twisted pleasure and selfish needs!"

"Fine, I'll try it on," I mumbled.

"She'll try it on?" Lucy repeated, then squealed, clutching Angela's arm and bouncing on her heels. "She'll try it on, Angela! You should be a motivational speaker. Last week, you convinced us to make men fear us if they value their lives. Today, you've convinced Adriana to wear something that shows actual skin."

"For the record, I always advise giving men hell, not poisoning their coffee when they turn their backs...unless you must."

"Don't give her any more ideas," I said, nudging Angela's arm.

"A drop a day keeps the doctor away," Lucy sang in a sugary lilt.

"Lucy!" Angela and I snapped in unison, whipping our heads toward her. She only let out a wicked little laugh.

Angela tugged the hanger from the rack and thrust it

toward me. "Alright, in you go," she said, her tone equal parts motherly and mischievous matchmaker as she guided me toward the dressing room curtain.

"I'm going, I'm going," I muttered, clutching the gown.

I slipped out of my dress, the fabric falling in a soft puddle around my feet. When I pulled the navy velvet over my hips, it slid against my skin like liquid night, clinging to every curve before flaring gently below the knees. I smoothed the fabric down over my stomach, my breath catching in my throat at the reflection staring back at me. The satin sheen picked up the low light, turning my reflection into something I barely recognized. I had never seen myself like this.

"Are you breathing in there?" Lucy called out, her voice sing-song and impatient.

"I think she fainted," Angela added. "Or she's hiding from us."

I pulled the curtain aside slowly, my fingers lingering on the fabric as though it could shield me a moment longer. Angela's brows shot up. Lucy gasped so loudly, heads turned from the other end of the salon, her hand flying to her chest as if she needed to hold her heart in place.

"Holy hell," Angela breathed, a cigarette forgotten between her fingers. "She looks like a goddamn movie star."

"Ava Gardner, who?" Lucy declared, circling me, a hand still resting at her lips. Her eyes glittered, her lips curled into a feline smile. "Adriana, if Joey doesn't drop to his knees the second he sees you in this, he's not a man, he's a corpse. And I'm his mortician."

Heat crawled up my neck. I turned to the mirror, hardly recognizing the woman staring back. The deep navy velvet seemed to ignite against my olive skin, pulling out a golden glow I didn't know I carried. The neckline plunged enough to suggest the curve of my breast, while the fabric molded to my waist before falling in a sweeping line that brushed my calves. The dress shimmered like moonlight on dark water.

I couldn't look away from my reflection. My throat tightened, and my pulse fluttered in disbelief. Was that really me?

"I don't know..." I said hesitantly, my fingers smoothing over the velvet as if the fabric itself might reassure me. "It's a lot. I don't think I can pull something like this off."

Angela stepped in behind me, her perfume—jasmine with a bite of smoke—curling around me. Her hand settled on my left shoulder, grounding me in place. "Good. Let it be a lot. You're allowed to take up space, Adriana. I'm so sick of men thinking they can take up all the room and we have to exist quietly."

Lucy leaned in on my other side, her smile dazzling in the mirror's reflection. She tilted her head, eyes sparkling. "This dress doesn't just say you're hot. It says you know you're hot."

I'd never considered myself hot. Attractive, at times. But mostly because the praise I got from Joey made me feel as such. But this, this was hot. "Alright. I'll take it. But I don't know if I'll wear it."

Lucy shrieked with delight. "I knew today was going to be a good day!"

Angela's reflection smirked back at me. "You're going to wear this. I don't care if it's to dinner or to do the damn laundry, you're wearing it. And Joey Romano is going to drop to his knees when he sees you in it."

"She needs shoes!" Lucy declared, already sweeping toward the shelves. Her white French-manicured finger trailed over glossy leather heels and delicate slingbacks before she spun back toward us. "So when he's down there, gasping for air, she can stomp on his heart with a brand-new pair of heels. It's magnificent, isn't it?"

I laughed, shaking my head, my reflection still foreign but a little less frightening now. "Sounds like you're the one who needs those shoes, Lucy."

Angela smirked around the cigarette she'd just lit, the flame from her lighter catching in her mocha eyes. She exhaled a slow stream of smoke. "Preferably something sharp enough to slice skin and show Ben Hudson exactly who the hell Lucy Giordano is."

Chapter Twenty-Seven

Antonio
Five days after Vincent's murder

The sun was shining bright in the blue, cloud-filled sky, baking the cracked red clay of the track. A few small kids shrieking on the swings, transistor radios crackling with rock 'n' roll, the clink of a baseball bat striking in the distance.

As I walked, the rhythm of my steps were slightly out of sync with Mia's. She was beside me, her dark curly hair pushed back in a ponytail, swaying behind her with every step. The heat had flushed a rose glow into her light brown cheeks, and her cotton sundress—white with tiny yellow flowers—fluttered at her thighs whenever the faintest breeze cut through the still, heavy air. A thin silver bracelet jingled against her wrist every time she tucked a strand of baby hair behind her ear.

"Are you hot?" I asked, wiping the sweat from the back of my neck.

She nodded, brushing a strand of dark hair from her forehead. "A little bit. But I'll be okay."

"Should we run over to Davidson's and grab something cold to drink?"

Her lips curved into a small smile. "I would like that."

We cut across the park path, the sound of a baseball smacking into a mitt fading behind us as we passed the iron park sign and stepped out onto the main road. I reached for her hand, intertwining my fingers with hers. Her palm was warm, her fingers smaller than mine, and when she glanced down at our linked hands, then up at me, her smile widened.

"I was wondering how long you'd take," she teased.

I smirked, keeping my eyes on the cars streaming past. "Timing is everything." She laughed, the sound soft and warm, as it worked its way into my chest, buzzing there like electricity. We waited for the traffic to thin. When it broke, I tugged on her hand, and we darted across the street together. Her laughter spilled out, bubbling, flooding my eardrums until it was all I could hear.

Outside Davidson's, Sal sat sprawled in a metal chair, his legs stretched out like he owned the whole damn block. (Perhaps, he thought he did.) His arm was slung around Val, who was perched sideways on his lap. Her purple shorts rode high against her thighs, her white striped blouse tied at the waist, and she leaned back against him, one hand curled around his jaw as if she had staked her claim on him and dared anyone to question it. A glass Coke bottle dangled loosely from Sal's other hand, condensation dripping down his wrist, dark spots forming on his trousers.

Sal's eyes found mine, and a smirk tugged at his mouth. Val didn't glance our way; she tipped her head back, laughing at whatever he murmured against her ear. I tugged Mia's hand tighter, pulling her with me toward Davidson's door. Sal tapped her leg with a finger. "Up, baby," he said, leaning down and pressing a peck to her cheek.

She giggled, brushing her hair behind her ear as she rose to her feet. "Hi, Antonio. Mia."

Mia waved, cheeks flushed, and I forced a half-smile, trying to keep my nerves from showing. My stomach twisted a little at the sight of them, but I didn't show it.

Sal ambled over, grin wide, and threw an arm over my shoulders. "What's up?" he asked, voice casual but loaded, as if he already knew more than he let on.

"Nothing," I muttered, shrugging him off. "We're hot, so we're going to get something cold to drink."

"Leave the kids alone, Sal!" Val called, her tone dripping with mockery. *I'll show her a kid.*

"Could I steal you for a minute?" Sal asked.

I hesitated before letting go of Mia's hand. "I'll be right back." I nodded at her. She smiled shyly, fingers laced behind her back, swaying from foot to foot. Sal tugged me toward the narrow side alley next to Davidson's, his shoulder bumping the brick wall as he leaned against it.

"I've got something lined up for you," he said, smirking. "You ready?"

"Yeah." I nodded.

"Think you can tell your mom you're crashing with Enzo again tonight? Don't let Enzo know you'll be staying over, or he'll get suspicious. I'll have Val cover for you."

I nodded again, my stomach tight with excitement and nerves. My mind raced, imagining the thrill of sneaking into the city at night, doing something I probably shouldn't, and yet wanting it more than I'd admit to anyone.

"Good. Meet me on the curb outside her place at seven tonight. We're going into the city. No one knows you there, and Joey never does business downtown. So, it's perfect."

The corners of my mouth lifted into a grin I couldn't contain. My chest felt like it was vibrating with anticipation, each heartbeat echoing in my ears. "Got it."

Sal clapped me on the shoulder. "Don't worry, kid. Tonight, you're gonna see how the city really moves."

We circled back to the front of Davidson's. Mia was standing there, her chin tucked shyly, but her brown eyes lifted to meet mine as I emerged with Sal. Val, on the other hand, stood waiting with her arms crossed over her chest, one hip jutting out, suspicion etched into every line of her face. Sal grinned, strolling over. He cupped Val's face in his hand and pressed a quick kiss to her lips.

"What were you doing, Sal?" she asked, narrowing her eyes.

"He had to tell me something, man to man," Sal said.

Val rolled her eyes, clearly unconvinced. "He's a kid, Sal. And I swear to God—"

I tugged Mia's hand, pulling her inside Davidson's before Val could unleash the rest of her wrath.

Davidson's smelled of sweet candy, cold soda, and peanuts. Metal shelves lined with glass jars of penny candies, chewing gum sticks in neat rows, and crisp packages of crackers. In the corner, a small wooden cooler whistled, filled with ice-cold glass bottles of Coke, Sprite, and RC Cola.

Behind the counter stood Mr. Davidson, with his round belly that stretched his suspenders, wire-rimmed glasses perched on the tip of his nose, and a warm, weathered smile that made the store feel like home. "Antonio! How you doing, son?"

"Stopping by for a cold Coke," I said. I lifted two cold Cokes, the condensation soaking my fingers. Mia's eyes glanced at me, lips curved in a small, contented smile. "We're just trying to survive the summer heat."

"It's blazing out there," he remarked. I grabbed a small paper bag of peanuts along with the two Cokes. Mia and I walked up to the counter, and I set the bottles and bag down.

As I dug into my pocket for change, Mr. Davidson waved me off with a smile. "It's on the house, Antonio."

"No, let me pay," I said, insisting. Joey had drilled it into me —always pay, always tip. Nothing in life was ever free.

Davidson chuckled and slid the bottles closer to me. "Joey was in here earlier, y'know. Talking my ear off about you."

"Oh yeah?" I asked, trying not to grin too widely, though it was impossible to hide. "Good things, I hope."

"Of course, good things." He said, his glasses sliding further down the bridge of his nose. "He said you've got the best arm Staten Island's ever seen. Said you're gonna make it to the big leagues one day."

I felt a flush of pride that Joey had said that about me. "Really?"

"Sure did," Davidson said, picking up a cloth and wiping down the counter. "But I told him, if you do make it big, don't forget the little guys back here. People like me."

I shook my head, smiling. "He's just boosting. I'm not that good. But even if I were, I'd never forget this place. We're like one big family."

"Dysfunctional," he said with a short, raspy laugh. "But that's the best kind, I suppose." *He wasn't wrong.* "And who's your friend?" he asked, leaning a bit on the counter, his eyes crinkling behind his wire-rimmed glasses.

"My name is Mia, sir," she said softly, her hand brushing against the edge of the counter.

Mr. Davidson nodded and extended a hand. She shook it politely. "Nice to meet you, Mia."

"It's nice to meet you, too," she replied, cheeks tinged pink from the heat and the attention.

"You kids, if you want to escape that heat, you can head back there by the coffee maker and sit down. Nobody will bother you," Mr. Davidson said, gesturing toward the small alcove at the back of the store.

I set the Cokes and the small paper bag of peanuts on the tiny two-seater table by the coffee bar. The vinyl seats were warm from the afternoon sun filtering through the front windows, and the small metal table wobbled as I nudged it into place. I slid into one of the chairs, and Mia took the other seat, brushing a strand of hair from her forehead.

I twisted the caps off the bottles, the satisfying *pop* ringing in the cool, shadowed corner. The condensation dripped onto the table, leaving tiny rings of water. I grabbed the bag of peanuts, hearing the crinkling paper.

"I'm going to teach you something life-changing," I said, dumping a few peanuts into my palm. "Two choices. You either chew them first and wash them down, or you pour them straight into the Coke and enjoy it that way."

Mia tilted her head, eyes sparkling as she asked, "Which way's your favorite?"

I shrugged. "Depends on the day and the mood. Today...I think I'll add them to the Coke." I poured the small handful into my bottle, watching them sink and float, bubbles fizzing around them. She giggled and followed suit, letting the peanuts plop into her own Coke.

"You've taught me about B.B. King, and now this...Coke-peanut concoction."

I grinned, raising my glass in a mock toast. "Stick around, and I'll teach you everything I know."

Her fingers curled around the cold glass. "What else do you know?"

I stared into her eyes, my thoughts wandering to a dozen places at once. "I think you're forgetting one other thing I've already taught you."

Her cheeks flushed a warm pink. "Well...that too," she

admitted, glancing down at the table for a second before looking back at me.

"Has Giovanni beaten me to it?"

She shook her head quickly. "I don't like him. I like you, Antonio."

"He's a sore subject. You're right, we should probably refrain from speaking his name."

She nodded, her fingers tightening around the bottle. "I don't want him to ruin this. Or what we're building."

I smiled, leaning back against the chair. "What exactly are we building?"

She batted her long eyelashes toward her eyebrows, a knowing smile on her face as she shrugged.

I chuckled, "Don't worry. Nobody's ruining what we build, least of all, Giovanni Accetta."

"What did Sal want from you?" she asked, her brows pinched as she twirled the peanuts in her Coke with the tip of her finger.

"Oh, nothing."

"Well, it didn't seem like nothing. And Valentina seemed mad. It's all rather suspicious."

I traced the condensation on my glass with a finger. "I was just buying a pack of cigarettes from him," I lied.

"Then where are the cigarettes?" she asked, tilting her head, curiosity flashing in her eyes.

"I have to get them later. Am I under interrogation or something?" I laughed anxiously.

"No, I'm sorry—"

"No need to apologize."

"This is really good," she said, tilting the bottle toward me before taking a sip.

"Yeah? I'm glad you're enjoying it," I replied, watching the sunlight catch the curves of the glass, the peanuts drifting in the fizzy liquid.

She took another sip, her eyes half-lidded as she leaned back in her seat. "And I've been listening to B.B. King. I really like his music. I lie on my bed and listen at night, wondering what you're doing...thinking about the day you kissed me."

A small heat crept into my chest. "That's strange," I said, lowering my voice, shifting my weight against the table, "because I do the same thing. Only I imagine what it would be like to kiss you again."

"I'm here right now. You don't have to imagine anymore."

"No...No I don't," I whispered. I pushed my glass aside and leaned across the table. Her eyes widened slightly as I closed the distance. "Mia..."

Her lips parted just a fraction, inviting me in without any hesitation. I leaned closer until our foreheads almost touched. Her flowery scent hit me, making my chest tighten. My lips met hers, soft at first, testing, learning before I pressed a little closer, letting the kiss deepen. Her hand rested against my shoulder, fingers pressing into the fabric of my shirt, while I kept one hand steady on the edge of the table. I could feel the faint tremor of her pulse through her skin, matching the quickening of my own heartbeat.

When we finally pulled back, a soft laugh escaped her lips. "Antonio..." she murmured, her eyes sparkling.

"Yeah?"

"I like you a lot," she said, her hand lingering near mine.

"I like you a lot," I whispered, brushing a stray strand of hair from her face.

* * *

The streetlights cast golden pools on the asphalt. Cicadas hummed in the trees lining the street, their song oddly soothing. My hands shoved into my pockets, replaying the kiss over and over in my head. Mia's lips were soft, warm, and sweet. I felt as if fireworks went off in my chest.

I lied and told Ma I'd be crashing at Enzo's tonight, and I hadn't mentioned anything to Enzo. Ma trusted me, and here I was sneaking out, following Sal into God knows what trouble downtown. I had to push the guilt aside for the sake of Joey's redemption.

I shifted my weight, kicking at a small stone on the curb, and my mind kept drifting back to Mia. Would she think about me tonight? Would she replay that kiss the way I had a dozen times already?

I heard the front door of Enzo's house creak open and close behind me. I jumped, my spine stiffening as I spun on my heels, expecting Enzo to be standing there, catching me in a lie. But it wasn't him. It was Val. She walked toward me barefoot on the warm sidewalk, the tips of her toes brushing the cool blades of grass at the edge. Her eyes lifted from the ground, scanning my face, until she stopped right in front of me.

"Hey," she said softly, her voice hesitant.

"Hey," I echoed, awkwardly.

She glanced down at the sidewalk, then back up to me. "Whatever Sal's got you wrapped up in...you need to stop before it's too late. I love Sal. But he's got habits. Dangerous habits. You don't want to pick them up."

"He didn't drag me into anything, Val."

Her brow pinched together, eyes narrowing as if trying to pierce through the confidence I was pretending to wear. "Do you even realize how dangerous this is? How fast things can go wrong?"

"I know you think you know me. I know you're trying to look out for me, and I appreciate it. But I don't need you to. I can handle this. Sal didn't rope me in. I'm not just some kid,

Val. I know what I'm doing. And I know why I'm doing it. And who I'm doing it for." Whatever innocence I'd once had was gone, or maybe it had never truly been there in the first place.

Her eyes glistened, sorrow radiating from her expression. "You think this is a good idea. But whoever—whatever—you're doing this for...they won't have to pay the price. This isn't something you want to get involved in. One day, you're going to look back, and you'll wish you'd never gotten in that car with Sal."

"Do me a favor, Val. Let me carry my own regrets. I'll handle whatever comes."

Her lips pressed together, and she shook her head. "Are you doing this to prove yourself to Joey because—"

"No. I'm not doing this to prove myself to Joey." *I'm doing this to save him.*

She sighed, shoulders slumping. "I just...I don't want to see you get hurt."

My hand connected to the side of her arm, and I gave it a firm squeeze. My face softened, pity bleeding into my expression. "I won't get hurt, but...thank you for caring, Val. That means a lot."

Her dark eyes lifted to mine. It felt like she wanted to say something more, or maybe even do something more, but the low hum of an engine cut through the night air. Headlights washed over us, blinding for a split second before settling like a spotlight. I jerked my hand away, shoving it deep into my pocket. Val straightened beside me, her arms folding across her chest, both of us turning toward the street. Sal's baby-blue Thunderbird purred up to the curb, its polished hood gleaming. The car eased to a stop at the sidewalk curb. Side by side, Val and I stood in silence, the weight of unspoken words heavy in the humid night air.

"Come on!" Sal called, his arm slung over the door, waving me forward. The convertible top was down, and doo-wop spilled from the radio. I hesitated, glancing back at Val. Her eyes locked on mine, almost pleading to stop me before I crossed some invisible line. But my decision was already carved into stone.

I pulled open the passenger door and slid into the seat. Sal leaned across the wheel, grinning wide, then blew her a kiss before gunning the engine. The Thunderbird leapt forward, tires skimming the curb as we tore away from the sidewalk.

The wind hit me like a slap in my face, tugging at my shirt, filling my ears with its roar. For a fleeting second, guilt stirred in my chest—a flicker of my conscience clawing to be heard. I shoved it down, pressed my head against the seat, and let the rush of speed carry me.

There was no turning back now.

Chapter Twenty-Eight

Antonio
Five days after Vincent's murder

S al's Thunderbird rumbled beneath us, the engine purred and growled with every shift of the gear, making my chest vibrate. The streets of Staten Island blurred past in a patchwork of brick houses. We cut through toward the ferry, the sky darkening above us, lights winking on one by one across the water. The summer air carried the salt bite of the harbor. Manhattan loomed in the distance, but Little Italy was where we were headed. The hum of doo-wop floated from the Thunderbird's radio. Sal had one hand on the wheel, while I sat back, letting the wind whip through my hair and sting my face. Every passing mile carried me further from home and deeper into something I couldn't yet name.

"So, was that your girlfriend? The cute little Spanish girl from earlier today?" Sal asked, his eyes slid toward me with a smirk, half on the road, half on my face. A toothpick bobbed between his teeth.

"I don't know," I said, leaning my elbow against the door, watching the blur of streetlights streak across the windshield.

Sal chuckled low in his throat. "What do you mean, you don't know? Have you asked her to be your girlfriend?"

"No," I admitted.

He tilted his head, grinning. "Do you like her? 'Cause you sure looked like you were into her, and she sure as hell couldn't take her eyes off you. But you know—" he paused, tapping the steering wheel with his thumb in tune with the doo-wop on the radio, "—I got a feeling you're about to be the hottest commodity on Staten Island. High school girls are gonna be all over you in the fall."

"We like each other. But I've never had a girlfriend. Right now, I'm just...getting to know her. We'll see what happens. Why do you think girls are going to be all over me?"

Sal barked a laugh, shaking his head. "Val tells me they're already all over you now. So I can only imagine once you've got a little more street credit under your belt. You're Joey Romano's son. That name alone gets attention. Add in the fact that you can throw a baseball halfway across the damn island. Women are gonna be lining up outside your door. I have to say, I'm jealous."

"Why would you be jealous? You have Val."

"Yeah, and I love Val," Sal said without hesitation. "But I'm still gonna live vicariously through you."

"You'll live vicariously through me?"

"That's right." He gave the wheel a spin with his palm as the car curved toward the Brooklyn side. "See, I was nobody before all this. Just another kid hustling for a dollar. I had no family name. I had no weight. When you think about it, I had nothing."

I turned my head toward him, catching the sharp lines of his profile in the glow of the dashboard lights. "Well, you seem popular now. Everyone in town's always talking about you."

Sal's jaw flexed as he shifted gears, his eyes fixed on the

road ahead. The toothpick stilled between his teeth. "Yeah," he muttered. "I didn't ask you, but are you nervous about tonight because we're almost there."

"No. Should I be nervous?"

"Nah. I won't let anything happen to you. I just figured maybe you'd be a little anxious about running with the big dogs." He nudged my arm with his elbow, playfully.

He doesn't know I've already done worse. He doesn't know I've been face-to-face with Vincent and made it out alive. "How'd you get into all this? You seem like you were born for this."

Sal's smile crooked wider. "Born for it? No. Molded by it, maybe." He kept one hand draped over the wheel, the other tapping a rhythm on the dashboard. "I grew up on the streets of Brooklyn. I'm only as good as the man before me. And that man happens to be Joey Romano. I'd see him on the news, in the papers, even on the radio. Like all of us, I became fascinated. But I used my own head. I asked myself...was he really as bad as they said, or was he greatly misunderstood?"

Sal's eyes flicked toward me. "Turns out, he was greatly misunderstood."

Something in my chest twisted hearing him lay it out like that. He spoke about Joey like he was a legend, like a myth pulled from the pages of some old tale. Maybe he was. Joey Romano, my father: the myth, the legend, the man everyone thought they knew but never really did. To Sal, he was a savior. To the world, he was a menace. But to me? To me, he was a father, a protector, an outlaw who carved his own rules into the earth. He was the man who gave me everything, who loved me without condition, and the man the world seemed hell-bent on tearing down.

"I remember the first time I went to his shop. I walked right in, no money in my pockets, and Paul was there asking me if I wanted to buy a car. I said I didn't have a dime to my name. He told me to come back when I did." Sal gave a short laugh, shaking his head at the memory. "I told him I wasn't there to buy a car. I wanted to see Joey Romano."

"Paul damn near fell over laughing at that request," Sal said, his own laugh rising over the hum of the engine. "He called Marco over, the two of them ragging on me, making me feel like some dumb kid. And then—" he paused, "—your mom came out from the back. She was visiting Joey that day. She smiled at me." He let out a low whistle. "And then Joey trailed behind her, walking her out. Right then, I thought...damn, this guy's got it all."

Sal's grin widened at the memory. "Joey asked who I was, and Paul answered for me, very sarcastic of him. Joey told me to hang tight and said he'd be right back. I stood there with Paul and Marco laughing in my ear, but Joey came back."

I could see it, picture the whole scene as if I'd lived it myself. "And then what?"

Sal drummed his fingers on the wheel, eyes glinting like he was back in that moment. "He listened to me—me, some skinny nobody kid—beg and plead and praise him. Then he handed me an envelope. Told me to pick a car off the lot so I could deliver a shipment for him." His palm slid affectionately across the Thunderbird's glossy dash. "So I picked this baby. Paul and Marco were just as shocked as I was. But I made the drop, brought the car back, ready to hand over the keys. And Joey told me to keep it."

He let out a satisfied sigh, the corners of his mouth lifting. "He said I'd be needing it for all the runs he'd have me doing to the city. And I suppose, I wasn't a nobody anymore after that."

Sal's voice still rang in my ears. Joey Romano—a man worth idolizing. A man who made others believe they were chosen, touched by something bigger, just because he noticed them.

Part of me swelled with pride hearing it. That was *my* father they were talking about. When Sal called Joey misunderstood, he wasn't entirely wrong. Joey wasn't the monster they painted him as. But contrary to popular belief, he wasn't untouchable either. Every mile this car carried me into the city, I knew I was fighting for his life.

The son of Joey Romano. The one who'd set him free. Not the son who betrayed him.

* * *

Sal eased the Thunderbird to the curb across from a narrow bodega. Little Italy didn't seem to know how to rest. It was 8:30, the hour when Staten Island would already be slowing down, porches dark and streets quiet. Here, the night was just stretching its legs. Neon beer signs buzzed over storefronts, glowing in red and green. The sidewalks overflowed with chatter, Italian mingling with English, sometimes loud enough to sound like arguments, but ending in laughter just the same.

The smell of garlic, frying sausage, and fresh bread floated out from the trattorias, mixing with the smoke curling from cigars outside the social clubs. Men in white shirtsleeves stood in doorways, their ties loosened, gesturing with their hands as if the whole block were listening as they spoke. Beautiful women in sundresses strolled arm in arm. A pack of kids darted past us, their shoes slapping the pavement, a soccer ball bouncing between them as they weaved through the crowd. An old man sat outside the bodega on a milk crate, rolling dice with two others, their laughter echoing down the block. The bodega owner leaned in his doorway, towel over his shoulder, shouting greetings to every passerby.

I leaned back against the seat, feeling a pull, like invisible strings tying me to this place. Staten Island felt small, half-asleep compared to this. Here was a world that was alive. The smells, the voices, the energy...it all felt like a heartbeat I wanted to sync my own to.

I stared at the men outside the Gallo's Social Club, how they carried themselves as if they owned the night. I thought about Joey, how this was his world, how he was spoken about here like a legend. How he must have walked these streets until he owned them. Until he became Joey 'The Shark' Romano. I didn't just want to visit Little Italy, I wanted to belong to it. I wanted its noise, its heat, its danger. I wanted this street to know *my* name...Antonio Romano.

"Alright, kid," Sal said, turning toward me, one hand still gripping the steering wheel, the other resting casually on the door. The streetlights from Little Italy danced across his face, highlighting the smirk tugging at the corner of his mouth. "Here's your first job. It's simple. Think of it as a test...a way to prove you're worthy for more jobs."

He popped open the glove box and pulled out a small envelope, the yellowed paper crisp in his fingers, handing it to me. "You take this to a guy named Frankie 'Bags.' He's got a dry-cleaning place off 180th. You hand it to him, and he hands you another envelope. That's it. You don't open anything. You don't say anything. You keep your head down, and you come straight back."

I tucked the envelope inside my waistband, the paper pressing against my hip. My fingers lingered on the door handle. "That's all?"

Sal nodded, his eyes narrowing as he studied me. "If you do this right, you'll get more work. But you're not Antonio Romano right now. You start at the bottom, just like the rest of us."

"So what's my code name?"

He squinted at me, brow furrowing. "What?"

"Everyone's got a code name, right? What's mine? What's yours?"

Sal laughed, a bark of surprise that made the car's frame vibrate. He leaned back, dragging long on his cigarette, smoke curling around his face. "Oh, shit. You're really taking this seriously. They call me Sally Boy. And I suppose we'll call you Nino. But you're not there for introductions. You don't speak. You make the drop and come back."

"Nino? Why Nino?"

"Short for bambino. You're still a baby in this life. You even got the little baby face. It's perfect."

I scowled. "I hate it."

Sal chuckled, the sound rough but amused, and slapped my chest playfully. "Hey, it could be worse. I could've called you Sweet Cheeks...Tony 'Sweet Cheeks.'"

I swung the passenger door of the Thunderbird open. My loafers hit the asphalt as I bolted across the curb, my chest heaving with adrenaline.

"Ciao!" called a voice from the bodega across the street.

I glanced over and saw the Italian man leaning against the entrance, a warm smile on his round face. "Hey there, bambino! Off on an adventure, huh?"

I waved quickly, the envelope pressing tight against my side, and continued running, the sidewalks of Little Italy blurring past me. I hit 180th Street and slowed down, scanning the row of buildings. Buildings stretched on both sides, storefronts glowing under streetlights. I stilled. Sal never gave me the name of the building, he'd just said "off 180th." A small dry cleaner shop with a sign that read **Fresh Pressed**. The windows were fogged from the hum of the press inside, and a faint smell of starched shirts and detergent wafted into the street. I pushed open the door, the bell above jingling, announcing my arrival.

Rows of neatly hung suits and dresses swayed slightly. The

walls were painted a pale mint green, and a ceiling fan rotated. A stack of folded linens sat neatly on a side shelf, and the rhythmic hum of a pressing machine in the back punctuated the otherwise quiet shop. Behind the counter stood a man in a gray suit, his hair slicked back. His posture was straight, and his face was stone cold. He glanced up, eyes sharp as knives, then returned to whatever he was doing with his hands. I assumed this had to be Frankie "Bags." The envelope in my waistband suddenly felt heavier, and my palms became slick with sweat.

I took a few steps forward, my loafers squeaking against the linoleum, and tried to calm the pulse thundering in my ears. The shop smelled like heat and detergent. I placed the envelope onto the counter, keeping my eyes locked on the man I assumed was Frankie 'Bags'. His stone-cold gaze lifted, met mine for a brief second, then flicked to the envelope. He walked over, snatched it, and shoved it into the breast pocket of his gray suit.

He opened the cash register and placed another envelope neatly on the counter. I grabbed it, tucking it into my waistband, and forced my gaze away from him, my pulse still racing as I made for the door. I ran back down 180th Street, blaring horns, distant laughter, Italian grandmothers yelling after children. My brown loafers pounded the sidewalk until my foot caught a crack in the concrete. I stumbled, scraping my knee as I fell. A man passing by stopped and pulled me upright, speaking quickly in Italian.

I didn't know much Italian, but the one word that came to mind was the only thing I'd ever learned. "Grazie," I said, before sprinting the rest of the way toward Sal's baby-blue Thunderbird. My chest heaved, lungs burning for more air, sweat sticking to my forehead, and I could feel the warm sting of blood on my kneecap seeping through my trousers.

"You delivered it already?" Sal asked, raising an eyebrow as I swung open the passenger door and slid inside.

I nodded, too winded to speak.

"That fast?"

Another nod.

"You sure it was the right place?" he asked, frowning. "Because I forgot to tell you the name of the joint...it's called Fresh Pressed. If you delivered to another place—"

I pulled the envelope from my waistband and tossed it into his lap to shut him up.

Sal blinked, stunned, before opening it. The flap revealed stacks of hundred-dollar bills, the green paper practically sparkling. I couldn't see exactly how much was inside, but you didn't need to be a mathematician to know it was a small fortune.

"How much is that?"

Sal's grin widened as he threw the car into drive. "Wouldn't you like to know." *Yes. In fact, I would like to know.*

Chapter Twenty-Nine

Joey
Five days after Vincent's murder

I stepped through the front door, and the house was quiet. Freshly cooked Italian food drifted up from the kitchen. The grand foyer stretched before me. I let my eyes wander over the space, but I didn't spot anyone. I moved into the living room, expecting Adriana or someone else to be lounging there. Only the tick of the clock.

The dining room table was set for two. Polished silverware and candles flickering. Adriana was at the kitchen counter, pouring two glasses of red wine. She was wearing a navy velvet dress that hugged every curve she possessed perfectly. Off the shoulder, showing enough of her breast to make my pulse spike, a diamond rhinestone glittered near her left shoulder. Her olive-toned skin looked almost luminescent against the deep navy of the fabric. Her victory curls framed her face, and her cat-eye makeup paired with the red lipstick made her look untouchable. Her hand tilted the wine glass toward me.

She was so incredibly beautiful. Breathtaking, even. Sin never looked so holy.

I took the glass and set it down on the counter. My gaze

roamed over her again, drinking in the way the navy velvet clung to every curve, before rising back to meet her eyes. "Where's my wife? And what have you done with her?"

"Perhaps you should find her," she murmured, her eyes sparkling with mischief.

It took everything in me not to rip the dress off her on the spot. "Are you trying to kill me tonight?"

A soft, bashful laugh slipped past her lips, curling through my chest and tightening around my heart. My hands found her hips, fingers sinking into the velvet as I pulled her close. Her body molding against mine. My hands slid around to her lower back, following the smooth dip of fabric over skin. She smelled of wildflowers. Her laughter lingered in the air between us like a melody I wanted to replay.

My forehead brushing hers. "You're dangerous in this dress, you know that?"

"Good," she purred, her breath hot against my lips. "I wore it just for you...to see if you could handle it."

My thumb traced the line of her spine as her fingers toyed with the fabric of my suspenders, sliding up and down with teasing slowness that made my pulse thrum in my ears. "Well, I love it so much, it's going to be a damn shame taking it off you," I murmured, my lips brushing the corner of her mouth.

"I like seeing how desperate I can make you first."

I tucked a curl behind her ear, my fingers brushing the soft curve of her cheek. "What did I ever do to deserve you, sweetheart?"

"I'm convinced you were always mine and I was always yours," she breathed. Her hand rose, placing itself over mine and pressing it to her cheek. "We were just two halves searching for the other, Joey."

"You think so, sweetheart?" I asked, my thumb brushing over her skin.

She nodded, a small, almost shy smile tugging at her lips. "I know so. I've never been more sure of anything in my entire life. You're my soul mate, Joey Romano."

"I think...I've been waiting my whole life to hear you say that. Even when I didn't know you existed, I believed I was waiting to hear you say that to me. I don't want a day to go by where I don't show you just how much you mean to me. How much I love you."

"Show me. Make me forget that life ever existed without you."

"Oh, I plan to," I whispered, lips brushing hers, my hands lingering at the curve of her waist. "I'll spend every day making sure you never question it. I love you."

She turned her head, pressing a kiss to the palm of my hand still resting against her cheek. I traced my lips along her temple. "Now...come upstairs with me."

I laced my fingers through hers and led her out of the kitchen. As we approached the bedroom, I opened the door, and she stepped inside first. The curve of her back framed by that navy velvet dress made her silhouette almost otherworldly, enough to drive any sane man to insanity.

She turned the corner of her mouth, quarreling in a teasing, knowing way that always made my pulse race. I closed the door behind us, shutting the world out.

Tonight, there was nothing but her and me. The rest of the world could wait.

Chapter Thirty

Adriana

Five days after Vincent's murder

Joey's hands cupped my face, tilting my chin up so our eyes locked. His gaze lingered on me like I was something sacred. Something to be worshipped. "Have I told you how beautiful you are tonight?"

A smile curved my lips. "Maybe a time or two. But I'm not opposed to hearing it again."

A smirk tugged at his mouth as he brushed his lips against mine. My fingers slid to the edges of his button-down, tugging him closer. "You want praise?" he breathed into the kiss. "Then you'll have to earn it."

Heat curled in my stomach as his mouth traveled lower, skimming along my jaw, trailing down my throat. Each kiss sent a shiver racing through me. His hands framed my hips, then his fingertips glided up my spine. My pulse stumbled when his fingers found the zipper of my dress. He dragged it down achingly slow. The fabric slipped from my body and puddled at my heels. My fingers tangled in his hair, urging for more.

"Everything I ever wanted is right here," he whispered.

His mouth claimed mine again, but it wasn't tender. It was

hungry. Possessive. His tongue demanded, coaxed, and consumed me. The kiss stole my breath and dragged a low sound from my throat. He walked me backward, never breaking the kiss, his touch mapping me as if he were memorizing my skin and bones. The bed caught the back of my calves. He pulled away, as his voice rasped out a quiet demand, "Lie down for me."

The sheets were cool against my back as I stretched out, watching him through heavy-lidded eyes. He took his time unbuttoning his shirt one slow snap at a time, a knowing smile curving his lips. My pulse pounded against my neck and ears. The fabric slid from his shoulders, baring muscle over tanned skin. His fingers dipped to his belt, easing it free, then unfastened his trousers and pushed them down his long legs.

He crawled over me, bracing himself on his forearms above me. His gaze roamed my face like he was trying to memorize every expression he pulled from me. His fingertips traced the length of my thigh, featherlight, dragging upward until they reached my core, already aching for him.

His fingers slipped beneath the fabric of my panties, parting me with a stroke that made my breath catch. When he found me, slick and aching, his touch unraveled me as a slow, relentless circle of his fingers dragged a whimper from my throat and sent my hips arching into his hand. A gasp escaped, but he caught it with his mouth, swallowing the sound as his kiss deepened.

"I want to remember this," he whispered against my mouth. "You. Like this. With me. For the rest of my life."

The words unraveled me. I clutched at the back of his neck, dragging him down to me. His fingers never stopped their torment, the steady rhythm pushing me higher until I trembled beneath him. His lips moved lower past my shoulder, throat, breast, each kiss claiming a vow that I was his. That nothing outside this room could touch us.

"Joey," I gasped, arching into him, my hands tangling in his hair.

"Tell me what you want," he murmured against the skin of my stomach.

"You," I breathed. "I want you."

A smirk curved his mouth as his chin pressed into my lower belly. My hands rested on either side of his face. "You don't think you should work for it?"

Heat continued to pool between my thighs. "Fine," I whispered. "I'll earn it."

I pushed myself up, forcing him to brace his knees against the bed. His eyes tracked me, curious, hungry, waiting to see what I'd do next. He didn't have to wait long. Confidence surged through me. I pressed a hand to his chest, guiding him back until his head sank into the pillows. His grin faltered as I swung a leg over, straddling his hips, my knees framing him. I hovered there, lips a breath from his, savoring the moment I had him exactly where I wanted him.

"Tell me what you want, Joey," I murmured, threading my fingers into his hair. "Tell me how to make you lose that smug grin."

His grip clamped on my thighs, hard enough to make me gasp. "You already got me on my back, sweetheart. What more do you want?"

I kissed him softly, then pulled back just enough for my lips to ghost over his. "I want to feel you inside me, Joey."

His restraint snapped. His hands slid up my back, pulling me down hard against him as his mouth crushed to mine. Nothing gentle about it now. Only fire, hunger, and the raw ache of need. I ground my hips against the rigid length of him, and he hissed into our kiss, fingers digging into my thighs. A groan rumbled deep in his chest when I pressed my palms into him and lifted just enough to trail kisses down his jaw, over the taut line of his throat.

I smirked when his head tilted back into the pillow, chin lifted, lips parted in quiet surrender.

That surrender didn't last. His grip moved to my hips, dragging me against him like he couldn't take another second of the torment. "That's enough," he growled. He flipped us, pinning me beneath him. A breathless laugh escaped me, swallowed quickly by the triumphant curve of his smirk as he slid between my thighs, pushing them wide apart.

His gaze seared over me before his hand wrapped around his cock, guiding his length between my folds, positioning himself perfectly. The first slow push stole the air from my lungs. He eased into me inch by inch, deeper and deeper, filling me until I arched with a gasp. My nails raked his back as his forehead dropped to my shoulder, a hiss tearing from him as he buried himself to the hilt.

"Fuck..." he breathed against my skin, his voice rough in my ear. His hands pressed my thighs wider, anchoring me as he began to move...harder, deeper, and mercilessly steadier.

Each thrust sent shockwaves through me, dragging cries I couldn't contain. His pace built with maddening precision, grinding against every place that made me shatter, then pulling back to do it all over again. My body clenched around him, desperate and aching for more.

"Joey..." My voice was broken, breathless, but he drank it in like it was everything.

"Say my name again," he rasped, his lips brushing my ear. "I need to hear it."

"Joey," I gasped, louder this time. His rhythm grew rougher and harder. His teeth grazed my neck, his voice a growl of devotion and desperation. He whispered my name again and again, each thrust carving it deeper into my soul, like he could etch himself into my very skin. My back arched, pleasure spiraling higher, almost unbearable to take any longer.

"Look at me," he demanded, lifting his head, icy blue eyes burning into mine. His thrusts quickened. "I want to watch you come undone."

The world fractured around us, heat and breath and the perfect rhythm of him inside me. My body trembled, breaking open beneath him, and I cried out his name as the release tore through me. His own groan followed, as he drove deep, holding me tight like he'd never let me go.

When it was over, he held me against his chest, one arm tucked beneath his head, the other curled around my body. His lips brushed the top of my hair, and I felt his heartbeat slowly return to normal beneath my palm. The room was quiet except for our ragged breathing. My body was still trembling, aftershocks rolling through me in waves.

His breath was hot and uneven, fanning against my hair. "Christ, you undo me."

My chin tilted up, smiling as I brushed damp hair from his temple. My chest rose and fell against his as I whispered, "You make me whole."

The feel of skin against skin, the way our hearts hammered in sync. His hand smoothed down my side, thumb tracing circles on my hip. "You're mine," he said softly.

"No, you're mine," I murmured, pressing a kiss to the warm skin of his damp chest.

He chuckled, low and tired, then tilted my chin up for one last kiss. Wrapped in his arms, feeling his chest rise and fall, the world outside didn't exist. There was only the promise that this moment would stay carved into my body and my memory long after the night ended.

Chapter Thirty-One

Antonio
Five days after Vincent's murder

The roar of the Thunderbird's engine had long since faded. My head rested awkwardly, sandwiched between the door and the leather headrest. The warm leather pressed against my cheek. The adrenaline from the night's runs and the heat finally surrendered to my exhaustion. I could hear the faint sounds of Little Italy settling down, but my mind was already drifting, images of flashing lights and envelopes of cash mingling with the memory of Mia's laugh and lips on mine. My chest rose and fell unevenly as I slipped deeper into sleep.

Sometime later, a hand pressed on my shoulder, shaking me gently. "Hey, hey, Nino," Sal's voice murmured, low but full of amusement. "Wake up. We're here."

I groaned, trying to focus through the haze of sleep. The convertible was parked in front of Enzo's house. Sal's hand remained on my shoulder. I shifted, my head rolling off the door, trying to shake off the drowsiness. "Mmm...already?"

"Already, Nino. I can't have you passing out on me after your first night on the job. I'm just kidding. Come on. Let's get you inside before someone notices you've been out running around me."

I pushed myself upright. My muscles ached from the adrenaline and the long run, my knee still stinging from the sidewalk scrape. Sal nudged me toward the curb, his hand lingering on my shoulder. I glanced up at the darkened windows of Enzo's bedroom as Sal pushed open the front door soon after.

Val was perched on the edge of the couch, her dark eyes trained on the door, waiting for us to arrive. The second she spotted me, she sprang to her feet and rushed forward. Sal opened his arms, thinking she was coming for him, but she brushed right past him and gripped my arms, scanning me like a medic assessing a patient. "What the fuck, Sal?" She spun on her heels and shoved his shoulder hard enough to knock him a step back.

I bit down on a laugh, trying not to show how entertained I was by her intensity.

"What did you do to him?" she demanded, her brown eyes flashing with concern and anger.

"Nothing!" Sal's hands shot up, his face wearing that guilty-but-confused expression. He dropped onto the couch with a grunt just as Val dropped to her knees in front of me, rolling up my blood-stained trouser leg without asking. *Not that I minded.*

"Go get a wet rag from the kitchen, Sal," she barked over her shoulder. He huffed out a sigh, dragging himself toward the kitchen with a muttered curse. Val's eyes never left my knee as she worked. "Are you okay?"

Never been better, I thought, though I didn't say it aloud. "I'm fine. It's hardly anything. I just tripped. My loafers probably weren't the wisest choice for running down the street."

Sal returned, handing her a damp rag. She grabbed it and

began dabbing at the scrape, blotting away the blood. "This is Sal's fault. If he hadn't dragged you into this mess, you wouldn't have gotten hurt."

"It's not his fault. He didn't drag me into anything. I'm okay, really. He's not that bad."

Sal popped one of the Red Hots Val had left on the couch into his mouth, smirking. "Thanks for having my back, Nino. Baby, he scraped his knee. You gonna call the cops about it? I mean, why are you freaking out like this?"

Val pushed herself up, hands planted on her hips. "Why am I freaking out?" she shot back, jabbing a finger into his chest. "Because I've been sitting here praying I wouldn't have to explain to his mother that you're an *idiot* who let him get hurt!"

Sal stood, jabbing a finger toward my knee. "Nobody can see that—"

"I can!"

"Sal's right. It's not that noticeable once we get it cleaned up."

"Go to the bathroom and leave your clothes by the door. I'll grab something from Enzo's closet and wash your clothes for you."

I headed for the bathroom, slipped inside, and turned on the shower. The steam fogged up the mirror as I peeled off my clothes and dropped them next to the door. The warm water hit my skin, washing away the sweat and blood caked around my knee. I didn't even hear Val come in until I heard her voice.

"I left you some clothes on the counter," she said softly.

My spine straightened. My entire body tensed as the reality hit. I was standing completely naked behind a thin curtain, and Val was on the other side of it.

"Okay. Thanks," I mumbled, trying to sound casual but failing miserably. The bathroom door clicked shut, and I exhaled again. Half of me wished she'd stayed. Wished she'd pulled back the curtain, dropped her clothes, and joined me. The other half knew that was a terrible, *terrible* thought.

I shut the water off, stepped out, and noticed a pair of Enzo's striped cotton boxers and a white ribbed tank top waiting for me by the sink.

Fuck my life.

I considered going home and faking some story about how I ruined my trousers, but I sucked it up. I put on the boxers, tank top, and what was left of my pride before stepping back into the hallway and into the living room. Val was curled up on the couch.

"Where's Sal?" I asked, scanning the room.

"He left," she said, letting out a breath. "Or...I told him to leave."

"Oh." I lowered myself onto the couch, leaving one cushion between us.

"Are you hungry?" she asked, glancing over at me.

I shook my head. "No, I'm good." I hesitated. "Well...except for the fact that I'm wearing Enzo's boxers. I'm probably gonna need extensive therapy just to recover from this."

She let out a soft giggle that was so damn cute it made my stomach flip. A grin broke out across my face at the sound of it.

Yeah. I was in trouble, considering I had a crush on my best friend's older sister.

"Can I ask you something? And will you promise to be honest?" Val's gaze was locked onto mine, her head tilted against the back of the couch, legs tucked underneath her, one hand wedged between her cheek and the cushion. Her shorts had ridden up, and the tank top hugged every curve.

"What's up?" I asked, trying to sound cool even as my heart beat harder than I liked.

"Why are you doing this? You don't have to. You could do

something else with your life. Something better than all this. You have the skills to be some famous baseball player. You don't have to become what Joey is just to be close to him."

Her eyes searched mine, begging me to hear reason, but I couldn't give her the comfort she wanted. The truth was, after tonight, I knew there was no other path. Being in Little Italy, feeling the rush of the streets, the high of what the mafia could offer, it felt like stepping into the part of Joey's world I'd been chasing all my life. There was no turning back.

"Don't you think it's kind of hypocritical for you to tell me not to do something when you're practically doing it yourself? You're with Sal, and we both know what he does. You think you're going to change him or something?"

"Of course not. I love Sal, his flaws and all. But I care about you, Antonio. I didn't know him before all this. I met him afterwards. I never had a chance to stop him. But you...you still have a choice. Once you take this path, once you take an oath, there's no walking away. You don't just quit. The only way out is death. And I've made my peace with that for Sal...but I don't want to have to make it for you."

Her words sank like stones tossed in the harbor. "You make it sound worse than it is. I'm not naïve, Val. I know it's not all good. I know there are bad things people have to do. But I haven't sworn anything. I haven't joined the mafia. I know what I'm doing. I know why I'm doing it. And your perception of that is wrong."

She looked gutted, as if I'd just ripped the heart out of her chest.

"You really think I'm ruining my life?" I asked.

Her dark eyes glistened. "Yes. I do. Because I don't see what you think the end of this looks like. Even if you're doing it to help Joey or whoever you think you're helping, what's the end goal, Antonio? Where does this lead?"

I'll clear Joey's name. That's it. That's all I want. Then I'll go back to life like before.

But even as the thought formed, I knew it was hollow. This wasn't some side road I could wander off of. This was the first step into something darker and too big for a thirteen-year-old boy to fully grasp.

Her voice snapped me back. "Did Sal pressure you?" she asked. "Because if he did, you can tell me. You don't have to be afraid of him—"

"I'm not afraid of him. And he didn't drag me into anything. Like I told you a million times before...I practically got on my knees and begged him for this opportunity."

"What about Enzo?" she pressed. "What will you tell him? Because we both know he'll find out."

"He won't find out. You don't have to worry about that."

"I don't know..." she sighed, her arms folding across her chest. "I could see him not only finding out, but happily joining in. You know how he is, rather impulsive with a short fuse. He'd blow this wide open just to prove himself."

"I'm not telling him. He won't find out. I'll make sure of it. You've got my word."

Joey's voice echoed in my head: *Don't give your word unless you plan to keep it. Otherwise, you're just another man people learn not to trust.*

"Your word?" she repeated, her brows arching. "You act like you're older than you are." *I feel older than I am.*

I shrugged, fingers tracing idle circles on my knee. "I'm mature for my age."

Maybe I imagined it. Maybe I wanted it too badly. But I could've sworn her eyes dipped, down to my mouth, lingering there before climbing back to mine. My pulse hammered in my ears. I straightened against the couch, silently begging her to close the distance. Because I couldn't. Nor would I.

Not first. Not with her. Not with Enzo's shadow hanging over us.

She pushed herself off the couch. My eyes trailed helplessly after her...the slow sway of her hips, the subtle tug of her tank top against her body, the way her shorts clung and shifted, climbing just enough to tease, to torture a raging teenager who thought he was ten years older.

"Goodnight," she said softly.

The second she disappeared down the hallway, my head dropped back against the couch. I dragged my palms over my eyes, groaning under my breath.

I wanted to touch her. To kiss her. To press her against me and feel every inch of her.

Instead, I was stranded here, pulse racing, heart on fire... wearing Enzo's boxers, and losing my goddamn mind.

Chapter Thirty-Two

Antonio
Six days after Vincent's murder

My eyes fluttered open to the sound of *The Flintstones* theme song playing softly in the background. Blinking against the light streaming in from the windows, I scanned the room. Val sat at the kitchen table with her back to me, slicing into a grapefruit. Enzo was cross-legged in front of the coffee table, halfway through a bowl of Frosted Flakes, with his eyes glued to the TV.

That is, until he heard me stir from the couch behind him.

He turned, grabbing his bowl and shifting to face me, one brow arched in skepticism as he took me in. "What the hell are you doing on my couch? In my clothes? My boxers, no less," he hissed, glancing toward Val to make sure she hadn't caught on. She kept eating, totally unaware. I rubbed the sleep from my eyes, sat up slowly, and raked a hand through my hair. He was still glaring at me, each crunch of his cereal more aggressive than the last.

"I came over last night. I needed to get out of the house. Val said you were already asleep and that I could crash here. She gave me some clothes and offered to wash mine for me."

He scowled. "Why the hell would Val do something like that?"

I shrugged. "I don't know. I didn't feel like going home, and I guess...she felt bad for me."

"Val felt bad for *you*?" he repeated, clearly not buying it. "What's going on at your place to make you leave in the middle of the night?"

"Uh...Joey and Ma weren't seeing eye to eye. I told them I was going to stay at your place." It was the best lie I could come up with on the spot.

"You left in the middle of the night, listening to your parents bicker? And they were cool with this?"

I nodded.

"You're lying."

"I'm not," I said, entirely too defensive.

"You are."

"No, I'm not, Enzo. What do I have to lie for?"

"Oh, I don't know. You always tell only half the truth about anything for as long as I've known you."

"That's not true."

Enzo snorted softly, tipping his chin as if daring me to keep talking.

"Come on, at least offer me something to eat."

He blew out a sigh, pushed himself up from the floor, drank the sugary milk from his bowl, and then asked, "Sugar on top?"

"Sure, why not?" I said, sliding farther into the depths of the couch. "Go big or go home."

As he passed Val in the kitchen to fix my bowl of cereal, he called over his shoulder in a deep, exaggerated voice, "They're grrrrreat."

I was grinning at the Flintstones on the TV when Val stood from the kitchen table. She strolled past me, muttering from the corner of her mouth, *Clothes in the bathroom* before disappearing upstairs.

Enzo came in a moment later, handing me a bowl of Frosted Flakes dusted with extra sugar. He dropped onto the couch as the front door creaked open. Sal slipped inside, his bright smile peeking through first before the rest of him followed, bouncing on his heels, too full of energy. He circled to the other side of the couch and slid in next to me just as I shoved a spoonful of sugary goodness into my mouth. Slinging an arm across my shoulders, he grinned ear to ear. "How's it going, Bambino?"

My eyes stayed glued to the TV as I kept shoveling in spoonfuls of cereal. Sal pressed his elbows into his thighs, eyeing Enzo on the other side of me. "Any more cereal for your future brother-in-law?"

"Sure, if the future brother-in-law knows how to make it," Enzo shrugged.

"That's no way to treat someone who's going to be family."

Enzo didn't bother replying. Sal pushed himself up and wandered into the kitchen as Angela trudged down the staircase. Her hair was a wild, lopsided mess piled on top of her head, her black robe cinched tight around her waist. Eyes halfshut, she looked like she was sleepwalking. "Good morning, boys," Angela muttered as she shuffled past us into the kitchen.

"Good morning," Enzo and I said in unison.

"Next time you have company, Enzo, you should be the one to sleep on the couch."

"No, really, it's fine. I slept great," I said quickly. Sal glanced up from where he was pouring milk into his bowl.

Angela waved me off. "That's beside the point. If you invite someone over, you ought to be welcoming. I bet you hogged the bed, Enzo." Her lips curved into a playful grin.

Enzo nodded absently, his eyes locked on the TV. Angela

dropped into a kitchen chair, lit a cigarette, and blew smoke toward the ceiling. Enzo's eyes still watching the screen, whispered out of the corner of his mouth, "It would've been nice to know I was having company, wouldn't it?"

"I'm sorry. I'll tell you next time," I whispered.

"Sal, start the coffee pot for me?" Angela asked, exhaling another stream of smoke.

"Anything for you," Sal replied with a grin, his mouth half full of cereal. He juggled his bowl in one hand while fiddling with the coffee pot in the other. I tipped back my bowl, drinking the last of the sugary milk, then carried it into the kitchen. After dropping it in the sink, I noticed Sal edging closer, still pretending to fuss with the pot. "Davidson's. Wait for me."

I walked back into the living room and paused by the TV. Enzo's gaze drifted up from the screen, locking onto me. "I think I'm gonna get dressed. Ready for the day," I said, jerking my thumb toward the hallway. I didn't wait for his reply before I turned, disappearing down the hallway and into the bathroom. Stripping out of Enzo's clothes, I pulled on my own and stepped back out, only to find him waiting by the door, his arms crossed over his chest.

"Going somewhere?"

"Oh, I thought I'd go meet Mia."

His eyes narrowed. "If you're hiding something, now's the time to confess. Your behavior's off, you show up in the middle of the night, and now you're slipping out suddenly."

I shifted on my feet, heat prickling the back of my neck. "I'm not hiding anything. I'm just going to meet Mia."

Enzo grinned and clapped a hand on my shoulder. "Good. Then let me get dressed, I'll come with you. I think I'll give Maria another shot."

My stomach dropped. My eyes went wide. No. Absolutely

not. If he came, everything would blow up in my face. I stammered, scrambling for words. My mouth opened, but nothing came out. The words got stuck somewhere between my brain and my throat, choking me from the inside. "You can't come."

His forehead creased. "Why the hell not?"

"Because...because things between Mia and me are getting serious, and I need some alone time with her."

Enzo's expression went flat for a moment before a grin cracked across his face. "Alone time, huh? Ha! I knew it. I approve of this behavior, you sly little devil, sneaking off like that."

I forced a smile, nodding, letting him run wild with his own assumptions.

"You'll fill me in on everything, won't you? All the details?"

"Yeah," I nodded again, the lie catching in my throat. When I stepped back into the living room to grab my shoes, Sal was nowhere to be seen. Angela sat on the couch, cradling a steaming cup of coffee, while Marco stood by the counter, pouring his own.

"Leaving already, Antonio?" Angela asked as I slid my feet into my brown leather loafers.

I smiled. "Yeah. I'll be back later."

I slipped out the door, but my heart hammered in my chest with every echo of the latch. Next door, Joey's Ferrari was gone for the day. Only Ma's Chevy sat in the driveway. I thought I heard the scrape of something in the yard, but when I glanced over, no one was there.

I started down the sidewalk toward Davidson's corner store, my loafers tapping against the concrete. Somewhere nearby, a transistor radio blared Elvis. A passing Ford and the rattle of loose screen doors punctuated the morning calm. In the back of my mind, I couldn't shake the thought of Rosa, pretending to be senile but probably keeping tabs on us.

Could she have been spying on me from the front yard?

Chapter Thirty-Three

Joey
Six days after Vincent's murder

The showroom gleamed under the morning sun, polished chrome and glossy paint reflecting the heat in long streaks across the floor. On the surface, it was every inch a high-end luxury car dealership: rows of sleek Cadillacs, shiny Buicks, and powerful Ferraris lined the parking lot, each hood propped open to show off a spotless engine. Behind the glossy facade, the numbers whispered "loan shark" more than "luxury wholesaler."

Lisa sat behind the front desk, shuffling invoices and flipping through the guest registry. She was Tommy's young girlfriend. Tommy leaned across the counter, grinning, spinning his usual flirty lines that made her blush and fidget.

Across the floor, Lee and a few others were hauling boxes into the back of an eighteen-wheeler we'd "borrowed" a few weeks back, a truck that had been mysteriously absent from a local lot but now bore our own stamps and labels.

Marco lingered near the espresso machine, a cup of steaming coffee in hand, chuckling as he skimmed the morning newspapers. Headlines speculated about missing trucks, luxury car heists, and mysterious "business dealings" in town, and he leaned back against the counter, shaking his head. "They've got no idea what's really going on, do they, Paul," he muttered, taking another sip.

Paul stood beside him, cigarette dangling from his lips, flipping through the latest inventory sheet. Smoke curled toward the fluorescent lights as he occasionally glanced at Marco, smirking at his running commentary. Every glance, every laugh, was part of the rhythm of running a showroom that had to appear legitimate to clients while quietly keeping its real customers satisfied. I walked over to Marco and Paul. "Hey, what's the headline say for today?"

Marco waved the newspaper. "'Romano Luxury Wholesale accused of smuggling Ferraris to Florida, hoarding stolen Cadillacs, and turning a showroom into a speakeasy—can you believe that?'" We all burst out laughing, the sound echoing against the high ceilings.

Paul shook his head, cigarette dangling from his lips. "Yeah, they've got no clue what's really going on here."

"A speakeasy?" Lee called from the back, pausing as he stacked crates into the swiped eighteen-wheeler. "*The Wise Guy* has been running since before I was born, and these idiots still haven't figured it out yet."

"Not a single idea," Marco said, raising his coffee cup. "Makes you wonder how boring their lives must be. Must suck to be a civilian."

Paul smirked, smoke curling around his head. "Ever think how bad they'd feel seeing us reading this paper for laughs?"

"I like to watch them guess," Marco added, taking another sip from his mug.

"Where the hell is Sal?" I asked, pouring myself a cup of espresso, the rich aroma filling my nose.

"He was at Angela's house this morning. He left before I

did, so he should be here," Marco commented, eyes still scanning the headlines with amusement.

* * *

Not long after I'd checked the wholesale shop for Sal, he walked through the front door, peeling off his aviators. Even at only eighteen years old, there was a natural swagger to him—a lean frame tucked into a mint green short-sleeved, crisp button-down, cream slacks, and loafers that clicked against the showroom floor. A young mafioso coming up under my watch, all charm and dangerous energy wrapped into one. He made his way toward Marco, Paul, and me, practically gliding across the floor with that wide, confident grin already in place.

"Speaking of the devil," Marco said, tossing the newspaper into the garbage bin with a smirk as Sal approached.

"The devil? I'm a fallen angel, what are you talking about?" Sal replied, beaming. "Good morning, Boss. Sorry, I'm late. I'm reporting for duty."

"Doc his pay," Paul said, smirking. "And work him to the bone."

"I agree," Marco added, nodding with mock solemnity. "Exactly what we should do."

"You two shut up," Sal said, laughing, hands on his hips. "Had a few hiccups this morning, but you know what they say...better late than never."

"Never late is better," Paul countered.

I gestured toward my office. "Sal, follow me."

He practically skipped after me, that wide grin plastered across his face. Sal's energy is always impossible to ignore. I stepped into my office and sank into the leather chair behind my desk. Sal shut the door behind him before he strode toward me, still smiling, his eyes taking in the room with the confidence of someone who knew exactly where he belonged.

"You got something for me, boss?" Sal asked, practically bouncing on his heels, his loafers tapped against the floor.

"I need you to make a collection for me."

Sal's grin stretched wider. "What's the details, boss?"

"Mickie Two-Times. Over in Little Italy."

Sal let out a low whistle, eyebrows shooting up. "That fast-talking prick?"

"He's late, *again*."

The grin slid from Sal's face, replaced by an understanding. This wasn't a routine visit.

"I want you to deliver the threat if he doesn't have what he owes plus interest for being late," I continued, leaning back in the leather chair. "And remind him the clock's ticking. He took out a loan to keep that meat joint of his running, and the only reason he's still open is because we let him keep it that way. You can let him know that it ends if I don't see a payment by the end of the week. I'm being generous with him."

Sal nodded, his posture tightening with focus.

"I want you to rattle his cage a little. He needs to understand this isn't a favor. I don't do favors. He wants to keep operating under our umbrella, he pays up. And tell him, if I have to get in my car and drive over there myself to collect the money he owes, he's going to wish he'd paid up."

"Got it, boss," Sal said, his voice steady but laced with a dangerous grin that made him look older than his years. He turned on his heel and slipped out the door. I thought about the next fire I'd have to put out, and this one was coming fast. I glanced at the clock. Barely enough minutes to savor a moment of silence before meeting Ben at the diner.

* * *

I was sitting across from Ben in the back booth at the diner. The place smelled like bacon grease, maple syrup, and fresh coffee. A slice of cherry pie sat in front of me, untouched except for the bite I was chewing. Ben, on the other hand, had gone all-in: cheeseburger, fries, and a chocolate shake sweating on the table.

"That's all you're eating?" he asked, popping a fry into his mouth.

"Yeah," I said, pressing back in the booth, my arms stretched wide as I took another slow bite of pie. "Adriana made us a late breakfast. I'm not hungry. Besides, I'm not here to eat."

Ben grinned, still chewing. "Not gonna let a man finish his burger, are ya?"

"The way you're inhaling that thing, you'll be done in no time."

He chuckled, then polished off the last few bites in record speed. Not a single fry left behind. He wiped his mouth with a napkin, folded it, and tossed it on top of his plate. "Well, I've got good news and bad news. A lot of it, actually."

I stared at him, waiting.

"Lucy told me Hector's got a mistress out in Queens. She's got three kids with him in some hidden apartment."

That might've been news to Lucy, but it wasn't exactly news to me. Hector had a whole damn rotation of side women. I guessed this was the brunette...the one who's Frankie Bags' cousin. I had seen them out a few times when I'd done business with Frankie Bags in the city.

"I checked it out. It's solid." *No shit.*

"Ben, do you know how many men have affairs on their wives? Too many to count when it comes to our kind. I do not care about Hector having a secret family. That's not news to anyone. Other than you, apparently. The angle here is Lucy. That's where the leverage is."

He nodded slowly, letting me go on.

"You gotta convince her to cry to her father. I mean… Christopher didn't earn the name The Butcher because he used to cut cold cuts back in '35. A man betrays his little girl like that?" I shook my head. "If it were my daughter, I'd gut the bastard and feed him to the fish. And I have a feeling Christopher would do worse."

"Well…that was the good news."

I raised an eyebrow.

"The bad news is, Lucy already threatened to do that. And Hector told her if she opens her mouth, he'll expose us…Our affair. You know what happens to me if that shit gets out. I'll be the one gutted and fed to the fucking fish. But I told her," Ben continued. "I told her to do it anyway. That I'd take the fall. That it was the only way for you to be free of this mess."

Ben's elbow hit the table, his forehead sinking into his hand as he let out a hot sigh. "She refused. I told her what really happened—that Hector killed Vincent, that turning him in could clear your name. She still said no."

I sat still, holding my breath.

"But she says Hector was asleep. Out at the horse races all night, gambling. Said he passed out drunk on the couch when it happened."

There's no way Hector had an alibi. If he didn't pull the trigger himself, he sure as hell sent someone to do it, and my money was on that snaggle-toothed motherfucker, Frank Costa, Renee's new victim. Or maybe the two of them hired someone else entirely. "No. That can't be. Even if Hector didn't do it, you know he had someone else handle it. You've gotta talk some sense into her, Ben. It's him or me. And I've got a new wife at home harassing me every time I walk through the damn door or try to sleep in my own bed. All this has done is stress Adriana out."

"Yeah, well...that *might* be a problem."

A crease formed between my brows. "Why?"

"Because when Lucy refused to go to Christopher, I did the only thing I could think of. I told her my wife is pregnant."

"What?"

"I thought it would make her mad," he said, rubbing his chest. "And boy, did it. She nailed me with a heel. Look at this." He tugged his shirt collar down to show a fresh welt on his collarbone.

"Ben, I don't give a fuck if Lucy tied you to a bed and whipped you with a stiletto. Why the fuck would you admit to something like that? At a time like this? And is she even pregnant? You told me you were trying to get divorced."

"She's not pregnant, but I panicked—"

I slammed my palm against the table. "You better un-panick and come up with something better than that. Why the hell would you say something like that?"

"I figured it'd make her hate both Hector and me. That she'd get so angry, she'd throw Hector under the bus to her old man. Christopher would have the blade to his neck, and then boom, it'd be my turn. And you'd be free."

My gaze locked on him, blank with disbelief. "You trying to get yourself killed, you dumbass? Don't sacrifice yourself this damn early in the game! I need you right now, Ben. I need you to help me figure out how we're going to prove Hector did this shit before he comes up with a way to convince Christopher it was me."

"I figured I'd be your savior. You could at least say thank you. All the shit I do for you—"

I glared. "Over my dead body, Bennie."

Ben grinned. "Oof. Haven't heard that nickname in a minute."

"Alright," I chuckled, pushing back from the table. "You're gonna find Lucy, and you're gonna tell her you're a dumbass. Then you're gonna tell her the truth. The *real* truth. The one you just laid on me. And we're gonna find a way to pin Hector *without* you dying in my honor."

"Well, that should be real fucking easy," Ben muttered under his breath as I stood up, slapping a fifty down on the table.

"Come on," I said, giving his chest a firm pat. "After all the shit you've done for me? Bennie, this is a piece of cake."

He rose from the booth beside me, shaking his head with a smirk. "You don't know Lucy very well, do you?"

Chapter Thirty-Four

Adriana
Six days after Vincent's murder

I smiled as I stood in front of the sign that read *Cosa Bella*. Lucy's newest addition to her beauty salon. The *Closed* sign hung in the window, along with a handwritten note taped underneath it: *No men allowed*. Which made me chuckle. I pushed the door open and stepped inside, taking a look around. Pink vinyl salon chairs lined the wall, each one stationed beneath those massive silver-domed hair dryers. The floor was checkerboard tile, glossy and spotless. A vintage carved wood bench sat near the front, repurposed and reupholstered in velvet blush fabric with gold accents—made by Lucy. The whole place smelled like hairspray, rose powder, and a hint of cigarette smoke.

Angela was perched on the bench, legs crossed, a cigarette smoldering between her red-tipped fingers. A box of Pat's Cannoli sat open beside her. She wore a slinky black dress and a cheetah-print scarf tied loosely over her freshly styled curls.

"Where's Lucy?" I asked, setting my purse down on the counter before taking a seat beside Angela on the velvet bench.

Angela exhaled a stream of smoke in the opposite direction and nodded her head toward the back of the salon. Before I could even wonder what Lucy was doing back there, she appeared, and her face said everything I needed to know. She was dressed in a teal mini dress, thigh-high white boots, and a wide cream belt cinched around her waist. Her hair was blown out to perfection, not a strand out of place. But her makeup told another story. Her winged eyeliner had smudged down her cheeks, mascara trailing like war paint. Angela nearly leapt up, sending the box of cannoli teetering on the bench next to me as she rushed to Lucy. I followed right behind her. Lucy was dabbing at her eyes with a crumpled tissue.

"It's no use," she sobbed, collapsing into our arms. Her arms wrapped around both of us, her forehead pressed against our shoulders. "I keep trying to fix my makeup, but I can't stop crying."

"Come sit down," I urged her. Angela and I helped ease her into one of the pink salon chairs. Angela took the tissue from Lucy's hand and began blotting her face for her. I grabbed a cannoli from the box and held it out as an offering.

"Thank you," Lucy sniffled, grabbing it and taking a bite.

"What happened?" Angela asked.

Lucy gave a short, bitter laugh, her mouth still full of cannoli. "What hasn't happened? Where should I start? My love life is a joke."

"Well, starting at the beginning would be splendid."

Lucy let out a long, dramatic sigh and sank back into the chair. "Hector's got an entire family in Queens, and Ben's wife is pregnant."

Angela's face fell. Mine mirrored hers. Our eyes locked, then darted back to Lucy—already shoveling another cannoli into her mouth.

"You mean to tell me," Angela said slowly, trying to process the bomb Lucy had just dropped, "that *both* Hector and Ben have been playing you?"

Lucy nodded as she continued eating the second cannoli. "Hector's got three kids and a mistress out in Queens. And Ben —" her voice cracked, and she looked up at the ceiling like she could force the tears back down. "Ben said he wasn't sleeping with his wife. And now she's *magically* pregnant, and he's one hundred percent sure he's the father."

I blinked, speechless. It didn't feel real, and it wasn't even my reality. Angela snorted, a dry laugh escaping her lips. "Men are the devil. If nothing else, that much I've learned."

All I could think about was Hector. Wouldn't this be exactly the kind of ammunition Joey needed to take Hector out?

"I don't care about Hector and his secret little family," Lucy scoffed. "He's completely useless to me, and he always has been. But Ben—" she shook her head, biting back another sob. "Ben *broke* me. He told me over a pay phone for crying out loud!"

"Do you want me to take care of him? You know I don't care if he's a crooked cop or not," Angela asked, dead serious.

Lucy shook her head quickly, "Is that your first response... violence?"

"Of course not," Angela flicked her wrist. "But if all these men can live by their own moral code, why shouldn't we? I believe in karma, but it doesn't work fast enough, so I help move it along. Nothing messy, mind you, but I could show you what I call the 'sleepy cocktail.' They'll never see it coming."

Lucy let out a giggle, hiding her mouth behind her hand, and I burst out laughing right after, unable to help it. "Angela, you little psychopath," Lucy sniffled, her dark eyes still glossy. Then she frowned, "Oh my God, don't make me laugh when I'm clearly in need of a good cry."

"I'm not trying to make you laugh. I'm being serious."

"Christ, Angela," Lucy hissed playfully, a smile still sitting on her lips.

"Okay, enough murder plots," I said, reaching over and taking Lucy's hand in mine. "Ben Hudson is a damn fool. And one day, that fool is going to choke on the regret of ever letting you go." Lucy's brow furrowed as her lips wobbled into a soft, heartbroken frown. She pulled me into a tight hug.

"Hell," Angela muttered, hip cocked to the side, holding a cannoli near her mouth, "with the way you look in that dress, he'll be crawling back the second he sees you again. And you'll offer him a sleepy cocktail."

"Okay, we're not offering sleepy cocktails to rogue cops. But you know what you're going to do?" I said, smiling at her. Lucy looked back at me, waiting for me to continue. "You're going to show him who the hell Lucille Giordano really is."

"And how am I going to do that?" Lucy countered.

I cupped her face, wiping the tears with the pads of my thumb, "You've done it before. You can do it again."

"Now that's what I'm talking about," Angela grinned, nodding in approval. "Maybe I should be one of those motivational speakers."

"See what you've done, Adriana?" Lucy smirked. "You've inflated her ego even more."

The three of us burst into laughter. "And the only one who may receive a sleepy cocktail is Hector. I'm surprised he hasn't been to bed yet," I remarked.

Lucy tossed her head back, "Me too, honestly."

Chapter Thirty-Five

Antonio
Six days after Vincent's murder

I'd been standing outside Davidson's for thirty minutes, the air shimmering above the asphalt like a mirage. I was shifting from foot to foot, trying not to check my watch again. Where the hell was he? He left before me, and he still hadn't shown up. A couple of kids biked past me, ringing their bells and laughing with one another. My eyes stayed glued to the sidewalk, hoping Sal would come around the corner any second.

Instead, Mia and Maria walked up the street. My heart jumped out of my chest at the sight of Mia. They weren't identical; Maria had a confident sway, dark hair catching the sunlight. Mia, on the other hand, was quieter, more reserved, but her eyes always seemed to see right through me.

I froze for a second, debating whether to look away. Pretend I didn't see them, perhaps. If I acknowledged Mia, I'd have to explain why I was standing here sweating and waiting on Sal for...another mafia job. I wasn't ready to drop that on her. Not after I convinced her the other day that Sal and I weren't doing anything fishy together.

I shifted enough to angle my body away, pretending to dust something off my spotless loafers while sneaking glimpses at her out of the corner of my eye. My stomach knotted, half because I was excited to see her, and half because lying by omission was a hell of a lot harder than I wanted it to be.

"Antonio? Are you just gonna pretend you don't see us?" Maria asked.

I straightened up, smoothing my hands down my pants before shoving them into my pockets. *Act normal, act normal.* "Huh? Oh...hey. Didn't notice you," I mumbled, forcing a casual grin.

"Are you waiting for someone?" Mia asked.

"Waiting for someone? What? No. I'm just...killing time," I stammered, hoping my voice didn't give me away.

Maria unlooped her arm from Mia's and grinned. "I'll go into the store and grab us something to drink so you can have some time alone."

Mia sighed, turning her gaze back to me. I forced my shoulders to relax. "So?" she asked, crossing her arms. "Who are you waiting on? And why are you so worked up?"

"Nobody. I told you, just...hanging around," I replied, trying to sound casual. Heat rose to my collar, my heart thudding in my chest.

Come on, act natural. Don't panic.

"Is it another girl? Are you waiting on another girl and don't want me to know?" Her dark brown eyes glinted with suspicion, glistening in the sunlight.

"What? Of course not. I wouldn't do that to you," I said quickly, shaking my head.

"So why can't you tell me who you're waiting on? You're lying to me again, aren't you?"

"Again? When have I lied to you to begin with?"

"When you told me nothing was happening between you

and Sal. Nothing shady, nothing questionable. Now you tell me you're just killing time out here, but you're clearly waiting on him," she said, her arms still crossed, gaze unwavering.

Busted. How do I even explain this one without making it worse?

"Nothing shady or questionable is going on between Sal and me. Why would you think I'm waiting on Sal? That's ridiculous—" I stopped mid-sentence, a sinking feeling crawling up my spine. *He's here. Sal's behind me, waiting. I just know it.* I closed my eyes for a second, trying to swallow the guilt, watching the betrayal etched across Mia's face. "Okay, well—"

"It's okay, you can go do whatever it is you're going to do. You don't have to explain anything to me."

"Mia, it's really not...It's..." I trailed off, unsure how to bridge the gap between the truth and what I could safely tell her. *God, why is this so complicated?*

She nodded, as if giving me permission to leave, though her eyes didn't soften. "Just go."

"Sal's just giving me a ride," I said, finally blurting it out, my hands fidgeting at my sides.

"So why couldn't you have said that?"

"I don't know," I admitted, lifting my hands before letting them fall limp at my sides. My head dropped, shame coiling in my stomach, before I lifted my eyes to hers, meeting the sadness swimming inside. "I don't know. I'm an idiot. I should have just said that."

Her gaze flicked away for a moment, then back to mine. "I don't believe you. I'll talk to you later."

"Mia," I said, stepping toward her, but she turned to walk over to Maria standing by the door of Davidson's, shoulders squared but small, almost fragile in the summer sunlight.

I rounded the back of Sal's baby blue Thunderbird and yanked open the passenger side door. The leather seat was already hot from sitting in the sun, but I slid in anyway, slouching against the cushion with my arms crossed tight over my chest. A sulk sat heavy on my face. Sal tapped the wheel with one hand, slipped on his aviator sunglasses with the other, and stomped his foot down on the gas. The engine growled, and the car shot forward, tires squealing as we sped down the main strip. From the corner of my eye, I caught Mia turning her head, watching us. My chest squeezed, but I didn't dare make eye contact.

"Trouble in paradise, bambino?" Sal's voice was light and teasing, the tip of his mouth pointed upward on one side.

I huffed, rolling my eyes toward the windshield. "Where the hell were you? You told me to meet you there. I've been roasting on that sidewalk for thirty minutes, waiting on you, and you're late."

Sal chuckled low in his throat, one arm dangling lazily over the wheel as he merged into traffic. "Relax, bambino. I had to swing by the shop first. We've got a good one today. Don't take your girlfriend problems out on me."

"She's not my girlfriend." My jaw tightened as I sank deeper into the seat.

Sal glanced over, a grin tugging at the corner of his mouth still. "Yeah? Does she know that?"

I rolled my eyes again, humming under my breath, fingers drumming against my crossed arms.

"If it makes you feel better, I was late because Val wouldn't let up on me. Same kind of lecture, you know, about what we've got going on, what it looks like, who's gonna start asking questions. So..." He flicked his wrist like it was nothing new to him, chuckling softly. "We're in the same boat, little brother."

"Do you think everything is funny?" I asked.

"Little bit," he said, shoulders rising in an easy shrug. "You're sitting in a brand new Thunderbird, brooding and sulking. You were practically burning holes in the sidewalk trying to avoid that girl's eye contact. But I know the feeling, that's why it's funny, all she has to do is bat her lashes at you, and suddenly you're tangled up in knots. I've been there. I am there with you right now."

A low breath slipped out as I brushed my hand across my jaw and looked away. "You don't get it. You think this is a joke, so I'm not having this conversation with you."

"Oh, I get it," Sal said, drumming his fingers on the steering wheel in time with the do-wap crooning out of the dash. "You want her because you're not better than any of us when it comes to a pretty girl. But if I had to bet money on it, I would bet you don't want her to know what you're tied up in. The problem is..." He angled his head toward me, grin crooked. "Girls like her? Bambino, they can smell lies. It doesn't matter how much cologne you splash on it, she'll know. I'm speaking from experience. She's got beauty and brains. And splash a little bit of innocence, and Nino, you're in trouble. They always say it's the girls with the nice bodies who come from good families to watch out for. No, the combination of beauty, brains, and innocence is deadly. She's smart enough to know when you're lying out of your ass, pretty enough to force you to come clean, and innocent enough that if you tell the truth, you'll be the one to take her innocence. So you see...you're in a tough predicament."

I pressed my lips together, staring hard at the blur of shops and street signs flying past the window. "So what am I supposed to do? Lie to her? Break up with her even though I've never asked her to be my girl? Tell her the truth? What?"

Sal barked out a laugh. "Christ, don't fucking tell her the truth. I thought I just made that clear. You don't tell anybody the truth. You just learn how to lie better."

I turned to him, forehead scrunched. "That's your advice? Learn to lie better?"

"That's my gospel," he said, shifting gears. "You think I'll tell Val where I've been every night? You think Joey goes home and gives your mother the rundown of every dirty deal he made? No. Fuck no. We tell them enough to keep them warm, keep them happy. The rest stays in the dark. It's not theirs to carry, even if they think they can handle it. You don't ever tell the full truth."

I exhaled through my nose, heat still in my chest. "That seems like terrible advice and like it would be a miserable relationship. I don't want to lie to the person I'm in a relationship with, whenever the time comes."

"You'll see what I mean when you get done with today, and have to drag your feet up to her doorstep and beg for forgiveness. And she tells you you're full of shit and she knows you're lying. And I want you to look at her, after what you've done, and what you know about the mafia, and you'll realize, you can't take her innocence. That would only add to the guilt you feel. So, silence is the cleanest lie you'll ever tell."

Sal's words sank in like lead weights. *Silence is the cleanest lie you'll ever tell.*

I wanted to argue with him, to tell him he was wrong, that Mia deserved the truth, that if I started a relationship with her, hiding things from her, it'd only blow up in my face. But the more I sat there, the more I realized part of me agreed with him.

What was I supposed to say to her? *Hey Mia, sorry I kept you waiting, but Sal and I are heading to Little Italy for another mafia-related run.* Yeah, that'd go over real smooth.

My chest felt tight, like my ribs were a cage I'd locked myself inside of. Sal made it sound easy—lie better, say less— but the thought of looking into Mia's deep brown eyes and feeding her some half-truth made my stomach churn. I could already see that look she gave me earlier, like she knew I was a fraud before I even opened my mouth. Maybe that was the real problem here. I wasn't like Sal. Or Joey. Or Marco. Or Paul. They carried lies like second skins. But I felt every one of them.

Still...what choice did I really have?

"What's the job for the day? You said it was a good one."

"We're making a collection. My favorite kind of job." Sal licked his lips before he smiled.

I cocked my head. "What's the difference between a collection and a drop?"

Sal steered with one hand, the Thunderbird humming under us. "A drop, like the one you did for Frankie Bags, is a runner's job. You move something quick, cash or goods, from A to B and try not to get noticed. Fast and clean is the key." He tapped the dash. "A collection is when you go inside. Face-to-face. For today, *Mickie Meats and More*, we pay Mickie Two-Times a visit about what he owes Joey. We don't make a scene about it. We pass a soft suggestion that Joey will come collect if the money ain't on the table by the end of the week. Nobody on the face of this earth wants Joey showing up to collect."

"What would my dad do if he had to collect?" I asked, testing the edges.

One hard glance, and I understood. He didn't have to spell it out.

"So how's this gonna help clear his name?" I pressed.

"Because we work in the city. Joey thinks Hector was behind Vincent. Hector's mixed up with Frankie Costa, but those two didn't pull the trigger themselves. They'd get someone from the city to do the dirty work. We're close; so we listen. We're eyes and ears on the street. If you want to prove Joey didn't do it, you need to know how things move. You can't do that hiding in the shadows, you gotta see it, hear it."

"So we're gonna threaten some gangster—" I started.

Sal barked a laugh. "No, no." He pointed a finger between us. "We aren't 'threatening' shit. I do the talking. You shut up, keep your eyes and ears open, and learn. You don't show up and start putting out fires, bambino. It's a build-up."

That damn nickname again. It stuck in my teeth. I bristled but kept my mouth shut. Learning or not, I didn't have to like being reminded I was still a kid in his world.

Sal nodded, fingers drumming a lazy rhythm on the steering wheel. "Mickie Two Times gets his nickname 'cause he's got a stutter, says everything twice. On top of that, the bastard talks so damn fast you need a translator just to follow along. Half the time, I don't catch a word he says."

I didn't doubt that one bit.

"He borrowed money from your old man to keep his place running under our protection. Now he's late. The first week, Joey let it slide, and gave him a warning. But today, we're dropping by to remind him he doesn't want Joey showing up next. He's got 'til the end of the week to pay or else."

"So my dad loans money out to people often or something?"

Sal's head snapped toward me, brows pulling tight, his face twisting like I'd just asked if fire was hot. "Wait, you're serious? *Christ.* Why the hell do you think they call him The Shark?"

I blinked. "I thought it was because he was violent."

Sal barked a laugh, shaking his head. "Well, sure, he can be. But your old man doesn't get his hands dirty unless there's no other choice. Most people are smart enough not to push him that far."

I knew. I'd seen it once. Even now, the memory came in flashes that I tried to shove back down.

"But your pops?" Sal smirked, leaning into the steering wheel like he was enjoying the revelation. "He's the best damn loan shark on the East Coast. He's got guys from Staten Island to New Orleans in his pocket. And they all pay, sooner or later. Trust me."

I turned to the window, watching the city blur past in streaks of brick and neon. I thought I knew who Joey was. I thought I had him figured out.

A shark. Not just feared but respected. Worshiped, even.

"He's a fuckin' legend, kid," Sal said, shaking his head like he still couldn't believe my ignorance. "You really had no idea?"

My throat tightened. "I do now."

* * *

It was an hour later when we finally pulled up to the curb outside *Mickie's Meats & More*, a narrow deli sandwiched between a tailor shop and a bakery. The storefront looked innocent enough with just a few faded posters in the window.

Sal and I stepped out of the Thunderbird. A couple of guys leaning against the corner gave him a wave and shouted, "Hey, Sal!" He tossed them a grin and a finger gun in return, soaking it up like a movie star walking onto set. He liked the attention. Joey got the same kind of nods, the same respect, but Joey didn't care for the spotlight. Sal, on the other hand, looked like he'd melt without it.

We pushed through the glass door and stepped inside the deli. It was narrow and dim, with black-and-white checkered floors that were scuffed in a few places. One brick wall ran the length of the shop, with a few vinyl booths lined up against it. The front of the store held the counter. The display case was full: cold cuts, sliced cheese, fresh Italian bread, and toppings. Above it hung a handwritten menu taped to the counter, listing eight sandwiches and one soup of the day. The air smelled like salami, vinegar, and fresh bread. My stomach growled, and my mouth salivated. Another reason I needed to be a part of the life that existed in Little Italy.

It was the perfect setup for something shady. Because it was so subtle and hidden in plain sight, nobody would have ever guessed what was lurking behind it all.

Behind the counter stood Mickie Two-Times, a stocky, middle-aged guy with a round belly and salt-and-pepper hair slicked back with pomade. He smelled like mortadella and aftershave, and wore a smile that was a little too wide to be sincere. He handed a customer a sub with one hand and took a few crumpled bills with the other.

If I didn't know any better, I'd think this was just your average neighborhood deli guy. That was the thing about these guys. They were built to blend in.

Behind Mickie, mounted above the register, was a wall clock stuck at 2:17 and a framed photo of him shaking hands with Frank Sinatra, both of them smiling in front of this very counter. The signature at the bottom was from Frank himself.

Mickie looked up, spotted Sal, and gave him a quick smile and a subtle jerk of his head toward the back. I followed Sal past the register and into the backroom. It was colder back there. The walls were lined with meat grinders, stainless steel counters, and a couple of industrial-sized freezers and ovens. In the center sat a dented metal table, draped in a lemon-patterned vinyl tablecloth like someone had tried to make it look homey.

Something told me those freezers didn't just hold prosciutto.

"I know why you're here, I know why you're here, Sal," Mickie blurted the second we stepped into the back room. "And I've got the cash. I've got it."

Sal crossed his arms, smirking like a cat waiting for a mouse to hand itself over.

Mickie waddled over to a small safe in the corner, punched in a code with his short sausage fingers, and pulled out a stack of cash. He turned and handed it to Sal. My eyes widened. I'd never seen that much money before being exchanged like second nature.

Sal flipped through it, nodding in approval. "You know Joey was getting impatient, Mickie."

"I know, I know," Mickie huffed, wiping sweat from his brow with a deli rag. "I'm sorry about that, it's just…well…it's been a slow couple of weeks. Real slow. The bread order came late, the slicer broke down—"

He continued to rattle off. Repeating words twice. Talking so fast, I barely caught one out of every four words. I tuned him out, my eyes drifting around the room, past the meat grinders, the freezer doors, the lemon-print tablecloth trying to dress up a room that probably saw more threats than sandwiches.

How many places like this were out there? Tucked between bakeries and tailors, running fronts for things no deli menu ever listed.

A sharp elbow jabbed me in the ribs. I flinched, turning to Sal. His brows were raised, gesturing with a twitch of his head toward Mickie, who was staring right at me.

"You the new kid?" Mickie asked again, a little slower this time.

"Nino," I said, nodding.

Mickie grunted. "You look twelve."

"Well, I'm thirteen, fourteen in December."

Mickie turned to Sal, and the two of them barked out laughs. "You bringin' me high schoolers now? What the hell is Joey into?"

Sal was bent at the waist, trying to ease his laughter. "Kid's got hustle."

"That's what Frankie Bags told me, but I wasn't expecting someone so damn young."

Mickie's gaze held me still, a quiet threat without a word spoken. Then he reached for something on the counter and picked up a thick white envelope, holding it out. "Alright then. Take this down to *Sammy's Cleaners* on Fulton. Don't open it. Don't fold it. Don't drop it. I'm going to time you. Tell 'em Mickie sent you. I want to see for myself if you're everything Frankie and Sal say you are."

I took the envelope, sliding it into the waistband of my trousers.

"And keep your eyes off the girl at the counter. I heard she likes to bite."

Mickie and Sal barked out another laughter that made me grind my molars.

Sal clapped a hand on my shoulder. "Now listen," he said, leaning close with a grin. "The girl's too old for you, Bambino. So make the drop and come straight back. And remember, she likes to mess with your head. Trust me, she tries me every time I'm in there."

I burst through the doors and hit the sidewalk of Little Italy at a run, weaving past shoppers, strollers, and the occasional stray dog. My chest burned, legs pumping, until I skidded to a stop at the corner. The street sign read **Fulton**. And there it was—*Sammy's Cleaners*, tucked beneath a faded blue awning with a little brass bell hanging above the door.

Time to find out who the girl behind the corner was.

The bell above the door jingled as I stepped inside. The place looked like it hadn't been updated since the 40s. The scent hit me first: a strange mix of fresh-pressed starch, mothballs, and cigarette smoke, like someone had been chain-smoking in the back while ironing shirts all day. The floors were black-and-white checkered linoleum, worn down in a trail from the door to the front counter. A plastic mat with curled edges sat crooked near the entrance, printed with the words *"Your Clothes, Our Care!"* in faded red.

To the left of the door, a metal coat rack leaned awkwardly in the corner. On the wall behind the counter, rows of clothes hung in plastic wrap on a motorized conveyor system that occasionally creaked and groaned as it moved. Most tagged with names, but others suspiciously blank. The countertop was a green Formica, chipped in one corner, and beside the old cash register was a jar of hard candies that looked like they'd been there since Truman was in office. A small radio sat beside it, playing low static between a doo-wop track. Behind the counter stood a young woman in her early twenties, leaning on one elbow, flipping through an old copy of *Photoplay*. She didn't look up when I entered.

There was a door to the back, slightly ajar, with the edge of a clothing rack just barely visible. Something about it felt off. Like this was the place where you could drop off a bloody shirt and no one would ask a single question.

She finally looked up from the magazine.

And now I see why I was warned about her because she was gorgeous.

Pale ivory skin that made her dark red lipstick pop. A rhinestone barrette sparkled in her jet-black curls. She wore a baby-blue cardigan, buttoned tight and tucked into high-waisted pants that showed off every curve. She wasn't just standing behind that counter, she was posing for me. Like she knew she was being watched and wanted to give you something to remember.

With this new awareness of every pretty girl who walked by, I wouldn't forget her either.

She batted her lashes. "Can I help you?"

I cleared my throat, trying to remember what the hell I was here for. "Mickie sent me."

She straightened, eyes dragging over me in a slow assessment. "Frankie Bags told me about you," she said, one perfectly shaped brow arched. "You're Nino."

I tried not to react, but I smiled a little on the inside. I nodded and pulled the envelope from my waistband, placing it on the counter.

She slipped it behind the register like it was nothing more than a receipt. I turned on my heel and headed for the door, remembering I was still on Mickie's clock. "Bye, Nino!" she called behind me, sing-song and sugary sweet. "Come back and see me sometime!"

Maybe the nickname wasn't so bad after all.

Chapter Thirty-Six

Adriana
Nine days after Vincent's murder

Angela and I stepped into *Cosa Bella*. The smell of fresh paint, fresh flowers, and Chanel No. 5 lingered in the air. The soft pink salon chairs sat in a perfect row under hooded hair dryers plugged in and ready to go. The checkerboard floor shined. And there wasn't a speck of dust in sight. Lucy had added fresh copies of Vogue and Glamour magazines next to the vintage bench she'd sat near the window. It was spotless. But Lucy was pacing the space like she had a hundred things left to do.

"I thought we were coming to help," Angela said, arching a brow as she pulled off her black lace gloves. "This place looks like Jackie Kennedy herself is scheduled for a blowout."

Lucy spun around, wearing a high-waisted pencil skirt and a ruffled blouse that cinched her tiny waist. Her heels clicked across the floor as she waved a hand in the air, a roll of ribbon in the other. "There's always something left to do. Look at this bow, it's crooked. And don't get me started on the placement of the hand mirrors. I don't care what the contractor said, they're uneven. I can see it."

Angela and I squinted at the perfectly placed round mirrors that weren't crooked at all before we exchanged a confused expression. It really was stunning. Every detail screamed glamour, from the blush-colored curtains to the old-fashioned cash register. It was a women's only sanctuary.

"Lucy," I said softly, "It's perfect. *Really*. I think you may just be nervous. In fact, you've outdone yourself. Have you been sleeping? I was here three days ago and the place was nothing compared to what it is now."

"I'm not nervous and I've slept just fine," she snapped. Then paused, sighing as she dropped the ribbon onto a nearby chair. "Alright, maybe I'm a little nervous and lacking a bit of sleep. It's not just a beauty salon, it's *my* beauty salon. It's my name at stake. My reputation. It *has* to be perfect."

Angela crossed her arms, eyeing Lucy. "Well, you've outdone yourself, sweetheart. It's 1960 and this place looks like 1965 walked in early."

Lucy cracked a smile, her shoulders finally dropping just a little.

"Now," Angela said, slipping her purse onto the bench, "how about we crack open a bottle of champagne and toast to your empire before your anxiety burns the curls right out of your head?"

Lucy grinned, slipping behind the cash register. She crouched down and pulled out three delicate coupes, setting them on the counter. Then she grabbed a bottle of Dom Pérignon, chilled and sweating with condensation, and gave us a mischievous look that promised trouble.

She popped the cork, and it shot into the air with a celebratory *pop!* A tiny spray of bubbles tickled her nose. She laughed, shaking the bottle like a pro, and tilted it carefully, pouring the golden liquid into the glasses so it frothed up over the rim in a perfect little cascade.

"Cheers, ladies!" she announced, holding the glasses high, her eyes sparkling as she wiggled her eyebrows at us. The bubbles danced in the light, fizzing and crackling like tiny fireworks. Angela and I laughed, clinking our glasses against hers.

"Finally. I've been dry since yesterday," Angela said, taking a grateful sip.

"To *Cosa Bella*," Lucy declared, her grin wide and bright.

"To new beginnings," I added, raising my glass a little higher.

"And to any man who dares cross us ever again...they will be six feet under," Angela said with a wicked smirk. "Because we've officially formed our own girl gang...right here in a girls-only salon."

We all burst into laughter, the champagne fizzing faster in our glasses.

"Do you hear yourself?" I giggled, shaking my head. "We sound terrifying when you say it like that!"

Angela lifted a shoulder as she took another sip of her champagne.

"You know, I think I'm going to throw a party when I open," Lucy said, practically bouncing on her heels with excitement. "A big one with jazz music, fancy cocktails, oysters on crushed ice. Every housewife in Staten Island will have to see how it's done. And Renee...will *not* be invited."

"Thank God," Angela muttered, grinning into her glass.

"Yes, or I'd have to be stuck mixing cocktails and secretly serving Angela's sleepy cocktail," I added, earning a shared laugh that made the room feel both wicked and dark.

I couldn't help the small thrill running through me. There was something intoxicating about this—us, laughing, planning, plotting little mischiefs in a world that usually demanded we play the nice girl.

"So," Angela said, swirling the champagne in her glass.

"What's the update on Hector and Ben? Because neither of them looked very dead to me when I saw them strolling a little too freely through town last night. Separately, of course. But still, they seemed alive and well, smiling and laughing without a single care in the world."

Lucy sighed and rolled her eyes, taking another sip before answering. "I didn't tell you the full story. But I confronted Hector. And he didn't even bother denying it. He told me he has a five-year-old, a two-year-old, and she's pregnant again. So, of course, I told him I wanted a divorce, and he looked me dead in the face and said if I tried anything, he'd have Ben killed."

Angela choked on her drink. "He what?"

"He said the only reason Ben's still breathing is because he's '*useful*.' But if my father ever found out about Ben and me...it'd be over. And I cannot have that sitting on my conscience. So I guess Hector wins like he always has. He gets to have his cake and eat it, too."

I felt my stomach twist, a cold knot forming in my gut. Every time Hector gets away with something, it's like a masterclass in fear. Somehow, we're all trapped in it, tiptoeing around the chaos he leaves behind. First, he paints a target on Joey's back and walks away, promoted. Now he has a family with another woman besides Lucy, and he still gets away with it.

Maybe...if Joey can't take him out, and Lucy is too scared, then I'll have to do it. Somehow. Some way.

"So I told Ben," Lucy continued. "And he"—she paused, shaking her head, frustration curling in her features—"he told me to do it anyway. To tell my father everything Hector's done. I said absolutely not, of course. And then, like a total lunatic, he drops the bomb that his wife is pregnant."

Angela gasped. "That dirty—"

"Oh, it gets better. He showed up here like a stray mutt, banging on the salon door. I stood right there and yelled at him to read that sign. He tore the sign off the door and tossed it in the trash. When I let him in, he confessed, saying it was a lie. His wife's not pregnant. He made it up just to push me to go to my father and get Hector killed, because he's convinced Hector had someone kill Vincent. But I told him I would never do that. No matter what happens, I will never do anything to jeopardize Ben's life. It means too much to me."

Goosebumps rose along my arms. I felt the air leave my lungs. "Joey told me the same thing," I said quietly. "He's sure Hector's behind it."

Lucy turned to me, grabbing my arm. "And listen, I love Joey, I do. But it's not that simple. If I go to my father, Hector will throw Ben and me under the bus, and I can't let that happen. Because..." She hesitated, then grinned. "Ben and I made up after he told the truth. But even if we hadn't made up, I know what would happen to him, and I can't do that. Hector is a coward. And he would never let me have any happiness if it came down to it."

I felt a cold pit form in my stomach. So that's it. That's why everything's falling apart behind the scenes. Hector gets to keep winning while everyone else is trapped in the fallout. And we're just...watching, powerless. If Joey can't fix it, and Lucy can't, then who will? My fists clenched. Somehow, I have to figure out a way to stop him before he ruins even more lives.

"Well...you could always put Hector to sleep with Angela's secret cocktail," I blurted, the words slipping out before I could stop them.

I didn't know if I meant for anyone to hear. My chest tightened, heat prickling at my neck, and for a moment I barely recognized myself. Who was I becoming? The thought sent a shiver down my spine, a mix of fear and a strange exhilaration.

Lucy's eyes widened, a sly smile tugging at the corners of her lips. Angela blinked, mid-sip, caught off guard by my suggestion. Silence hung in the air for a second, heavy with possibility and danger.

This wasn't just a joke. Maybe it could work. Maybe it shouldn't. But part of me couldn't help wondering…what if it did?

I forced out a soft, almost nervous laugh. Angela threw her head back and cackled. "You scared the hell out of me for a second!"

"I thought she was serious!" Lucy gasped, pressing a hand to her chest, still laughing.

I smiled over the rim of my glass, letting the laughter settle around us. *Perfect. They're already thinking about it, imagining it. The ideas are in their heads now.*

All I need is patience. Let them stew in the possibility, let the notion grow like a spark in the dark. By the time anyone realizes I planted it, it'll already be too late, or too tempting to resist.

I took a slow sip, letting the bubbles tickle my throat, and enjoying the quiet power of a well-placed suggestion.

Chapter Thirty-Seven

Antonio
Nine days after Vincent's murder

A glass bottle of Coca-Cola sweated in each of our hands, the fizz catching the sunlight as I tipped it back between laughs. In the middle of us sat a crumpled brown paper sack, steaming with boiled peanuts. Shells snapped and cracked, piling up in the grass at our feet.

Enzo leaned back on the bleachers, his hands tucked behind his head. "Man, this is it. The life. No school, no homework—thank you very much, Michael—just boiled peanuts, cold Coke, and sunshine."

Michael shifted, his grin tugging at the corners of his mouth. "Well, speaking of life...I've got something to tell you two." He paused as his eyes bounced from Enzo to me. "I asked Alessia to be my girlfriend last night."

Enzo shot upright. "You what?"

I nearly choked on my Coke. "I'm sorry, come again?"

Michael flicked a peanut shell at us. "See? I knew you'd both be idiots about it."

"I'm not being an idiot," Enzo said, trying to look serious, but I could see the grin twitching on his face. I snorted into my Coke, which only set him off howling.

Michael groaned, dragging a hand down his face. "You guys are so annoying sometimes."

"Don't look at me," I protested, pointing my Coke bottle at Enzo. "He started it."

"Started it?" Enzo gestured at his chest, wide-eyed. "You're the one who laughed first!"

"Only because I saw you about to explode!" I shot back, snickering.

Michael shook his head, muttering, "And this, right here, is exactly why neither of you has a girlfriend."

Enzo smirked. "Not wrong. Maria was a terrible kisser anyway."

Michael's brows shot up. "You ever think maybe that was you?"

Enzo lifted one shoulder in a lazy shrug. "Could have been. But hey, I'm keeping my options open. Maybe I'll snag someone older when school starts up again."

I barked a laugh, though deep down I thought the same. "Yeah, right. Nobody's giving a freshman the time of day."

Enzo tipped his Coke bottle in salute. "We'll see. I mean, come on. Look at me." Enzo jumped to his feet, waving his hands down his body like he was presenting a prize on a game show. His all-black shirt clung to him in the heat, the short sleeves rolled up, jeans cuffed at the ankles, and scuffed black boots. A thin gold cross swung at his chest.

"You're an idiot, that's what I see," Michael shot back. "Too immature. And probably too shitty of a kisser to impress anyone older."

"How would you know?" I challenged, sizing Michael up with a smirk. "How much kissing have you actually done with Alessia?"

"Yeah! Tell us, lover boy. How much and how far?"

Michael shrugged, the corners of his mouth tugging into a smug grin.

Enzo and I both shot up straight. "No way!"

"What about you?" Enzo spun on me, his eyes narrowing. "Whatever happened with you and Mia?"

Damn it. Mia. The name alone twisted in my chest. I scratched the back of my neck, avoiding his stare. "Nothing. Just a kiss."

Enzo exhaled hard and dropped back onto the bleacher, relief written all over his face. "Thank God. Because if either one of you beats me to it—especially Michael—I'll lie myself down in the road and let the Buicks roll over me. I couldn't live with Michael becoming a man before me."

"You don't have to 'do the deed' to become a man," Michael scoffed.

Enzo barked a laugh. "Oh, come on. He didn't get more than a peck on the lips, and now he's calling it a deed? Jesus, who talks like that?"

"What would you know?" Michael snapped, his ears going pink.

I threw an arm around Michael's shoulder. "Face it, Enzo. Michael's already a better man than either of us."

Enzo sat back down, shrugging. "Probably."

"Hey." The voice was soft, but it sliced right through me. A chill rushed up my spine as I turned. Mia. She stood at the bottom of the bleachers, sunlight catching the edge of her dark hair, swept back in a high ponytail.

Enzo's forehead scrunched, his eyes going wide. He muttered into his Coke, "Shit."

"Antonio?" Mia's gaze locked onto mine. "Can we talk?"

My eyes wandered up her body before finally landing on hers. She wore a pale yellow sundress that swayed in the breeze, the hem brushing just above her knees. Her sandals slapped softly against the pavement, toenails painted a coral pink. The heat had curled strands of hair at her temples, framing her face. I swallowed hard and nodded, sliding off the bleachers to follow her. Each step down the metal rungs echoed like a warning bell in my mind. We slipped to the side of the bleachers, away from Enzo's gawking stare and Michael's smirk.

Fuck. I knew I'd have to confront her sooner or later. I knew I'd have to explain myself. There's no hiding in this town, it's too small, too many eyes, too many mouths running faster than cars down the strip. Another reason I needed to get out when I was old enough.

Her arms folded tight over her chest as she kicked at a pebble, sending it skittering across the pavement. "It's been three days," she muttered, not looking at me.

I know. I've been avoiding this moment for seventy-two hours straight, counting every hour that passed. My eyes dropped to her coral-painted toenails, anything to keep from meeting her stare. But I could feel her gaze cutting into me like a spotlight I couldn't escape. "I wasn't sure how to go about this. I know you're upset. And I—"

"You thought avoiding me was the best decision. That way, you didn't have to deal with my feelings?"

My head snapped up, eyes locking onto hers. "That's not what I said."

"You didn't have to say it."

"You're putting words in my mouth. Words I wasn't even thinking." *Liar. Fuck. That was exactly what I was thinking. Sal was right.* And as I tugged at my bottom lip, looking at her straight on, I knew she could see right through me.

Her chin lifted, eyes glassy with anger. "So you weren't hoping this would just...disappear? That I'd forget the shady behavior. That I'd forget you dodging me like I don't matter. That I'd forget the way you keep lying to me?"

Yes. Fuck. Yes. That's exactly what I was hoping. But my voice came out smooth, acid burning my throat as I forced the words: "No. Of course not." I gestured between us, my hand dropping when it felt useless. "I'm trying, Mia. I don't...I don't know how to do this." My voice cracked enough to betray me. "I like you. I know you like me. But I don't know how this works."

Her arms tightened around herself as she held in the storm building inside her. "You're not supposed to act the way you do, for starters."

Her words sliced through me. My chest felt heavy, my breath shallow. My mouth opened and then closed. What could I even say? "Mia, I don't want to lose you over this. Tell me what to do. Tell me how to fix it."

She shook her head, her voice trembling, but her eyes never left mine. "Don't put that on me, Antonio. You're the one who has to decide if I'm worth telling the truth to. Not me."

Holy. Fuck. This is what Sal meant. She's radiant in that yellow dress, sunlight seems to live in the hem, and those big brown eyes look at me like I'm the only person who can fix whatever she's hurting from. Innocent. Expectant. Smart enough to see through my bullshit.

And I can't tell her. What the hell do I say? *"Oh, you want the truth? Sure. I shot the only man I ever called father in a blind rage because some mafia boss was fucking with my head. Joey covered for me. Then that boss is murdered, and everyone points fingers at Joey, so now I run errands for Sal to try to clear his name. Also, three days ago, when you caught me lying, I was out doing shady shit in Little Italy, and instead of feeling guilty about living a double life, I kind of liked it."*

Yeah. That would go over well. I think not.

"Are you even going to say something?" she asked, and the words snapped me back from the edge of my own spiral. I don't even know how long I'd been staring at her like a ghost.

"I'm sorry," I blurted, because it was something, anything I could pull out. "I'm sorry for being an idiot." *That's more like it.*

"Sorry isn't good enough. I want the truth."

No fucking way am I telling her the truth. No. Absolutely not. Not happening.

Mia's jaw clenched. "If you don't want to tell me, then don't talk to me. Don't look at me like nothing happened. Don't pretend everything's normal." The sun caught the wet rim of her lower lashes, and for a second she looked ten times more fragile than she had any right to be.

I wanted to bang my head into the concrete. I couldn't scrape together a single thing to tell her that would sound true. Every lie I thought of tasted hollow. I don't know how to lie. I don't know how to tell her the truth. And it felt like both choices were poison: tell her and watch everything break, lie and watch whatever little trust was built rot away. I clenched my jaw until my teeth ached, because there was no clever line, no smooth dodge, nothing that made this less than the disaster it already was.

"I'm not—" I started, then stopped. "Okay...Okay. I'll tell you part of it. My dad's been...busy. Sal works for my dad. And so I've been helping Sal with work for my dad. So, I've been helping out at the shop. It's stupid, and I should've told you." Even as I hear myself repeat the half-lie, I don't even believe it.

"You're working for your dad but with Sal?" she asked, slowly as if testing how the syllables fit together.

"Yes." *Kind of.*

"What do you do with Sal for your dad?"

My throat went dry. Fuck. Am I sweating? "We...sell cars."

"You sell cars?"

"Paperwork, too."

"You sell cars and do paperwork?" she repeated, jaw working like she couldn't decide whether to laugh or cry.

"Yes." *No.*

She let out a breath that might have been a laugh if it wasn't so raw. "You know what? Fine. Keep your secrets, Antonio. But don't expect me to wait around until you decide to grow up." She started to walk past me.

"Wait—" I said, lunging after her, but my feet felt like they were moving through syrup.

She stopped, turned, and the sight of her holding back the waterfall behind her eyes hit me like a fist in my gut. "You can follow me, or you can go back to your peanut shells and Coke. Either way, I'm done being second place to your secrets. And the worst part is that I actually liked you. A lot. And for someone who says he hates Giovanni, you're not much different."

Her words slammed into me harder than any punch. I watched her walk; the space between us swallowed up in a few long strides, the hem of her yellow dress swinging with each step until she was just a silhouette down the sidewalk. The space between us stretched and stretched until it felt impossible to cross.

I knew then and there, if I ever stayed involved with the mafia, I would never, ever be in a relationship. I refuse to lie to someone who's begging for the truth. I refuse to see that helpless, innocent look in another person's eyes. And I refuse to be the one to strip that innocence away again from another pair of wide, trusting eyes.

"You do know Alessia's the daughter of a man who once shattered Tommy's nose with a pool cue for calling him '*Cat*' in front of a room full of people, right?" I could hear Enzo remark to Michael.

I didn't catch Michael's response as I dragged myself back to the bleachers and sank down beside him, but Enzo kept going. "Doesn't that go against everything you're always preaching?"

Michael frowned. "What's that supposed to mean?"

"You're the guy who swears he's gonna get out of here. College degree, clean life, pension, white picket fence." Enzo gestured with his Coke bottle. "Dating Paul's daughter doesn't exactly scream escape plan. Feels more like a one-way ticket to being chained here for good."

Michael scoffed, "You make it sound like I'm marrying her tomorrow. I said we're dating. I asked her to be my girlfriend last night, for crying out loud. Not take my last name. Things are getting a little serious in the way that we like each other, yeah, but no one's picking out china patterns."

"Well..." Enzo jabbed a finger at him, "You so much as annoy her, and you're dealing with Paul. Make her cry? Forget a pool cue, you'll be breathing through a tube. You're on his radar the second you lay a finger on his only daughter. That's not a path I'd be strolling down if it were me." He threw his hands up. "But hey, go nuts."

"I don't plan on making her cry."

"Yeah, well...that's usually out of your control," Enzo muttered. His eyes slid over to me, and a grin tugged at his mouth. "Right, Antonio? Looks like you just proved the point with Mia."

I let Enzo's jab about Mia slide. "Nothing could happen to Michael. He's mafia royalty."

Michael winced. "Don't say shit like that." He shoved my shoulder hard enough to make me rock. "You know how much I hate being lumped in with all that."

"God forbid we call him a Mafia Prince," Enzo said with a smirk, raising his Coke bottle like a toast.

Michael groaned and sulked, then tried to redirect. "What happened with Mia, anyway?"

My body tilted forward, elbows digging into my thighs, fingers dragging through my hair before gripping the back of my neck. I stared at the peanut shells scattered between my shoes. "It was short-lived. Better this way."

"Why? I thought you liked each other," Michael said.

"Nah." I forced a smirk that didn't stick. "She liked me more." I didn't buy it. "I'm not right for her."

"Not right for her?" Enzo barked out a laugh, confusion wrinkling his brow. "You're Antonio Romano. Joey Romano's only son. The prodigy. If I were The Shark's kid, hell, if I were a so-called Mafia Prince, I'd wear it like a crown and make it my entire identity."

Michael rolled his eyes at Enzo's "Mafia Prince" comment. "You'd wear it like a crown because you're an idiot. That's why. And because you've got no idea what it feels like to be me, Enzo. It's not a crown, it's a shackle."

"Fair," Enzo said, cracking open another peanut, "but I'd take advantage of being a mafia prince and play it in my favor." Enzo tipped his Coke bottle toward Michael. "Oh, listen to him, talking like some tragic anti-hero. *'It's not a crown, it's a curse.'* Man, Alessia must eat that shit up. Girls love a brooding guy with a family secret. You should feed into this."

"Would you shut up?" Michael muttered, though the corners of his mouth betrayed him.

I smirked, finally glancing up from the peanut shells. "Enzo's not entirely wrong. You asking Paul's daughter out isn't exactly subtle. If you're not careful, you're gonna fulfill your prophecy."

Michael rolled his eyes. "It's not like that. I'm not fulfilling any prophecy. I like Alessia, she likes me. It's as simple as that."

Enzo grinned. "Oh, yeah. Paul's basically built out of pool

cues and rage with the code name 'Cat' for sneaking up on you in the dark of night. What a catch, Michael. I didn't know you were such a rebel."

"It's not like I asked her to marry me, for crying out loud. We're just dating. That's normal. People date. Just because the two of you don't date, doesn't mean the rest of us don't," Michael huffed.

"Not people in families like ours," I muttered before I could stop myself. "That's why I'm not dating Mia anymore. She should date someone from a normal family. Mia deserves better than this crap. Better than me."

Enzo pointed at me. "See? Antonio gets it. You're out here planning your white picket fence and pension, but the second you piss off Alessia, or worse, Paul, you'll be buried six feet under the picket fence. There's no way I would risk that to get to second base with a girl."

Michael barked a laugh. "You wouldn't know what to do with second base if it smacked you in the face."

"I'd figure it out," Enzo said, puffing his chest. "And when I do, it won't be with some girl who's about to get me whacked by her dad. Unlike you."

"You guys don't get it. Alessia's different."

The smiles slid off Enzo, and I's face when we realized how serious Michael was about Alessia. "Different how?" I asked.

He shrugged, a small smile sneaking across his face. "She listens. She sees me. And I'm almost convinced she's the only one who sees me."

Enzo whimpered, clutching his heart. "God, you're in deep. Next thing we know, you'll be writing poetry in your notebook. *Roses are red, violets are blue, Alessia's dad's got a pool cue, and he'll break me in two.*"

I cracked up, Coke fizz shooting up my nose. Michael shoved Enzo's shoulder hard, but he was laughing too.

Enzo lifted his Coke high, a wicked grin spreading across his face. "To us...the idiot"—he thumped his chest with his free hand—"the love-sick mafia prince"—his brows shot at Michael, who groaned but couldn't hide the smirk tugging at his mouth—"and Joey Romano's cold-blooded prodigy son." His eyes locked on me as I lifted my bottle, and the three of us clinked together in a sloppy little triangle.

"Staten Island's finest, ladies and gentlemen!" Enzo bellowed toward the whole park, arms spread like he was on a stage.

Michael shook his head, muttering, "You're an embarrassment."

"Correction," Enzo said with a bow, "I'm the glue holding this circus of embarrassment together."

Chapter Thirty-Eight

Joey
Nine days after Vincent's murder

Sal was in the front parking lot going over an invoice with a guy from the docks, and I could hear Marco and Paul cracking jokes near the back garage, where we had a cherry-red '59 Cadillac Coupe DeVille parked for a "friend" who'd fallen behind on payments. I walked into the lounge, poured myself a cup of black coffee, and barely had time to take a sip before Tommy came to tell me, "Boss, Christopher is here."

Seconds passed before I could hear Christopher's dress shoes making their way through the front to the lounge. "Joey," he smiled, extending his arms wide. "Look at this fucking place." His eyes bounced around, a smile glowing on his features.

I pulled him into a quick hug. He grabbed my face with both hands, giving my cheek a light tap before stepping back. He turned slowly, taking in every inch of the office—leather chairs, polished wood desk, walls lined with framed photos of classic cars and newspaper clippings of our recent successes.

"I was passing by, and I saw the new sign," he said.

I nodded. "*Romano Luxury Wholesale* now. We specialize in high-end vehicles only. No more small-time bullshit."

Christopher turned in a slow circle, taking it all in. "Luxury's where the money is nowadays, huh?"

"The kids nowadays want luxury cars only," I said, sipping my coffee.

Christopher's eyes gleamed with pride as he shook his head, smiling from ear to ear. "You've come a long way, figlio mio."

"I learned from the best," I said, tapping his shoulder.

"I'm proud of you. You've made us all millionaires, Joey. I want to see this Cadillac I've been hearing about through the grapevine."

We walked through the shop as I pulled my keys out of my trouser front pocket and opened the garage door, letting sunlight pour over that gleaming cherry-red beast.

As he stepped forward to admire it all, he added, "Keep making moves like this, Joey, and the future of this family might just be sitting behind your desk someday. Hector's going to need someone solid by his side when I'm dead and gone."

"You've got plenty more years ahead of you," I said with a light chuckle as we climbed into the car. I started the engine, easing us onto the main strip.

"That's kind of you," he said, glancing out the window, "but I've got more behind me than I do ahead. There comes a time when a man knows that."

A few seconds of silence stretched between us before he asked, "How's your family doing, Joey?"

"Everyone's good. Adriana's doing incredible and, my boy, Antonio is the best damn baseball player this town's ever seen."

"That right?" he said, turning his head back toward me with a grin. "Baseball, huh? You must be proud."

"Proud doesn't even begin to cover it," I beamed. "Kid's got a swing on him that'll make scouts be all over him in a few years' time."

He chuckled low in his throat. "Good. Keep him pointed at that diamond. The world's got enough of us breaking the rules and calling it a living."

I nodded. "That's my plan. Keep him clear of this mess. Let him have a life that's his own."

"You know, talking about young kids staying off the streets, I've been meaning to ask you something I heard on the street."

My brows stitch together as I glance over at Christopher, "Yeah, what is it?"

His eyes meet mine as I coast down the strip. "You happen to know a runner who goes by the name Nino? I was told he's high school-aged."

I tried to place the name, but nothing came up. I shake my head. "No, it doesn't ring a bell. Why?"

"A couple of the guys say he's the best runner they've ever seen. Some say he's connected to your crew. Some say he's connected to the Moretti family and Frank's crew. Others think he belongs to another family entirely."

"Well, if he is mine, he hasn't introduced himself yet. And I'm not a fan of including kids in my operation. But I'll keep my ears open. Let you know if I find anything."

Christopher nodded, resting a hand on his round belly. "Do that. Something tells me whoever's got this kid...they've got more power than they realize, and we need to keep the power in *this* family. I'm not a fan of kids on the street, but if he's going to be on the street, he needs to be with the right family."

We circled back through the city, and I pulled into the parking lot of *Romano Luxury Wholesale.* I parked next to a 1960 Cadillac Eldorado Biarritz convertible. Black exterior, cherry-red leather seats, white-wall tires that gleamed. Custom gold trim on the grille.

I turned the engine off, stepped out of the car, and gestured for Christopher to follow. "All yours. It's a gift to show my gratitude. And for all you've done for me. A man like you should be cruising around this city like the king that you are. I'll have one of the guys deliver your car, but you leave in this."

He walked toward it. Ran a hand over the hood and let out a low whistle. A grin stretched wide over his lips.

"You're gonna turn heads from Brooklyn to the Bronx," I crossed my arms, a smirk riding my lips.

He opened the driver's side door, slid inside, and ran his thick fingers over the steering wheel. His eyes looked over at me. "This family's in good hands, Joey. Because we got you. I've always known that. Get in. Let's drive up to Pat's for some cannolis."

I circled around and slid into the passenger seat, deja vu hitting me like I was a kid all over again. The engine purred to life, and we backed out of the lot, the tires kissing the pavement. It didn't feel like he was the boss. It felt like I was twenty years younger, just a kid he found wandering with no direction, and a man who gave him one. Now we were riding through the city we'd carved with our own hands. Two kings of Staten Island, rolling down streets that would remember our names forever.

A short while later, we stepped inside Pat's Bakery. The place smelled like heaven. Fresh cannoli cream, warm almond biscotti, and freshly brewed espresso. Behind the glass counter, shelves were stacked with Italian cookies in every color (rainbow, amaretti, pignoli). The espresso machine hummed in the background. Pat stood behind the counter, a copy of *La Gazzetta dello Sport* folded open in front of her.

"Ah! Cristoforo!" she called, stepping out from behind the counter, arms open as she wrapped his large body into a hug, kissing each of his cheeks before it was my turn. "And Joey! Dio mio, the city's *finest* men in my bakery! Tell me, what have I done to deserve the honor?"

The room bloomed with a warm laughter that transported me back to my childhood when I stood in this very same bakery, but Pat was twenty years younger, more attractive to a rebellious teenage boy with her Italian accent and bold personality.

Christopher and I sat at the table near the window, where the sun poured through the white lace curtains. Pat returned with a silver tray, two cannoli, three rainbow cookies each, and two tiny cups of espresso. "Compliments of the house," she said, placing the tray down. "And if you want more, you just say the word, and it's yours."

"You spoil us, Pat," Christopher said, grinning. She smiled and patted his shoulder as she sauntered back to her Italian sports magazine.

Christopher took a sip from his small espresso mug. "You know, I wanted you to become the underboss so we could run this family together. But then you got pinched, and I had to have Vincent step in." He paused. "I never told you, but that crushed me. To see you locked away in your prime. That hurt me, Joey." He patted his thick hand against his chest. But all I could think about was how I was framed by Vincent and Hector. "And Hector's my son-in-law, but he's always been working alongside Vincent and me, so it only made sense that he would take the role as underboss."

I looked down at the cannoli, then back at him. "I understand. I learned a lot while I was away. And even if they hit me with a life sentence, I would have never broken the oath I made to this family. I wish it could have been different, but—" My voice trailed off, but my mind screamed, I was the fall guy, thanks to Vincent and Hector.

"My biggest fear is that one of the guys will flip. Just to avoid getting canned. But I've never worried about that with you." He looked me in the eye. "You're the only one I trust, Joey. The other night, when I questioned you, it was just out of protocol. But the truth is, I'd like you to be the consigliere."

"I would be honored."

He exhaled, nostrils flaring at the weight of the emotions flowing between us. "We'll set a meeting up in a few nights to announce it. Does that sound good to you?"

I nodded. "I couldn't be happier right now. It's an honor to be your right-hand man."

"I'm the lucky one, Joey," he said, taking a bite of one of the rainbow cookies. "I wanted to ask you about the update from Ben. What's he worked out with what he thinks was behind this?"

"He hasn't figured out who did it yet. He's still working the case. He says the NYPD's been wracking their brains, but I think they're close to giving up. Which is what he needs to have happen so he can figure it out for himself."

"You know, Vincent was upset about you bringing Ben in. But I think that's the best damn thing this family's ever had. He's a real stand-up guy. I like him. It's a genius idea to have someone who plays both fields."

He plays both fields, alright. "Yeah, he's solid. Ben's...Ben's one of a kind."

The pride in my chest swelled, dizzying me, but the knot in my stomach made it impossible to savor the moment like I'd always imagined I would. Being Christopher's consigliere meant keeping the family polished on the outside and burying the filth where no one could find it. But what happens when the filth is the underboss himself, and Christopher doesn't see it?

Chapter Thirty-Nine

Adriana
Nine days after Vincent's murder

The front doors of the Giordano estate creaked open before Angela or I could even knock. Mrs. Dobbins, Lucy's housekeeper, stood in the grand marble foyer, her expression taut and eyes a little haunted. It had only been a few hours since we'd left Cosa Bella, laughing and toasting Lucy's success, but her frantic, disgruntled phone call had us both bolting out our doors.

"She's upstairs," Mrs. Dobbins said.

Angela and I exchanged a glance before stepping into the house. The estate was its usual museum of wealth—crystal chandeliers dripping like icicles, gilded mirrors that seemed to watch from every wall, velvet upholstery so plush it swallowed the light. But as we climbed the staircase, the sweetness of Lucy's Chanel No. 5 hung in the air, poisoned by something acrid, like smoke and raw nerves.

Lucy's bedroom door was ajar, and inside lay devastation. The room looked as though it had been caught in a hurricane of rage: a vase of long-stemmed roses shattered in the fireplace, petals bruised and blackened in puddles of water; a mink coat smoldered in the grate, filling the air with the bitter stench of scorched fur; stilettos littered the carpet like shrapnel; the silk sheets twisted, as if two bodies had fought a war on top of them.

In the center of it all stood Lucy. Barefoot, her black curls tumbled in a storm around her face, mascara streaked down her cheeks in crooked rivers. The skin across her chest was flushed with angry welts, and a cigarette quivered between two fingers, ash bending dangerously close to her knuckles. At her wrist was the unmistakable imprint of a hand, red and raw, as if branded there.

Angela and I rushed toward Lucy. She was standing there in the wreckage, body present but spirit gone, her eyes glassy, as if whatever had happened between this morning and now had carried her somewhere far away.

"Is that a handprint on your wrist?" Angela asked.

Lucy lifted her wrist, glancing at the red mark, then flicked the last of her cigarette into a crystal ashtray perched on the vanity, its fractured mirror throwing back warped shards of her reflection.

"Did you kill the bastard?" Angela pressed. "Did you hide his body and need our help? Because I sure as hell hope so, considering he had the nerve to touch you."

"Unfortunately, I didn't kill him." Lucy's voice was flat, detached, her gaze fixed on something beyond either of us.

Angela plucked the open bottle of vodka from Lucy's mirrored bar cart, while I moved through the wreckage, side-stepping shards of broken glass until I perched on the edge of the tufted chaise. Lucy was a storm contained inside herself, smudged mascara, trembling hands, that welt of a handprint branding her wrist. Watching her, all I could think was how miserable it must be to live gilded and trapped, forced into the orbit of a vile man. I'd long given up that for better days. Lucy could too. If only she'd end Hector.

"I'm fine," Lucy said at last, waving her bruised wrist. "I just had to get a few things out of my system. My father came for lunch after we left Cosa Bella, and Hector had the gall to gift me a mink coat, putting on a performance in front of Daddy like he's some doting husband. And the moment Daddy left, he told me he's off to the city to see Cassandra." She spat the name like poison. "If you were wondering about the other woman, there she is. *Cassandra.*"

Her voice wavered, then hardened. "I told him I wanted a divorce. I told him I hated him. I reminded him he's gotten everything he wanted, he's the underboss now, and he doesn't need me anymore. He's got his whore in the city; he should go to her. But you can see how that turned out." She held up her wrist again, her laugh brittle as glass. "It got violent. He told me I'm stuck with him until he's done with me. And worse, if I ever try to have him taken out, if anyone harms him before his 'time,' he's made arrangements. He's given orders. Someone, probably that buffoon Frank, will kill Ben."

Angela spun on her heel, marched into the hallway, and leaned over the banister. "Mrs. Dobbins! Would you get some olive brine up here?"

"No, I want my dirty martini without the brine."

Angela reentered, folding her arms across her chest. "So you want just a shot of vodka then?"

"Not a shot." Lucy scoffed, lifting her chin, the ghost of her old arrogance breaking through the cracks. "Christ, Angela, that's tacky. I want it in a proper glass. With ice."

Angela rolled her eyes and hollered again down the staircase. "Mrs. Dobbins! Bring bread and butter too!"

"Angela, I'm carb-free again!" Lucy shrieked.

"You're drinking chilled vodka with no food in your system and losing your mind over a man who wears pinky rings and has three kids with another woman. What kind of friend would we be if we let you ruin your liver over that pig?" Angela challenged, her eyes blazing with fury.

"She's right," I said, trying to soften the moment, forcing a small smile to curve my lips.

Lucy groaned, strands of her black hair falling into her bloodshot eyes. "Fine, I'll eat a piece of bread. One. Small. Piece." She held up a single finger for emphasis. Angela rolled her eyes, perched on the edge of the messy bed.

Mrs. Dobbins appeared silently with a silver tray, delivering softened butter, a few slices of fresh bread, and chilled glasses filled with ice cubes. Once she disappeared, Angela took over, pouring vodka like she was behind the bar at *The Wise Guy*.

Angela handed out the glasses. I reached for the bread, spreading butter thickly over three slices before passing one to each of us. We coaxed Lucy down to sit on the edge of the mattress. She slumped forward, her shoulders heavy, legs dangling, hair falling over her face. From this vantage, I could see every detail, her bloodshot eyes rimmed in smeared black liner, her lips pressed tight, and the trembling of her fingers as they brushed the glass of vodka.

It reminded me of myself back when I first arrived on Staten Island, broken, breathless, unsure of survival, when Joey Romano became my anchor, my saving grace. Now, life was cruelly ironic; I had become the reason someone else had to grow harder, colder. I forced the thought down, pressing it into a corner of my mind. No sense dredging up ghosts when the living still needed you.

Lucy let out a shaky sigh, wincing as the vodka burned down

her throat. "Can we not talk about my life? Can we talk about your life instead, Angela? How do you do it, Angela?" Her gaze locked onto Angela. "How do you have Marco falling over his own damn feet for you? How do you walk into a room full of untamed men and suddenly they all sit up straighter? They all respect you. They never cross the line. I'm a joke. I'll always be silenced."

Angela smirked into her glass, swirling the ice until it clicked against the sides. She sipped slowly, savoring the cold burn before speaking, each word lethal. "Those men have seen too many women cry, beg, and plead. And you know, I've done that once before." She paused, the weight of her gaze on Lucy. "It didn't get me a damn thing, just a bruised heart and a sore throat from all the screaming and pleading. So now I don't cry. I certainly won't beg. And if a man wants to know how I feel... well...he'll find out when he's on his knees asking for permission to breathe the same air as me."

Lucy turned her head, eyes locking onto mine with a mix of desperation and curiosity. "How did you tame Joey Romano on the Staten Island Ferry? I've known Joey most of my life. He's never loved anyone besides himself. He's never wanted to be tamed or settle down. But you...you did something to him. You got your happy ending, and so did he. I want the same thing. I want to be free of this. I want to be happy again. I want Ben and me to have a happy ending."

"I don't think it was about taming," I said softly, the muted sunlight glinting off the shattered crystal on the vanity. "I think...Joey and I were looking for something we didn't know we'd been missing. Maybe we're two halves that make a whole. Or maybe it's about finding someone who sees the parts of you that no one else ever could. Because we see each other, all our parts. You have to do some really hard things to get your happy ending. I thought I'd never have it. But I did. And it's possible for you too. You just have to come to terms with some really hard decisions."

The room fell into silence, the weight of our life choices pressing down around us. Vodka and crushed flowers lingered in the air, mixing with the warmth of our bodies huddled together. It was somehow comforting—a cocoon keeping the darkness at bay.

Angela's crimson nails tapped against the empty glass with a wicked grin. "I mean...worst case scenario, we poison Hector."

Lucy let out a bitter, incredulous laugh, the sound bouncing off the cracked mirrors. "Jesus, I can't kill him. Did you not hear anything I said? He'll have Ben killed. And that would kill me. So I suppose I get no happily ever after."

"We could always euthanize whoever he ordered to place the hit on Ben, too," Angela added, one brow arched.

Lucy nudged my shoulder with mock disbelief. "Oh my God. She's terrifying. Isn't she, Adriana?"

I shrugged, brushing a strand of hair from Lucy's face, letting a small smirk tug at my lips. "It's not the worst plan I've ever heard."

Lucy gasped, theatrically clutching her chest. "Wait. Look what you've done! You've convinced Adriana that your antics are acceptable."

"Well, then we've only got one more to convince, don't we?" Angela smiled wickedly.

Lucy rested her head on Angela's shoulder."How many men have you...what did you call it...put to sleep permanently? Euthanize a man?"

"Now come on, Lucy. A woman never tells all her secrets." Angela smirked.

We all burst into laughter then, full-bellied and unrestrained, echoing across the room's chaos, the shattered mirror, the scattered petals, the burned mink coat in the corner, the jagged crystal catching fragments of light. Breadcrumbs stuck to our fingers, vodka glinting in our glasses, the scent of burnt fur and spilled alcohol. Surrounded by the ruin of the afternoon, the absurdity of our survival, and the closeness of one another, I realized: this was what survival looked like for women like us. Though at least we had one another.

Chapter Forty

Antonio
Nine days after Vincent's murder

The late afternoon sun hung low over the trimmed lawns of Enzo's front yard. I wiped sweat from my brow, squinting against the glare as I wound up and sent the baseball hurtling toward Enzo. He caught it, grinning my way. The sound of leather smacking leather echoed across the lawn. A low hum cut through the summer stillness, and I turned my head just in time to see Sal's baby blue Ford Thunderbird rounding the corner, convertible top down. He eased the car onto the curb. His aviator glasses caught the last rays of sunlight, reflecting them in sharp streaks across his face. The ball sat heavy in my glove for a moment.

Sal leaned casually against the driver's side door of his baby blue Thunderbird, one ankle crossed over the other, arms folded. His aviator sunglasses perched atop his head, catching the golden rays of the late afternoon sun, reflecting them in a sharp streak across the driveway. "Don't worry about me! I'm just scoping out talent for the Yankees!" His smirk tugged at the corner of his lips, arrogance radiating off him.

Enzo and I snickered, ducking as I tossed the baseball

toward him. The ball cut through the humid air, and Enzo caught it in his glove.

From the front porch, Angela stepped into view wearing a fitted sleeveless blouse tucked into a high-waisted, knee-length skirt. Strappy leather sandals clicked against the concrete, black cat eye sunglasses perched on her nose, red lipstick across his lips. "Enzo, I'm going to work. Be good for Val. And don't let Antonio sleep on the couch again," she called.

Enzo rolled his eyes, offering a half-smile, and Angela waved toward Sal and me before slipping into the driver's seat of her black 1960 Chrysler 300F hardtop. She started the engine, the growl of the V8 cutting through the quiet neighborhood, and rolled her window down. "Enzo! Would you go bring the mail inside for me?"

"Sure, Mom," he called back, trudging past me to the mailbox. He fished out the day's letters, the paper rustling against the metal, before heading inside through the front door.

Sal whistled behind me. "You got an arm on you, Nino!" I twisted to face him, the sun glinting off his sunglasses. "We got another job in Little Italy, Nino. Think you can tell your mom you're staying with Enzo again?"

"Yeah, she doesn't care. It's summertime," I said, shrugging. "The problem is...how am I going to pull it off with Enzo?"

"Once he's sound asleep, you sneak out. But you've got to get him down before nine," Sal said, his grin widening.

"How do you expect me to do that?"

"I'm sure you can figure something out. I'll bring over some junk food. You guys get nice and full, pass out, and you sneak out to the city."

I muttered my agreement, the late afternoon sun bouncing off the Thunderbird's polished chrome. "Okay...sure, I can manage that."

Sal tipped his head back, shading his eyes with one hand. "You've made quite the name for yourself over in Little Italy."

"What do you mean? I've only done two jobs."

"Technically three. But I'll tell you later," Sal said, motioning behind me with a knowing grin. I turned to see Enzo and Val stepping onto the driveway. Enzo's brow furrowed suspiciously as he walked toward me, his hands shoved into the pockets of his rolled-up jeans. Val moved past us to meet Sal, her summer dress swaying as she walked.

"What was Sal saying?" Enzo asked, eyes narrowing at me, a mix of curiosity and wariness in his expression.

"Nothing, just his usual stupid jokes," I shrugged. Enzo gave a slow nod, though I could tell he wasn't entirely convinced. "Want to walk over to my house and ask my mom if I can stay over tonight?"

"Yeah, sure," Enzo hummed, brushing a stray lock of dark hair from his forehead. The two of us walked across his lawn. As we approached my house, a sudden scuffle by the flower bed froze us in our tracks. I thought perhaps a stray cat or raccoon had wandered too close. But then Rosa emerged, standing upright with a deliberately confused smile. I wasn't buying it.

"Hey, boys!" Rosa said cheerfully, her wrinkled hands cradling a bouquet of freshly planted chrysanthemums. "Look at these beautiful flowers I've planted, white and violet. Did you know these flowers are associated with mourning and funerals? The white ones, especially. I planted the violet ones for your mother. She used to love wearing that violet dress of hers. Seems she might've upgraded her fashion lately. Anyhow, with all that's happening on the streets of Staten Island, the white ones seem fitting. Be careful, boys, or they might end up like Vincent, won't they?"

A chill ran down my spine. Had she been listening to Sal and me? Was she spying on me? Enzo pressed closer to my side, his eyes wide like he'd just seen a ghost. I nodded and walked past her, careful not to let my unease show, as she held up a single white chrysanthemum like a warning. I opened the front door and closed it behind us.

"Okay, there's no denying that old woman's off her rocker," Enzo hissed. "She's losing it. She doesn't even make sense."

Oh, she makes perfect sense. But I wasn't going to tell Enzo that. She's either senile or onto me, and I had a feeling it was the latter.

Ma rounded the corner, her hands clasped as she adjusted her apron. "Oh, it's you. I thought it might have been Rosa. I don't know where she wandered off to."

Enzo squinted toward the front door.

"She's in the front yard by the flower bed," I said.

Ma sighed and shook her head. "Not again. She's always wandering off." *Right.*

"Well, I was going to ask if I could stay at Enzo's tonight," I said as she marched toward the front door.

"Of course," she said, smiling over her shoulder. "Enjoy your summer. High school will be a hard adjustment, so enjoy your time off while you can."

I watched as Ma guided a confused-looking Rosa into the house, Ma's arm gently wrapped around Rosa's shoulders. But I knew something was off about the entire encounter, the hidden meaning behind Rosa's words, the sly warnings hidden. As Enzo and I made our way back to his house, my backpack bouncing against my shoulder, I couldn't shake the feeling that summer on Staten Island was about to get a lot more complicated.

Sal and Val lingered at the curb, the streetlights painting shadows over them. His hands were wrapped possessively around her waist, holding her close, and her chin tilted up to meet his hungry gaze.

Enzo muttered just what I was thinking, "Get a room, you two. Good God."

Val giggled, her laugh bright and airy, cutting through the humidity.

"I'm going to pick up some food for the night. Anything in particular you want?" Sal called over her head toward us.

Enzo spun around, ears perked at the mention of food. "What did you have in mind?"

Sal smirked, though it felt like more than just a smirk, more like a knowing glance aimed at me, a silent confirmation that our plan was about to unfold perfectly. "Anything you want, little bro."

"Pizza sounds good!" Enzo said eagerly, before we stepped inside the front door.

For the next few hours, Enzo and I lounged on the living room floor, pizza boxes stacked on the coffee table, plates of breadsticks and pasta salad strewn about. Marilyn Monroe's beautiful features flickered across the screen in *The Seven Year Itch*, but my attention flitted between the movie and Enzo, who had soon eaten his fill. It wasn't difficult at all to keep him content, stuffed, and on the verge of sleep.

When we made it upstairs, he finally slumped against his bed, and I crept quietly toward the living room. Sal sat there waiting, his hands drumming on the polished wood table in a rhythm that felt part menace, part encouragement. "There he is. Staten Island's golden boy..." he said with a grin as I approached. In a mock announcer's voice he added, "Nino the Bambino, ladies and gentlemen, fastest damn runner we've ever seen."

I rolled my eyes, forcing down the grin threatening to spread across my face.

"Ready?" he asked, pushing himself off the couch.

I nodded, and together we stepped outside. Joey's Ferrari

hadn't yet made it into the driveway, an oddity I noted but pushed aside, sometimes he worked late. I slid into the passenger seat of Sal's baby blue Thunderbird, the leather warm from the sun earlier in the day, and he started the engine with a low, powerful growl. The roar of the car seemed to echo down the quiet street as we eased into the night.

"So, what was it that you wanted to tell me?" I asked, the anticipation making my stomach twist.

Sal's eyes gleamed as he glanced over at me. "Word on the street is...there's a new runner in town. And this runner knows how to get in and out in a millisecond. Some of the guys are already trying to poach him. But everyone's asking the same thing: Who the hell is Nino?"

The rush of pride and exhilaration washed over me. I shouldn't like the attention. I shouldn't let it go to my head, but I did. I liked the feeling of being chosen, of being seen, of being needed. My fingers tightened slightly on the edge of the seat as I stared out into the dark streets, eyes wide, starry, and completely alive.

Sal kept his hands relaxed on the steering wheel, as he turned slightly to glance at me. "They're saying whoever trained him must've known what they were doing. But the best part is," he nudged my shoulder with a crooked grin, "they don't know you're connected to Joey. They just think you're some new blood making a name for himself the old-school way. The old-timers are impressed. And I sit there hanging onto every word they say, knowing full well who Nino is."

I should've felt disgusted. Or ashamed of myself. But the tight knot in my chest unraveled just a bit, replaced with something more alive than ever. I'd never felt more in control, more needed, more...seen. This was for Joey, I reminded myself, for his name, his honor. Once it was done, I'd return to the normal rhythm of life: school, baseball practice, being a kid again.

Yet, even in that small triumph, a quiet fear flickered inside me. Afraid I was losing sight of the goal. Afraid I liked this (being chosen, being Nino) a bit too much. Afraid I needed it more than I ever thought I would.

The soft hum of Sinatra filled the car as Sal reached over to turn the radio up, the warm tones of the trumpet and husky voice of Ol' Blue Eyes. "Let's go show 'em, Nino," Sal said, his grin wide. Pride shone in his eyes, the kind of pride that made you feel invincible, like you were part of something larger than yourself. Maybe he was proud because he had a hand in it, because he'd shaped my reputation before I even knew I had one.

"Can I ask you something?" I said, my voice hesitant, almost swallowed by the low rumble of the engine.

"What's up?" Sal replied, eyes forward on the dark street.

"Why'd you join the mafia? Why didn't you do something else with your life?"

Sal was quiet for a long minute. "I didn't grow up like you, Nino. I didn't have anyone keeping me warm at night. No one made me sandwiches before school, or asked how my day went. No one gave a damn if I made it home safe. So I found a family. I admired Joey. I thought he was a real stand-up gangster. I wanted to be part of something, to be noticed. And I've already told you the story, but Joey made me a runner. He treated me like I belonged in his crew. He knows how to make a community. How to make someone feel like they matter. And I didn't think any other path in life would come with the same rewards."

I stared at the dashboard, the faint reflection of streetlights bouncing off the chrome details, imagining the streets Sal spoke of, imagining the work he did to prove himself, the choices he must have made, the loyalty he earned in exchange for it all.

"Do you ever regret it?" I asked, my voice almost swallowed

by the purr of the Thunderbird's engine and the soft crackle of Sinatra in the background.

Sal's eyes didn't leave the road. The corners of his mouth tightened for a moment, a shadow passing over his expression, before he finally exhaled. "Sometimes," he shrugged. "But not enough to stop. Not ever enough to stop. The pros outweigh the cons, as they say, Nino."

A mixture of awe, fear, and thrill of being alive in a world I was only beginning to understand coursed through my veins.

"Don't get it wrong, not a single second of my life do I regret walking into Joey's shop. I wish I would've found this family sooner, in fact," Sal said, his voice steady with conviction. The words carried so much weight they made the hair on the back of my neck stand up. "It's like a secret society of brothers. If you're loyal, you've got fifty loyal brothers standing behind you, ready to do anything for you. I couldn't regret that kind of loyalty. Joey gave me a life. He gave me a name. An identity. A place in this world. So I don't regret it but it does come with cons."

"How did you know it was the right move?"

Sal smirked faintly, his knuckles tightening on the wheel. "You don't. You don't know if anything is going to go in your favor. But that's just the game of life, you do it anyway. I knew I wanted to be part of something bigger than me. I wanted my name to mean something. When people heard the name Salvatore Genovese, I wanted them to know exactly who the hell I was, and what I stood for." His tone was steady, as if the name itself was a crown he'd fought to wear.

I kept repeating in my head that this was for Joey. That I was only here to clean his name, to fix what I'd broken. That when it was over, I'd walk away. Go back to baseball, to a life where the biggest thing that mattered was a swing and a hit.

Though the truth pressed harder against my chest with every beat of my heart.

I liked the way it felt when people whispered about me. The way the older girl at Sammy's looked at me like I was someone bigger than life, legendary. I liked being Nino the Bambino, the name rolling off tongues like I was a walking headline, not just a kid.

That frightened me more than anything because I wasn't sure I wanted to let this go.

Chapter Forty-One

Joey
Nine days after Vincent's murder

I slid into the corner booth at *The Wise Guy*. Paul dropped down beside me, nursing the toothpick between his teeth, while Marco slid in across from me. Ben took the seat next to Marco. Angela had already brought us a round of Old Fashioneds. Smoke curled from the next booth over, The Everly Brothers' floating through the air. I'd called them here with a hushed promise of "news." No one knew what that meant yet, but I could feel their eyes on me, waiting.

I lifted my glass, let the bourbon wet my lips, and finally said, "As you know, Christopher came to see me today. We spent some time together."

The table leaned in as silence pressed between us.

"He told me a meeting's coming soon. A big one. And at that meeting...he's naming me consigliere." Not just a seat at the table, a hand on the wheel.

Paul let out a sharp whistle, shaking his head in disbelief. Marco slapped the table hard enough to rattle the glasses. "About damn time," he said, a grin splitting his face.

Ben smirked, eyes narrowing like he'd been waiting for this moment. "I knew it. Christopher's no fool. He couldn't keep Hector as his only right hand forever. Not with you back, and better than ever."

I took a slow sip, letting the bourbon burn steadily down my throat. "This stays between us until it's official. When the announcement comes, it changes everything. We're not just dealing cars and collections anymore. We'll be shaping the family even more than what we already have. Which means eyes, inside and out, will be on us every second."

Paul leaned forward, toothpick clicking against his teeth. "That was my next question. You'd think this would be nothing but good news, but I wonder what Hector's saying behind closed doors. I suspect he's not happy, or maybe this is part of whatever game he's been playing, which I can't imagine is a good thing for us."

"Yeah, that's what I'm thinking too. Which is why we've got to be careful. Every step from here on out has to be more calculated than the last. One loose thread, and we unravel. I don't know what Hector is playing at, but until Ben finds out, we have to be careful."

Marco turned his head toward Ben. "So, what's the update, officer?"

Ben huffed, leaning back in the booth with a humorless chuckle. "Update? I've been spending every damn hour trying to quiet the NYPD. You think they're just gonna forget? Their white whale, the underboss they've been chasing for decades, gets his head blown off in broad daylight. That doesn't just disappear off the books."

"Of course not," Paul muttered. "Which means until we figure out who the hell pulled that trigger, we're sitting ducks."

I felt the truth settle in my chest: being named consigliere wasn't just a crown. It was a target. Strategically painted on my back by none other than Hector himself.

"Speaking of which," I began, setting my glass down onto the table. The smoke from Paul's now-burning cigarette curled between us. "I was told about a new runner. His name's Nino. Word is he's been doing some runs in the city. For who? I don't know."

Marco raised a brow. Paul leaned back, arms crossed. I gestured to the three of us. "Now, we don't do much in the city. Which is why I want Ben to keep an eye out, see who this kid belongs to. Because here's the thing, nobody seems to know. And that bothers me."

"He shows up right after Vincent gets clipped, completely anonymous, and supposedly he's young. High school age. Which can't be good. But I wouldn't put it past Hector, or Frank, or any of the other families to put a kid on the street. Hell, for all we know, they're reckless enough to let him be the one who took Vincent out."

Paul exhaled a long stream of smoke as his brows knitted. "Christ. A kid doing work like that? That's bad news all around."

Ben nodded in agreement. "That's a very good point. I'll keep my eyes open. Ask around, move quietly. If I hear anything, I'll let you know first."

Marco grinned wide, his eyes gleaming with mischief. "Alright, so is that all the work shit we gotta hash out tonight?"

I frowned, my forehead tightening. "Why?"

"Because," Marco said, "this deserves a toast. This deserves a goddamn celebration. We're talking about you becoming a consigliere, Joey. That's not small news. That's champagne-bottle, Sinatra-on-the-radio, dance-on-the-table kind of news. So let's get the serious talk out of the way and drink like we're kids again."

Paul groaned, pressing the finger with his cigarette into his temple. "We're in our thirties, Marco. Nobody parties like that anymore. Our backs give out just bending over to tie our shoes at this point."

"Speak for yourself," Marco shot back, pointing his glass at him. "I can still go three rounds with bourbon, cards, and women, then wake up for work like it never happened. And if tonight isn't the time for it, when is? Joey's moving up in the family. That deserves every last drop of whiskey in this place."

Ben smirked, swirling the ice in his glass. "If Marco starts singing again, I'm walking out."

"Then drink faster so you don't have to hear it," Marco said, raising his glass. "To Joey. Our consigliere. To the future of this family."

Marco tipped his glass toward Angela's retreating figure, his words slurring as he said, "Now that's service. Joey, when you're consigliere, you oughta make her our personal bartender."

Paul snorted, tipsy as well. "You'd make anyone your personal bartender if they poured as heavy as Angela."

By the third round, Marco was telling a story I hadn't heard in years, about the time he tried to impress a girl (who I assumed to be Angela, though neither would ever admit to such) by sneaking her into a shiny Ford coupe he "borrowed" off a side street. "I barely made it down the main strip before the damn engine coughed, backfired, and died right there in the middle of traffic," he said, throwing his hands up. "Next thing I know, a couple of cops are helping push me to the curb while this girl has taken off running."

Ben chuckled into his glass. "You're a walking cautionary tale, Marco."

Marco leaned across the table, finger jabbing in mock accusation. "And don't act like you're a saint, Paulie. I remember you trying to climb Pat's Bakery window when we were sixteen because you bet Joey you could steal a tray of cannoli without getting caught."

Paul's face reddened, and he groaned. "Christ, you still bring that up? That was twenty damn years ago."

"Yeah, but Ben wasn't around then, so he doesn't know that you didn't succeed. That you, in fact, fell into the alley trash cans," Marco said, howling with laughter.

The table rocked with Ben's low chuckle, Paul muttering curses under his breath, and my own laughter. For the first time since Christopher dropped the news, I let myself feel what it meant. Not the weight of the role. Or the danger with Hector. Just the pride of being chosen.

Marco leaned back, arms spread like a king on his throne. "This is it, boys. Tonight's proof. We fucking made it. From petty thief to alley trashcans to sitting here in an underground speakeasy, celebrating Joey as consigliere." He pointed at me, eyes glassy and red. "You won't forget us, little guys, when you're sitting at the big table. Will ya?"

I shook my head, smirking. "You're not little guys. You're the only guys."

Under the haze of bourbon and laughter, we weren't hustlers, or criminals, or men with targets on our backs. We were friends. Brothers.

* * *

I crept through the front doors of the house. The place was dark, except for the foyer lamp. I slipped out of my dress shoes and carried them toward the staircase, trying to keep steady even as the bourbon drummed behind my eyes. Fifteen years— it had been that long since I'd drunk this much. The hall light snapped on. I winced, squinting.

"Joey?"

Adriana stood at the top of the staircase, framed in silk, her robe tied at her waist. The sight of her made my chest swell. Her thick brows fused together as she took me in, my loosened tie, the way I clung to the banister. I started up the steps, each one heavier than it should've been. By the time I reached her, her hands lifted to my face, palms cupping my cheeks. She tilted my head down toward hers, thumb brushing the line of my jaw.

"Joey..." she whispered, searching my eyes. "Are you drunk?"

"Sweetheart," I murmured, sliding my arms around her and pulling her flush against me. I kissed her hard, tasting whiskey and smoke on my lips. I pressed my forehead to hers, grinning like a fool. "You waitin' up for me?"

"Well, yes," she breathed, her fingers clutching at the lapels of my suit. "I just wasn't expecting you to come home like this."

I couldn't hold it back. The words spilled out, rough with intoxicating pride. "Christopher made me consigliere."

Her eyes widened. "What?"

"Yeah." I lifted a hand to cradle her cheek, thumb tracing her skin. "I'm sittin' at his right hand now. Advising the family. Guiding the whole damn thing, sweetheart."

Her lips found mine again, urgent and hungry. I pressed her back against the hallway wall, my hand tangled in her hair as I deepened the kiss. She smiled against my mouth, whispering, "You deserve it. After everything you've been through... everything you've done for them...you deserve this and more."

My hands found the tie of her robe, tugging lightly. "The only thing I ever did right was finding you and making you my wife."

Her cheeks flushed as she bit down on her bottom lip. She slid her fingers over mine, stilling them. "You're drunk, Joey," she whispered, though her smile betrayed her. "Come on. Let's go to bed."

"I'm only drunk on you, sweetheart," I murmured against her lips before bending at the knees and scooping her into my arms. She gasped, then laughed into the crook of my neck, clinging tighter as her legs wrapped around my waist and her arms locked around my shoulders.

"You're going to drop me," she whispered, her breath warm against my ear.

"On the bed, maybe," I chuckled, kicking the bedroom door open with my foot. The knob smacked the wall, loud enough to make us both stifle a laugh. I set her down, then shut the door. Turning back, I gripped the sides of her waist, then tugged at the silk tie of her robe. The fabric loosened, slipping apart beneath my hands. I peeled it back from her shoulder and pressed slow kisses down her neck, tasting her skin as I traced the line of her collarbone.

"You don't know what you do to me," I rasped, my hands settling on her hips, guiding her backward until the backs of her legs brushed the bedframe. I let my palms roam down, cupping her ass, kneading before my thumbs hooked into the waistband of her panties. I crouched low, tugging them down the smooth line of her thighs.

Her hands threaded through my hair, fingertips grazing my scalp before tilting my chin up. She stepped free of the fabric, and when I lifted my head again, my lips hovered at her stomach, my gaze locked on hers.

"Joey..." she breathed.

"Shh, sweetheart," I whispered, kissing just below her navel. "Let me take care of you. Celebrate with me, because this is good news for us."

I rose to my full height, sliding her nightgown up, the silk whispering against her skin before I pulled it over her head. I bent, cupping her breasts in my hands, peppering kisses across them until her back arched into me, urging me further.

I eased her down onto the sheets, her body surrendering beneath mine. Soon, I was bare too, covering her with my weight, our skin burning against each other. My mouth traced every curve of her stomach, tasting her, breathing her in, while my fingers gripped at her hips, anchoring her to the mattress.

Her breath grew quicker, filling the air with soft whimpers, her thighs shifting restlessly against me. I glanced up at her through half-lidded eyes, a wicked smirk tugging at my mouth as I hovered just below her waist.

I let my breath fan over the delicate skin of her inner thigh, watching the shiver ripple through her. She threaded her fingers tighter in my hair, tugging me closer with a wordless plea. I smiled against her, kissing a path along her trembling flesh until her hips lifted from the bed, desperate for more.

"Patience, sweetheart," I murmured, my voice low from whiskey and want. "I wanna taste every inch of you tonight."

A whimper left her throat when my mouth finally found her sweet core, teasing her with slow strokes. She gasped, head tipping back against the bed, her hand flying to clutch the sheets. The sound she made lit a fire in my chest, hotter than any bourbon could ever burn.

I tightened my grip on her thighs, holding her open, keeping her right where I wanted her as I coaxed more of those sounds from her lips. She writhed beneath me, her cries spilling out as I lapped at her core, until I pulled away to look up at her, lips glistening with her arousal, both of our chests heaving. "I could do this all night."

Her answer was a moan, pulling me back to her glistening core. My mouth pressed against her clit, drawing circles around it as two fingers curled inside of her. I savored the way she arched and trembled for me, the way her body bent toward mine as if she couldn't get close enough.

When she finally broke apart in my arms, her cries filled the air, kissing her thighs as she rode out her high. When I climbed over her again, pressing my mouth to hers, she kissed me like a woman undone, tasting herself on my lips.

"Joey," she whispered against my mouth, her nails digging into my back as I settled between her thighs. "Please...I need you."

I brushed my forehead against hers, my breathing ragged. "Sweetheart, you've got me. You'll always have me."

"No, no, no," she whimpered. "I need you."

Her plea hit me like a spark to gasoline. I kissed her hard, swallowing her desperate little whimper, before guiding myself against her heat. I dragged the head of my cock along her slick folds, teasing her until she was trembling beneath me, legs hooked tight around my hips.

"Tell me you want it," I rasped, my teeth grazing her lower lip.

"I want you, Joey. Please."

That was all I needed to hear before I pushed into her, inch by inch, burying myself until I was seated deep inside. Her body clenched around me, pulling me in tighter, and my head fell to her shoulder with a groan torn from my chest. "Fuck, you feel so good..."

Her nails raked across my back as she arched into me, urging me to move. I pulled back slow, savoring every drag of her body around mine, before thrusting forward again. The rhythm built in hard, steady thrust, her breaths breaking into ragged cries that only drove me harder.

I cupped her face in my hands, forcing her eyes on mine as I rocked into her. "Look at me, sweetheart. You should see how perfect you look right now."

Her gaze locked with mine, eyes wide and shining, her lips parting with each thrust. I kissed her again, hungry and messy, swallowing every sound she made. Her walls fluttered around me, and I knew she was close. "Let go for me," I groaned into her mouth. "Come with me, sweetheart."

Her cry tore through the room as her climax gripped her, her body trembling violently under mine. The sight, the feel of her unraveling around me, dragged me over the edge. I buried myself deep one last time, spilling into her with a guttural moan, holding her tight as if I could fuse us together.

Neither of us moved as we came down from our high, tangled in heat and breath and the pounding of our hearts. I pressed my lips to her temple, whispering against her damp skin, "You're all I'll ever need, sweetheart."

She smiled faintly, her body melting into mine as I eased us into the pillows, still inside her, unwilling to let go. Her chest rose and fell against mine, every breath shaky as she clung to me. I smoothed damp strands of hair from her face, brushing my thumb across her cheek. She looked up at me through heavy lashes, her lips still parted, and all I could do was stare. My palm slid down her side, over the curve of her hip, holding her close.

I pulled the blanket over us, gathering her against my chest. She tucked her head beneath my chin, her legs tangled with mine. My hand stroked up and down her back.

"I meant it, sweetheart," I murmured into her hair. "Everything I'm building, everything I'm fighting for, it's all for you. For our family. Nothing else matters to me."

Her fingers traced the lines of my chest. "Promise me that nothing will happen to you...promise me you'll come home to me. Hector is dangerous, and I can't live with myself if something happens to you."

I tilted her chin up so she could see the conviction in my

eyes. "Sweetheart, there isn't a throne in this world that could keep me from our bed."

A soft laugh escaped her as she nestled back against me, finally letting her body relax into sleep. I lay awake a little longer, holding her, breathing her in, and vowing to myself that nothing—not even Hector—would ever come before her.

Chapter Forty-Two

Antonio
Eleven/Twelve days
after Vincent's murder

I tugged at the collar of my shirt as we walked up to the restaurant, Manhattan's humidity clung to me even though the sun was long gone. Ma had pressed my clothes earlier that afternoon for dinner in the city. I wore a crisp white button-down tucked into charcoal-gray trousers that had a sharp crease running down the legs. My shoes were freshly shined, black oxfords. A narrow tie sat snug at my throat, and my dark hair was slicked back with Brylcreem pomade. Joey said a man's appearance was his first calling card.

The glow of neon signs lit up the Manhattan block, but Vino e Pasta stood out with its gold-lettered script above the door, polished brass handles, and a valet out front who tipped his hat the moment he saw Joey. The second we stepped inside, I felt swallowed up by the place: the whispers of conversation, the smell of garlic and butter, the red wallpaper patterned with gold filigree. Waiters in pressed white jackets glided between tables carrying silver trays stacked with wine bottles and dishes of pasta. A violinist played in the corner, his music threading through the air.

"Mr. Romano," the maître d' said, bowing his head the moment his eyes found Joey. His voice carried a mix of respect and caution, because he knew exactly who he was speaking to. "Your table is ready."

"Grazie," Joey said with a small nod. He rested a hand at the small of Ma's back as the maître d' led us deeper inside. I trailed behind them, taking in the sights and wonders of this luxurious place.

We didn't stop in the main dining room. Instead, the maître d' drew back a heavy velvet curtain and revealed a secluded section near the back, round tables lit by soft lamps and more privacy. I noticed how the waitstaff seemed to stand taller, their eyes flicking to Joey every few seconds as if to make sure not a thing went wrong. But also strangely admiring him in the flesh.

Ma slid into the chair Joey had pulled out for her. Joey sat beside her, his arm draped along the back of her chair. They looked...happy. Happier than normal. At first, I thought this was an act for the public, but their eyes glowed like they were in on some secret I wasn't. Something was happening that I didn't know about.

I sat in my chair, smoothing the crease in my trousers. My soda fizzed in the crystal glass, the bubbles fizzing under the lamp on our table. Around us, the low hum of the restaurant carried on, cutlery clinking, muffled laughter, the violinist's bow sliding over the strings. Behind the velvet curtain, it felt like our own private sanctuary.

A heavyset man in a tall white hat and an apron pushed through the curtain. His face was broad and beaming, cheeks pink from the heat of the kitchen. "Signor Romano!" he exclaimed, his voice booming in the otherwise peaceful space. He walked straight to our table, wiping his hands on his apron before offering both to Joey. "Always an honor when you come to my house."

Joey stood, gripping the man's hands with both of his. "Chef, it's an honor to be here tonight with my family." He turned toward us, his chest puffing with pride. "This is my wife, Adriana. And my son, Antonio."

The chef turned his gaze on me, eyes crinkling at the corners. "Ahh. He looks just like you." His thick finger wagged toward me.

Heat rose in my face, though I tried to play it cool. *He looks just like you.* I let the words settle in my head like a medal pinned to my chest. I wasn't his by blood, but I'd studied him enough to be his prodigy son, as Enzo likes to call me—his walk, his slicked back hair, his mannerisms, the way he carried himself like every room already belonged to him. If the chef saw the resemblance, maybe it meant I was getting it right.

Joey clapped a hand on my shoulder, grinning wide at me. "You should see this kid on the baseball field. Best swing in Staten Island, in fact, all of New York."

The chef laughed, his belly shaking. "Is that so? You must be proud."

"Scouts are gonna be all over him before he's eighteen," Joey went on, his eyes gleaming with pride. "Line drives, home runs, you name it. He's the future, this one. The city doesn't know it yet, but he's going to show them the best extension of me."

I forced a smile, nodding as though I deserved every word he said about me. Inside, though, a knot tightened in my stomach. Because while Joey was telling the chef about my clean swing, my steady hands, my bright future, I couldn't stop thinking about the nights I'd been sneaking around Little Italy.

I wanted to be like Joey. I wanted to make him proud. But instead of baseball diamonds, I'd been stepping into his shadows, shadows he'd never want for me. And the more runs I did, the more I realized even if I cleared Joey's name, I didn't want to give it up.

Sal told me to be a better liar, he didn't tell me I had to become a better actor, too. But I laughed when they laughed. I lifted my glass when Joey toasted to my bright future.

Joey had already loosened his tie, his dark jacket draped over the back of his chair. He leaned back, one arm stretched along the top of Ma's chair, a glass of red wine balanced in his other hand. Ma radiated happiness, her dress shimmering like the champagne in her glass, her hair done up in curls that framed her face. "How's summer going, kid?"

I forced a grin. "It's been good so far."

"What happened to that girl? Mia?" Ma asked, taking a sip of her champagne.

Joey smirked, and I guess whatever expression I formed on my face looked believable, though I felt all the blood drain from my body as soon as she asked that question. "She's just a friend."

"I thought you took her to the cinema?" Ma questioned

"As friends, ma."

"Come on," Joey's lips brushed Ma's cheek, the corner of her mouth curved. "Let the boy figure himself out without our questions. He's too cool to talk to us about girls anyway."

Between courses, waiters came and went with an attentiveness I hadn't seen before. A basket of warm bread appeared. A plate of clams, steaming and fragrant, landed on the table next. Every waiter who came by glanced at Joey a little longer than normal.

Ma leaned closer to Joey, lowering her voice, though I could still hear. "You look so happy. And I love seeing you happy."

His eyes softened when they met hers, and even I could see the look in his eyes that said everything without saying anything at all. Joey reached over and tucked a strand of hair behind her ear, his thumb lingering against her cheek. "How could I not be?" he murmured. "I've got everything I've ever wanted...sitting at this table with me tonight."

I glanced down at my plate, pretending to fiddle with my fork, but a smile tugged at my lips anyway. The waiter returned with our main courses, pasta glistening with oil and garlic, veal so tender it melted at the touch of a fork. Ma laughed at something Joey whispered in her ear.

* * *

I pressed the blow dryer against my forehead until my skin felt like it might blister. My cheeks burned, sweat beading at my temples. I tucked cubes of ice down my undershirt, pressing one against the back of my neck until my skin prickled and my shoulders trembled. Shivering and flushed all at once. I caught my reflection in the mirror, my tan skin now pale enough under the bathroom light, brown eyes ringed from lack of sleep. I almost convinced myself I really was sick. I suppose I was advancing in my acting skills.

"Antonio!" Ma's voice carried up the stairs.

I shuffled to my bed and pulled the blanket over me as she appeared in the doorway. She clucked her tongue at the sight of me, sweat shining on my forehead. "Ma..." I croaked, layering it on thick. "I don't feel so good."

Rosa appeared behind her, her eyes narrowing and squinting. "He's dying," she announced gravely.

"Rosa!" Adriana gasped, whipping her head over her shoulder to give her a stern look.

Rosa shrugged, muttering under her breath, "A spoonful of olive oil, a garlic clove, a nap, and he'll live."

Ma sighed, stepping into my bedroom. She brushed her hand over my damp forehead. "You're burning up. You'll have to stay here with Rosa and get some rest." She kissed my temple and swept out with Rosa, who was muttering about how she didn't mean to say "dying," she was just confused. *Yeah, right.*

The bedroom door shut a few minutes later, leaving me in silence. Relief unfurled in my chest. Sal was right, if anyone from the city recognized me as Nino, the whole thing could blow up. I hadn't been lying back for a few minutes when I heard my bedroom door creak open again. Then Enzo's face appeared. He slid inside, shutting the door behind him.

"You're not going?" he asked.

"No, I'm too sick." I put on a weak cough for effect.

Enzo flopped into the chair by my desk, frowning. "Sick? You're always MIA lately. What happened to our summer plans? What happened to running around town, staying out all night, raising hell this summer?"

His words dug at me. We *had* promised a summer to remember. But he didn't know what I knew. He didn't know about the runs in Little Italy, or about working with Sal, or about trying to clear Joey's name since Vincent's murder.

I shrugged from beneath the blanket, my voice low. "Maybe it's just a stomach bug, and it'll pass. We can do something tomorrow night."

Enzo leaned back in the chair, crossing his arms. "Yeah, well, Michael's changed, too. He already was a snooze fest, but add on his first love, and now it's unfuckingbearable. All he wants to do is talk about Alessia's hair, Alessia's smile, and how Alessia laughs at his dumb, weak jokes." Enzo made a gagging sound and rolled his eyes.

I laughed under my breath, but it came out weak. "Guess we're all growing up."

"Growing up?" Enzo scoffed. "Don't say it like we're fucking forty. We're supposed to be running around, having the summer of our lives. Not sick in bed and listening to Michael write poetry about his little girlfriend."

I smirked at that, though guilt tugged at me again. The ice melted slowly against my skin, soaking my undershirt, sending another shiver through me. I swallowed, wishing I could tell him everything, but instead I just stared at the ceiling, listening to Enzo whine about how this summer was lame. Nothing weighed heavier than the secrets I was keeping from him

Chapter Forty-Three

Adriana

Twelve days after Vincent's murder

Dresses draped across the foot of Lucy's grand four-poster wooden bed. The hangers dangled off the corners. Heels in every height, shape, and color were scattered across the floor. Lucy stood in the entrance of her massive walk-in closet, buried in gowns as she cursed under her breath.

"Why is it," she huffed, her voice muffled as she pulled a hanger free, "that I own three hundred dresses but not one worth seducing a detective in on the grand opening of my salon?"

Angela was sitting at the vanity with legs crossed, and a thin trail of smoke curling from her cigarette holder. Her dark, backless dress was sin poured into satin. "You're going to get poor Detective Hudson killed if you wear that one dress, Lucy. Because there's no way he's going to be able to continue this act in front of your father, that nothing is happening between you two."

"Angela's right, Lucy. As soon as he sees you in that gown, he's going to have a heart attack."

Lucy emerged from the closet with a deep crimson velvet dress in her hand, holding it up to her body and staring in the mirror. Her lips curled deviously. "Is it too much?"

"It might be too little," Angela replied.

I stifled my laugh. "We bought that dress weeks ago. And I've already worn mine, so you have to wear yours tonight."

"You know what's funny? How ironic it is for me to be the daughter of Christopher Giordano, and I'm madly in love with a detective? It's something to be planning outfits to seduce Ben in while Hector tries to fool my father that we're still in love after all these years. When in reality, we've never been in love."

I stepped closer to the mirror, helping her zip up the crimson dress. "We can't help who we love, Lucy. That's the beauty of it, because without it, the world would stop spinning. Love is the only thing that can withstand time."

Lucy looked at me in the reflection of the mirror. Her expression was full of softness, and I smiled at her, running my hands down her arms. "It's rather romantic when you think about it. Isn't it? I know what he's giving up when he's with me. You don't spend years sneaking around New York City with a man just for fun. I love him with all my heart. And he loves me, too. Now, if only we could claim that in front of the world...life would be perfect. Wouldn't it?"

Angela stubbed out her cigarette, walking over towards us. "We could make that happen. All we've got to do is put Adriana or me on cocktail duties, and Hector will be out like a light."

"It can't happen soon enough, that's for sure," Lucy muttered as she adjusted her deep neckline.

The three of us locked eyes in the mirror. I flashed an innocent smile, crossing my fingers that the seed in Lucy's head would sprout into fruition soon. Not only for her happiness but for Joey's safety.

* * *

Twenty minutes later, I was walking through the front door. As I climbed the stairs, I passed Antonio's bedroom and caught a glimpse of him propped against his headboard, spoon in hand, eating the pastina I'd made him earlier. When I reached my and Joey's room, I noticed the door was cracked slightly. Slipping inside, I found him standing at the vanity mirror, buttoning his white dress shirt, brown suspenders hanging loose at his sides. He ran a comb through his damp hair, slicking it back. Aftershave mixed with the warm spice of cologne drifted from the bathroom into the bedroom, surrounding me and flooding my senses.

He set the comb down and turned, smiling. "Hello, sweetheart."

"You look so handsome."

"And you look as beautiful as ever, sweetheart."

I crossed to the vanity, unclasping my pearl earrings and laying them down next to his comb. Joey's hands slid to my waist, turning me around to face him, and pulling me against him. My arms wrapped around his neck. "I have to change," I whispered.

"Do you need help with that?" His crystal eyes danced over mine, mischievously.

The corners of my mouth lifted. "I think I can manage."

"I don't think so. I think you need my help," he murmured, dipping his head to capture my lips before trailing kisses along my cheek, past my ear, down the curve of my neck.

A laugh slipped out of me, breathless. "Joey, you just got dressed. Your hair hasn't even dried yet, you'll mess it up."

He chuckled low, the sound rippling through me, making my thighs press together. "I can get dressed again. I can do my hair again."

His mouth trailed lower again, down my neck, across my collarbone, lingering at the swell of my chest. Heat pooled under every brush of his lips, but I cradled his face in my hands, coaxing his eyes back to mine. My fingers smoothed the strands of hair that had fallen across his forehead. "We can't be late," I whispered.

His lips curved into a faint pout before a sigh slipped free. Reluctantly, I eased away, leaving him to finish dressing while I retreated into the bathroom. When I emerged, I was wrapped in the gold satin gown I'd laid out earlier. Bias-cut and body-skimming, it clung in all the right places, the sheen catching the lamplight like molten gold. Around my throat rested the pearl necklace Joey had given me on our very first date.

Joey froze mid-motion, cufflinks forgotten. His gaze dragged slowly upward, starting at the slit of the hem, following the line of my legs, the curve of my hips, the dip of my waist— until it locked with my eyes. His jaw ticked, and he exhaled like the sight of me had knocked the wind clean out of him. "You're trying to kill me," he muttered.

I tilted my head, smiling coyly as I braced one hand against the wall, slipping on one heel, then the other. "If I were trying, you wouldn't have lasted this long."

His laugh came low and husky, his eyes never leaving me. "You know," he said, gaze dipping to the shimmer of satin hugging my hips, "you could've let me help you into that dress."

I batted my lashes at him. "And risk not making it out the door tonight? Absolutely not."

His eyes darkened, desire burning from within. "There'll be so many people, no one would even notice if we came in late."

I sauntered closer, my palms sliding up the expanse of his chest, feeling the strength taut beneath the fabric. He held me at the waist, fingers curling possessively into the satin.

"Sweetheart," he murmured, his gaze dropping to the curve of my hips, voice thick with want, "how do you expect me to stand through an entire party when all I'll be thinking about is peeling you out of this dress?"

My palms settled flat on his chest, feeling the tension rise and fall with his breath. I leaned in, brushing my lips just below his jaw. "You'll just have to suffer for a little bit. But you can think of it as foreplay, because I'll need your help taking it off later." His whole body went rigid, his eyes closing as a low, quiet curse slipped out. I walked past him with a small smile tugging at my lips.

At the vanity, I freshened my lipstick and smoothed the soft wave of my hair back into place. In the mirror, I caught Joey behind me, dropping heavily onto the edge of the bed with a groan as he bent to tug on his dress shoes. "Jesus," he muttered, almost to himself. "I need a damn drink already."

"You know, a few days ago..." I began casually, eyes on his reflection as I dusted powder over my cheeks. "Lucy called and said she needed Angela and me to come over." He was bent at the waist, fiddling with his cufflinks, but I saw his body go still. "When we got there, the house was a wreck. Her room looked like a hurricane had torn through it. She said she and Hector got into a fight. She told us he threw a vase at her. And attacked her."

Joey's head snapped up. "What?" His voice cracked into a cough of disbelief. "He threw a fucking vase at her? And what the hell do you mean he attacked her?"

I turned from the mirror, slowly meeting his eyes. "She said it happened after lunch with her father. Apparently, he played the doting husband. Then he ran off to see his other family, and when she asked for a divorce again...that's when he snapped."

Joey shot to his feet, his whole frame jerking tight, defensive lines etched into his shoulders. His arms folded hard across his chest, jaw clenched like he was chewing back every vicious word clawing its way up. His face soured, dark and stormy, all pretense stripped away. "Adriana. Sweetheart. What do you mean by snapped? Did he lay a hand on her? Are there marks?"

My throat constricted. "Yes. She had bruises. She's hiding them tonight."

He let out a sound that was half laugh, half sob, and ran both hands through his hair. Then he began to pace, a hard, efficient line across the room. "Are you fucking kidding me?" he muttered. "And Ben...Ben didn't notice any of this?"

"She didn't tell him. She's terrified. Hector threatened her. He said if anything happened to him, someone would make sure Ben was taken care of. Lucy says if she had to guess... she'd say that someone is Frank."

Joey stopped as if I'd struck him. His back rose and fell in heavy, angry breaths. For a moment, he stood there, all contained violence, like a tightly wound spring. "I'm going to fucking kill this guy." His hands dragged down his face, as if trying to scrape the rage off. "I swear to God—"

A hot, blinding part of me wanted him to go, wanted him to tear the world open and set things right. Thank God, I thought, relief flaring. He was finally going to do something. Someone needed to.

"Joey." I stepped up beside him and laid my hand on his arm. "Just don't do anything tonight. If anything happens to Ben, Lucy will never be okay. You need a plan before you go in and attack Hector."

He met my eyes, and for a heartbeat, the fury dimmed into something colder. "Don't worry. I'll behave tonight. But I'll make sure Hector and Frank pay for this." The promise was a blade sheathed in civility. He forced himself to breathe, to fold the anger back into a contained, dangerous calm. "Are we ready? I don't want to be late now."

I smiled, slipping my white fur shawl over my shoulders as we passed the bed. "I just want to check on Antonio first."

Joey nodded, and together we walked quietly down the hall. I eased Antonio's door open, finding him fast asleep, his chest rising and falling in an easy rhythm beneath the maroon quilt. Stepping closer, I brushed a stray curl from his forehead and kissed his forehead softly. Joey lingered in the doorway. When I stepped back out, we crossed paths with Rosa in the hallway, a dish towel slung over her shoulder. I touched her arm, giving it a squeeze. "Call Cosa Bella if anything feels off. We'll come straight back."

"I've been checking on him every half hour," she said with a reassuring nod. "No fever yet. You two go enjoy yourselves, he'll be just fine."

Joey gave her a grateful pat on the shoulder, and we continued down the stairs. Our steps fell in time with each other, the soft sound echoing through the quiet house. Outside, the night air rushed against us, but Joey's hand slipped into mine. I looked up at him, and he flashed me a soft grin that made my heart lift with ease.

Chapter Forty-Four

Joey
Twelve days after Vincent's murder

Tomorrow night Christopher would make it official. I'd be named consigliere of the Giordano family. But with every passing day, and now with the revelation that Hector had laid hands on Lucy, it was getting harder and harder not to take him out myself, consequences be damned.

As I pulled into the parking lot of Cosa Bella, the place was overflowing. Cadillacs and Lincolns lined the street like a showroom of power and wealth.

I stepped out and rounded the car to open Adriana's door. Extending my hand, I helped her out. That gold satin gown clung to her petite frame and caught the light of the street-lamps, gleaming like molten metal under the glow of the night. My chest swelled with pride, and I couldn't wait to have her on my arm, to watch every head turn the moment we walked in.

She slipped her hands around my arm and pressed close against my side. "Ready, sweetheart?" I looked down, smiling.

She glanced up, her brown eyes warm and shining, the corners of her lips curving in answer. All I could think about was how much I loved her, now and always. The sight of her in that gown, the trace of her flowery perfume, the feel of her touch against me, it was almost enough to make me forget about Hector. *Almost.*

Inside, Cosa Bella was packed wall to wall, shoulder to shoulder. Every wiseguy within a hundred miles had shown up, each one accompanied by either his wife or his mistress. The men were in tailored suits, hair slicked back to a sheen. The women dripped in diamonds and pearls, their perfume mingling with the bite of aftershave and expensive cologne.

In true Lucy fashion, the place was pure spectacle—a hot-pink explosion from floor to ceiling. Servers glided through the crowd with silver trays of champagne, flutes brimming with Dom Pérignon. Soft jazz curled through the air, blending with the hum of laughter and murmured conversations. Waiters weaved between guests, balancing trays of oysters on crushed ice, prosciutto-wrapped figs, and boxes of Italian cookies fresh from Pat's Bakery.

I spotted Paul near the back wall, his wife, Florence, tucked at his side, chatting with Mickie Two Times and Frankie Bags. Frankie with a cigar smoldering between two fingers and a glass of scotch in the other. Marco leaned in on their conversation, laughing at something, while Angela waved across the room toward Adriana and me.

"Looking sharp, boss," Sal called as we passed, raising his glass. He was planted with Tommy and Lee, already halfway through their drinks. I gave him a nod, keeping Adriana close. She offered a soft smile to the men before leaning into me, the warmth of her body a grounding force against the tension coiling in my chest. I smirked and guided her toward the back, my hand firm on her lower back.

Christopher and Sammy from the cleaners held court by the makeshift bar near the back door. Beside them, Hector puffed on a cigar. At a card table outside, Enzo and Michael sat with Ben, who looked one hand away from losing his shirt. Across from them, Lucy laughed at something Pat said, entirely unaware of the stares around her. Ben's eyes, however, were glued to her, shamelessly so, like Hector and Christopher weren't even standing a foot away.

My face wore an easy, practiced smile, but beneath it, my blood burned hot. The secret she'd revealed before this—the truth about Hector—was gnawing at me, making restraint a difficult task. Every time I caught sight of him, I had to force my hands to stay on Adriana's back. Paul finally noticed us. Passing his cigarette to Florence with a wide grin, he stuck two fingers in his mouth and let out a whistle. "Well, look who finally showed up. James Dean with Ava Gardner on his arm."

I chuckled, leaning slightly toward Adriana, letting the social banter mask the fire simmering just below the surface. She squeezed my arm, and the world felt like it could be perfect. But Hector's presence was a shadow over the glamour, a reminder that the night was a careful dance between indulgence and danger. Especially, with his smirk in the background as he listened to Christopher tell some story to Sammy.

Adriana's laugh rang in my ear as I released her arm and crossed to Paul, pulling him into a firm hug before gripping his shoulders and giving him a once-over. "Figured if you're rolling out the red carpet, I had to show up ready for it too."

Florence stepped forward, beaming as she drew Adriana into a warm hug. "You look gorgeous, Adriana. Lucy and Angela told me you helped turn this place into what it is. You all outdid yourselves. I can't wait to get my hair freshened up now."

"Oh, I shouldn't take the credit," Adriana replied with a soft smile. "Angela and I were mostly emotional support. Lucy was the mastermind."

Florence laughed, looping her arm through Adriana's as she led her toward Angela and Marco, not even a foot away.

Paul and I followed behind them, and I made my rounds—hugging Frankie Bags first, then Mickie Two Times. I caught the flicker of anxiety in Mickie's eyes but offered a nod and a firm pat on his chest, a silent gesture that said the past was behind us. I watched the tension ease out of his shoulders almost immediately.

"You two look phenomenal tonight," Angela said as I pulled her into a hug. "You might not want to let Adriana out of your sight," she added with a knowing smirk.

I chuckled under my breath, my eyes drifting toward Adriana, who was now hugging Mr. Davidson. "Believe me," I murmured, "I haven't blinked since she walked out of the bathroom in that gown."

"What a shame Rosa couldn't be here to see what Lucy did to her flower shop," Marco muttered, taking a slow drag from his cigarette and shaking his head in mock disappointment. "It looks like someone puked up Pepto Bismol in here."

"Oh, stop it," Angela said, swatting at Marco's shoulder.

"Where is Rosa, anyway?" Frankie Bags asked, turning toward us.

"She's home watching Antonio," Adriana said. "He's got a virus. Nothing serious, but enough to keep him in bed since this morning."

"The last time I was in this place..." Marco began, cigarette perched between his fingers, one arm crossed under the other, his leg cocked casually to the side. "I came in to buy flowers for someone special, and Paul was passed out on that bench by the door...cigarette still lit in his hand. The idiot burned a hole clean through his trousers."

Our circle erupted, laughter blooming like wildfire. Everyone except Paul, who tried to mask it with a scowl, but the attempt only made us laugh harder. "I was recovering from bronchitis, you prick," he grumbled, his voice tight with faux annoyance.

Angela's eyes narrowed playfully at Marco. "Who was the special someone, Marco?"

Marco smirked. "Wouldn't you like to know."

"Oh, come on," she teased, her voice rising with curiosity.

"I forget her name, but she was wild in bed, and loved that bouquet of wildflowers Rosa whipped up for me."

Laughter erupted again. But I knew exactly who those wildflowers had been for. Marco had bought them for Angela. I remembered stopping by her house that week, seeing the bouquet on her kitchen table. Marco's shoe had been kicked carelessly next to the coffee table, and I had deliberately looked away, pretending not to connect the pieces.

Paul clapped a hand on my shoulder, grinning ear to ear. "You all remember Joey used to run numbers out the back? He was the loanshark a decade before the media caught on. I say we put a statue up in his honor. Bronze, slicked-back hair, and a fedora. Lucy would probably love it."

"The man, the myth, the legend," Marco added, raising his drink. "Joey 'The Shark' Romano...loan sharking with more commitment than any guy I've ever met. That's for damn sure."

Laughter rolled through the group. I glanced at Adriana standing beside me, dressed to the nines, laughing like she'd always belonged here. She didn't just love me in spite of my flaws. She loved me because of them.

A loud pop cracked behind me, followed by cheers.

I spun to see Lucy outside, champagne bottle in hand, spraying it with reckless delight. One heel kicked up, her body posing beneath the glowing Cosa Bella sign. Christopher stood a few feet back, Nikon F ready. The camera flashed, and I knew tomorrow morning that image would likely be on the front page.

Hector looked three drinks in already, nursing another glass with a glassy-eyed grin. Ben lingered nearby next to Mr. Davidson, snagging a shrimp off a passing silver tray of shrimp cocktail and olives. His eyes never left Lucy, even as he murmured a response to whatever Davidson said.

Christopher helped Lucy onto the counter by the register as she strode inside, her champagne flute cradled in one hand. She cleared her throat and beamed at the crowd like a burst of sunlight. "Thank you all for coming," she said. "Cosa Bella has been a dream for a long time, and seeing all of you here tonight feels like that dream has finally taken its first breath."

A wave of applause and whistles rolled through the crowd. Adriana stood beside me, her eyes glistening as she watched Lucy, completely captivated in the moment. Paul clapped so hard his hands were nearly red.

"I couldn't have done this without two truly incredible people...Angela and Adriana," Lucy continued. "I won't make you come up here since there's hardly room, but I just wanted to say: I love you both. And I couldn't have done any of this without you."

Adriana brushed away a few stray tears with the back of her finger. Angela slid an arm around her shoulders, giving a tight squeeze, then cupped her hands over her mouth and shouted, "We love you!"

Lucy smiled down at them, then turned her gaze to the rest of the room. "Thank you to my family, especially my father." She grinned at Christopher, still close enough to steady her on the counter. "To Rosa, for trusting me with the keys and believing I could make something beautiful of this place. And to my sweet boy, Michael Christopher Giordano, for making me a mother, and for teaching me to believe in myself." She blinked quickly, dabbing at her eyes as she mentioned Michael, who crouched in a corner next to Enzo. She didn't mention Hector. Instead, she lifted her flute high, and the crowd followed her lead. "To Cosa Bella."

"To Cosa Bella!" The crowd echoed, voices ringing with warmth and celebration.

Christopher stepped forward to help her down from the counter. He reached into his coat pocket and fumbled with a tiny box, drawing every eye in the room toward him. "My little girl. My princess. My Lucille. You've always been the light in our home, the light of my eyes. And now look at you...lighting up the whole damn block." Soft laughter rippled through the guests. "I'm proud of you, Lucy. Your mother would've been, too." He kissed her temple and handed her a black velvet box. Lucy hugged him before lifting the lid to reveal a pair of diamond earrings.

"Daddy," she breathed, pressing a quick kiss to his cheek before holding the earrings up for everyone to admire.

Hector stumbled forward, ruining the moment with a careless grin and a fresh glass of champagne in one hand. The other hand gripped Lucy's waist like she was property, not a woman. In his eyes, love was possession, not devotion, and it took everything in me not to bulldoze the crowd to take him out.

"I just want to say," he slurred, a cocky smile tugging at the corner of his mouth, "my wife didn't just open a salon. She built a fashion legacy. That's Lucille for ya." He pressed a sloppy kiss to her cheek, and Lucy recoiled, forcing a smile as he handed her an envelope. She peeked inside, a flicker of surprise and even delight crossing her face, but her posture was stiff, shoulders tense. The crowd cheered, clapped, and pretended they hadn't noticed. "I'm proud of you, baby," Hector muttered before swaggering toward the door and slipping out into the night.

My eyes immediately found Ben, standing near the front, only a row of guests between him and Lucy. Hands shoved into his pockets, shoulders slouched, his gaze locked on her like she'd cast a spell he couldn't break. A man in love with a woman he couldn't have. I knew that feeling all too well—how it twists your chest, how it makes your stomach tighten. For a moment, I'd thought that could've been Adriana and me. But life had other plans. Better plans. Unfortunately, Ben and Lucy hadn't been so lucky.

"Be right back, sweetheart," I murmured into Adriana's ear. She frowned, but Angela slid into my place quickly, chattering about something I didn't catch.

I wove through the crowd until I was shoulder to shoulder with Ben. He glanced at me, offering a hollow smile. "Enjoying your night?" he asked.

I nodded, taking a sip from my champagne flute. "It's alright. How's yours?"

His eyes flicked downward for a moment before he forced a smile back into place. "Oh, it's a good night. No doubt about that."

"I want you to meet me at Tino Gallo's after this." I patted his shoulder lightly and slipped past him toward Lucy. Her back was to me, deep in conversation with Frankie Bags. Frankie noticed me first and gave a subtle nod in my direction. Lucy turned, and a smile lit her face.

"Joey," she said, pulling me into a quick hug. "I'm so glad you guys came out tonight. You two are the best-looking couple here tonight."

"Thank you. But I wanted to ask you if you would meet Adriana and me at Tino Gallo's."

Her brows drew together in confusion, but she nodded. "Sure. Michael is going to spend the night with my father. So I'll meet you there as soon as I can."

I slipped back to Adriana, still talking with Angela. I stepped behind her, hands settling on her hips. She caught my hands, threading her fingers between mine, and guided them across her stomach, leaning back against my chest. Angela's attention drifted toward Enzo—my cue to get us out of there.

"Let's get out of here, sweetheart," I murmured against her ear. "I want to take you into the city."

She tilted her head up, eyes locking with mine. I pressed a soft kiss to her lips, fingers tracing lazily along the small of her stomach. "What's in the city?" she asked.

"Me," I smirked. "And you."

She kissed me again. "I want to check on Antonio first before we go anywhere."

"We'll stop by the house," I promised. "Make sure he's okay. Then we head out." She squeezed my hand in agreement. I stepped around her, took her hand in mine, and guided us through the crowd, tossing out polite goodbyes over my shoulder as we moved.

Just before we reached the door, I spotted Lucy across the room, laughing at something Davidson said. Our eyes met, and I gave the faintest nod, signaling her to follow as soon as she could. A knowing smile tugged at her lips. Adriana noticed the exchange and gave me a sideways glance as I opened the door for her.

"What's going on?"

"I invited Lucy and Ben. I told them to meet us there. I hope that's okay."

"Of course, it's okay."

I helped her into the passenger seat, shutting the door behind her before walking around to the driver's side. The engine groaned, and I cranked the air on. The headlights cut through the night as we pulled away from *Cosa Bella*.

Chapter Forty-Five

Adriana
Twelve days after Vincent's murder

Joey sat in the driveway, the car engine humming, as I rushed inside. Rosa was curled up on the couch in front of the television, a steaming cup of tea in her hands. She glanced over her shoulder and smiled when she saw me. "You're back early," she said, setting the cup down on the coffee table. "Where's Joey?"

"He's waiting in the car. I just wanted to check on Antonio before we head into the city for a little date. Would that be okay with you? We shouldn't—"

"Oh, Adriana, he's sound asleep. I haven't heard a peep since I went up to get his empty soup bowl. He's fine. You go enjoy your night, he's safe with me."

Guilt nipped at me, but Rosa had a way of quieting it. "Okay. Thank you, Rosa."

"You need it. Go on now. Enjoy your night while you're still young and in love."

I slipped into the passenger seat. Joey turned toward me, a grin spreading across his face. "Everything alright?"

"She says he's asleep. She told me to enjoy the night with you."

"Then that's exactly what we'll do," he said, shifting the car into reverse and pulling out of the driveway. As we cruised down the block, Joey turned the radio down low. Staten Island was alive tonight, cars lined the streets near Cosa Bella, people lingering outside on the sidewalks, soaking in a few more hours of glamour under the summer sky.

Joey reached over and took my hand in his, lifting it to his lips. He pressed a kiss to my knuckles before lowering our entwined hands into his lap, his thumb tracing gentle circles across my skin.

"I might need a few more kisses from you."

He chuckled, the sound low and teasing. "Just say the word, sweetheart," he said, his eyes returning to the road. "And I'll give you anything you want."

"Anything?" I lifted my brows, leaning slightly closer.

His gaze drifted over me slowly, appraising, lingering. "Anything. There's nothing I wouldn't do for you. Want more kisses?" He lifted my hand again, brushing his lips across each knuckle in turn. When his mouth trailed up the back of my hand to my wrist, a shiver ran up my arm.

I let out a breathy giggle, and he chuckled, his eyes still on the road as he lowered our joined hands into his lap. His thumb found a rhythm, and I melted a little deeper into my seat with every sweet touch. I adjusted the vents to have more cool air rush over my heated body.

"I know a good way to cool you down," he smirked.

I rested my elbow on the console, my chin propped on my knuckles, watching him. His grin was devilish, but his eyes flicked to mine with a flash of innocence. "And what would that be?"

He shrugged, though the grin never wavered. "It involves a whole lot of me...kissing you."

"Yeah?" I tilted my head, playing coy.

"Keep giving me that look, and I might just pull over and show you exactly what I mean."

"Joey," I laughed, swatting playfully at his chest.

"All you've got to do is say the word, sweetheart," he murmured, voice low. "It's dark out...a nice summer night, perfect for cooling each other off...right here in the backseat."

I sat up a little straighter, crossing my arms with a teasing glare. "Is that all you think about?"

"When I'm around you? Yeah. Hell, even when I'm not around you, I'm thinking about being around you."

"Is that so?"

"That is so," he replied, blue eyes glinting with amusement.

"I want this on the record. Joey Romano says he thinks about me *constantly*."

"I'll put it in writing," he replied, taking my hand in his. "I'll tattoo it on my chest if you want."

I laughed, letting my fingers weave between his. "Who would've thought Joey Romano could be such a romantic?"

"Romantic?" His voice dropped an octave. "I wouldn't go that far."

"No?" I arched an eyebrow.

"Nah," he said, his thumb tracing circles on my palm. "The things I'm thinking about right now...they've got nothing to do with opening doors or pulling out chairs for you."

"Mm, shame. I do like a gentleman."

"Oh, I can be a gentleman," he said, a smirk creeping back across his lips. "I'll always make sure you finish first...like the gentleman I am."

My cheeks flamed before I could even try to hide it.

"I love when you blush like that," he murmured, his eyes gleaming.

I turned to the window, pretending to ignore him, but I could feel the grin tugging at my lips, and, worse, I knew he could see it. "Say the word," he whispered, squeezing my hand, "and I'll take the next turn off. Ten minutes. That's all I need to ruin you exactly the way I want."

I turned back to him, lips parted in shock. "Joey Romano," I gasped. But I was too flustered to speak further, especially because the intensity in his eyes made it clear he meant every word, and the thrill of it made me want to follow along with whatever he had in mind.

* * *

We pulled up in front of a neon sign glowing in bold cursive: *Gallo's*. Joey was out of the car before I could even unbuckle my seatbelt. He opened my door, and when I stepped out and tightened my fur shawl around myself, his hand slipped around playfully to palm my ass. I yelped, shooting him a glare.

"It was too tempting, I'm sorry," he said with a wink, his fingers lacing through mine as he led me toward the entrance.

The entryway was narrow and hardly lit, but I could make out the dark green and navy wallpaper along the walls. A young doorgirl stood ready beside the coat rack, poised to take our coats. We handed them over, and the music and hum of conversation beyond the corridor grew louder with each step. I leaned closer to Joey as we walked. Looking up at him, a teasing smile playing on my lips, I murmured, "So you do open doors like a gentleman?"

His gaze lingered on my lips. "I also know the restrooms are just past that corner on the left. And I could take you in there right now...show you all the other ways I plan to serve you tonight."

Heat rushed to my cheeks as the hallway opened into the heart of Gallo's.

The room sprawled wide, plush booths lining one side, a bar overflowing with every liquor imaginable on the other. Card tables crowded the center, stacks of cash resting at men's feet, cigars or cigarettes balanced between fingers. Women perched in laps, laughter and smoke swirling through the air. Every man wore a smirk like he owned the world, and in this room, they pretty much did.

Ben sat at the bar, nursing a drink. He gave Joey a subtle chin nod as we approached. Eyes landed on Joey first, and then, inevitably, on me. A spotlight of attention seemed to blaze down, isolating us in the middle of the crowd. I didn't know everyone here, but they knew me. Because of Joey. Like a queen entering the court of a king.

Within seconds, a wave of men descended, greeting Joey with backslaps and whistles, clinking glasses, parting the crowd as if the room itself had rearranged for our arrival. We moved through them like royalty, and I couldn't help but glance up at him, knowing all eyes followed him...and, by extension, me.

Rising from a downstairs lounge was the man himself, Tino Gallo.

Tino strode toward us, his arms open wide, gold rings flashing on every finger and thick chains draped over his chest. His suit was flashy, his grin toothy, and his swagger impossible to ignore. He wrapped Joey in a bear hug like a proud father, slapping his back with exaggerated force. Joey chuckled, tugging him toward me, one arm still draped around Tino's shoulders.

"Tino, this is my wife...Adriana," Joey said, his voice warm. "Sweetheart, meet Tino Gallo."

I smiled, extending my hand. "Nice place you've got here, Tino."

He took my hand in both of his, pressing a kiss to the back of it. "Grazie, bella. And look at you, Mio Dio, just as stunning as Joey promised you'd be."

Joey slid his hand to the small of my back. "What can I say? I'm a lucky man, aren't I?"

"You are," I replied, my eyes flicking up to meet his.

Tino laughed. "I like her already," he said, clapping Joey on the shoulder.

"She's the only one who knows how to keep me in line." Joey teased.

Tino chuckled, wagging a ringed finger at me. "Keep it up, bella. The rest of us need Joey behaving."

I laughed, giving Joey's chest a playful pat. "Someone's gotta do it. I suppose I can take that job."

Tino roared with laughter. "She's a good one! Alright, you two enjoy your night, but don't pay for a damn thing. Everything's on the house."

"Tino—" Joey called after him, but Tino just waved him off, grinning, and disappeared into the crowd.

Joey's arm tightened around my waist, pulling me against his side. He pressed a kiss to the top of my head, his voice dropping low so only I could hear. "You really are trying me tonight, aren't you?"

I lifted my chin, wide-eyed and innocent. "Whatever are you referring to, Mr. Romano?"

A low growl hid in the breath. My smile widened at the sound. "You're going to pay for this," he muttered.

"Pay for what?" I blinked sweetly, letting my fingers trail along the length of his tie.

His jaw flexed, tongue flicking along the inside of his cheek as he stared down at me. I loved it, seeing him unravel like this, and knowing I was the cause. "You keep playing sweet," he warned, voice husky, "and I'm going to have you pressed against that bathroom wall before the night's over."

I leaned in, letting my lips brush his ear. "Then maybe I should keep playing," I whispered.

When I stepped back, I could feel his gaze burning into my back as I made my way to the bar, where Ben was sitting. Joey followed, forcing himself to behave...mostly. Ben stood as I approached, offering a surprised smile. "I wasn't expecting to see you tonight, Adriana. But this is a nice surprise."

I slid onto the barstool beside him with a sly smile. "Figured it was time to get out of the house...and see where Joey's hiding in case I feel like spying on him."

Ben let out a dry chuckle, and Joey's hands found their familiar spots, one resting on my lower back, the other on my upper thigh, as he leaned forward to order from the bartender. "Negroni for her. Old-fashioned for me."

Ben raised his glass to his lips. "It's good to have you out with us."

Joey smirked. "Oh, we've got someone else coming."

Lucy walked in with her effortless way of commanding attention. I couldn't tell if it was her name, her beauty, or the way she carried herself as if she owned every space she entered. Maybe it was all three. Either way, when she stepped through the doors, every eye in the room turned, but none more intently than Ben's. His eyes locked onto hers, and Lucy froze for a brief half-second, surprised, before regaining her signature composure.

Joey took a slow sip of his old-fashioned, a grin tugging at his lips. "Looks like everyone's finally here."

I watched Lucy and Ben silently drink each other in, their attention cutting through the noise like they were the only two people in the room. A smile stretched across Lucy's face—

wider, freer, more genuine than I had seen in days. Ben's grin threatened to break entirely, his teeth biting at the corner of his lips as he tried to play it cool. Lucy strolled to the bar, confident and precise. "Dirty martini. Rinse the glass with vermouth, don't add it."

Joey pressed in behind me, his chest flush against my back. One arm wrapped around my waist, his other hand brushing against mine. His voice was a low rasp in my ear. "Wanna go win some money, Mrs. Romano?"

I tilted my chin, meeting his gaze with a sly smirk. "Oh? Is that what we're calling it now? Winning money?"

He chuckled before Tino's booming voice carried across the room. "Watch out, people! The Shark is here to take your money!" He pointed right at us, laughing, and Joey raised his glass with that cocky grin I adored.

The next few hours blurred. I perched on Joey's lap as he commanded the poker table, exchanging sly banter and calculated bluffs, winning hand after hand with deadly focus and infuriating charm. Ben and Lucy flitted about the room like restless spirits, first at the bar, then dancing near the jukebox, then drifting to play a few hands before disappearing again, leaving the rest of the room to speculate where they'd gone. Joey's laugh rumbled from his chest, warm and triumphant, as Tino cursed under his breath and slid a gold watch across the table in defeat. The sound vibrated through me, making my body shiver slightly atop him.

I giggled as Joey wrapped his arms around my waist, nestling his face into the crook of my neck. His stubble grazed my skin, and I hooked an arm over his shoulder, pulling him impossibly closer. Bourbon, cigars, and spiced cologne swirled together in his scent. "You're my lucky charm, sweetheart," he murmured against my skin.

I pulled back, my hands resting on the sides of his neck, meeting his eyes. "Is that so?"

"Mhm," he hummed, pressing a kiss to my lips as his hand slid beneath the table to squeeze my thigh. "You havin' fun, sweetheart?"

"Mmm," I teased, "I don't know yet. I'll let you know after you teach me how to cheat at poker."

He let out a low, gravelly laugh, tilting his head back enough for it to rumble through the room before his dark, gleaming eyes locked on mine. "I don't cheat, sweetheart. You married a fuckin' winner."

I bit my lip, letting my fingers trace along the side of his neck. "Well," I smirked, "maybe I'll just have to take you down next time."

A devilish grin tugged at his lips as he leaned closer. "That's not the only thing you'll be taking tonight." My cheeks flushed, thighs pressing together, and all he did was chuckle, knowing exactly what he was doing.

Lucy and Ben were on their way to Ben's apartment, courtesy of Joey's careful orchestration. The crowd had thinned, the chips stacked heavily in Joey's favor.

"C'mon," he said, rising to his feet, tugging me along with him. His hand slipped possessively into mine, gripping tight.

"And go where?"

His lips brushed the shell of my ear. "Home. So I can show you exactly what happens after all that teasing."

I let out a soft laugh, my pulse quickening, and allowed myself to be pulled out into the sultry summer night, knowing that tonight was far from over.

Chapter Forty-Six

Joey
Thirteen days after Vincent's murder

Tonight was the night. The night I'd been waiting for. Not just a captain anymore. I was about to become consigliere of the family. Soon, underboss. One day, boss. I always knew I was a visionary, and I was in it for the long haul.

Inside Vino e Pasta, the red wallpaper, gilded with delicate gold filigree, bathed the room in the kind of warmth only old-world Italy could pull off. I'd been here two days ago, celebrating early with Adriana and Antonio, but tonight was different. The waiters in their white jackets moved between tables, and the same violinist in the corner drew a soft, melancholy tune from his instrument. I could feel the tension in my shoulders ease a fraction. Familiar territory, yes, but with stakes I'd never felt before. From across the room, the maître d' acknowledged me with a look that said he already knew why I was here.

"Mr. Romano. Right this way."

We moved through the dining room, past men in tailored suits and women in gowns that caught the low lighting. The noise faded behind us as we approached the back, where the familiar pair of heavy velvet curtains hung. He pulled them aside, and the room beyond glowed in candlelight. Spacious and intimate, the Giordano crime family members were scattered throughout, laughter and conversation filling the space, until I stepped through. Every head turned, and the chatter died.

This was it.

The room didn't just acknowledge me as Joey, it recognized me as something more. The heir. The *trusted* one. The man poised to guide this family into the next chapter. Ironically, I was the man they had tried to pin a murder on two weeks ago, and now I was the one about to help run this family. Hector sat beside Christopher, eyes darting to mine, disgust written across his face.

Christopher rose from his seat, the chatter fading to an expectant hush. He glanced at me, pride softening the usual steel in his eyes. "Joey," he said, and I could hear the respect in that single word. He crossed the room in long strides and pulled me into a firm embrace, one arm around my shoulders, the other on my back. The hug was brief but measured, a signal to the room that everything was official.

When he stepped back, his eyes swept the gathered men, and his voice cut through the tension with ease. "Everyone here knows why we're gathered. Tonight, we make something official." He paused, letting the silence hang. "Joey Romano will become Hector, and I's right hand. The consigliere of this family. If there's a problem or a dispute, Joey will take care of it."

The first problem I was taking care of was...Hector. Our eyes settled upon each other as he stood, wearing a fake smile and clapping loudly. The room erupted, voices rising in cheers and applause of respect. I kept my face steady, letting the acknowledgement wash over me, knowing that every glance, every nod, every hand extended was a vote of confidence in me and my loyalty. But I couldn't help but wonder if Hector had strategically placed me here for his own plot.

Christopher clapped a hand on my shoulder again. "You've earned this, Joey. I trust you. Hector trusts you. Everyone in this room trusts you. And from this day forward, you're not just part of the family, you're a part of running it."

The applause slowly faded, replaced by men moving toward the buffet along the walls. The savory pull of octopus pizzaiolo, spicy rigatoni vodka, and fresh bread filled the room. Plates in hand, everyone grabbed food and found seats, settling in for the night's feast. I took a moment to let my eyes sweep the room, committing every face, every expression, to memory.

Paul slipped in beside me at the buffet, his tray already half-full. "Operation Ice Box tomorrow night?" he murmured, leaning close so only I could hear.

I glanced around, ensuring no one was paying us any mind, then nodded. "Sal has it mapped out and ready to go. Ben says this is the guy."

Paul's eyes glinted. "Good. We've been waiting on this for a while. Everything goes smoothly, and this thing's over and plays in our favor."

I nodded again, scanning the room one more time before letting my gaze settle on him. "I'll handle my part. You handle yours. Sal's got the timing down. We hit this guy clean. And we clear my name once and for all."

Paul clapped me on the shoulder. "Fuck, Joey, we're so close."

I gave the smallest smirk. "It feels like it. Doesn't it? Being the consigliere isn't about sitting in the back. It's about knowing everything before it happens. That's how we stay ahead." *Of Hector.*

He nodded, a quiet understanding passing between us. We

moved along the buffet, plates in hand, just two men among the family, already thinking two steps ahead.

Ben pulled at a loose thread, and it unraveled straight to Hector. A slip of a name from Vincent's housekeeper during an interrogation, but Ben lurked in the shadows, stitching scraps together until the pattern was clear: the last man to see Vincent alive had ties to Hector's port business.

Hector and Vincent had always fenced through DiSanti's docks, moving things off the books, cutting corners, cheating the system. Vincent's murder changed the calculus, somebody had to move the goods, someone expendable and quiet. It made sense that Hector would hire a hand from the margins: an immigrant tied to his mistress in the city, paid in pennies and secrecy to do the dirty work. This wasn't a one-man job. Hector's arrogance meant he used other people as shields. That shield was about to be pulled aside.

We drew up a simple plan with teeth. Intercept the docks. Find the eighteen-wheeler the mystery man was driving for Hector's black market stolen goods. Take the truck. Kidnap the driver long enough to make him talk, *whatever* it takes to pry the names and secrets out of him. Clean out the load and send an empty rig back to Hector. Let him wake up to the smell of humiliation and know, without question, that somebody's onto him.

It wasn't revenge for revenge's sake. It was precision, a lesson wrapped in a warning, and I would make sure Hector understood exactly who had pulled the string.

Chapter Forty-Seven

Antonio
Fourteen days after Vincent's murder

Sal's baby-blue Thunderbird idled at the curb outside Enzo's, with the top down. He leaned back against the headrest, elbow draped over the door, a cigarette balanced between his fingers as smoke floated into the summer air. The Flamingos crooned *"I Only Have Eyes for You"* from the radio, and Sal hummed along, half-lidded and content. I pulled open the passenger door and slid inside. He sat up, turning the volume down, grinning at me as he started down the road. *"Cosa Bella's* opening was fucking incredible the other night, Nino. The whole place lit up like the goddamn Copacabana. It's a damn shame you had to miss it."

"Well, I'm really glad you enjoyed yourself. I had a fucking blow dryer pointed at my forehead, shoving Ice Cubes down my shirt, trying to convince Rosa and Ma I was one foot in the grave."

Sal barked out a laugh. "Well, whatever you did worked. The way your ma and Joey were carryin' on last night about how sick you were? Shit, I was proud of your Oscar-worthy performance, Nino."

I smirked. "I had to work *twice* as hard to sell it to Rosa all night. You have no idea what I've been through, so whatever we're getting into right now needs to make up for the torture I've endured."

Sal chuckled, glancing over at me for a second before his eyes returned to the road. "She's got dementia, doesn't she? That's what everyone says, at least. You know, this morning, I saw her in the front lawn eating an orange like it was an apple."

I shook my head. "That's what she *wants* you to think. She's as sharp as a tack. She just uses the confusion skit when it benefits her. She's got the whole town fooled...except me. And I swear, it took every ounce of dedication I had in me to convince her. I'm not even sure I pulled it off. I think she just got tired of watching me set myself on fire and then freeze myself to death."

Sal was laughing hard now, gripping the steering wheel. "Jesus Christ, Nino. You're a full piece of fucking work. But I do have some exciting shit I plan for us to get into tonight."

My spine snapped straight against the seat as I looked over at Sal, who was grinning like a possum. "What is it?"

He smirked, glancing at me from the corner of his eye. "Operation Ice Box."

I blinked. "What the hell is that supposed to mean?"

"I wasn't sure if I should drag you into it," he said, shifting in his seat like he'd been waiting all day to spill it. "But I think this is what you've been waiting on. There's a refrigerated eighteen-wheeler docked at Red Hook. Supposedly, it's got French perfumes and imported caviar in the trailer. We're meeting the guys there tonight to boost it and get it to the warehouse."

My brain stalled. "And how exactly is this supposed to help me clear Joey's name?"

"DiSantis has his crew at the dock. They're posing as inspectors and dock workers. Even Tommy and Lee are down there waiting on us. You and I are gonna climb into the back of the truck when it gets pulled for a surprise inspection. From there, Tommy and Lee will get the rig to the warehouse. At the warehouse, a second truck's waiting. We offload everything and kidnap the driver."

Hijacking an eighteen-wheeler and kidnapping the driver and goods? "I'm still not hearing how this clears my father's name."

"It turns out the guy behind the wheel was working with Vincent. The guy behind the wheel is now working for Hector, and supposedly, he was the last one who saw Vincent alive. The housekeeper slipped up and told Ben during one of his interrogations. Ben's been tailing him and connected him to Hector's operation at the ports. So the guy knows what happened to Vincent, or he was the one who killed Vincent. And our job is to get this to the warehouse, and Joey will take care of it from there."

A crooked smile appeared at the corners of my mouth. *I'm about to hijack an eight-wheeler. Kidnapping the driver. Steal the goods. And clear Joey's name.* My pulse is so loud in my throat I can hardly hear anything else. I shift in my seat, trying to look casual when every part of me is anything but. Half of me wants to laugh, and the other half wants to throw up. I want to run and hide, and also drive straight into my first mafia operation with my eyes wide open.

Sal laughed and nudged my arm. "Welcome to the family, Nino. There's no orientation packet. Everybody earns their stripes the same way."

I pressed back into the seat, my pulse hammering, and my mind spinning out of control. The kid everyone thought needed bed rest is now long gone. The city was waiting for me to prove my worth. Joey was counting on me to help pull this

off and clear his name, and tonight, I would finally do what I set
out to do.

* * *

We pulled up to the dock and started down the long stretch of
concrete, in time to see the eighteen-wheeler pulling in. The guys
were already in position, in fake customs uniforms and clipboards.
Like clockwork, they flagged the driver down and motioned him
to stop. I'd never seen anything run so smoothly before. I guess
that's why they call it organized crime, because these guys were
calculated. Efficient. Everyone had a role to play, and they played
it like a well-oiled machine. Sal and I crept up the side as Tommy
popped the trailer doors open for a "routine inspection." Without
a single word, Sal climbed in first, and I followed his lead. The
second those doors slammed shut, the panic hit me.

It was freezing. I mean, bone-deep, my lungs might freeze,
Arctic death trap freezing fucking cold. All I could think was...
I'm dead. I'm going to freeze to death in here, and when they
finally open the doors, they'll find me and Sal frozen solid, two
dumbass ice sculptures, toppling over and shattering into a
hundred little shards. I couldn't see him. I couldn't see
anything, for that matter. Not that I gave a damn about seeing
Sal right now. Because I was too busy losing it. Perhaps if I
could see Sal, I might not be panicking as badly.

My chest was tight, and my breath came out short and fast.
My heart was thudding like a drum, and part of me clung to the
only warmth I had left—my racing heartbeat. Either it would
keep me alive, or it'd pound itself into overdrive and kill me
right here in the back of a frozen truck.

Oh fuck.

This can't be how it ends.

I was profusely sweating, somehow, even though the cold cut through me like knives. My throat was so dry I couldn't swallow back the lump that had formed. My trembling hands ran through my hair, trying to think, trying not to scream. Because the truck was moving now. There was no getting out.

Why the fuck didn't I ask Sal how far the damn warehouse is?

"Sal," I croaked. I'd curled into myself, knees pulled tight to my chest, arms locked around them. "Sal...how far's the warehouse?"

"I don't know. I think about ten miles."

Ten fucking miles?

My heart kicked up harder. Jesus Christ, how long have we even been in here? Ten miles might as well be ten hours. We could be human fucking popsicles in ten minutes. I was shaking so bad my teeth were knocking together. My fingers were numb already, and I couldn't tell if the burning in my legs was from the cold or my own fear of dying this way. Maybe it's both. I can't tell. My brain is in survival mode, and my body is already giving out from my point of view.

"Sal," I hissed again, a little louder this time. "We're gonna fucking die in here, man."

"No, we're not," he said like it was nothing. Like we were sitting in a warm diner and not a damn meat locker on wheels. "Just relax, Nino. We're getting closer."

"Relax?" I stared into the dark, like I might actually see him through it. But then the panic flooded back because I couldn't see shit. "The only thing we're close to is freezing to death. You ever been locked in a fuckin' freezer, Sal? Because I haven't. Not exactly how I imagined goin' out."

The next thing I hear is a long string of laughter followed by wheezing.

"Hey, come on, Nino," he coughs out between his wheezes.

"You're tougher than this. I've done this many times, and I'm still alive to do it again."

"I'm thirteen fucking years old!" I snapped like a short fuse, my teeth chattering still, my entire body convulsing. "I haven't made it through fucking high school, and now I'm about to freeze to death over a crate of caviar and perfume?"

Sal couldn't respond because he couldn't stop cackling and wheezing. I couldn't see him, but I could hear him laughing so hard he was rolling against the walls of the truck. "Okay, okay," he breathed out. "You want me to hold your hand? You need my touch, bambino? Would that make you feel better?"

"If it's warmer than mine, maybe!"

He snorted again, then all I felt was something being thrown at my face. I grabbed it and noticed it was Sal's suit jacket. Oh, this guy's deranged. He's going to freeze to death for sure by giving me his damn coat. "It's my coat. Put it on."

"I'm not takin' your—"

"Shut up and take the damn coat, bambino. I'm fine. I told you I've done this countless times before."

"No," I said, throwing the coat back towards him. If I'm going to die of hypothermia, I'm going to do it with my dignity intact. "I'm fine," I said as my teeth chattered. I could barely feel my feet. My jaw hurt from clenching, and my fingertips were for sure frostbite. "Why the hell do they keep this thing so cold?" I muttered.

"Because we're sitting on a couple of million dollars' worth of European bullshit. Perfume, caviar...I think there's butter in here, too."

At this rate, I couldn't understand why any of that shit matters over me losing my life.

"I'll give you some extra pocket change once we get our cuts for the job." All I can think is I won't be alive to spend a single dollar of it. "And Tino Gallo's gonna flip when he sees what we brought him. Because that's our next job, bambino... you get to meet Tino Gallo."

I don't see how we're going to survive to get a single thing to Tino Gallo.

"This is your shot to prove yourself. You're making a name for yourself, Nino. I'm impressed, and so is everyone else. Just think, after tonight, we'll clear Joey's name, which is what you wanted all along."

"Yeah, well," I shivered. "I didn't think it'd involve losing my fucking fingers."

Sal choked out another laugh, "At least when you tell this story someday, you'll sound like a hardass to the old timers."

When I thought my life was over, the truck jerked to a stop. The doors flue open. More cool air rushed in, only it doesn't sting as bad as the cold air inside the back of the rig, and certainly not when I'm gasping for air like I've been drowning under water. Lee is the only person I see, and he hands me a ski mask. "Put it on before you get out," he instructed. Right. Because whoever is outside this freaking rig could recognize me. The good thing is, Lee also has a ski mask half on, so it's not like I'll be the only one. Plus, I'm so cold right now, any extra fabric is a gift. So I tugged it over my face as Sal practically rolled out, doubled over, laughing like a maniac. I stumbled after him, dragging in breath after breath. "Sweet fucking Jesus." I gasped, dropping to my knees.

The second I looked up, everything froze. Because we're not in some random warehouse. *No.* I'm standing inside *the* warehouse. The same one I followed Joey to months ago. My mouth is bone dry again. The blood feels like it's drained from my body, but it doesn't appear on the concrete. The warehouse has been renovated. Overhead lights above a massive table surrounded by chairs. But only one chair matters: the one that's been dragged to the center.

A man is tied to it, his arms twisted behind the backrest, legs roped to the legs of the chair, duct tape slapped across his mouth. His eyes are wild, darting around like he's praying for some miracle that clearly isn't coming. Across the warehouse, I clock the other 18-wheeler. Identical to the one we just crawled out of. A few of the guys are already swapping crates, working fast, as if it's all just another Tuesday night for them. Because I suppose it is. But not for me. Sal finally stumbled toward me, wiping tears from the corners of his eyes, still wheezing from laughter. He clutched my shoulder for balance, and I shoved him off, scowling.

"Oh, fuck, that was the funniest shit I've ever experienced, Nino," he choked out, laughing again.

I glared at him. "Yeah, just hilarious. What happens now?"

Sal slung his arm across my shoulders as if we were at a family cookout and not in the middle of a warehouse with a man tied up in a chair. "Now?" he said, steering me forward, toward the man in the chair. "Now you learn what really happens behind the scenes, Nino."

The guy's soaked in his own sweat, rocking against the ropes like he still thinks there's a way out. If I know anything, it's that he's out of fucking luck tonight. I glanced around. Mobsters are everywhere. Nobody I know, like Paul or Marco. So these must all be low-level mobsters. But not a single one is flinching, blinking...nothing. Because this shit is normal for them. Hijacking rigs, stealing goods, and kidnapping drivers.

Sal dropped his arm, grabbed a nearby chair, and straddled it backward, his arms folded over the top. He looked stupid, but I kept my mouth shut. Because I'm not stupid enough to push my luck in a room full of gangsters, low-level or not. Tommy walked over and ripped the duct tape off the guy's mouth in one go. The sound is brutal, like skin tearing, and the man gasped hard, his lips red and raw. His accent was thick. European maybe. Russian? Hungarian? I don't fucking know.

"Please," he begged, his chest heaving. "Please, I didn't know—"

"Do you work for Hector?" Sal asked him casually.

The guy shook his head and kept begging and whimpering. "Please—I swear—I don't know anything."

"Answer the fucking question!" Sal shouted. I jumped because I've never heard Sal raise his voice like that. But now I notice there's a gun in Sal's palm. I don't even know where he pulled it from. Only that one second, nothing, the next, a muzzle aimed at this guy's face. Now, I'm not shivering. I'm whipping the sweat from above my brow.

The man yelped. "Yes! Yes, I do some jobs for him...sometimes!" he sputtered. "Small things. I didn't know this would happen..."

I watched as his face went pale, his legs went limp under the ropes. It hits me like a brick in the chest: this guy's gonna die tonight. And I'm gonna have to watch. Sal's now got this devious smirk that makes the hair on the back of my neck stand up. I've never seen this side of Sal.

"Good," Sal hummed, cocking his head sideways. "Did that job include killing Vincent Accetta so Hector could secure his spot as underboss? Or maybe so he could take over the docks?"

"No, no, no," the guy chanted, shaking his head in rapid succession. "I didn't kill anyone. Hector didn't kill anyone."

"So who did?" Sal asked, his tone eerily calm, which made my skin crawl.

"I don't know," the guy blurted out.

"You don't know?" Sal stood, his chair screeching before he kicked it aside. It clattered to a stop right in front of my feet. My eyes dropped to it, then snapped back up just as Sal pressed the gun into the man's temple.

My heart stuttered. *Oh no. I'm not ready to see this.*

"It was a woman!" the guy cried out. His eyes squeezed shut as if he were waiting to see his life flash before them. "She came in after I left. I don't know who she is...very pretty. Maybe someone Vincent's been seeing."

Sal's brows drew together in confusion, and I felt it too. *A woman? No way.*

"A woman?" Sal echoed.

The guy nodded frantically. "Yes! I swear. I don't know her name. I've never seen her before. Never."

Vincent Accetta was taken out by a woman? It sounds like bullshit. But...something in his panic feels like the truth.

"Joey's here!" Tommy shouted from across the warehouse.

Sal froze. His eyes snap to mine like a deer in headlights.

Oh shit.

The gun lowered from the guy's temple, only to swing toward my chest. My body locked up. His mouth is moving, but I don't hear a damn word. The next second, he whirled and pointed toward the open back of the 18-wheeler.

Somehow, my legs began to move. I dove into that freezer box like it was my salvation, and Lee slammed the doors shut behind me. Everything went dark and silent as soon as the doors shut behind me. This time I didn't panic. I sat down, my breath fogging up in front of me.

If ten minutes passed, I didn't feel them. Sal was right. The more time you spend in a frozen truck, the less you feel it.

In that numbness, one thing becomes clear. I don't just want to clear Joey's name anymore. I want to live the same lifestyle Joey lives. I want to sit at that long, dark table under shitty lighting. I want to be part of something that runs deeper than loyalty and thicker than blood. I want the oath and everything sinful that comes with it. Even if it means being buried under crates of black-market caviar.

Chapter Forty-Eight

Joey
Fourteen days after Vincent's murder

I spot some of the guys off near the loading dock, heaving crates into the back of a waiting eighteen-wheeler. Lee climbed into the driver's seat of the other rig and tore out onto the road like a bat out of hell, the tires screeching into the night. I stalled watching him take off, my eyebrows tugging together.

Tommy leaned against one of the wide doors, the one he was holding open for me. A cigarette hangs between his lips, and he flashes me a grin as I approach the doors. Something about him feels off. I can't quite put my finger on it. Perhaps it's nothing. Perhaps, it's the fact that everything I've worked for is finally lining up, finally tipping in my favor, and everyone, including Tommy, knows it.

"Nice suit, boss," Tommy said, smoke curling from the side of his mouth.

I passed through the door. It creaked shut behind me with a heavy clank, but Tommy stayed outside, keeping watch. Not that it was necessary because Ben's got the front of the street on surveillance. No one's getting past him. I saw him on my way onto the street. The warehouse is full, every low-level guy in my crew, which is now Paul's crew, huddled around the edges of the room, all facing the center as if they're waiting for a boxing match to go down. Probably because a very unfair boxing match *is* about to go down, and I'd say the bets are in my favor tonight.

Right in the spotlight, tied to a chair, is our star.

He was mumbling to himself, his eyes clenched shut, chin tucked as if he were praying to a God who won't be here to save him. I can't understand Russian, so I don't have a clue what he's saying. However, there's no mistaking the fear in his voice. That kind of fear's universal, and you don't have to speak someone's native tongue to know this is a call for mercy. I stalked toward him, my eyes on him like a hawk circling its prey. His hands are bound tight behind the chair. There's sweat on his brow despite the slight chill in the metal warehouse.

I remember three days ago when Ben came into my office that morning, his eyes were lit up like he'd just cracked open the case of the century. He said he'd made a break in the Vincent's case. By break, he meant, he'd found the middle man. It turned out Hector had a side hustle in black market goods. Which wasn't anything I didn't already know. But I did find out he was not turning over most of his profile or revealing the full scope of his operation. Every guy standing in this warehouse had dipped their hands into hijacking cars and high-end stolen shipments. That's rookie shit. Petty cash. For a man like Hector, the underboss of a crime family, it's downright pathetic.

I've poured millions into the family. I've kept the lights on for this family. I've made sure the books look clean enough to pass through City Hall and still line every judge's pocket. Yet, every week for years, my place at the table had been under threat by amateurs with illusions of power.

This isn't about some stolen French perfume or caviar, or butter. This is about what's mine and who thinks they can take it from me. After tonight, a lesson will be learned.

The name sitting in front of me is a Russian man whose name is Aleksei. The housekeeper said he was supposed to show up the morning Vincent was killed, supposedly right after she left for groceries. She couldn't say for sure if he ever made it there or what happened while she was gone. Now, here I am, standing in the middle of this warehouse and sitting dead center, tied to a chair like a lamb to slaughter, is none other than Aleksei. Whatever he's still whispering under his breath sounds like a Russian prayer.

I know he's the hired hand, the one who pulled the trigger on Vincent, and the reason I've had a target on my back for two weeks now. The plan must have been simple in someone like Hector's mind: take out Vincent, secure his spot at the table as underboss, and then take me out. But if Hector wants to swim with sharks, he'd better know how to deep dive because I don't just bite. I fucking devour, and now it's Aleksei's turn to confess like I'm the god he's been praying to for the past few minutes.

I bent down, trying to meet his eyes, but he wouldn't look at me. He kept whispering that Russian prayer under his breath. My brows knitted together as I grabbed him by the collar and gave him a hard shake. He only chanted louder. So I gave him something worth praying about. I released his collar, and his head dropped forward, limp. My other hand moved, and I reached behind me and pulled out my .38 caliber revolver. Then I crack it across the side of his face. His jaw twisted faster than his skull, spit flying, blood trailing from the corner of his mouth. His groan was guttural, half-choked, and finally, his eyes opened.

I grinned as though we were old friends. "Hi there, Aleksei," I murmured, grabbing a fistful of his hair and jerking his head back until he was looking at the ceiling. The barrel of my revolver pressed into the soft flesh under his chin. "I don't think we've been properly introduced. My name's Joey Romano. But some folks call me The Shark. Does that ring a bell?"

There's a gash on his cheek, red sliding down his neck like melted wax. If he walks out of here—which is a big if—he'll be wearing that bruise for weeks.

He tried to nod, but he isn't going anywhere unless I let go of him.

"Please..." he croaked, his voice gravelly from pain. "Take anything...take it all..."

A wicked laugh trailed past my lips. "Oh, that ship's already sailed. You could have crates of diamonds and a truck full of black market kidneys parked outside, and I wouldn't blink. This isn't about what you have, Aleksei."

His eyes lock onto mine, wide and pleading. "I have a family..."

"So do I," I snapped. "A teenage son. A wife. They pray every goddamn day that I make it home alive. But the man you work for...Hector? He's got other plans for me in mind, doesn't he?"

The revolver pressed deeper into his throat. I could feel his pulse pounding against the muzzle.

"You wanna live?" I asked. "Then here's what you're gonna do. You're gonna stay tied to that chair. You're gonna sleep here tonight. And come morning, you're gonna confess, loud and clear, that Hector hired you to take out Vincent Accetta. And you're going to do this in front of a very special someone. Ever heard of Christopher The Butcher Giordano?"

He stared up at me, his chest rising in short, shallow gasps.

"You do that," I muttered, "and maybe he'll let you walk out of here in one piece. But he didn't get the nickname by chance, so if I were you, I'd get to confessing."

"But I didn't kill anyone," he muttered, his eyes shut like he was bracing for another hit, and I considered it. But decided against it.

"Are you calling my guy a liar?" I asked. *Ben wouldn't dare lie about this.*

"No," he breathed, blood trailing down his jaw, dripping onto his shirt. "I was there, but I didn't pull the trigger...but...I think I know who did."

For a second, I toy with the idea of ending it now, just blowing his brains out and walking away. But that would be too easy and too stupid. If I kill him, I lose the only shot I've got at surviving this mess. Hector will come for me, and I'll have nothing to stand on. "Why were you there? Because I know you were there that morning. I want to know why."

"I was delivering diamonds from my truck. Hector sent me to do it. Vincent and Hector worked together."

I waited for him to keep going.

"I dropped them off, like Hector told me to. When I left, I crossed the street and got in my car. That's when I saw a woman pull into the driveway. She got out and walked straight toward the house. I was just about to drive off. But for some reason, I didn't. I watched him open the door and let her inside. That's when I drove off."

He swallowed back some of the blood pooling in his mouth, and his voice cracked. "She was the last one there. Not me. I swear on my family. You've got to believe me on this."

Everything inside me stilled. My breath. My thoughts. My goddamn heart.

I let go of his hair. His head slumped forward. My arms fell limp at my sides. "That's not what the housekeeper said. She said she went to pick up groceries, and Vincent told her to come by a little later because you were coming by. She never mentioned a woman."

"I swear to you," he begged, tugging wildly at the restraints. "I saw her with my own two eyes. I didn't think...I didn't know she was gonna...Please, I didn't kill him! I'm telling you I didn't do it!"

His voice faded into background noise. Because my mind was already racing through every woman I've ever seen near Vincent Accetta, and only one stood out...one with motive, rage, and access.

Renee.

It's not impossible to assume she'd do something like this. There's no doubt in my mind she isn't ruthless enough to kill her own father in cold blood if it meant taking me down with him. Perhaps they got into an argument when Vincent didn't take me out soon enough. So Renee took him out so she could frame me, take everything from me in one clean move. That would make sense that she would say those things to me at the funeral, so the target on my back would grow bigger and more visible. I'm an idiot for not considering this sooner.

I narrowed my eyes back onto Aleksei. "What did this woman look like?"

"She was probably in her thirties. Dark hair, tanned skin. Wearing a dress...I think it was violet, but all I really noticed were the buttons undone at her chest. I figured she was someone he was seeing. She was beautiful...so I stuck around, watched until he let her in. All I know was that she was attractive."

That didn't narrow down anything. But it ruled out Renee. *Maybe.*

"Was she curvy?" I asked, locking eyes with him. If he says yes, it's Renee. But if he doesn't—

"No. Slender. Medium height."

Renee's short with wide hips. I wrack my brain, and it hits me...it's the only woman I've ever suspected. Slender. Medium height. Dark hair. Tanned skin. Early thirties. Access to Vincent. And most importantly...motive.

Lucy fucking Giordano.

"Fuck," I spat, rage boiling over as I lifted the revolver and slammed it down onto the concrete at my feet. Metal cracked, pieces scattered. Aleksei flinched so hard he tipped over in his chair and hit the ground with a thud.

"Get the fuck over here and help him up!" I barked, my voice slicing through the warehouse. My fists dug into my hips as I paced. Sal scrambled to lift him. "Was he happy to see her? Did he look like he trusted her?"

"Yes," Aleksei panted. "He let her in right away. He was smiling and happy to see her."

I raked both hands through my hair and started circling like a caged animal. My heart crashed into my ribs, and I couldn't stop thinking about the avalanche that was about to fall on me. I kidnapped Aleksei, who works for Hector. Now Hector's going to want my head, and the worst part is, I can't deliver Hector to Christopher like I planned, because it wasn't Hector.

It was Lucy.

Unless this guy's lying, but from the sound of it, I doubt it. I know when someone's bullshitting me, and this? Oh, this is the truth. I've got two options—go against everything I stand for, which is not involving women, and deliver Lucy despite that, or take the truth to my grave and let Hector win this game of chess we've been playing for far too long.

I needed to think fast. Damage control. "Sal, take him to the hospital. Get him patched up and seen about. Give him my cut of the shipment." Money should keep him quiet about this encounter. I spun around to face the other men in the room, my finger wagging at each of them, "What happened here tonight is something you don't speak about. If you do, I'll find out, and if I find out, it'll be the last thing you ever tell anyone."

Sal hesitated, blinking like he'd misheard me. I've got enough money that handing over a few grand to keep this guy quiet is more of a gift than a burden.

I crouched down and gripped Aleksei's swollen jaw, making him yelp out in pain. "You just got sixty grand delivered to you in exchange for your silence," I growled. "You'll tell Hector you were robbed by some Russians. Pick a name, anyone you hate and want karma to handle."

He nodded frantically.

"And when I come back for you—and I will—you answer on the first ring, and you do every fucking thing I say. Or you'll find out why they call me the Shark."

I leaned in closer, my lips right at his ear as I growled. "Here's a hint...I always come back to collect. Do you understand what I'm saying to you right now?"

"Yes, yes, yes!" he chanted, trembling against my touch. "I understand! I understand!"

I released his chin with a shove and rose to my feet, turning on my heels. Men lined both sides of me like statues, their eyes lowered as I walked by. I shouldered through the warehouse doors, letting them slam open as the night air slapped me in the face. I sucked in a deep breath. Because now I've got one thing left to do.

Figure out what the fuck my next move is.

Chapter Forty-Nine

Adriana
Fourteen days after Vincent's murder

I turned back to the sink, but my eyes lingered on the TV screen where grainy footage played, a shadowy figure ducking into a car, flashes of sirens, yellow tape billowing in the wind. The words *Another Possible Mafia Involvement* scrolled across the bottom of the screen.

My stomach churned.

It was getting harder to ignore the world pressing in around us. Harder to tell where it stopped and began. I heard the front door open and close again shortly after. There were no footsteps at first, only the soft sounds of movement. I assumed it was Joey, slipping in quietly. When I heard his dress shoes against the hardwood growing louder with each step, there was no mistaking that it was Joey.

A smile tugged at my lips as I continued chopping some fresh lemon slices for my nightly cup of tea, pretending I hadn't noticed the scent of his Old Spice drifting closer and closer. A scent I knew better than my own perfume. Out of the corner of my eye, I saw him stride into the kitchen. He came up behind me, placing both hands on the counter on either side of me, caging me in. He leaned in, brushing his lips against my cheek with a grin I could feel more than I could see.

"Are you trying to get stabbed?" I muttered, still focused on the lemon.

His breath was warm against my neck as he chuckled. "Depends," he said. "Is that how we're doing foreplay now? I might be into it." He pressed a kiss to the side of my neck. His lips brushed the shell of my ear, his warm breath curling down my neck. "I got you something," he murmured. "Turn around, sweetheart."

I had to shift awkwardly in the narrow space, maneuvering my body as he remained planted in place. My hands found his shoulders, and then he leaned in closer, pressing me gently into the counter. His lips found mine, soft at first, then much deeper. I reached behind his neck, pulling him down into me, and his tongue parts my lips. The kiss turned molten, slow, and consumed me completely. His hand slid up my spine as our mouths moved together in perfect sync.

He pulled back enough for me to catch my breath, and that's when I saw it over his shoulder—a lotus plant sitting on the counter behind him. My lips twitched into a smile as I met his eyes again. He was already smiling back at me. "Do you see something you like?"

I fanned my lashes, grinning. "Is that a lotus plant?"

"It is," he said. "For old time's sake."

Something fluttered in my chest as I pulled him down again, my lips seeking his in a kiss that's more eager now than the one before. He kissed me back but paused, his forehead resting against mine. His hands trailed from the counter to my hips, his thumbs brushing my waist as his lips grazed mine with every word he spoke. "There's more, sweetheart."

I glanced over his shoulder again as he stepped aside, and this time I saw the rest of it. Next to the lotus plant: A glass bottle of Diorissimo by Christian Dior, the pale floral fragrance whispering of that feminine springtime flowery scent I adore so much. A block of Beurre d'Isigny, in its parchment wrap, is my favorite French butter that's smooth as velvet and pairs well with Rosa's homemade Italian bread. A tin of Caviar d'Aquitaine, a lustrous black pearl caviar from southwestern France that Lucy has taught me to add on top of the homemade Italian bread, and French butter.

I moved forward, my fingertips trailing over the cool metal tin and butter wrap. I opened the fridge and tucked them inside. When I turned back, Joey was still watching me, one hand in his pocket, the other resting casually at his side.

I lifted the Dior bottle, removed the cap, and spritzed it on my neck, then dabbed my wrists and pressed them together. His eyes found mine again. His head was slightly tilted as he watched me. "Thank you. Where did you get butter and caviar from?" I laughed. It seems so strange to bring this home close to nine at night and so out of the blue.

He shrugged one shoulder, straightened up, and stepped forward. His hand slid to the back of my neck, fingers threading into my hair as he drew me close. "Oh, you know I have my ways," he hummed, his lips brushing mine. "I figured you'd enjoy it with Angela and Lucy."

His mouth claimed mine again. He kissed down my chin, tracing a path to the curve of my neck. He stopped there, his breath warm as he inhaled me like he couldn't get enough. His hands slipped to my hips and started to roam. As though he were reminding me exactly who I belong to. I tried to compress the breathy sigh in my lungs, but it slipped past my lips anyway. He met my gaze, his arms wrapped securely around me, while mine stayed looped behind his neck, keeping him close. "How was your day? Did you miss me?"

"I always miss you," I mumbled. "The question is...did *you* miss *me*?"

A devious smirk spread around his handsome features, and his blue eyes sparkled with mischief. "I always miss you."

The tea kettle started to sing next to us, and Joey reached off, removing it as it turned the burner off. "Where is everyone?"

"Rosa is in bed, and Antonio is with Enzo and Michael."

"Does Antonio even live here anymore, with how much time he spends at Angela's or Lucy's?"

"It's summertime. Plus, he doesn't want to be here with us. You said it yourself, he's too cool for us."

Joey's chuckle was low, almost a growl. "I know. He should be out with his friends..." His hand slid up, brushing a strand of hair off my shoulder, his fingers lingering against my skin like he couldn't quite let go. His eyes swept over me before locking back on mine. "But I was thinking, no one's down here to interrupt us. Just you, me...and that lotus plant making me feel a little nostalgic." His mouth curved into a wicked smile. "Do you remember the kitchen counter? The way you were gasping my name while I had you spread out beneath me?"

He leaned in, his breath warm against my ear. "You've got me thinking about that right now. The way you look, this new hairstyle, the way your lips are begging to be kissed...you're even more irresistible than that night. And all I want is to lay you back and remind you exactly how good it felt."

Joey's fingers traced along my collarbone. His thumb brushed the edge of my neckline, fingertips brushing my skin. "You have no idea," he murmured, his lips grazing my skin, "how hard it is not to take you right here, right now."

My pulse jumped when his hand slid lower, splaying

against my waist, tugging me flush against him. The heat radiating off his body made my knees feel weak. The memory of the kitchen counter blooming in my mind as his mouth found my throat. Each kiss dragged slower, hotter, pulling me deeper until I was completely at his mercy. He tilted my chin up with his knuckles, forcing me to meet his dark, hungry stare.

"I want you like that again. Right here. Right now."

Chapter Fifty

Joey
Sixteen days after Vincent's murder

There's a saying: *when it rains, it pours.*

Well, that doesn't even begin to cover the state of my life.

Two days ago, we intercepted Hector's dock operation. Paul had gone to check on Aleksei who was sixty grand richer but still nursing the bruises from the pistol-whipping I'd given him. To cover himself, Aleksei fed Hector a story: he claimed the truck had been hijacked by Russian men posing as dock inspectors, that he'd been blindfolded the whole time, but recognized a voice. Whoever he handed over was someone Hector quickly erased from history.

The problem was that Hector might play the fool, but he's too conniving to swallow Aleksei's lie. In this business, nobody's word holds weight for long, and I knew the clock was already ticking. It wouldn't take Hector long to start suspecting me.

I walked into Christopher's estate, a place that looked like it belonged in the pages of *Life* magazine. The house was sprawling with polished oak floors and wide hallways cooled by an old rotary fan. Family pictures lined the walls and crowded the shelves, sepia-toned portraits beside more recent color photographs in brass frames. Michael as a small child in his Sunday best, a wedding photo of Hector and Lucy, family vacations at the shore...snapshots of a wholesome life that made the man seem like nothing more than a devoted husband and father. If I didn't know better, I might have believed it. Though Christopher Giordano wasn't just the boss of a crime family. He was *The Butcher*, the most feared name in the city's underworld.

The housekeeper approached. She was a thin Danish woman, her hair pulled into a neat bun, the faint accent in her voice a hand-me-down from her mother, who had served this house before her. She folded her hands politely and smiled. "Mr. Giordano is outside waiting for you, sir."

I smiled and nodded, stepping toward the back door. The screen creaked as I pushed it open, and the sun hit me full force. Christopher lounged in a patio chair, his laughter booming so loud it tangled with the chatter of birds in the trees. His round belly shook with every chuckle.

Across from him sat Hector, leaning forward with his hands braced against his thighs, that rehearsed smile plastered across his face. The second he noticed me, his spine snapped straight. His dark eyes fixed on mine, nostrils flaring like a bull about to charge.

Christopher's short, round frame waddled into my line of sight. He spread his arms wide, a grin stretching ear to ear, and pulled me into an embrace that smelled faintly of cologne and cigar smoke. "Joey! Come, come! Sit with us!"

Christopher steered me toward the empty patio chair, and Hector rose reluctantly, the scrape of his chair loud against the stone. *Sit the fuck down, or I'll use you for target practice* was all I could think, but with Christopher looming between us, waiting, we both slipped on our masks. Two smiling fools, embracing stiffly, recoiling just as quickly, like siblings forced to hug and make nice in front of their parents.

We settled into our seats. A moment later, the housekeeper appeared, balancing a silver tray with tall glasses of lemonade. She set them down, and Christopher flashed her a grin that drew a faint blush to her cheeks. Any man could read that exchange without needing it spelled out. Lucy's mother had been gone for years, and Christopher was pushing sixty. Whatever arrangement he had with his housemaid wasn't my concern.

"So," Christopher sighed, thick fingers curling around his glass of lemonade, "I don't think it's news to you, Joey, that things are getting messy around here. Two days ago, the docks were intercepted by the Russians. Hector believes he found one of the guys—"

"But it's deeper than that," Hector cut in, dark eyes narrowing, his voice low and dangerous. "And I think we can all attest to that, can't we, Joey?" His glare pinned me in place. Either he knows I was involved...or he suspects.

I forced my voice steady. "Why are we doing business with Russians anyway?"

"We aren't," Christopher said, his fingers tapping the glass. "Vincent was, without my knowledge—"

My eyes bounced from Christopher to Hector. He lounged back in his chair, lemonade raised to his lips, but his stare on my side profile was sharp enough to cut steel.

"Now that Vincent is gone," Christopher continued, "and Hector has revealed everything he found out to me, I've had him make sure we put a stop to it. The Russians have always been our enemy. But Hector suspects they got upset by this news, which is why our shipment got hijacked."

"How did you find out Vincent was doing business with the Russians?" I asked Hector.

Hector's gaze burned into me. "Word on the street. I control the docks now, but I hadn't been there in a long time. When I finally visited, some guys filled me in on what had been going on. I put a stop to it immediately."

I nodded slowly. *You lying motherfucker.* "But this is your rig that was stolen?"

"It belongs to the family," Hector said, "but I'm in control of it now that Vincent is gone."

I pressed my back against the patio chair, biting at my cheek to keep from smiling at the anger flickering across his face. "And the driver? Do we know him well, or is he working with the Russians too?"

Christopher's forehead furrowed as his eyes bounced between Hector and me, waiting for an answer.

Hector sat up straighter, his finger wagging as he tried to play it off. "You know, I'm not sure. I think he's one of our guys. I'll have to check on that." His eyes never left mine as he continued. "The driver was kidnapped, blindfolded, beaten, from what I've heard. We lost the shipment, and all the money with it. I can't imagine what that thief will endure when we find out who was behind it. I've already taken one guy out. Though he swore up and down he had nothing to do with it. Usually, they start singing when they're close to death. But not this one. He died swearing he didn't know anything."

Hector leaned forward, his hand thumping the patio table, and I could feel the heat in his gaze. "You know what I suspect, Joey? Whoever was behind his dock operation...was behind the killing of Vincent."

"I wouldn't doubt it one bit—" Christopher began.

I leaned forward, the space between Hector and me shrinking, the air thick enough to choke on. *We're so close to ripping each other's throats out.* "Why would we assume the two acts are connected? It seems we need more dock oversight to ensure things are running smoothly."

Hector smirked into his glass of lemonade, the faintest curl at the corner of his mouth, but I saw it. I saw the malice hidden behind that grin. "Because Vincent was in charge of that rig. Surely it's no coincidence that the one rig he controlled was the one that got hijacked. And as far as more oversight, I'm taking care of that as the underboss of this family, I've got it handled."

Christopher's hands rose, steepling over the table. "I agree. This isn't a coincidence. This was planned and plotted. We need eyes and ears on the streets. We need to figure out who's behind this...someone out there is trying to take us down."

Oh, you're right about that. The person plotting our downfall was sitting right across from us, smiling into his lemonade. My blood ran molten. At this rate, I'd do anything to stain my new suit with his blood if it meant I could rip him apart, piece by piece.

* * *

Everything was coming to a head, and I was coming up empty-handed. Sooner or later, someone would pin the hijacking on my crew and me. Hector had already convinced Christopher that whoever orchestrated it was also behind Vincent's death. But that wasn't the truth. Now, Hector had me cornered, my options shrinking like sand through my fingers. I could come clean about the hijacking, but doing that meant revealing what I had discovered: Lucy was the one who killed Vincent. What kind of man would I be if I handed her over just to save my own skin? Just because Hector didn't pull the trigger himself, or so Aleksei claimed, didn't mean he wasn't guilty of other things. If I could find a way to expose who he really was...maybe then—

"Joey?" Adriana's voice cut through my spiraling thoughts. I jerked my head so fast I half-expected my neck to crack. Through the fogged glass, I saw her shedding her clothes, her slender silhouette blurred by the steam. My head fell back into the water, letting it pound my face, masking the stress still lingering in my chest. It wasn't enough to drown out my thoughts, but it was something I could cling to amidst the thoughts in my mind.

The shower door opened, and Adriana slipped inside. Her wet body pressed against mine, arms wrapping around my waist. I looked down at her and forced an easy-going smile to light up my features. As if everything were fine. Because if there's one person I won't let see me fall apart, it's her. Water streaks across her face. Her brow was drawn in concern as she looked up at me, her breast brushing my bare chest, sending any rational thought out the damn window.

"You okay?" she asked.

I wrapped my arms around her. "Yeah. I'm great now." It wasn't the truth, not fully. It's easier than unloading the war going on inside my head. She can see through me. She knows the parts of me no one else does—the rough, the dark, the broken pieces I don't show anyone. So naturally, she doesn't believe me when I say I'm great.

"I know something's wrong, Joey. You've been quiet through dinner. You've been in the shower for twenty minutes now. You're tense and stressed. I know something's wrong. So please just tell me what it is."

Her hands rose to comb through her thick black hair, the curls unraveling under the water into the soft, frizzy texture she never lets anyone else see. Perhaps I don't tell her enough, but it's my favorite sight of her. The thought of anything happening to me, of leaving her alone in this world, makes something sharp twist inside my chest. She wouldn't be okay, and I know that, like I wouldn't be okay if anything happened to her. We're soulmates, and life means nothing if she's not here to quiet the noise in my head.

My hands skimmed up her slick, wet sides until they settled between her neck and jaw. I tilted her chin up toward me. "Nothing's wrong, sweetheart. I'm just glad you decided to join me," I murmured, brushing her lips with mine.

The kiss was soft, nearly innocent, but her body pressed against mine was anything but that. Her nipples graze my chest, her bare curves molded perfectly to me, and suddenly, everything I'd been thinking before she stepped into this shower is gone. I don't want to feel any of it. I want her to take away the stress.

"Joey." My lips trailed down the curve of her neck. One arm around her waist, the other cupping the firm curve of her ass. She's flush with me. I'm hard, aching, desperate to lose myself in her. "Joey, I *know* something's wrong. I want you to tell me what it is."

I know I can't dodge her forever, but perhaps I can buy a little time.

Nothing's wrong if we don't talk about it, and I've become a master at pretending. I'll acknowledge it after I've gotten a second to breathe her in. After my nervous system stops screaming because she's got the ability to calm it. "You don't understand how badly I need you," I growled into her ear.

It's true. I need her in ways I can't even explain or understand. Right now, I need her legs around my waist, her moans ringing in my ear, her body taking me in until there's nothing else but the sound of water and skin and relief. Until this blush pink shower stall becomes the only place on earth that matters.

"Joey, no. Stop."

A groan slipped out as I released her. My arms dropped to my sides. My back hit the cold tile wall. My face turned up to the stream, letting the water slam into me. Her hands slid to either side of my neck and forced my gaze back down. Her makeup has washed away, her olive-toned skin flushed from the steam, and her thick brows drawn together. Wet black hair fell down her back, frizz creeping in. Her rawest form and the only innocent piece of my life I seem to have left. She's my past. My present. And I hope she's my future.

"I'm serious," she said. There's no teasing in her tone. "I want to know what that was at dinner."

I searched her eyes, hoping she would let up on her interrogation if she saw the exhaustion in my eyes. I think that's what makes her press harder. "Sweetheart, I've had a long day. There's nothing wrong other than I'm tired from the day and I want to press my wife against the shower wall and have my way with her, but she won't let me." I hope the pout on my face pulls at the strings of her heart, but they don't.

She blinked. "I don't believe you, Joey. I know when something is bothering you."

I blinked the water from my eyes. "Nothing." I don't even believe myself. I try again, clearing my throat. "It's nothing, Adriana." Wrong tone again. *Fuck.* My molars ground together. The frustration simmered under my skin like a pot about to boil over at any moment. Now I've got two options: say it again and pray it lands right or confess. Admit that it's not nothing. That it's something. A big something. Risk tainting the only innocent one in this mess.

Adriana's eyes studied me. I couldn't help myself. "Nothing," I said one last time.

She watched me for a second longer before giving me a small nod. Then she turned, opened the glass shower door, and stepped out, slamming it shut behind her.

"Oh, fuck me," I groaned under my breath, water still pouring down.

It could've been so simple. She could've made me forget the hell I was enduring. I could've had her against the tile, her moans echoing in my ear. But no. Now she's mad. Now I've got a pissed-off wife.

I slapped the water off and yanked the door open, grabbing a towel. I dried off fast and wrapped the towel around my waist, moving quickly, but apparently not quick enough. I hear her in the bedroom. Drawers opening and closing loud and hard. I raked my fingers through my wet hair, trying to slick it back, but it fell forward again, soaked and stubborn. Least of my worries. I've got bigger problems at hand right now, and a list of them at that.

I stepped into the bedroom and stopped dead at the threshold. Adriana's already dressed in the *loosest* sense of the word. A light green babydoll nightgown, the one with the little ruffles on the hem, dances against her still-damp skin. It's sheer. I bit down on my bottom lip when I saw the matching green panties beneath the fabric. She's got no bra underneath, either, and definitely no intention of making this easy on me.

She doesn't wear this to sleep.

She wears this to drive me fucking insane, and she may get her wish.

Because now? Well, I guess now I'm fucked. She knows I'll say whatever she wants to get that nightgown off her. Or maybe I won't. Maybe I could keep it on her as I fuck her senseless for getting such an attitude with me.

Either way, I'm ready to confess. I'm willing to do whatever she wants me to do. To say whatever she wants me to say. To get on my knees and beg for her forgiveness if I have to.

She plopped down at the vanity, tugging a brush through her wet hair.

"Sweetheart, can we talk?"

I'm aware of how desperate I sound. I'm desperate to fix

this. I'm desperate to feel her against me, stripping back every layer of stress hidden in my chest, and she could with one simple act. I've got a very specific idea of how this night ends, and it doesn't include me sleeping on the couch. *Again.*

She didn't answer my plea. She keeps brushing, more violently now. A sigh slipped past my lips, and I leaned against the doorframe, my arms crossed over my damp chest. "You're not going to bed mad at me. I won't let you do it."

"I'm not mad at you," she snapped. "And I am going to bed as soon as I'm done with my hair. You can't stop me."

I chuckled because she's so damn cute when she's fiery. "If you keep raking that brush through your hair like that, you won't have any left to do anything with, sweetheart."

The brush slammed onto the vanity, rattling against the marble. Her eyes snapped to mine, daring me to choose my words wisely. She spun to face me, arms crossed over her chest. One leg crossed over the other, every inch of her posture radiating challenge.

I couldn't focus on anything else. My gaze kept drifting to the hem of her skirt, riding higher and higher up her thigh, and the way her arms pressed against her chest, hinting at the curve above, threatening to spill over. Every movement, every angle of her body, caused my cock to harden even more, and I had to fight to keep my thoughts tethered.

"There. Happy?" she hissed. "You have my full, undivided attention even though now my hair's going to dry like this and I'll have to wash it again."

I tugged my lip between my teeth to keep the smirk from painting across my features. "Your hair looks fine like that, sweetheart. What's the point of curling curly hair anyway? Aren't you just making more work for yourself?"

"You wouldn't understand beauty standards. You're a man," she scoffed.

I shrugged. "Maybe. But for the record, you look beautiful exactly like this. I love to see you like this."

Her nose scrunched. "Well, society disagrees. Natural curls aren't exactly 'glamorous wife of Joey Romano' material. I'm supposed to look a certain way."

"Says who? I'd like to speak with whoever told you Joey Romano's wife had to bend to society's rules and standards."

She rolled her eyes. "You wouldn't understand, and you're making a joke out of this to deflect from whatever it is you're hiding from me!"

She's right, but I've already barked up this hill, and I'm not going to stop until it goes deeply south and I'm forced to bend to her will. I lifted both hands in surrender. "Excuse me, but I thought I told you long ago that society doesn't mean shit to us. We make our own damn rules."

She jumped to her feet, and my eyes tracked every inch of her slender frame, taut stomach, olive skin still damp from the shower, and the curve of her perky nipples pressed against the sheer fabric. My thoughts threatened to derail entirely.

"It doesn't work like that!" she snapped, breaking through my haze.

"What do you mean it doesn't work like that?" I countered, forcing my gaze to meet hers, though my focus wavered badly. "I'm one of the head players in the largest organized crime family the United States has ever seen. We make our own rules, our own constitution, our own terms and conditions, and whatever we say is final. So if you want to dye your hair purple, you can. And if anyone has a problem with it...they'll have to deal with me."

Her eyes narrowed, and her head shook. "That's the problem. You only see the world from your point of view...the point of view of a man in a male-dominated society. You make the rules—"

"We make the rules," I shot back, my finger wagging between us.

"No," she said, stepping closer, brown eyes blazing. "*You* make the rules. You put yourself in a position that shines a spotlight on me. I live under a microscope, judged constantly by everyone in this town. Women are always underestimated, pushed aside. And then you think that just because you hold a higher position, you can let your ego run wild within this home. You think you don't have to explain yourself, because I'll just know when to back off. But you're underestimating me—as men always do—and it won't end in your favor."

I pushed off the bathroom door frame, closing the distance between us, my hands resting on her arms to ground us both. "You're right, sweetheart. You're always right. How could I ever forget or underestimate the woman you are?"

I spun her so we faced the vanity mirror. "Look at yourself. You're a fashion sensation. Curls, wild and free, whatever you want, I'll make it happen. Staten Island won't know what hit it." She tried not to smile, but I caught the twitch at the corner of her lips. "And you're my wife. Your hair is perfect just the way it is. Your attitude, on the other hand, might get you into some trouble, but we can negotiate something."

My fingers traced the curve of her waist over the nightgown, and I felt the slightest relief at the warmth of her skin beneath my hands. I leaned in closer, letting my voice dip low, just over a growl against the shell of her ear. "This little nightgown? You know exactly what it does to me. Don't you, sweetheart?" Our eyes stayed locked in the mirror, fire and desire sparking in the reflection.

I let a teasing smirk play on my lips. "Careful. You might find your little rebellion doesn't last long...because when it comes to us, society doesn't matter. Not when we're the ones running it. You know, maybe I should just bend you over and fuck you until you remember we make our own rules and the rest of the world lives by them."

I had her right where I wanted her. Her body pressed against mine, finally relaxing, the fire in her brown eyes giving way to desire. For a moment, there was no Hector, no Lucy, no looming disaster.

"What I want to know," she murmured, "is what's really going on with you. I'm your wife, Joey. And if you meant everything you said just now, then you shouldn't hide anything from me."

Some things are better left hidden.

"I want to know. Or else..." Her words hung between us, eyes locked on mine in the mirror.

My brows drew together. "Or else what?"

"Or else I won't speak to you until you tell me."

I blinked, stunned by the weight of her words. "You're not serious."

Her lips pressed into a firm line, and she stepped away, sitting in the chair in front of the vanity. I'm a man at a crossroads now, and I've got no damn choice. I have to come clean.

I scrunched my face, pressing my fingers into my temples before dropping my hand. Adriana ran the brush through her hair, the strap of her nightgown slipping down her arm, and she made no move to lift it back, perhaps deliberately to torture me.

"Remember when I asked if Lucy could have had any involvement in what happened with Vincent?" I said. She nodded, waiting. "Well...how do you know for sure Lucy didn't do it? Maybe she did it before you all went shopping. Or maybe afterward."

She spun in her chair so fast I had to step back. The fire in her eyes nearly singed me. I've faced killers, done ten years in the can, stared death in the face, but that glare knocked the breath out of me. She shot to her feet. "Because Lucy wouldn't kill anyone! She doesn't have it in her!"

Adriana rarely yells. She plays the game right with mind games, silent treatments, cutting stares that cut deeper than words ever could. Right now, she's shaking with fury, her voice raw and loud, and I know I've crossed into dangerous territory.

"Yes," I pressed, "but how do you *know* she doesn't have it in her?"

"Because she's my friend, Joey. I know she didn't do it!"

"She's my friend, too. I've known her longer than you have, Adriana. I know Lucy, she's impulsive. She's overly emotional at times. And that's a deadly pairing. She feels everything all at once, and she doesn't always know how to handle it. When she's upset, she doesn't think, she reacts. I would know. I've seen it."

Adriana's closing the space between us as I've finished the last word. "Exactly! So if she did something like that, it'd be written all over her face. She'd give herself away! It would be obvious. You wouldn't even be asking me this right now."

I paused. My voice dropped to a near whisper. "Sweetheart...It was a woman who killed Vincent...Supposedly."

The words seem to hit her hard. Her whole body goes still. As though she's been knocked out without the fall. I reached out, brushing her arm, and her eyes snapped to mine. They're wide with horror I can't place. "How do you know that? How'd you find that out? Who told you that?"

"The housekeeper told Ben during an interrogation."

Her eyebrows shot up. "The housekeeper? The housekeeper wasn't even there."

"No. But she knew Vincent's schedule."

"Tell me exactly what she said," Adriana ordered. It's not a request. I know, I won't be able to keep Operation Icebox from her much longer.

"She said Vincent had a meeting that morning with someone named Aleksei. When Aleksei was leaving, he saw a woman walking in."

Her head tilted. "So what? That doesn't prove anything. How do you know this Aleksei guy isn't lying? How do you know the woman he saw was the one who killed Vincent?"

I don't have an answer. Not a good enough one, at least. "He might not be telling the truth, but I've got a good feeling he is."

"Then how do you know it wasn't the housekeeper who killed Vincent? She's a woman. It could've been her."

"It wasn't. Aleksei said the woman he saw was in her thirties, with dark hair, tan skin, slender build. She was wearing a violet dress with the chest undone."

Adriana shakes her head, doubtful. I get it, but I can't ignore what my gut's telling me. "That could be anyone, Joey. I know it wasn't Lucy."

"Yeah, it could. But I've got to figure out who it was because if I don't, Hector's going to make sure I disappear. He hates me, and he's not going to stop until I'm out of the picture. So I need to be smart about this. I have to figure it out before he does."

Adriana stiffened again. I hate this part. I didn't want to tell her any of this, but it's come to that. I reached for her hand. "Don't worry, sweetheart. I'm close. You've got to trust me. I've almost got this figured out."

Her eyes met mine. The tension in her jaw faded, and she forced a toothy smile. And then the thought hits me like ice down the spine.

She...she wouldn't cover for Lucy.

Would she?

Chapter Fifty-One

Antonio
Sixteen days after Vincent's murder

I'm standing in the middle of the warehouse. It's pitch black and freezing cold. My heart is slamming against my ribcage. I know this feeling. It's familiar. It's exactly how I felt in the back of the semi-truck.

Where did the table go? The chairs? The lights? Where the hell is everyone?

I pressed my hand against the wall, fumbling along its surface in search of a light switch, cursing myself for not paying attention when I was here days before. My hands are shaking in fear. I feel something wet beneath my bare feet.

Bare feet? Where the hell are my shoes?

I bent down, touched the cold puddle pooling around me, and rubbed the thick liquid between my thumb and two fingers. Up close, even in the dark, I can see it, dark and red.

Blood.

My stomach lurched. Sal must've killed that man tied up in the chair. Or worse, Joey did. The air rushed out of my lungs. My throat feels like a collapsing tunnel. How the hell did I end up back here? Then, I hear footsteps.

Thank God. Someone's coming.

I spun around as the light flicked on overhead. I shielded my eyes with the back of my hand. When I lowered my hand, I saw them. A wall of people. Not just people, the same guys from a few nights ago. No one says a word. I'm standing in the middle of the warehouse, soaked in blood. It's everywhere. On me. Around me. But the man who was tied to the chair is now gone.

Did they get rid of him? What do they want with me? I've done everything right.

Sal lifted a finger to his lips and whispered, "Shhhhhh."

I didn't move a muscle. I held my breath. I kept my mouth shut. Joey appeared out of nowhere. I don't even know how he got in here. I don't understand how he appeared out of thin air. The moment I saw him, my entire body locked up. Half of his face is there. The left side is blown apart. A bullet hole gapes in his chest. The same shot I gave him, but this looks worse. He limps toward me as blood spills across the floor, rising, climbing up my legs as if I'm standing in a tank filled with it.

It isn't water. It's Joey's blood.

"You were supposed to save me, kid. But you killed me. You betrayed me." He collapsed onto the floor after he said it.

I screamed, shaking my head, my eyes shut tight in horror. When I opened it again, I was standing outside. There's snow falling from the gray sky. It's freezing. I have no coat. No shoes. I stood in the middle of the empty street, trembling, barefoot in the snow. I don't know how I got here. But I know one thing for sure. If I don't move fast, I'm in trouble.

I see the house in the distance. I take out running for it until I'm at the front door. The lights are on. I hear Ma's laughter through the windows. Relief floods my system. I reached for the doorknob and twisted it. It doesn't open.

I pounded on the door in panic. "Ma! Open the door!" I

start hitting harder until my knuckles split and bleed, but no one comes. Room by room, the lights flicker off inside the house. But not my bedroom. That light stays on.

I spin around to run to Enzo's. Or Michael's. Someone. Anyone. But when I turn, I'm no longer on the porch. I'm back at Red Hook. Stepping off the semi-truck. All the guys are there, cheering and clapping. "Nino! Nino!" Their faces start to stretch. Distort. Skin melts like candle wax. Their eyes hollow out, black voids where their souls should be. Their mouths gape open in silent screams. I tried to run, but my feet won't move. They're locked in place. Cemented to the ground. I see someone coming toward me. When I squint to get a better look, I realize it's a small boy. He's maybe ten. As he steps into the light, I feel my bile travel up my throat.

He has my brown eyes. My thick eyebrows. My messy brown curls. Oh fuck. He's me.

I tried to back away, but I'm literally cemented to the pavement.

"You said you wouldn't be like them," he said. His voice trembled, and he was crying. There's a revolver in his hand, the same one I used on Joey. Now he's pointing it at me. I shake my head, my eyes blown wide, and I'm terrified. "Don't—" I started, but I couldn't finish. I glanced down. Blood is soaking through my shirt. I pat at my chest, searching for a wound. I feel no pain. I found no bullet holes. There's blood spilling out of my body somehow.

When I look up again, the boy is gone. Now I'm back in the warehouse. Joey's dead on the floor in front of me. His face is pale. What's left of it anyway. I'm on my knees, and the floor beneath me is slick with blood. I couldn't tell if it's my blood. Or Joey's blood. Maybe it's both. Now I can't seem to get up. Every time I tried, I slipped, and soon everything was spinning.

I hear a voice. "I saw you."

I whipped around. A woman is standing behind me. Her face is hidden in shadow. I knew her voice, but I couldn't place it. I opened my mouth to ask who she was, but all that came out was a scream. I'm not sure if I'm screaming in the dream anymore because when I wake, I'm soaked in sweat, gasping for breath, my throat hoarse from screaming.

The clock blinked: 2:03 a.m.

It was another nightmare.

I pushed myself out of bed and padded quietly to the door. I cracked it open. The house was peaceful. Everyone asleep. The soft lighting from the hallway spills across the floor, guiding me to the bathroom. I slipped inside, shut the door, and locked it behind me. My hands gripped the counter as I leaned in toward the mirror.

Who the hell am I becoming?

That dream felt too real.

I twisted the faucet on and splashed cold water on my face, hoping to wake up the part of me that still feels like I'm trapped in a nightmare. I'm going to save Joey. That dream it's just my head messing with me. I'm not going to hurt him ever again. I'd never let anything happen to him. As far as I know, I cleared Joey's name the other night. I can rest knowing I made right on my wrong. That nagging voice in my head keeps telling me, even if I've cleared Joey's name. I'm not done. This isn't over. In fact, it's only the beginning—that I'm not becoming someone else. I'm becoming who I was always meant to be.

A soft knock rattled the door. I nearly jumped out of my skin. "Are you alright in there?" Rosa's voice is soft, but it sliced through the silence and left goosebumps scattered along my arms. I pressed a hand to my chest, catching my breath, and shut off the faucet.

"Yeah," I called back. "Just finishing up." I dried my face with one of Ma's decorative towels. Unlocking the door and stepping into the hallway, I find Rosa still there, with her arms crossed.

"Do you need anything?" she asked.

I shook my head. "No, I'm good. Thanks." I started walking back toward my room. "Goodnight, Rosa."

I've almost reached my bedroom door when her voice stops me cold. "You're the spitting image of him."

My heart dropped into my gut.

Please don't be another goddamn nightmare.

I closed my eyes, bracing myself for whatever came next. Though when I open them, I'm still in the hallway. Rosa's still there, watching me with her arms crossed. "Who? Who am I the spitting image of?"

She sighed. "Your Father. Joey."

I swallowed. My pulse pounded like it wanted out of my throat. My hand traveled to my neck, trying to calm it. "What do you mean? Maybe you should get some rest."

"When he was a teenager," Her words stopped me from turning the doorknob and slipping back into my bedroom, "he had nothing but me and what little I could give him. I tried to help. But Joey always had plans of his own."

I'm frozen solid. I have to check if I'm not back in that nightmare where my feet are cemented to the floor.

"You remind me so much of him," she continued. "I used to find him in the bathroom late at night. His hands were under the faucet, scrubbing with water so hot it blistered his skin. I didn't know what was wrong at first. I figured whatever trauma he went through before I took him in must've been worse than I thought. But it wasn't the past he was trying to scrub off. It was the present. The crowd he'd gotten mixed up with. The things he was doing. That's what he wanted gone."

Her words closed in around me. Maybe Joey had been innocent his whole life. Maybe it was life that did him wrong. I felt something rising in my chest, threatening to choke me, but I swallowed it down. "I'm not doing anything wrong, Rosa. I was just using the bathroom."

"Does your mother know you have those nightmares?"

I spun around to face Rosa. Her eyes searched mine, and I wondered what she found when she looked into their darkness. "The truth would devastate them, Antonio. Especially Joey. I hear things, and I'm asking you...If you're involved in something—*anything*—stop before it ruins your life. Like it did his."

"I appreciate everything you've done for me, Rosa." I try to keep the emotion out of my voice, but it threatens to choke the life out of me. "You should remember, this is a small town. People talk. Not everything they say is true. You know that better than anyone."

She shook her head in disbelief. "You even sound like him. Oh, you're going to destroy them when they find out what you've done, and I pray I'm long gone before the day comes."

I opened my mouth, but nothing came out. I knew if I said one more word, it wouldn't be words I let loose. I turned around and walked straight into my bedroom, shutting the door behind me. I threw myself onto the bed, wanting to crumble, but there was no point. Not when I'm this deep in, and I don't want to be set free.

One thing's clear: Rosa doesn't have a *single* ounce of dementia.

She knows *exactly* what's going on.

Chapter Fifty-Two

Joey
Seventeen days after Vincent's murder

I rolled over in bed, reaching out for Adriana, hoping to bury my face in the soft curtain of her frizzy black hair, to breathe in that sweet, flowery scent she always wears. My hand, however, found nothing but cool sheets. She wasn't in bed with me anymore. I sat up, scanning the bedroom. It was empty, still wrapped in the light of early morning. I pulled on my robe and made my way downstairs. As soon as my feet hit the bottom step, I heard Rosa. "Want cream, Adriana?"

I already knew the answer before Adriana spoke. "Yes. No sugar." And it can only be Borden's.

That made me smile as I followed the sound and found her in the living room, curled up on the couch in her robe. Rosa was busy in the kitchen. It all felt so domestic, so normal. I almost forgot that I'm in a world of shit outside of this house. I almost forgot the terrible thought that flooded my mind last night...the thought that Adriana would knowingly cover for Lucy. Her brown eyes find mine. "Good morning, sweetheart," I said, pushing the thought out of my mind. There's no way she would do that. I can't allow myself to think such thoughts because I'm paranoid. I leaned over the couch, placing a hand on the back cushion and bending down to press a kiss to her temple. "The bed's cold without you."

Rosa rounded the corner, holding a mug in her hands. "I couldn't sleep," Adriana said.

"Good morning, Joey," Rosa chimed cheerfully, her face brightening when she saw me. "Care for some coffee?"

I nodded. "I'll take some, thanks." I prefer mine without cream or sugar.

A newspaper is folded in Adriana's lap, face down, so I can't see what the headlines say. I gestured toward it as I planted myself next to her. "Are you reading that?"

"I'd rather not read anymore of it," she muttered, tossing it onto my lap.

Right there on the front page is my mugshot from 1950. The headline read: *Joey Romano: Guilty as Charged.*

A dry laugh slipped past my lips as Rosa returned with my mug of hot coffee. "What exactly is Joey Romano guilty of, Rosa?"

She chuckled. "Well, being a charmer, for starters."

I nudged Adriana with my elbow, trying to coax a smile from her. She didn't find us funny. She took a long sip of her coffee, her eyes somewhere far away. Rosa disappears into the kitchen again. "Come on, sweetheart. I thought we worked it all out."

"We did," she sighed, but her eyes didn't meet mine.

"Then tell me what's going on in that head of yours? If I have to tell you, it only seems fair you have to do the same." It's a joke, but the annoyance on her face tells me I'm pushing my luck again.

She let out a sigh and lifted the newspaper off the coffee table, holding it up between us, my old mugshot staring back at me in black-and-white ink. "Do you ever wonder what life would be like if *this* weren't our world?"

I smirked. "Are you saying you don't like waking up to my face in the morning paper anymore?"

She didn't crack a smile. I took the newspaper from her hand and tossed it onto the coffee table. "Come on, sweetheart. That mugshot wasn't even my best one. You should have seen the one from 1939 or 1942."

Her lips twitched, the faintest pull of a smile trying not to show. "I'm being serious, Joey," she said into her coffee mug.

I reached over with one hand and found her thigh, giving it a squeeze, while my other hand cradled my mug. "Every day, I thank God you're in my world. I don't waste time thinking about lives we'll never get to live. It's a luxury people like us don't have. And without you, none of it would matter anyway. Whether it's this life or some other one, I'd still find you. I'd still choose you. That's what I know. And that's what you should know."

When her eyes meet mine, there's a quiet tenderness in them. "How would you even know it was me in another life?"

A low chuckle rumbled from my chest. "Because I couldn't forget you. Not in this life. Not in any of them. You give me a reason to keep going. You're my compass, so I'd find you, sweetheart. There's no question about that."

She tried to keep her walls up, but I saw the tiniest crack in her armor. A smile finally broke through. That's all I needed.

* * *

I stood in front of the vanity mirror, fixing the cuffs of my suit. My reflection looked like a man in control, but my gut said otherwise. I hadn't spoken to Aleksei since that night. How the hell was he still breathing? If Hector hadn't had him slaughtered, it meant Aleksei was useful to him, valuable in a way I hadn't figured out yet. That told me everything I needed to know: Hector was onto me.

I could already see the trail he'd carve, name after name, blood soaking every stop along the way. He'd torture, he'd murder, he'd leave them with a tragic choice: stay quiet and endure the punishments Hector deemed fit...or open their mouths and endure the ones I delivered. Either way, it wasn't a fair game. And I was the one caught in the middle because—

"Joey?" Adriana's voice cut through my thoughts.

I turned. She was framed in the doorway, her hair loosely tied back, curls slipping free around her face. She'd changed since we'd had coffee downstairs, looking softer now, but her eyes carried something deeper beneath the surface.

"Yeah, sweetheart?" She stepped into the room and shut the door behind her. That simple sound of wood against the frame felt like a lock clicking shut on the rest of the world. "Can you stay with me for a little bit today?"

I paused, cufflink half fastened, weighing what she was really asking. My mind spun with Hector, Aleksei, Lucy, but here was Adriana, planting herself in the middle of it, her voice steadier than she appeared to feel.

"I need to go to the grocery store, and I don't want to go alone. You can come with me, then go to work. But I'm not going without you."

It wasn't about the grocery store. Perhaps, she wanted to keep me in her orbit, close enough to make sure I didn't make the missing headlines. Last night's argument had cracked something between us, something neither one of us spoke about. I knew better than to argue. I wasn't in the mood to dig myself into another hole either.

"Whatever you want, sweetheart."

* * *

The summer heat clung to us the second we stepped outside. I opened the passenger door for her, and she slid inside without a word, clutching her purse in her lap. I rounded the hood and climbed behind the wheel. The leather seat stuck to the back of my shirt as I started the engine. I reached across the bench seat and caught her hand in mine. Her fingers didn't soften, didn't lace through mine like they usually did. Her gaze stayed fixed out the window, lips sealed, profile unreadable as the breeze lifted a curl from her cheek. I tapped my fingers against the steering wheel, each beat sharp and hollow in the heavy stillness. I'd faced down killers with less tension than what filled this car.

I tried to think positively about this. Negative energy feeds off negative energy. If Adriana wasn't going to lighten up, then I had to be optimistic for both of us. On the plus side, we were about to do something we'd never done before—grocery shop together. "You know," I said, rolling the wheel with one hand, "this feeling's kinda nice."

Her head turned, black cat-eye sunglasses hiding half her face, but I could see the scrunch in her nose. "What feeling are you referring to?"

Delusion, probably. I smirked. "Domestic bliss. Running errands with my beautiful wife. Maybe we can argue about what kind of bread to buy."

"That's what you think this is? Arguing over bread? Please. I don't buy that processed junk. Rosa bakes it fresh twice a week. When have you ever seen Wonder Bread in our kitchen?"

Fair. I was trying too hard to play normal when maybe we were anything but. I shrugged, glancing at her side profile, olive skin glowing in the summer light, plump lips painted a perfect red, curls slipping from her scarf. "Alright. So maybe we argue about which box of cereal to grab. I'll push for Frosted Flakes, you'll push for Cheerios, and we'll see who caves first."

"You're out of your mind." She leaned her elbow against the open window, the hot air rushing in and pulling at her scarf. "You're talking about breakfast like we actually eat it together. You don't even sit at the table most mornings anymore."

"Then maybe I'm trying to change that," I murmured, tilting my head until it rested on the back of the seat. One hand steady on the wheel, the other still tangled with hers, though she wasn't giving me much back. "Maybe I like the idea of being normal and domesticated."

She turned, and I caught her arched brow over the edge of her sunglasses. "Why are you trying to act like we're normal people all of a sudden, Joey?"

I chuckled under my breath, though the question landed heavy. Normal people didn't ride around in Ferraris. Normal people didn't wake up every morning and see their faces in the newspapers. But maybe we could pretend for a morning.

I shrugged, still smiling. "I mean, if you ignore the mugshots in the paper, the news trying to paint me as the villain, and the fact that you're half-convinced I'm not coming home every night...then yeah, I'd say we're about as normal as it gets." My joke fell flat, missing its mark entirely. I tightened my grip on her hand. "Come on, sweetheart," I coaxed. "Show me that pretty smile. It was just a joke. I thought it'd make you laugh."

She sighed, leaning her head back against the car seat. "Can we just get this over with?"

I tried again, forcing a grin. "I like your hair today. Did you take my advice? Should I make it mandatory that every woman in Staten Island copies this look?"

She let out a sharp huff, lips pursed, but didn't bother rewarding me with an answer.

I pulled into the grocery store lot, and before I could even throw it in park, Adriana had already opened her door, stepping out with her chin tucked, sunglasses shading her eyes, her summer dress cinched at the waist. She smoothed her skirt with one laced gloved hand, her purse clutched tight in the other. I caught up, sliding my palm to the small of her back, and together we crossed the lot. The automatic doors opened, and we stepped into the blast of too-cold air and harsh fluorescent light.

That's when it hit me dead in the face.

My mugshot.

Front page.

The same damn paper we'd seen on the coffee table this morning, only now it was stacked high in the metal rack by the entrance. My younger self stared back at me, cuffed wrists, that same cocky smirk I'd give anything to erase right now.

I let out a low chuckle. "Well, would you look at that?" I tilted my head toward the stack of papers by the entrance. "Guy cleans up alright. Don't you think, sweetheart?"

Adriana didn't dignify me with a word. She stormed over, heels clicking against the flooring, and yanked the top papers off the stack. One by one, she slammed them back down face-first, hard enough to rattle the rack. Then she attacked the next pile, flipping every last copy over.

A few heads turned. A mother clutching her son's hand froze mid-step; two men by the produce section glanced over their shoulders. As soon as their eyes landed on me, and then on Adriana's furious movements, they looked away quickly. Nobody wanted to get involved in mafia business. Adriana strode back, hips swaying with every step. She bumped me with her hip as she snatched the basket straight from my hand.

I let out another laugh, falling into step beside her as we pushed deeper into the aisles.

"Real subtle, sweetheart," I murmured, low enough for only her to hear.

She stopped dead in her tracks and spun, a burning fire in her eyes. "You really think this is funny?"

"Funny? No. But watching you terrify half the store with that attitude? Now that's something."

She huffed and fished a folded list out of her purse with all the grace of a dagger being drawn. Without another word, she marched on, tossing items into the basket like each can and box had personally wronged her. By the time we turned into the cereal aisle, I threw my arms up as if I'd stumbled on the Holy Grail. "Oh, look at that, sweetheart. The promised land. The cereal aisle!"

"Behave," she warned, already scanning the shelves with the precision of a general surveying troops.

I plucked a box of Corn Flakes and held it up proudly. "This one screams American family. Picture it, sweetheart... you, me, Antonio, a few more little rascals, Rosa, and a white picket fence with a dog named Sparky. We eat our Corn Flakes and watch cartoons on Sunday Mornings. We pay our taxes on time. We don't see our mugshots in the papers. What do you think?" I smiled like I was the poster boy for Corn Flakes.

Her lips twitched, fighting a smile. "I think the only thing missing from that picture is you actually showing up for breakfast and paying your taxes."

"Ohhh," a laugh rumbled low in my chest. She tried to smother her smile, but it tugged at the corners anyway. I stepped close enough that my shadow fell over her, lowering my voice until it was more of a murmur. "You know what? I'm not leaving the house until I have breakfast. Every morning. You'll be so sick of me hanging around that you'll start shoving me out the door." I cocked a brow, smirking. "As for the taxes...well, sweetheart, I'll do my best. But the line of work I'm—"

Her laugh broke free this time, light and free, as she swatted at my chest.

"Which one do you want?" I asked, sweeping a hand dramatically at the wall of cereal boxes.

"I don't eat cereal, Joey. Antonio and Rosa love Cornflakes, Frosted Flakes, Cheerios...any of those are fine."

"I didn't ask about them. I asked you. You've gotta pick one."

She huffed, crossing her arms, her chin tipped up in defiance. "Nope. You pick. I told you, I never eat it."

I leaned in, my voice dropping low. "I'll decide...if you pick first."

Her lips parted, her eyes flicking to mine like she couldn't decide if I was serious or just trying to drive her crazy. She let out a tight breath. "Fine. Cornflakes."

I tapped my chin, drawing it out, enjoying every second of her exasperation. "Mmm...see, I was leaning more toward Frosted Flakes."

Her mouth twitched, the laugh bubbling before she could contain it. She caught it behind her hand, shaking her head. "Joey, you're being ridiculous. Just get the damn Frosted Flakes. I'm not eating either one."

I plucked the box off the shelf, tossed it into the basket with a grin. "Frosted Flakes it is. See? We make a great team, sweetheart. Breakfast of champions...and lovers."

Adriana rolled her eyes, bumping my arm with her elbow, smiling.

"You know," I murmured, leaning down so only she could hear, "I heard that laugh back there. I know you're trying to give me a hard time, but—"

"Would you cut it out?" she said, swatting at me, though the corners of her mouth betrayed her every time.

"You gonna make me if I don't?" I teased, winking. Her smirk lingered. As we moved down the aisle, it vanished. "What's wrong now?" I asked.

"Nothing." Her eyes dropped to the scuffed tile floor, hands gripping the cart.

"Adriana..." I sighed, slowing my steps to match hers. "Would you just tell me, so maybe I can fix it?"

Her eyes scanned the crowd, wary. "Everyone's staring at us."

"Yeah, that's nothing new. Especially after you made all that commotion at the front, flipping those papers over."

Her gaze snapped to mine, intense. "The papers with your mugshot, you mean? This isn't admiration, Joey. This is people trying to pin a murder on you. And you said it yourself, Hector is closing in."

She brushed her shoulder against mine as we edged forward in line, the heat from her touch sending a jolt through me. I could feel the subtle press of her body against mine with every step, the faint scent of her perfume mingling with the sterile air of the store. Her hand rested on the cart, fingers tightening and loosening as if holding back the fear she refused to voice.

I helped her load the groceries onto the conveyor belt, my fingers grazing hers. The cashier, a young girl no older than sixteen, gave me a wary glance, her eyes wide as if she could see the danger lurking just beneath my calm exterior. I flashed her a big, disarming smile. "Good morning."

She swallowed hard, the motion tight in her throat. "Good morning."

Adriana's hand shot to her side, swatting my thigh in a subtle, silent plea to stop. I obeyed, though the smirk on my face refused to fade. My chest still throbbed with the heat of her closeness, the press of her shoulder lingering. Every subtle movement she made—tilting her head, brushing a strand of hair from her face—felt like a challenge, daring me to keep my composure.

The conveyor belt rattled under the weight of the groceries. The tension between us was unspoken, but I felt it deep in my chest. Once we got outside, I opened the door for Adriana and helped her into the passenger seat. Then I loaded the groceries into the back and returned the cart. Sliding into the driver's seat, I barely had time to settle in when she asked, "Why did you scare that girl?"

I chuckled. "I didn't scare her. Maybe I intimidated her. And that was hardly my own doing. But nothing could intimate anyone as badly as you flipping my mugshot over like you did."

Her voice dropped to a hiss. "Joey, this isn't a joke. What I think you should do is just take Hector out. You can—"

"Wait. What?"

"—do it without anyone knowing. Make him disappear." Her eyes locked onto mine, deadly serious. "For all anyone knows, whoever killed Vincent could have killed Hector. They'll assume it was you if they want, but at least you'd be in control. You've got to act before he does something irreversible."

"Adriana..."

"Do you see how they stare at me? Everywhere I go, like I'm some freak in a cage. They already think you're a murderer. I'd rather live with that than end up a grieving widow because Hector decided to do God knows what to you."

I ran a hand over my face, momentarily stunned. "It's almost over anyway. When the truth comes out, which it will very soon, the joke's going to be on all of them."

"Yeah...I'm sure. And what do you think the truth is? That

some woman took Vincent out just because some gangster said so? And that woman is Lucy? So what...are you going to turn her over?"

"What? Of course not—"

"Then what's the alternative, Joey? You don't turn her in and take the blame yourself? You can't be serious right now."

I pinched the bridge of my nose, my heart hammering. Every instinct in me screamed that if Hector found out the truth, I would be as good as dead. And Adriana...she'd be in the crossfire too. My jaw tightened. "I didn't say that."

"You didn't have to. You implied it. And if you think I'm going to let that happen, you're crazy." Her voice trembled, a mix of fury and fear that made the air between us feel suffocating.

"Nothing's going to happen to me." I kept that thought like a shield, but the truth rattled around in my gut. I couldn't just sit back. "I'm not turning Lucy in. I don't even know if what was said is true. I—"

"Just kill him," she snapped, her hand grabbing my arm, pressing me with an intensity that made my pulse spike. "Get it over with so we can move on with our lives!"

Her proximity was kinetic. I could feel the heat of her body, the press of her hand, the way her brown eyes were flaring with desperation. Yet, her demand tore at me. Every part of me wanted to protect her, but I couldn't let my hands get dirty themselves on Hector...not yet. Not until I had a plan in place.

I swallowed, letting the tension thrum through my chest. The grocery store faded into the background. People, carts, and shelves become irrelevant. My fingers flexed against hers. "Adriana...you know, I'll protect you. I'll take care of Hector, and our lives will go back to normal, soon enough."

It wasn't exactly the truth, but sometimes a little white lie makes life easier to swallow.

Chapter Fifty-Three

Adriana
Seventeen days after Vincent's murder

Joey dropped me off at home, helped unload the groceries, and then headed to work. I couldn't sit still in that house, not with everything bouncing around in my head. So I grabbed my purse and headed straight to *Cosa Bella.*

The moment I stepped inside the salon, I was hit with a wall of noise and the scent of hairspray and cigarettes. The place was packed because this wasn't just a salon, it was a status symbol. Every woman in the city either went here or wished she could. Lucy was behind the register when I walked in. A few women turned to look my way, and just as quickly turned back. Maybe it was the fact that I was Joey Romano's wife. Maybe it was the state of my hair. Either way, the judgment was immediate.

"Good morning, Adriana," Lucy called out.

"Good morning," I hummed, scanning the room. I'd parked right next to her car, but she was nowhere to be seen. "Where's Angela?"

Lucy smirked, tilting her head toward the back of the salon.

"Funny story. Marco stopped by to fix that light in the back... and apparently, Angela decided he might need some assistance. It's been a while, so...I'll leave the rest to your imagination."

"Well, I really need my hair done. I know you're busy, but—"

"Adriana, I am never too busy for you. We make room for Mrs. Romano here at Cosa Bella." She rounded the register and clutched my arm. Looping her arm through mine, resting her head briefly on my shoulder as she guided me toward the back. "Come on. I'll personally get you washed and styled back to perfection, my darling."

"Thank you, Lucy," I said, grateful as I sank into the padded chair. I leaned back, letting my neck settle into the sink's groove while she unraveled the frizzy mess I'd pulled back in a desperate attempt to look presentable.

"So," Lucy said as she worked. "What's going on with you? You look like you've been through hell." She lowered her voice, glancing around to make sure no one was listening. Then she leaned in, her breath brushing my ear. "I'm guessing Joey told you what he found out," she whispered. "Ben told me this morning. I don't think I believe it. You know they love to blame women for everything."

I nodded. "Who does Ben think it is?" I asked, glancing up at Lucy as her manicured fingers combed through my wet hair.

"I was interrogated until I almost slapped him straight into 1970," she said, and I burst out laughing. I could just imagine it —Lucy had zero tolerance for being accused of anything, especially by Ben, of all people. The idea that Joey or Ben could even think Lucy would be involved in something like this was ridiculous. "He thinks it could be Angela. Honestly, he had me convinced, too. She's quick to..." Lucy raised her hand and dragged it across her throat in a slicing motion.

"I asked her," Lucy said, lowering her voice again. "She

swore up and down it wasn't her. Angela wouldn't dare lie about something like that. Not to me. Sooo...I think it was Renee."

"It has to be. But Joey says the description doesn't match."

Lucy scoffed. "Oh, please. Who needs a description? We know how vile she is. And if it wasn't her, she's at least thought about it. Which basically makes her guilty. And if it wasn't her, the list of women that man wronged could be endless."

"That's true. He was terrible. I think he got what was coming to him."

"Oh, no doubt. And the woman who delivered it should have a national holiday named after her, unless it is Renee," she said, working the shampoo into my scalp. "Oh! Speak of the devil! Were your ears burning?" Lucy grinned, her eyes drifting toward the front of the salon. I followed her gaze, and Angela and Marco stood behind the register. "Please tell me you actually fixed it, Marco," Lucy called out.

Marco gave a charming little shrug. "Everything's fixed, Lucy."

Lucy tilted her head, smirking. "I only asked you to fix one thing. What else needed fixing, Marco?"

He let out a laugh as he headed for the door. "I don't know what you're talking about. See ya, Lucy!"

Angela sauntered over and gave my knee a gentle pat before sliding into the chair beside me. "Why are you always trying to mess with him?" she asked Lucy.

"Well, excuse me for not realizing it takes two people to fix one flickering light switch," Lucy muttered, rinsing the suds from my hair. She glanced down at me with a knowing look. "Since when did you become so openly friendly with Marco anyway?"

Angela gave a casual shrug. "Since now. Marco's a good man."

Lucy and I both turned our heads toward Angela. It wasn't like her to hand out compliments to men. "What's going on here?" Lucy asked, raising an eyebrow. "Is he that talented at changing light bulbs?"

I couldn't help the soft laugh that escaped my lips.

Angela smirked. "He's *very* good at...changing light bulbs," she said, and for the first time since I'd known her, I saw the faintest blush creep into her cheeks.

Lucy gasped, loudly enough to turn a few heads across the salon. "Wait a minute," she said, eyes wide. "Is there a development in this relationship you want to share with the class, Angela?"

Angela let out a slow sigh. "I've always had a soft spot for him. I guess...time will tell. But for now, my lips are sealed until any serious developments have been made."

"But you're open to something happening? I never thought I'd see the way, you'd let him off his leash—"

"He's not on a leash!"

"—And sit at the table with you in public. Goodness, gracious." Lucy exclaimed, pretending to fan herself. I snickered. "Adriana wasn't here to see him follow you around our entire life with puppy dog eyes and drool collecting at his collar."

"Adriana, ignore her. Marco did not have drool collecting at his collar. Nor did he have puppy dog eyes. And anyway, this isn't a new development. We've had...relations...before. But things seem to be getting more and more serious. How am I supposed to explain that to the kids? He's their godfather."

"And the only father they've ever *really* known. Let's be honest. Marco has done more for you and the kids than Vin could have ever done."

Angela sighed and nodded. "Val has two years, and Enzo

has four before they are adults and out living their lives. What is another four years of waiting?"

"Another four years, Angela!" Lucy exclaimed.

"Angela, what about your happiness? Wouldn't the kids want that for you?" I asked, my eyes bouncing from Lucy to Angela. "They love Marco. They must know something is happening between you two. So really...why the wait?"

"They're both terrified of commitment," Lucy said from the corner of her mouth.

Angela waved Lucy's comment off, but I had a feeling it was the truth. "Is this what you two were gossiping about when you asked me if my ears were burning?"

"No," Lucy said. "We were talking about how Ben suspected I killed Vincent. And I was appalled that he thought I could do it. And then I thought perhaps you'd done it, but you said you didn't—"

"Wait, you two really think I would shoot a man? Poison, perhaps. That's more of my cup of tea. And even then, the only man on my radio of a sleepy cocktail is Hector."

If only someone would give Hector that sleepy cocktail. "How's it going at home, Lucy?" I asked as Lucy grabbed a towel and gently wrapped it around my head, patting my hair dry before guiding me to a styling chair in front of the mirror.

"You mean with Hector?" she asked, and I nodded. She started brushing through my damp curls. "He's hardly ever home. Thank God for that. And when he is, I start seriously considering Angela's offer. But he leaves before I can decide."

"What are you waiting for? He's vile." Angela asked with a teasing grin. Though it was just a joke. I secretly wished it would manifest into reality.

Lucy chuckled under her breath as she ran the brush through my hair. "I think I'm waiting on the final straw. I have

Michael to consider. What am I going to tell him? I murdered your father?"

"Christ, no!" Angela spat. "You'll say he died of a heart attack."

"I'll say he had a heart attack?" Lucy repeated. Angela nodded.

"Have you ever followed him into the city to see this little family he's supposed to have?" I asked. Angela was behind her, perched on the edge of the chair, inspecting her manicure, but when I asked the question, both their eyes bounced to mine.

"No, I haven't."

"It's just a thought. But maybe that's the last straw." *One could only hope.*

Angela straightened up, her posture no longer relaxed. "That'd be more than the last straw. That'd be the fire that burns the whole house down."

Lucy didn't say anything right away. Her eyes bounced between Angela and me, like she was watching a chessboard, trying to anticipate the next three moves. "I prefer to live two separate lives," she said, brushing a bit of hair off my shoulder as she worked.

"I know. I did too. For years. But eventually, the walls between those lives cracked. And I'm much happier now."

Angela moved to Lucy's side, resting her hand on her arm. "And we're here for you. Whether you poison your husband or let one of us do it."

"We are," I echoed. "Whatever you need. Whenever you need it. You've got us. Because Angela and I...we've both been through terrible marriages. And there is light at the end of that tunnel."

Lucy didn't respond right away. Though I could see it in her demeanor, the way her hands paused mid-brush, the way her eyes stared off into space, the crack was forming in the armor.

The seed was planted and starting to sprout.

Chapter Fifty-Four

Antonio
Seventeen days after Vincent's murder

I followed behind Sal as we walked into *Gallo's*. He took one last drag of his cigarette before flicking it onto the sidewalk and grinding it out with his loafer. He pushed open the door and stepped inside. I was right behind him. Near the entrance stood a coat check girl. She was tall, thin, and had a jet-black pixie cut.

"Hey, Sal. Want me to take your coat?" she asked with a coy smile.

"We're not staying long," Sal said, brushing past her. I hesitated for a second, glancing back at her, once more, before following.

The hallway was dimly lit, with some dark, moody wallpaper. I guess it fit the whole mafia vibe, but a little light wouldn't have hurt either. Somewhere beyond this hallway, I could hear the muffled sounds of conversation and laughter.

When we stepped out of the hallway, it opened into a large room. There were booths lined along the far wall, each one filled with men who looked like they were knee-deep in serious business. A bar sat in the corner, the bartender lazily wiping down the counter. In the center were scattered poker and card tables, mostly empty, though I could imagine the place got packed when rich mafia men with too much money were looking to blow off steam.

I scanned the room, wondering if Joey had ever come here. Obviously, Sal wouldn't have brought me if he came here often, but maybe back in the day, this was his hangout spot. If he had ever spent time here, I imagined he'd claimed one of those booths, part businessman, part outlaw. As we weaved through the space, my eyes landed on a staircase tucked into the far corner. That had to be where Tino Gallo held court.

We didn't get far before I heard a voice call out behind us. "Sal, Sal!"

I didn't have to turn around. I knew who it was.

Mickey Two Times.

"Nino, Nino," he grinned, stepping up to us with his usual double-speak. "How you doing, kid?"

"What's up, Mickey? I'm in a time crunch," Sal said.

"Word is, there's heat coming down from the 14th Precinct. Someone tipped off—"

Sal held up his hand to silence Mickey and reached into his coat. From the left pocket, he pulled out a small tin of caviar. From the other, a glass bottle of perfume. He shoved them both into my hands. The moment I touched them, something cold slid up my spine. I was back in the dark of that 18-wheeler. Surrounded by the same caviar and perfume. When I got home that night, Joey had already gifted Ma the same caviar and perfume. I wondered if she knew it was stolen. I shook my head, shoving the memory out of my head. "Nino, take that to Tino downtown. Tell him I'll be right there."

Nodding, I headed for the staircase. As I reached the bottom step, the temperature seemed to drop. It was darker down here and cooler. A mini bar sat tucked beside the stairs, its glass shelves catching what little light there was. Why the fuck was this place so dark? Across from me was a living room setup with a few leather couches and a coffee table. Past the bar stretched a long hallway, lined with closed doors. I had no idea where Tino might be. The whole place felt like an underground fortress. No voices. No movement. Only a heavy silence.

I took a few cautious steps down the hallway, past one of the doors, when I heard something behind me. A door creaked open. Footsteps followed. I spun around, clutching the perfume and caviar tighter in my arms.

Black boots. NYPD uniform. A badge that read Hudson.

Ben fucking Hudson.

My throat went dry. My palms started sweating. My arms tightened around the stolen goods.

A second man appeared behind Ben, shorter, dressed in a gray suit and fedora. Gold cross around his neck. A thick pinky ring flashed with every step he took towards us. He floated through the room as though he owned every square inch of it. He was smiling wide.

This had to be Tino Gallo.

He stopped next to Ben, who turned toward me, thumb pointing over his shoulder. "Who's this you got here?"

Tino's eyes met mine. I froze. He didn't know me. I'd never met him. My heart thudded as I lifted the perfume and caviar. "I'll be damned," Tino let out a breathy laugh, gripping Ben's shoulder before stepping forward. "Ben, this is Nino...How you doing, kid? Pleasure to meet ya, I'm Tino." He extended a hand.

I peeled my eyes off Ben long enough to shake it. "This is for you," I mumbled, holding out the goods. "Sal's on his way. He's just upstairs speaking with Mickie Two Times."

Tino held the perfume up to the light, turning it in his hand with a look of approval. "My wife's gonna love this," he said, placing it carefully on the bar counter.

Ben crossed his arms, squinting as he seized me up. "He looks a little young, doesn't he?"

Tino glanced back at me, folding his arms to match Ben's posture. His brows dipped as he studied me. He lifted a shoulder. "I was younger when I started," he said with a smirk, pointing a finger at me. "This kid's kind of a legend, you know. He helped pull off Operation Ice Box. He's been making all the runs lately."

Ben's neck snapped toward Tino, his brows pulled tight. I let out a quiet huff and scratched the back of my neck. "Joey's Operation Ice Box?"

"Yeah," Tino replied, chuckling. "Why?"

"I didn't do much," I muttered, my eyes dropping to my shoes.

I could feel Ben staring at me, burning a hole in my forehead, but I kept my gaze down until I had no choice but to lift it. The second our eyes locked, it was as if he'd grabbed me by the throat and forced me to look. "You sure do remind me of someone," he growled. "Do we know each other by chance, *Nino*?"

I tried to swallow, but my mouth was dry. I had to say something, *anything*. "I get that a lot." I forced my spine straight. "But I don't think we've ever met, officer."

Ben didn't move, he just kept staring, his hazel eyes seeming darker now, or maybe that was just in my head. Tino burst out laughing, throwing his arms up as if it was the funniest thing he'd heard all day. "Don't call him officer," he wheezed. "You can call him Ben or Hudson. He's on our side, Nino. He's not *that* kind of officer."

I nodded, even though I already knew. He was my father's

right-hand man. "My bad, Hudson. It's good to know you're not *that* kind of officer who would turn me in."

Ben nodded slowly. His lips pulled tight. Jaw grinding.

Tino's gaze bounced between us. "You two sure you don't know each other?" He wagged a finger between us.

"No, I don't think so," Ben said, his eyes never leaving mine. "He just looks like someone I know real well. A spitting image of a good friend of mine, actually." *Joey.*

I needed to get the hell out of there. "I'll go find Sal. I think Mickey got him held up."

"Oh yeah," Tino muttered, already distracted as he slid the caviar into the bar fridge. "Mickey will keep him there all day, telling the same story twice."

I forced myself to slip past Ben. Though I could feel Ben's breath on the back of my neck the whole way. As I reached the second step up, he called out— "Hey, Nino."

I forced my eyes to meet his and my feet to stop their desperate pursuit to get the hell out of there.

"Be careful. I hear there's sharks at every corner...and they're getting suspicious."

Tino didn't even glance our way, he was too busy with the fridge.

I knew what Ben meant. It wasn't just a warning, it was code for Joey 'The Shark' Romano. He was watching and circling. He was growing suspicious. I didn't wait to see if Ben had more to say. I bolted up the stairs and across the room, spotting Sal exactly where I left him, legs spread, arms crossed, nodding blankly as Mickey rambled on. Sal looked half-dead with boredom. Any other day, I would've found it hilarious how desperate he seemed to escape the conversation. Right now, I was the one looking for an escape.

The second I reached them, both their mouths stopped moving. "Tinowantstoseeyou," I blurted.

Sal's brows pinched as he slung an arm around my shoulders, guiding me back toward the staircase with a wave to Mickey. "See you around, Mickey!" Sal called over his shoulder. "What the hell took so long?" he hissed. "I was sweating over here after hyping you up. I told the whole city that Nino is the fastest we've ever seen. You were supposed to deliver the goods and come straight back for me. Instead, you left me with Mickey. I thought we had created a brotherly—"

"Can't you get yourself out of a conversation without my help?"

He scowled. "He had something for Joey and asked me to pass it on. But Jesus, I thought he'd never get to the point."

Joey.

Ben.

Ben's downstairs.

I'm fucked.

"I need to leave. We need to leave. Give me the car keys."

Sal laughed before he realized I was dead serious. "I'm not giving you my car keys. You'll leave my ass behind. No fucking way."

"I'm serious. We need to go. Now."

He narrowed his eyes. "Why? What happened?"

"Ben's here," I muttered, glancing toward the dark staircase. "He's down there with Tino."

"What?" Sal barked. "What the fuck did he say? Is he gonna tell Joey?" He raked a hand through his hair, then dragged it down his face, muttering curses, trying to keep himself from unraveling.

"I don't know. But I need to get home. I need to get out of here." Sal looked down the stairs like Ben might come storming up at any second.

The sharks were circling.

And I was bleeding.

Chapter Fifty-Five

Joey
Seventeen days after Vincent's murder

I crossed the parking lot and pushed open the door to *Romano Luxury Wholesale.* I expected to hear the usual sounds of the guys bullshitting over coffee, someone shouting from the back, and a radio playing low. Everything was quiet. The faintest smell of morning coffee still lingered in the air, but Paul was the only one in sight, slouched in the lounge chair near the front. My heels echoed as I padded across the floor. From the back, I could hear faint commotion, boxes shifting and muffled voices but nothing like the usual rowdy noise. "Where is everybody?"

Paul glanced up and lifted a shoulder. "They're in the back. Why are you just getting in?"

I'm not telling Paul I had to go grocery shopping with Adriana, and that's why I'm late. I'm not telling Paul I had to help Adriana unload the groceries and kiss her forehead before I left. I'm not telling Paul I think my own wife could be covering for Lucy. Instead, I jerked my head toward my office. "Come on. We can talk in there."

Paul pushed himself up with a groan and followed me in. I

rounded my desk and dropped into the chair behind it. He shut the door and sank into the seat across from me. "Where's Marco?" I drummed my fingers against the desk, then steepled them, pressing my mouth to my hands for a moment before dragging them over my slicked-back hair.

"I haven't seen him since the warehouse last night. I figured he'd show by now. He was stopping by to help Lucy and then making a few runs—"

"I think it was Lucy, Paul."

Paul's brows slammed together. "Lucy? You mean, Lucy Giordano? You think she killed Vincent?"

I nodded. He stared at me, tension thick in the silence stretching between us. "I can't prove it. And maybe I don't even want to. But I suspected her from the very beginning, and after thinking about the description Aleksei gave me, I think it was her. I think she's got the motive and power to pull this off. I think she's got people covering for her." *And I think I'm fucked, but we'll keep that one to ourselves.*

"Why would she do something like that? What could possibly be the motive before it?"

"I don't know exactly. You know how Vincent was. He was always spying, and maybe he saw her and Ben. At this point, who, other than Christopher, hasn't seen the two of them together? So perhaps, he saw and was blackmailing her as he always does, and you know she'll do anything to protect Ben, so maybe she killed him in a rage, and Ben helped her cover it up because you know he would."

Paul blinked, like he was measuring just how far off the rails I'd gone. "That's some theory. But no woman pulled this off. You couldn't get me to believe that with a gun to my head. A woman walks into Vincent's house and shoots him? Please. She'd be drenched in blood. They don't handle this kind of thing, Joey. Aleksei's feeding you shit. He's the one who did it, and Hector's the one who put the gun in his hands and stuffed his pockets with cash."

"Even if that's true, I can't force Aleksei to confess. You were there, you heard him. He wouldn't back down from that story."

"Because he was paid to stick to it. That's how these guys work. Throw some money their way, and they'll swear the sky's green. You just handed him sixty grand to keep his mouth shut, and notice...he didn't breathe a word of it to Hector. You should know better than to trust men who can so easily be bought."

"But if you think Ben had any part in this, you need to rule that out now. Make him say it to your face, drag it out of him. Don't go down for something you didn't do. You already spent ten years in the can for the family; you can't trade your life again. I won't let that happen. We live by rules, codes, loyalty, but there's a line. And if—and that's a huge *if*—Lucy did it, then Ben takes the fall. I doubt it's true. Women don't usually get mixed up in this kind of brutality. But *if* she did, Ben is the man, and he takes the blame. That's the way the game's played."

Paul's words dug in deep, like gravel under my skin. Rules. Codes. Loyalty. That was the gospel we were raised on, wasn't it? The bread and butter of this entire secret society we ran. The longer I lived by it, the more I realized it was just another leash—one meant to keep men like me chained to the fire until there was nothing left but smoke. They called it honor, but what it really meant was sacrifice.

Sacrifice your time, your blood, your future. Ten years gone in a cell, and for what? So the family could sleep easily while I rotted?

Paul made it sound simple. If Lucy pulled the trigger, Ben would swallow the bullet for her. End of story. I knew it wasn't that clean. Blood never washes off that easily, no matter whose name you pin it on. If Lucy really did it...then all those codes and rules we swore by weren't worth the paper they were written on. Because it would mean everything I thought I knew about loyalty was a lie. It could mean Ben had betrayed me again to save Lucy.

* * *

Adriana was upstairs. Rosa was in the kitchen. Antonio was sprawled on the couch in front of the TV, his eyes glued to the TV. When the doorbell rang, I already knew who it was.

Ben.

I heard Rosa's footsteps move toward the front door and then her voice, warm and polite, "Joey's just finishing something up. He'll be out in a minute." *Exactly what I told her to say.*

I wanted him to sit there for a few minutes, let it stew. Let the silence stretch until his brain started spinning with all the things I might say, all the reasons I might have called him over. Five minutes passed before I pushed back from my desk and stepped into the living room. Ben stood up the second he saw me. He trailed behind me to my office. After we stepped inside, I shut the door behind us. He took a seat across from me, slouched in the chair with his elbows on the armrests, fingers laced in front of him. His posture was casual, but I could see it in his eyes, he was on edge.

"What's going on, Joey? Paul said you needed to talk. What do you need to talk about?"

I nodded. "It's about Lucy."

His brows pulled together as he sat up straighter now. "What about her?"

"I need to ask you something, and I want the truth. I don't want you to bullshit with me." I pressed my forearms onto my desk, eyes locked on his. "Would you cover for her? If she did something wrong?" *Like kill Vincent.*

He hesitated going over the question in his head.

"Answer the question, Ben."

"I wouldn't let anything happen to her."

"That's not an answer. Please don't deflect away from the question. I asked you not to bullshit with me—"

"What is this about?"

"Answer the question." My tone was sharp now. "Would. You. Cover. For. Her?"

He rubbed the back of his neck. "I guess so. Sure, I suppose I would. But you'd cover for Adriana, wouldn't you? So, yes, I'd cover for Lucy. Why are you asking this?"

"So you'd provide her an alibi, even if you knew she killed Vincent?"

That made his eyes widen. "What? No. Fuck no. She was with me." He stood up from his seat, his fingers pressed into his chest. "That's not an alibi, it's the truth. You think I'd lie about something like that?"

I pressed my palms into the desk and rose to my full height, "You just said you'd cover for her. I know you'd cover for her. I know you love her enough that you wouldn't let anything happen to her. I love my wife enough not to let anything happen to her. I know if it came down to my wife, I'd turn on anyone in a heartbeat. I know you'd do the same when it comes to Lucy. So how the hell am I supposed to trust that what you're saying is the truth?"

"This is a trick fucking question. Some psychological mind-fuck you're trying to pull." Ben spat. "I'm telling you the truth, Lucy and I were together that morning."

"But that's the thing. She wasn't with you. She was meeting Adriana and Angela to go dress shopping."

Ben let out a loud, frustrated breath. "Yes, but she left my place to go there. She was late getting there. Angela and Adriana had already picked out their dresses before she even showed up."

"Wouldn't that be enough time to shoot Vincent and show up like nothing had happened?"

He groaned, throwing his head back. "Jesus, Joey, no. She didn't do it. Give it a rest. Let's just fucking kill Aleksei and Hector and be done with all this."

"You'd look me in the face, knowing what I stand to lose, and swear you wouldn't lie to me? That you wouldn't cover it up if she did something that could bury me?"

"I'm telling you the truth. Fuck!" he snapped.

"It's hard to trust you, Ben. You've betrayed me once. How do I know you won't do it again?"

His mouth dropped. "That was years ago. And I would hardly consider that betrayal. I've been on your side since day one, you know that. So why the hell are you coming at me like this? You're fucking losing it!"

"I'm a fair man, Ben. You know this. But fair only stretches so far when it's my neck on the line."

"I'm *not* your enemy, Joey."

"I'd like for you to go," I gritted out.

"Here's a thought," he said. "You can kill me. You can have me clipped, if that's what you want. But maybe you ought to start paying more attention to what's happening in your own house instead of everyone else's." He turned and stormed out, the door slamming behind him. I stared at the space he left, the echo of his words rattling around the room.

Chapter Fifty-Six

Antonio
Seventeen days after Vincent's murder

I sank onto the couch and flipped on *The Andy Griffith Show*, pretending to lose myself in primetime. I laughed at all the right moments, or at least I think I did. Truth was, I was sweating bullets. If Ben came in here ready to expose me, I was screwed. The doorbell rang, and I practically leapt out of my own skin. Rosa answered it, and Ben stood in the doorway. His eyes locked on mine the second he stepped inside. Neither one of us blinked.

"Thank you, Rosa," he said without taking his eyes off me, but the smile he gave her was only for show. He walked into the living room, his presence sucking the air right out of it. He stood directly in front of me until I had no choice but to look up. "Hello, Antonio. You sure have gotten taller."

I felt Rosa's gaze shift to me. Though I couldn't meet her eyes. Rosa and Ben stood across from me, trying to back me into a corner, but Joey always said a man who backs down is no man at all. Rosa shook her head, disappearing toward the kitchen. Ben sat next to me on the couch. I leaned forward, propped my elbow on my knee, and rested my cheek against my fist.

"You sure are getting grayer," I said, eyeing the silver streaks on both sides of his head.

He laughed loudly, but humorlessly. "And just what do you think you're doing with Sal?" he muttered, his voice low enough that only I could hear. "And how the hell do you think this ends well for you? I don't think it's any secret to you, but your father is practically the head of the largest crime organization the U.S. has ever seen, and you're sneaking around expecting to never be caught by him?"

"Just so you know, Sal hasn't dragged me into anything. He isn't grooming me for something that I didn't volunteer tribute for."

Ben huffed, shaking his head in disbelief. "What kind of kid signs himself up for the noose is what I'd like to know?"

"I didn't sign myself up for the noose, officer. And anyway, it's none of your business. I'm not getting into it with the likes of you."

"You think you've got it figured out? But you're walking into something you can't walk out of. It would be wise to stop this little act you're doing before it's too late."

It was too late. Even if I liberated Joey's name, I was too deep to stop now. "You're not my father. You're just a rogue cop on my father's payroll."

That shut him up, but the way his jaw clenched told me he wasn't done with me yet. "You do realize I could tell your father? He's going to find out. You're not as slick as you think you are. He's about to call me into his office, and I could tell him. He's already heard about you. He's asked me to keep an eye out for a runner named Nino. And wouldn't you know it... Tino said he was finally meeting the infamous Nino today, so I stopped by and waited to meet him myself. You can imagine my surprise when I realized Nino was you."

My jaw locked, teeth grinding, eyes narrowing into a glare.

I couldn't tell if Ben meant to intimidate me by saying Joey was onto me, or if he was really being honest.

"You're a thirteen-year-old with a code name. Sounds pretty fucking stupid to me." Ben scoffed, then barked out a laugh. "If Joey finds out I knew what you were doing and didn't say anything, that puts me in the crosshairs too. And if you think Sal's going to save the day. I hate to break it to you, Sal's a dipshit who can't tell his head from his ass."

I didn't get a word out before the sound of Joey's footsteps echoed down the hall, sharp against the floorboards. Both our heads snapped toward the noise. Ben rose, tugged his coat into place, and slipped into Joey's office without another glance at me.

The office door flew open not ten minutes later. Ben emerged like a storm, slamming it shut behind him. His stare found me, cold and cutting, before he turned on his heel and walked out the front door without a word. My heart was pounding in my chest. *What the hell happened in there?*

I pushed myself off the couch and stalked towards Joey's office. Raised my hand, knocked before twisting the knob, and pushing the door open. Joey was leaning over the desk, elbows planted into the desk, one hand gripping his slicked-back hair, the other massaging his jaw. "Come in."

I slipped inside. "You okay?"

Joey dropped his shoulders with a sigh as he pushed away from the desk. His shoulders were tight, and his usually slicked-back hair was disheveled from his own hands. He looked exhausted, drained in a way that was hard to see. "I'm okay, kid." He forced a smile. "Ben and I were just handling some business stuff. It's nothing to worry about." *Only I was worried.* "How are you doing? I feel like we hardly have time to spend with each other since you're always gone with Enzo and Michael." *You mean, Sal?*

"I'm fine. I just wanted to check and make sure you were okay." *And Ben didn't tell you what I'd really been up to.* "Is everything okay between you and Ben? He seemed very upset when he stormed out."

Joey's head tilted, his shoulders hunching as if carrying the weight of the world. He drew in a breath, cheeks puffing as he held it, then let it out with a sharp exhale. "Oh, it's nothing," he said, waving a dismissive hand and blowing a playful raspberry. "Sometimes business gets heated."

"Did something happen?"

"It was just a little back and forth. But it's nothing for you to worry about."

Only I would worry about it. Worry until it ate at my sanity, until I couldn't stand it anymore and had to dig in myself. Until I had to fix it. That was who I was—the fixer. The one who filled the cracks before anyone even noticed they were forming. I hated that part of myself. Yet, it was also my strongest trait.

It meant I'd always be at war with my own instincts.

Chapter Fifty-Seven

Joey
Eighteen days after Vincent's murder

I didn't get much sleep last night. My mind kept replaying every word from the argument with Ben. I tossed and turned, staring at the ceiling, feeling the weight of what he'd said press against my chest. The anger, the frustration, the doubt, it all mixed together, leaving me restless and wound tight. Even when I finally closed my eyes, sleep was a stranger. Every corner of my mind was haunted by what-ifs, by what could go wrong if I misstepped.

By the time morning came, I was still on edge. I pulled out of the spot and headed toward *Romano Luxury Wholesale.* Normally, I wasn't a speeder. I liked going under the limit, maybe because that was the only thing in my life I could control, the pace of it. Everything else flew by without warning, without permission. Not today. Today, I floored it, weaving through traffic like I was in a high-speed chase, letting the tension fuel my speed.

The second I hit the lot, I slammed the brakes so hard my body snapped against the seat. Marco and Tommy were outside, mingling with a couple of customers eyeing one of our luxury beauties—a 1960 Jaguar Mark IX, and a 1960 Rolls-Royce Silver Cloud II. My pulse still thrummed from the drive, my mind already moving into business mode, but the memory of last night's argument lingered like a shadow I couldn't shake. I killed the engine, shoved the door open, and was out before the car stopped rocking.

I barreled past the receptionist desk into the lounge, where Paul was on the couch, flipping through paperwork. "Paul!" I barked, jabbing a finger toward my office. "In the office. Now." Paul's eyes flicked up, suspicion coloring his face, but he rose from the couch, gathering his papers as if nothing were urgent. "Where's Sal?"

"I don't know," he shrugged. "He said he had some runs to do."

I blew out a hard huff. Out of the corner of my eye, I caught Lee watching me from the back. Today was his lucky day. "Lee!"

His brows jumped as he jogged over. "Yeah, boss?"

"I want you in my office."

I spun on my heel and strode off. Paul was already inside, planted in the chair, his eyes still glued to those damn papers. He'd seen me like this too many times to bother pretending to be rattled. Lee shut the door behind him, staying planted in front of it. I moved to the window, my elbow braced on the sill, and my hand pressed over my mouth.

"What's gotten into you?" Paul finally muttered, glancing my way. "I'm guessing things between you and Ben—"

"I want you to bring Aleksei to me," I said, my eyes on the street outside. Paul let out a sigh, pushed himself up, and left through the office door. Lee lingered, waiting for his orders. "You," I said, turning toward him, "go to the newspaper stand. Find whoever's working and get me the issue from the opening of *Cosa Bella*, the one with Lucy on the front cover."

Lee nodded and slipped out, shutting the door behind him.

Now it was just me. Alone with my thoughts. My mind kept circling the same ugly conclusion: Ben had betrayed me. Every instinct I had screamed against it, and yet, there I was—praying to God, the universe, whoever might be listening—that I was wrong.

* * *

It didn't take long for Lee to deliver the newspaper with Lucy's face splashed across the front page, right there in front of *Cosa Bella*'s grand opening. The part that killed me was having to wait half the damn day for Paul to bring Aleksei to my office. By the time Paul finally walked in, I didn't even hear whatever greeting he tried.

"Bring him in here," I barked.

Paul turned, heading back to the lounge where he'd left Aleksei. I stood behind my desk, all composure long gone, when they came in. Paul planted himself in front of the office door. Aleksei took the chair across from me.

"How you doing today?" I asked, even though I didn't give a damn about small talk. This wasn't the time or place, and he sure as hell wasn't the person. But I wasn't about to jump straight into, *Does this woman look familiar to you?* without a little lead-in.

"I'm doing okay," he said. "How are you?"

"I could be better. But that's why you're here." Or, more accurately, why Paul dragged him here. Not that Aleksei would fight either of us on something I ordered. I slid the newspaper across the desk. He picked it up, scanned it, his brow knitting like he was trying to make sense of what I was asking. "Well...Does she look familiar?" I knew he was going to say yes.

"No," he said, handing the paper back. "She's pretty, whoever she is."

Ha. "She's Hector's wife. Her name's Lucy. I thought maybe she was the one who shot Vincent."

"I've never seen nor met Hector's wife. But it wasn't her," he replied without hesitation, as if he were positive of it.

I was usually good at sniffing out a liar, but Aleksei didn't look like he was lying. "You realize what happens if I find out you're lying?"

"Yes," he said, nodding.

"You're one hundred percent sure this isn't the woman you saw?" I slid the newspaper back across the desk toward him. He let out a long sigh and picked it up again, his eyes scanning every inch.

"She didn't look like this. Similar in some ways, sure, but this...this isn't the woman I saw."

"What's similar?"

"I suppose everything except the face and the hair. They're not the same woman. Unless this woman"—he pointed at Lucy on the front page—"changes her hairstyle and does something to her face, it can't be her. I have a good memory. This isn't her."

Steam hissed out of my nose in frustration. There was no way Lucy wasn't involved. UnlessPaul was right.

Paul was pressed against the office door, arms crossed, a look of pure annoyance plastered across his face. Our eyes met, and I realized I'd fallen off the rails. I'd been wrong. Aleksei was playing me. Of course, a woman couldn't have done this, and Aleksei was still working with Hector, still trying to bring me down. My chest tightened, and my heart sank.

Fuck. Fuck. Fuck.

"Paul, go to the front desk and tell Lisa we need to close for a short lunch break."

His eyebrows shot up. He knew exactly what was coming. If Aleksei wasn't going to tell me the truth, I was going to have to pry it out of him...in the back...with a pair of pliers.

I watched Paul shuffle down the hall, each step echoing in the office. The second the door clicked shut behind him, the silence hit me. My mind raced, twisting through every scenario, every possible lie Aleksei could be spinning. Every second he didn't confess, every hesitation felt like a knife twisting in my gut. I can't believe I had gone off the rails and allowed him to convince me that a *woman* killed Vincent.

I ran a hand through my hair, gripping the edge of the desk until my knuckles ached. My heart thumped, loud and erratic, as if it knew what I was about to do. I could hear my own breathing, shallow and uneven, trying to convince myself I could control the outcome. The line had already blurred the moment I realized Aleksei was playing me. If I kill Aleksei, how do I know Hector won't find another way to come after me, and how will I take Hector out without raising more suspicion?

Seconds stretched into minutes. I felt the walls closing in, the anxiety pressing against my chest. I could almost imagine Hector laughing somewhere, thinking he'd gotten the upper hand and driven me mad with the help of Aleksei.

The door creaked open. Paul stepped back in, his eyes calculating. My eyes snapped back to Aleksei, who finally seemed to realize the gravity of the situation. He wasn't leaving today. At least, not alive if he made the wrong move. His face drained of color, and Paul's hand slipped to the revolver tucked in his waistband.

"What's happening? You're going to kill me for telling the truth?" Aleksei panted, twisting sideways in the chair. His eyes darted between Paul's gun and mine, both pointed squarely at him.

"Who said anything about killing you?" I asked, gesturing

with the revolver for him to stand. "We're going to talk...that's all."

Aleksei rose unsteadily. "I swear to you...on my children... it wasn't that—you know what? Maybe it was her! I think you're right! It was her!"

I chuckled, shaking my head. "See? That's the problem. I can't really trust you. All this lying—"

"You're going to kill me for the truth! What am I supposed to do?"

"—makes it difficult to trust you."

"Let's go," Paul snarled, revolver still trained on Aleksei, gesturing toward the office door.

"Please," Aleksei begged.

"You can do this one of two ways," I growled. "You go like we asked...or you die right here. I don't have a preference."

He hung his head, his steps hesitant, and followed Paul out of the office. The gun pressed firmly between his shoulder blades, Paul guided him toward the back of the warehouse.

I dragged in a breath, readying myself for what was about to happen when I heard Paul shout my name: "Joey! Come here!"

Grabbing the revolver, I bolted out of the office, through the lounge, and down the hallway that led to the back of the warehouse. Aleksei stood facing Adriana, and I's wedding picture, Paul's gun still sandwiched between his shoulder blades. "Say it again," Paul pressed the muzzle further into his back. "Say what the hell you just said."

"She did it," Aleksei said.

I felt Paul's gaze land on me, but the room was spinning. My stomach lurched so hard I thought I might puke right there on the floor. He lifted his arm and pointed right at Adriana's perfect, smiling face. "*Her*. She was wearing the violet dress. It was her that I saw."

"Joey," Paul said.

I felt my pulse slam in my ears. My chest rose and fell faster, each breath jagged and shallow. "How do you know it was her?"

"It's the hairstyle. It's the face. The smile. The height. It was her. I'm telling you." His gaze locked with mine. "It. Was. Her."

Paul shoved the gun into Aleksei's back, steering him down the narrow hallway. Aleksei twisted, panic in his eyes. "I'm not lying! You've got to believe me! She did it! You can't kill me! You have to believe me!" *That's exactly why I have to kill you.*

Without warning, Paul slammed the revolver into Aleksei's temple. He crumpled to the floor, groaning. I exhaled, the sound more like a low groan than a breath. My tie felt like a noose, choking me, and I yanked at it, trying to loosen the pressure before the walls of the hallway closed in. I strode down the hall, dragging my hands through my hair, forcing myself to breathe.

"Let me take care of him," Paul said. I met his eyes, feeling like someone had control of a remote, fast-forwarding and slowing down every second of my life all at once.

I glanced down at Aleksei sprawled on the floor, aimed, and pulled the trigger. The crack of the gun was deafening in my mind, though Paul's voice floated through one ear and out the other. I took longer strides back down the hallway, every step shaking the edge of my control. My eyes lifted to the portrait of Adriana on the wall...her sweet, serene smile a reminder of what I was protecting.

This was what Ben had been talking about.

This wasn't his home.

It was mine.

Chapter Fifty-Eight

Antonio
Eighteen days after Vincent's murder

I shifted on the stoop, the sun pressing down on my shoulders, sticky heat creeping beneath my collar. My shirt clung to my back, stiff and buttoned neatly. My hair was slicked back so perfectly that it barely moved when the warm breeze passed. I raised my hand and knocked, knuckles sharp against the wood, then dropped my arm brushing it against the side of my pressed shorts.

The door swung open, and Enzo finally appeared. Leaning against the frame, a shadow in a black shirt, hair piled high and perfect, one loose curl dipping low on his forehead. "Well, if it isn't fucking Nino."

My grin vanished, slipping right off my face. My stride stumbled, shoulders caving as if someone had cut the strings holding me upright. Heat drained out of me in a rush, leaving my skin cold and my features heavy, carved in stone. I could feel the color bleed from my cheeks, my pulse stuttering in my throat as every ounce of confidence I'd been carrying scattered to the floor.

"What are you doing here?" Enzo asked, folding his arms over his chest. "Shouldn't you be with Sal?"

"I wanted to tell you. So many times."

"I knew you were up to something."

"I was trying to protect you."

A dry, empty laugh fell from his lips. "Protect me? You think I'm some fucking wimp who needs saving from your stupid little secret? Or did you just not want me to outshine you? You wanted the spotlight for yourself, didn't you?"

"No. No, of course not. I promised Val I wouldn't say anything."

"Oh, so Val knows too?" I didn't answer. I didn't have to. He didn't wait for an answer. The laugh that slipped out of him was flat again. "And you keep a promise to her when I'm your so-called best fucking friend?"

"I—I'm sorry," I stammered.

Enzo threw his head back and let out a laugh. His palm snapped out toward me, fingers spread as if to punctuate the mockery. "Wow. Now you're sorry? Sorry, worked the first time you dragged Giovanni—Giovanni, of all people—into one of your wild schemes. But this?" He stepped closer, his grin gone as quick as it came, his voice cutting down to a growl. "No. Fuck that, Antonio. You can keep your fucking apologies."

I guess I deserve that. "Would you just listen to me? Would you just let me explain? I promised Val I wouldn't drag you into this. I was just helping Sal clear Joey's name, and I've accomplished that, so I'm done." Liar, the voice in my head rattled out. "That's all this—"

"So Val gets to be in on it, but I don't? Who the hell do you two think you are, scheming against me?"

My chest caved in. "It's not like that—"

"Sal's practically my brother-in-law. My father died as a

member of this family. Marco's part of this family. My grandfather, every uncle I've got is a mafia man through and through. My mother might as well be a made woman. Before you showed up, you treated the whole thing like a bedtime story to scare kids. Your mother marries Joey, you get patched in as some laughable prodigy son, and now you run around pretending you belong? Lying to my face while I sit here getting played? You think I'm that stupid?"

"No, no, no," I chanted, my hands raised. "I don't think you're stupid. You're impulsive—"

"And what do you call yourself?"

"Especially when you're angry and provoked. I couldn't tell you because I knew you'd take this too far. I was just doing it for two fucking weeks—" I thrust up two fingers. "Two weeks. I did what I had to do, and I'm done."

Enzo's jaw worked as he shook his head, dark eyes blazing. "Impulse? You haven't seen anything yet."

"En—" I started, but the door slammed in my face, the sound reverberating down to my bones. I stood there, staring at the wood, my throat burning. My legs felt heavy, as if I'd just gone ten rounds in a fight I hadn't trained for.

I'd meant well, at least in the beginning. But somewhere along the way, it stopped being about protecting Joey's name. It became about the rush. The thrill of moving through the city with something no one else knew about. It was a piece of Joey's world I could claim for myself. Now, I'd just blown a hole in the one friendship that had been solid since the day I'd set foot in this screwed-up place.

The sharp squeal of tires tore me out of my thoughts. I turned just as Joey's Ferrari swung into the driveway, the nose of it dipping with the weight of the stop. Joey threw the door open, fury written across every line of his face. He peeled himself out of the driver's seat and all but sprinted toward the front door, shoving past like a storm about to tear through the house.

What the hell is happening today?

Chapter Fifty-Nine

Joey
Eighteen days after Vincent's murder

In the car, I wrecked my brain trying to figure out how she could've done it. I didn't even remember her owning a violet dress until, sitting at a red light, it hit me. The day Paul tried to stop me from going to Vincent's house after I found out he'd been murdered, she'd pulled into the driveway, wearing a new dress. I'd told her she looked beautiful. But that wasn't the dress she left the house in earlier that day. The thought twisted my stomach. I wanted to believe she hadn't done it, that I'd go home, open the closet, and find that dress tucked away among the others and some kind of explanation.

I whizzed into the driveway, killed the engine, and went straight through the front door. The smell of sizzling garlic and olive oil hit my nostrils first. I didn't take off my shoes. I didn't remove my jacket. I took the stairs two at a time to our bedroom. I yanked open the closet doors. One by one, I pulled out every violet dress she owned, laying them across the bed. None of them had a white collar. None of them were *that* dress.

The bedroom door opened behind me. I knew it was her before I turned around. Some part of me hoped she'd be wearing it, that I'd turn and find all this was all in my head. When I turned, I found her in a colorful floral dress with her kitchen apron tied at her waist. Her gaze shifted from me to the dresses on the bed, then back to me. "What are you doing? And why do you have blood on your suit?"

It felt like someone had shoved a knife into my chest and was slowly twisting it. I glanced down at the blood splattered along my suit. What I care about right now is finding the blood splattered violet dress she had on when she killed Vincent. "Where's the violet dress with the white collar?"

She hesitated. "I'm not sure. Why?"

"I just want to know. Surely, you've got it in here some-where." *Please, don't let this be true. It's got to be here somewhere.*

"I think I lent it to Lucy or Angela."

Angela is taller and curvier than Adriana, nothing of hers would ever fit Angela. Lucy was flashy, draped in sequins and fur, a walking chandelier. Adriana's style has always been clean, simple, and elegant. There was not a chance in hell the two of them shared clothes.

I shook my head, closing my eyes, pushing the air out of my lungs in a slow, heavy stream. When I opened them again, Adriana was still in the doorway, still in that floral dress and apron. She hadn't moved. I'm not sure she's even blinked. "Did you do it?" I asked. But the words died halfway out of my mouth—*Did you kill Vincent?*—and just hang there between us.

Her gaze is as steady as ever. "Do what?"

I pinched the bridge of my nose, pressing my eyes shut. "Well, I'm almost certain you did it," I said. It's not for her to hear, it's for me to hear. Because I've been convinced it was

Lucy or Hector or anyone other than her who could have done this. The truth was...it had been her all along. The only questions left were: "Why did you do it? How did you do it?"

Her eyes darted around the room, as though she were looking for someplace to hide. Water trembled on the edge of her big brown eyes. "Fuck," I spat, slamming my hand against the vanity beside me. She flinched at the sound, the crack of my palm filling the room. The sting of it caused me a little comfort, but it soon vanished.

"Why did I do it? Because I'm sick of leaving it up to a man to do things when men are the ones who cause the problems!" The tears finally spilled over, streaking mascara down her cheeks before she swiped at them.

"I was going to take care of it," I gritted my teeth.

"Yeah," she nodded, her chin trembling. "But *I* took care of it for you."

"I told you not to get involved in this life." My chest rose and fell in hard, quick bursts. My nostrils flared with every breath.

"Oh, that's rich," she laughed bitterly through her tears. "I'm already involved. I'm your wife!"

"Exactly!" I roared, throwing my arms wide. "My wife! My wife has no goddamn business killing people in broad daylight, least of all the head of the fucking family!" My chest heaved as I clawed at my shirtfront, yanking the bloodstained fabric. "You want to know whose blood this is?" I shook the ruined jacket for emphasis. "It's a man's blood. A man who could've told every last soul in Staten Island and New York City that my wife killed Vincent!"

"Oh, so it's fine for you to do it? When you kill someone, it's *'business.'*"

Business, sure. Protecting her? Absofuckinglutely. "These two acts are not the same, and you know it!"

Her voice rose to meet mine. "You think you've kept me out of all this? Every night I sit waiting for you to come home, every time the phone rings, you think I don't worry, it has something to do with you? You've been dragging me through this life since the day you met me, so don't stand there and pretend I'm some delicate thing you've been protecting."

I stepped closer, pointing a finger at the floor between us. "When I saw you on that ferry—bruised, beaten—I killed that bastard. Not for you...for me," I jabbed at my chest. "Because I will always see you as someone I have to protect. And I will protect you, and any member of this family, even if it costs me my life. But what you did by killing Vincent and then watching me spiral is unbelievable. You painted a target on my back so big the whole goddamn East Coast could see it."

Her chin lifted, defiant even with tears carving tracks down her cheeks. "I didn't know what to do! I didn't know how to tell you. I thought—God, I thought—you'd kill Hector, and it would be done. It was killing me to watch you be blamed for something *I* did. I suppose I have to live with that for the rest of my life, but I don't regret it. That man hurt my son. Am I supposed to sit here and look pretty while you get around to it? No. I promised myself a long time ago I'd take whatever the men of this world do to me, but Antonio? I will kill to protect him."

"You don't understand what you've set in motion, Adriana. You've started something I might not be able to stop." My voice cracked on the last word, rage barely masking the fear crawling up my throat. I was as good as dead when Hector discovered I had killed Aleksei, and Adriana was behind Vincent's murder. Or perhaps, I'd have to kill Hector before he could beat me to it. Yes, that's—

"I've *begged* you to just run away with me, as a family. We've got the money, the resources. We could disappear to Europe tomorrow. Start fresh. Start over. You won't listen!"

"You really think we can just do that?" I stared at her, dumbfounded, like she'd completely lost her mind. The truth is, we've both lost it, spiraling down this twisted path because of my ties to the mafia, because of the blood I've let stain my hands, because I've only dug myself deeper into a life neither of us can escape.

"You're the one who said we make our own rules."

"I guess you took that and ran with it, didn't you?" Her mascara was smeared, lipstick faded. I wanted to reach for her, to pretend this moment wasn't happening, but it was. "You knowingly put a target on my back. You're my wife. You're supposed to have my back, not paint a bullseye on it."

"I do have your back! If you'd pulled the trigger, they'd have killed you. No one would suspect me. It had to be done, Joey. I did it for Antonio. For you. For us. Vincent wanted to destroy you, destroy our family. He thought I was there to warm his bed. That's the last thought he ever had before I pulled the trigger."

Her voice trembled on the confession. I watched her chest heave, her whole body shaking. Part of me feels relieved knowing she took him out. The other part is boiling, furious that she acted alone.

"You can tell them it was me," she whispered.

I stared at her, stunned. "I'll *never* do that. I will not walk into a room and say *my* wife killed Vincent Accetta. I'll take the blame myself before I let that happen."

"I'll tell them you're lying—"

"And they'll think you're crazy!"

"I don't know why you can't just kill Hector and make it look like he planned the whole thing. It's not that hard to believe. You know, Angela's right, you men think you run this town, but all you guys do is dig your own graves." She stormed out, slamming the door hard enough to rattle the glass on the vanity. Her words keep echoing in my head, not Angela's opinion, because I can practically hear that woman whispering poison into her ear, but the part about Hector. Killing him. Framing him.

It's reckless. But...it might just work.

Chapter Sixty

Adriana
Eighteen days after Vincent's murder

The bedroom door rattled behind me when I slammed it shut. The sound shot straight down my spine. *Breathe. Just breathe.* I chanted in my head as I brushed the tears off my cheeks. My chest wouldn't listen, rising and falling in sharp, broken bursts as I walked down the hallway. The wallpaper swam in my vision, yellow roses bleeding into stripes, and my throat burned from holding back sobs.

I wiped at my cheeks with the backs of my hands, smearing more black marks across my skin. I could feel the thick, greasy streaks and cursed myself for wearing a heavy cat-eye wing this morning. *What a joke.* I probably looked more like one of those clowns from the Macy's parade than Brigitte Bardot. I inhaled, pressing the sob threatening to spill down deep into my lungs. My hands trembled as I gripped the banister to keep from folding in on myself.

Get it together before you hit the bottom. Nobody needs to see you like this.

My heels clicked against the first step as I descended, my

eyes on the floor, my lashes lowered heavy with ruined mascara. When I reached the landing, the flicker of the television caught my eye, *The Andy Griffith Show* playing.

I heard Rosa's heels approaching as my hand latched onto the doorknob. "Christ, Adriana," her voice floated in, laced with concern. "Are you okay?"

"I'm fine. I'll be back. Don't say anything to Antonio if he comes home tonight. He's supposed to have gone to Enzo's," My voice cracked in the middle as I said it. A hiccup slipped out before I could stop it. I kept my eyes on my hand that held onto the doorknob. I couldn't look at her with my face streaked like this, black rivers of mascara cutting through the powder on my cheeks.

"You shouldn't drive like that," she pleaded. Perhaps, not. Though I had already made up my mind. I didn't trust my voice not to break all the way this time. I turned the knob and slipped out before she could say anything else to try and stop me. Or worse, before Joey came down begging me to stay.

The humidity slapped me in the face, but I didn't feel it. I didn't feel anything except the roaring in my head and the pounding in my chest as I hurried to the car. I slid into the driver's seat, yanked the door shut, and jammed the key in the ignition. The engine coughed to life, loud and unsteady like my own breath. My hands were trembling so hard I had to grip the wheel with both hands to keep steady. I didn't even know where I was going. I only knew I couldn't stay.

The car was in reverse when the front door burst open, and Joey stepped out, shutting the door behind him. He raced over towards the driveway as I began to back out. I could hear his voice as he shouted, "Come back inside, sweetheart!" I backed the car out all the way, leaving him standing there. As he had left me standing in the same spot the day he backed out to go see Vincent, right after I'd killed him, and when all of this was set in motion.

It's ironic how life always comes full circle. How the tables turn.

Through the blur of my tears, I caught one last glimpse of him in the rearview mirror—his button-down shirt half unbuttoned, blood still splattered across it, his tie hanging loosely, his sleeves rolled up to his elbows, his hands clutching both sides of his hair like he was about to rip it out. He was shouting, waving his arms as if that would stop me.

But *nothing* could stop me.

My chest heaved like something wild was trapped inside it, clawing to get free. The moment the house disappeared from view, the tears I'd been choking back spilled over. I gripped the steering wheel so tight my knuckles went white, my forehead nearly met the steering wheel as I sobbed out ugly, broken sobs that didn't sound as though they belonged to me.

The car drifted down the quiet streets of town, past men in fedoras locking up their storefronts and women gripping their purses tighter as they walked to their cars. They all looked so normal, *so calm*. Yet, here I was, falling apart behind the wheel because I was Adriana Romano, a woman who made her own rules and had to live by them. The streetlights blurred through my tears as I sped past *Cosa Bella's*. The windows were dark, and Lucy's car wasn't parked out front.

Closed.

I kept driving, my mind a tangled mess, until the glowing sign of *Davidson's Corner Store* cut through the late evening. Cars were parked outside. Men and women dressed in flashy clothes funneled inside the door. They weren't grabbing a soda from Davidson's, they were heading to *The Wise Guy*. I pulled up right out front, killing the engine. I sat there, gripping the wheel as if it were the only thing keeping me from falling apart.

My body molded into the cushion of the seat as I pulled down the sun visor and glanced at myself in the mirror. I was horrified by the image I saw staring back at me. It was much worse than I imagined.

My black mascara and heavy liner had bled down my cheeks, streaks like something out of a bad picture show. I cringed at the sight as I reached for my purse in the passenger seat and rummaged through it until I found the handkerchief. White silk, now destined to die in my hands with the amount of eyeliner and mascara I was going to try and rub off. I dabbed under my eyes, swiped across my cheeks, but it was no use. The makeup smeared worse.

The harder I tried, the uglier it got, until my throat closed and the sob came out raw and violent. My shoulders shook as I bent forward, pressing my forehead against the steering wheel. The horn let out a pitiful honk that made me cry harder.

The horn blast must've carried farther than I thought because I heard footsteps and voices. I wiped my eyes with the back of my hand, trying to quiet the hiccupping sobs. The icing on the cake would be for people to see me, Adriana Romano, sobbing my eyes out.

"Jesus, is that Adriana?" one of them said.

"Yeah," Sal replied. There was a moment of silence before I heard his shoes scuff against the pavement. I could see him from my peripheral vision as he approached the driver's side door. He tapped his knuckles against the glass. I rolled the window down a small crack, embarrassed beyond belief, my swollen eyes meeting Sal's easy grin. He leaned down enough to see me. "You okay?"

"I'm fine," I lied. "I'm just a little upset. It's nothing. Go enjoy your night and forget you saw me."

His eyes whisked over my face, down to the damp handkerchief twisted in my fingers, then back to my swollen dark eyes again. "Where's Joey?"

"At home," I muttered. "I'm fine, Sal. Please, just go inside and don't tell anyone you saw me this way."

Sal studied me, then nodded to himself. "Come on, get out and come inside. I can't leave you here like this. It'll wear on my conscience."

I shook my head, panic rising in my chest. "No, I, no, I can't. I look like a mess. I can not go inside there and have anyone see me like this."

He smiled, one arm resting above the window, his forehead leaning against it while his other hand pressed against the open edge where I had completely rolled the window down. "You can clean up in the bathroom. I'll make sure nobody sees you, alright?"

My chin trembled as I nodded. He opened the car door for me, offering me his hand as I pushed myself out of the car and followed him to the entrance of Davidson's. Lee held the door open for us, and I kept my head down, not making eye contact with anyone.

Sal guided me straight into the restroom, and I stood in front of the mirror, grabbing a paper towel and running it under the cold faucet water. The paper towel was rough against my skin, but I scrubbed anyway until every last streak of black mascara and eyeliner was gone. My eyes were raw and puffy now, rimmed pink from tears and rubbing. I stared at myself in the mirror under the bathroom light. My jet black hair is now slightly disheveled, my cheeks flushed, and no makeup left on my face.

When I opened the bathroom door, Sal and Lee were leaning against the wall waiting for me. They straightened up when they saw me, Lee offering me a soft smile while Sal gestured for me to follow. "Come on," Sal said, gesturing his head towards the storage closet. "You'll feel better once you're inside and with Angela."

Sal glanced over his shoulder at me before pressing his palm against a brass button hidden near the molding. The closet door swung inward, but instead of shelves stacked with mops and bleach, it revealed a tunnel lined with warm amber lights. The air was cooler as we drifted from deep underground. The sound of my heels clicked faintly against the concrete floor. At the end stood two massive oak doors, polished and dark as espresso, with a single street sign bolted above them: *The Wise Guy.* Sal pushed one of the doors open and motioned me inside.

"Thank you," I muttered to Sal as I forced a smile. The two of them sauntered off together towards a booth where Paul sat. My eyes landed on Angela, perched behind the bar like a queen holding court. She was leaning forward, her cigarette dangling from two fingers as she teased Marco across the counter. He was eating it up like a kid with candy. The second Angela's gaze slid to me, all the flirtation drained from her face. She saw me, and that was enough to make the back of my throat burn. I hated how well she could read me. How well she could read everyone.

Angela stubbed out her cigarette into a glass ashtray and murmured something to Marco. He nodded, stepping behind the bar as she came around to me. Her hand found my arm, and she guided me towards the red curtains behind the stage.

Behind the curtains were a couple of guys at a card table, cigar smoke dancing through the air. "Everyone out," Angela shouted. They didn't even look at her twice before grabbing their chips and clearing the room. That's the thing about Angela. She didn't ask, she told you. It was strange how she only had to say two words, and a room full of gangsters scrambled.

Angela eased me into a chair. "What the hell happened?" she asked, crouching in front of me.

I try to get the words to come out, but my throat tightens, strangling every confession before it can escape. "It's nothing. Joey and I—" a hiccup cuts me off, trembling between sobs. "Just got into a little argument."

"Did he hurt you?" Angela's eyes swept over me, searching for bruises that weren't there.

Joey wouldn't do that. He was covered in the blood of a man who threatened to expose my actions. I shook my head furiously. "Nothing like that."

"Then tell me what it is." Angela's perfectly painted red nails are resting on my knees. Her voice softened, coaxing me like a child. "What has he done? What has happened?"

"It's not what *he's* done—" the words burst out with a guttural cry, my palms smothering my face. "It's what *I've* done, Angela."

The silence that followed was suffocating. I could feel her stare burning through my fingers, waiting for the truth to crawl out. Before I could speak another word, the curtain whipped open.

Chapter Sixty-One

Joey
Eighteen days after Vincent's murder

When it sank in that Adriana wasn't coming back, I found myself behind the wheel, crawling through town, squinting at every car that passed as if it could be hers. I'd already made the rounds, Angela's place first, where Enzo and Val were parked in the living room, then Lucy's, where she answered the door with Michael and Antonio hovering behind her. I had to work overtime on the act, wearing a smile that didn't feel in the slightest believable, pretending Adriana and I were solid. I still don't know if Lucy bought it.

I drove over to Davidson's and spotted her car parked outside. I jerked the wheel hard and swerved into the lot as the tires screeched. I didn't even have the engine turned off completely before I was out the door, slamming it so hard the whole car rocked. I jogged to the entrance, as my heart was pounding and my mouth was dry. I shoved my way into the hallway that led straight to *The Wise Guy*.

A couple of low-level wise guys were loitering, dressed up in their best suits, slicked hair, and girls draped on their arms.

I barreled right past them, shoulder-checking one hard enough he stumbled back into the wall. I pushed through the doors to *The Wise Guy* and stumbled inside, scanning for Adriana.

My eyes landed on Marco behind the bar, shaking up a cocktail. He could barely pour a beer without foaming it over, no way in hell he knew what went into a Manhattan. That could only mean one thing: Angela had handed him the bar. She was with Adriana. I charged toward him.

"Where's Angela and Adriana?" I barked. Marco kept his eyes on the glass, poured it sloppily, and slid it across the counter to Lee. My palms slammed against the bar, causing heads to turn my way. "Where the fuck are they, Marco?"

He slowly lifted his hand and pointed toward the stage curtain. I was already moving before he'd fully raised his arm. Cutting through *The Wise Guy* like a blade, past the crowd and the music and the stale air thick with cigarette smoke. I knew every eye was on me, and I didn't give a damn. I yanked back the curtain and slipped behind it.

Adriana sat hunched in a chair, crying into her hands. Angela knelt in front of her, stroking her arms, whispering that everything would be okay. Both of their eyes snapped to meet mine. Angela stood to her full height, which for a woman was quite tall, especially in those heels.

"Get out!" she ordered, jabbing a finger toward the curtain. "You've done enough damage tonight. She can't even tell me what happened! She's a wreck! Get out! Leave!"

"I'm not leaving without my wife." *It was that simple.*

Adriana's voice broke through the tension. "It's okay," she said, sniffling. "I'll talk to him, Angela."

Angela's eyes locked onto Adriana's, then back to me, a blazing fire in them. She brushed past me hard, her shoulder crashing into mine. She paused right there. Shoulder to shoulder with me. Her eyes burned into the side of my face before she stormed off, leaving me alone with Adriana.

I rushed toward her. She was slumped in the chair, her shoulders caved in, her arms hanging limp at her sides. Her face was blotchy and wet, her mocha eyes swollen from crying, and her mouth parted as she tried to catch her breath. I stood before her, cupping her face in both hands and tilting her chin up to meet my eyes.

"Come home so we can figure this out, sweetheart," I whispered. "I'm sorry if I upset you. But we can't talk about this here." My thumbs brushed the dampness from her cheeks. "I have a plan. We can get out of this. I promise you, sweetheart." She didn't say anything. She looked at me with those wide, broken eyes. I sank to my knees. My hands slid up and down her thighs. I leaned in until my forehead rested against hers.

"You did what you thought you needed to do. That's okay," I murmured. "I don't fault you for that. I just wanna know what happened. And I want you to know I've got a plan to put this behind us for good." I pulled back enough to look at her. "I love you, sweetheart. Nothing's gonna change that. I want you to know that."

She gave me a faint nod. I pushed myself up and pulled her with me, wrapping an arm around her and tucking her close into my side. Her body sagged against mine as she walked alongside me. The room seemed to go quiet as we stepped out from the stage. People tried not to stare, but the silence was loud enough. A few eyes darted our way. I spotted Sal by the door and tossed him the keys to Adriana's car. "Drive it back to the house," I ordered. He caught the keys and nodded.

I helped her into the passenger seat of my car. She leaned back against the cushion, looking small and spent. I slid into the driver's seat and started the engine. As we pulled onto the road, I reached across and took her hand in mine and held onto it tight. The drive was quiet. Her head rested against the back of the seat, her breath slow and tired. When we pulled into the driveway, I turned toward her, her fingers intertwined with mine.

"Sweetheart," I pleaded. "Look at me." She turned, and her eyes met mine. "Take me back to that day. Tell me *everything*, so I can fix this for us. Because I can. I have a plan. I just need you to tell me what happened."

Chapter Sixty-Two

Adriana
Eighteen days ago

"Joey, where'd you put the money? I don't want to be late to meet Angela and Lucy at Mariani's," I walked into the living room and found him sitting on the couch with his shoulders slumped. He was staring out the glass window where Rosa was watering the garden in the backyard.

"On my desk, sweetheart."

I walked over and stood behind him, my fingers pressing into his tense shoulders. He tilted his head back against the back of the couch until his icy blue eyes met mine. Those eyes I loved so much looked dim. Full of sadness, he was trying to mask. "What's wrong?"

His lips tilted up, but they didn't touch his eyes. "Nothing, sweetheart. Go enjoy your time with Angela and Lucy."

"How can I, when my husband is clearly carrying something on his mind, and he won't tell me?"

He let out a rough chuckle, lifting his hands to draw my face down to meet his. His lips brushed mine as he pressed a kiss against them. His lips were soft and lingering, as if he needed the kiss more than he wanted to admit to me. "Buy something special for me, yeah?" he murmured against my lips.

"Like what?" I smirked as I leaned forward and pressed a kiss against his tense jaw.

His smirk bloomed to life. "You know what I like." Joey loved taking lingerie off more than seeing it on me, but I wore it anyway, if only to watch the hunger spark in his eyes. "Cash should be on the desk, sweetheart." My lips pressed a final kiss against his neck as I took in his warm scent and pushed myself straight up.

We'd come a long way from those early days when I'd found a duffel bag full of cash in his backseat and panicked. Now I understood: cash was how Joey moved through life. I made it to Joey's office and spotted the cash right away. But something else caught my eye. A manila folder. Last night, Ben had brought over a manila folder and then left. The manila folder was half-covering a sheet of paper, and there was something bulky weighing the folder down.

I grabbed the cash first and slipped it into my purse. Then I picked up the folder. It felt heavier than it should. I spotted two things at once in that instant. My gun inside. The one I had used when I tried to kill William. Beneath it, a registration slip with William's name printed in bold letters.

"Sweetheart?" Joey's voice called from the couch. My head jerked up toward the door. "Did you find the cash? I thought I left it on my desk."

"Uh...yeah! Just touching up my lipstick!" I called back. I tucked the gun and the cash deeper into my purse with my heart pounding. My mind was racing.

I'd known Joey had *"taken care"* of William long ago. I didn't need confirmation of that. I'd known it the day I did his laundry and spotted the bloodstained cuff. When I asked, he'd only said, "Don't worry about it. Don't worry about anything or anybody anymore." That had been code. William was gone, buried somewhere no one would ever find him.

I had kept that gun for protection. After marrying Joey, I'd forgotten about it. There hadn't been a use for it anymore. *Or so I thought.* I forced my features into a calm mask as I walked back into the living room. Joey was lounging on the couch, arms folded behind his head, trying to look relaxed. His smile hadn't yet reached his eyes, though.

"I'm one lucky man," he said as he took in the sight of me in my deep violet dress that had a white lace collar.

I forced a smile, "I forgot to ask you. How close is Ben to figuring out who shot you?"

"Oh, I think he's figured it out."

"Do you know who? Has Ben caught the shooter? Has it been taken care of?"

His eyes narrowed. "Is there a reason you're asking this right now when you just said you didn't want to be late in meeting Lucy and Angela?"

"Well, I know we never really talked about it, but I just wanted to make sure Will—"

Before I could finish, Joey's smile vanished, and he cut me off. "William's long gone, Adriana. We don't need to think about him *ever again*. He didn't do this. We've figured out who did it. And we've taken care of it."

I nodded, but my mind kept spinning. *How did Joey end up with that gun? Why had Ben delivered it? And if William was gone, who had tried to kill Joey?*

I had forced myself out the front door and into the car. I reversed out of the driveway. Somehow managed to meet Angela and Lucy on time. When I'd first arrived, it was just Angela holding a new black dress she'd purchased as she waited for Lucy and me to arrive. I floated through the store wearing a smile that wasn't real and grabbing the first dress I saw. The world around me felt hazy, like I was floating through it. Lucy finally walked in late, but she was always late, so that wasn't anything shocking. I sat there watching and waiting for Lucy to find a dress that met her standards, which meant we'd be here all day. My purse felt heavier with the gun inside as it sat in my lap.

"How's it going with you and Ben?" I asked Lucy, trying to sound casual.

The way Ben looked at Lucy and the way she looked back left little room for judgment in whatever was happening between the two of them. "Oh, we spent the night in the city," she gushed as she admired her figure in the full-length mirror.

I forced a smile, but my jaw ached from the strain, the clench beneath it betraying every ounce of the act. "Has he mentioned anything about the investigation? Joey's staying tight-lipped about the whole thing. But Ben stopped by last night, so I thought I'd ask you."

Lucy turned to meet my gaze. "You know...he said he had to drop something off. He said it was something he found. Some kind of evidence. I think he's getting close, though. We were far too busy with other activities to talk about that."

My heart nearly stopped. The smile slid off my face in an instant.

"Are you okay?" Angela asked, her hand caressing my arm as her eyes studied the side of my face.

I swallowed back the lump forming in my throat. "I'm...not feeling well."

"Christ, are you pregnant already? This is why I'm one and done," Lucy chimed in. "I was horribly nauseous with Michael."

"Let's get you some water," Angela offered, scanning the shop.

I didn't need water. I needed to get home. *Now.*

"I'm lightheaded. I think I need to leave."

"I'll drive you home," Angela insisted.

"No, no. You two finish up. Lucy hasn't even found a dress yet," I urged, standing up and smoothing my violet dress over my body. The strap of my purse seemed to weigh me down with the thought of what was inside.

"I don't care about a dress. You're not well. That's more important," Lucy frowned.

I shook my head. "I'll catch up with you later. I'm fine to drive myself back."

Before either of them could argue with me, I spun on my heels and hurried out. I practically ran to the car, climbed inside, and sped off. The only thing on my mind was getting home. I raced up to the door, my heart hammering away in my chest. My hand hovered over the knob when Joey's voice rang out, sharp and furious: *"You tried to kill me! Why?"*

I knew *exactly* who was on the other side with him. *Antonio.*

His voice rushed out fast, mixed with panic and pleading. *"He made me. You don't understand, Joey!"* The sound that tore me in two was Antonio's wailing sobs. "Vincent's been blackmailing me for *months*," he choked out. "He said if I told anyone, he'd kill Ma. What was I to do?"

I leaned back against the brick wall, needing it to hold me upright as Antonio spilled everything, all the torment I had so blindly overlooked. The fear. The manipulation. The hell Vincent Accetta had put him through. It was as if someone had a remote to my life and had put it in fast forward. The next thing I knew, I was back in my car with tears streaming down my cheeks. I didn't remember getting behind the wheel. I didn't remember driving and parking in Vincent's driveway.

I pulled down the sun visor, flipped open my purse, wiped my eyes with my silk white handkerchief, and dabbed on fresh powder. The gun sat heavy inside, as though it was burning through the leather of my purse. I unbuttoned the white lace of my dress so that enough of my cleavage showed. I glanced in the mirror one last time and then grabbed my purse and the shopping bag, stepping out of the car and walking to the front door. I rang the bell, and moments later, Vincent answered, a smile tugging at his mouth before he swung it wide. "Adriana."

The sound of him singing my name made my skin crawl. The thought of him thinking I was here for fun and not to kill him for hurting my son set me on fire. I forced a soft smile and batted my lashes at him. "I'm sorry to bother you, but my car ran out of gas while I was running errands. And it got quite hot waiting on the tow truck," I said, my fingers idly brushing the loose, unbuttoned collar of my dress as I fanned myself.

His eyes dropped to my chest right on cue.

Men...so predictable.

"Does Joey know you've stopped by?" he asked, his weary eyes lifting to meet mine again.

I tilted my head, smiling innocently. "He doesn't know *everything* I do."

The smirk that curled across his face made it difficult not to pull the gun out and shoot him right then and there. "Come inside, I'll get you some water," he said, swinging the door open wider so I could pass. I felt his gaze drag across every inch of me. He thought he was about to get *lucky.*

The thought only made my blood boil hotter. I smiled and sat on the couch, deliberately adjusting my dress so that the tops of my thigh-high stockings peeked out. His eyes slid up my legs before he turned toward the kitchen.

When his back was turned towards me, I rose from the couch and remarked. "What a beautiful house."

"Would you like a tour?" he asked over his shoulder as he continued to walk into the kitchen.

I reached into my purse, my fingers curling around the handle of the revolver. "Oh, I'd love one. I think I'll need your bathroom very soon." I smiled as I pulled back the hammer, the click slicing through the air between us. Vincent spun around. His eyes widened as he faced me. The revolver was leveled straight between his eyes.

Bullseye.

"Well, I really underestimated you."

I suppose so.

I was sure he and everyone else would underestimate me. So my finger squeezed the trigger, and a bullet flew through the air. Blood and brain matter flew everywhere. Blood sprayed across me in sickening arcs. His body fell forward with what was left of his face at my feet. I looked down at the horrific sight and took off running towards the kitchen sink, retching down the drain. I cupped my hands and filled them with cold water before I splashed them against my face, watching vomit and Vincent's blood drain down the sink disposal. I ripped my violet dress off and wiped the blood from the visible parts of my skin with my wet hands before I raced back towards the couch and pulled out the new dress from the shopping bag and tugged it onto my body. I shoved the bloody dress into the shopping bag. Joey had taught me how to get blood out of clothes—*hot water, vinegar, and hydrogen peroxide.*

I could hear his voice in my head now: "Leave no trace, Sweetheart."

Oh, I wouldn't. I'd sooner throw this dress away than try to scrub it clean. People always underestimate me, but they forget one thing: there's no fire like the kind a mother lights when she's protecting her child.

Chapter Sixty-Three

Joey

Nineteen days after Vincent's murder

The next morning, I drove to Ben's apartment in the city. I had spent the whole night lying in bed, Adriana curled against my chest, staring at the ceiling and replaying everything in my head. Guilt twisted in me like a knife. I wanted to give her and Antonio a fresh start. Yet all I'd done was drag them deeper into my mess and turn them into extensions of me.

I parked, took the stairs two at a time, and knocked hard on Ben's door. My knuckles against the wood were sharp and impatient. I heard his footsteps before the door creaked open and immediately wished I hadn't. Ben stood there half-asleep and half-naked, wearing nothing but a pair of boxer briefs. The door swung open wider than it needed to, giving me a front-row view of something no best friend should ever have to see. I turned fast, my eyes on the apartment across the hall.

"What the fuck!" Ben barked, his voice still groggy. "I thought you were Lucy and you'd forgotten your keys or something!"

"Sorry to disappoint," I muttered, lifting a hand in mock

surrender, my knuckles toward him. "Mind throwing on some clothes and inviting me in?"

The door slammed shut behind me. A few minutes later, Ben came back, this time in a tracksuit, looking more awake. He stepped aside and let me in. The place smelled like wine and Lucy's perfume. Two empty glasses sat on the coffee table, and a pair of high heels lounged by the couch. I stepped over them and dropped into the cushion while Ben ran a hand through his hair. "What'd you come here for?" he asked.

"To apologize."

Ben laughed a loud, fake, and over-the-top bellow. He even clutched his chest as if I'd just told him I was joining the priesthood. "You?" he said between chuckles, pointing at me. "You came all the way over here to apologize to me? Why don't we cut the bullshit and skip to what you really want me to do?"

I smirked, pulled out my cigarettes, and stuck one between my lips. I flicked the lighter and took a deep inhale of the nicotine. Then tossed the pack and lighter onto the table in front of him. "I'm sorry for accusing Lucy of something she didn't do, and I'm sorry for threatening you. My behavior was erratic and uncalled for."

Ben's brow lifted. A slow grin tugged at his mouth as he nodded along. "And?" I stared at him, trying to dig through my brain for whatever else he thought I owed him. Apologizing wasn't my strong suit, and Ben damn well knew it. "You're sorry for talking to me like I'm some fucking jackass."

"I'm sorry," I said, blowing smoke between us. "For talking to you like you're some fucking jackass."

"Now," Ben smirked, his eyes narrowing on mine, "what is it you need me to do?"

"Nothing, you jackass." I let out a dry laugh, and he followed right after. "I...just wanted to ask how you knew it was—"

The front door banged open before I could finish. Lucy walked in with a brown paper bag in hand, her voice sing-song as she kicked off her heels. "Bennie, babe! I got us bagels! Time to wake up!" Ben cleared his throat so fast it sounded like a choke. I bit back a laugh at the nickname, but the look he shot me could've burned a hole through my skull. Lucy froze when her eyes landed on me. "Oh my God! Joey? What are you doing here?"

I gave her my most polite smile. "Well, isn't this like old times?"

"What are you doing here?" she asked.

"I suppose you didn't grab a bagel for me?"

"Of course not," she scoffed. "Seriously! What are you doing here? I thought you two weren't even speaking." She shifted her weight, one hip cocked, her arms folding tight across her chest.

"I came to make amends with *Bennie*," I said, letting the smirk creep onto my face.

Ben groaned, running a hand down his reddened face. "It shouldn't take long," he muttered to Lucy.

She huffed, spun on her heel, and disappeared into the kitchen. Ben's eyes cut back to me. "You were saying?"

I leaned forward, tapping ash into the tray, and my voice dropped. "How'd you know it was Adriana?"

Ben's brow furrowed. "What do you mean? How did I know it was Adriana?"

I probably looked as confused as Ben by his reaction. *Was he dodging because Lucy was here?* "You know," I said, watching his face. "The comment you made, about me needing to focus on what happens in my own house instead of everyone else's. How did you know it was Adriana who killed Vincent? When did you figure it out, and why didn't you tell me? How could you let me accuse Lucy when it was—"

Ben choked on the drag he'd just taken, coughing hard, as his hand thumped against his chest. "What the fuck are you talking about?" he rasped. "I had no idea Adriana killed Vincent. How the hell do you know it was her?"

"Aleksei...Paul brought him to the office. I showed him a picture of Lucy—"

"Of course you did!"

"You'll be happy to know he said it wasn't her," I shot back, stubbing out the last of my cigarette in the ashtray. "He didn't even recognize her. I had to tell him who she was. But then..." I leaned forward, lowering my voice. "I thought he might be playing me, so when Paul was taking him in the back, he saw the wedding picture in the hallway and claimed it was Adriana."

Ben's eyes stayed locked on mine, his expression blank as he continued to listen.

"It turns out she found out Antonio was the one who shot me. She came back, planning to confront us both. But instead, she overheard me tearing into Antonio and heard him admit what Vincent had done. So she went over there. He let her in. The bastard thought he was about to get laid." I let out a humorless laugh. "Instead, she put a bullet between his fucking eyes."

Ben's mouth hung open. He didn't move. He didn't even blink once I finished.

"So...I need your help. I killed Aleksei yesterday. The only way out of this is to take out...you know who."

Ben smirked like Christmas came early. "Oh, gladly. I've been dreaming of this day for ten fucking years."

Wait.

"If you didn't mean that comment about Adriana, then who was it about? Antonio?"

Ben hesitated and nodded. "It was just me getting back at

you for you coming at Lucy and me. It was a mean way to stick it to you...don't even think about it. Let's leave that in the past." He waved his hand at me, brushing it off. "The real question is, how the hell are you gonna take Hector without starting World War Three?"

"Coffee, Joey?" Lucy's voice cut through the air. She stepped into the living room, holding two mugs. Ben and I exchanged a glance that said the same thing: *I hope she didn't hear a damn word.*

"Sure," I muttered, forcing a tight smile. "Thanks, Lucy."

She nodded, bright and oblivious, and bounced back into the kitchen. If anything, the past twenty-four hours have taught me it was that women couldn't be trusted either. They may look oblivious, but that's what made them dangerous and over-looked by all of us.

"The way I see it, Aleksei takes the fall for everything. I'll tell Christopher it was him who shot me and who shot Vincent...the cleanest, most believable cover story. I'll see Christopher as soon as I leave here; Hector won't be there, so I can lay out what happened. I'll also tell him Aleksei's tied to Hector, that he's working with Hector and connected to Hector's mistress, who has three kids by him. Once Christopher hears that, there won't be an ounce of mercy left for Hector."

Ben leaned back, gripping the coffee mug in his palms. "You're forgetting something. Hector's not going to go down alone. He'll tell Christopher everything about Lucy and me. About how I was a plant, how I fell for his daughter in that goddamn jail cell back in '43, and how I'm still seeing her in '60." His eyes met mine, steel in them. "And I'm not gonna deny it. That's not who I am. So he'll kill me too."

"No, he won't."

"He will, and I'm okay with that. I've lived a good enough life."

"I'll make Christopher believe Hector can't be trusted. He's proven he's a traitor—why the hell would Christopher take his word now when all he's done is betray him?"

Ben studied me for a moment longer. The silence stretched between us as we sipped on our coffee. We both knew what this was: a gamble big enough to burn the whole house down.

"Let's hope you're right," Ben said.

Let's hope. Because if I'm not, I'll lose one of my best friends because of it.

Chapter Sixty-Four

Antonio
Nineteen days after Vincent's murder

After the blowout with Enzo, I watched Joey storm into the house, his shirt streaked with blood. Then Ma came running out shortly after, tears spilling down her face, and an hour after that, Joey showed up at Lucy's door asking if she'd seen Ma. My stomach twisted into knots. I didn't need anyone to spell it out for me, whatever had gone down was bad...really bad.

I ended up crashing at Michael's place last night, but sleep didn't come easy. My head kept replaying Enzo's words, Joey's bloody shirt, Ma's tears, all of it stacking up like bricks pressing on my chest. When Michael asked me what happened between Enzo and me, I brushed him off, said I wasn't ready to talk about it. He bought it. Probably because he didn't want to talk about anything except Alessia anyway. His mouth was practically glued to hers, and when he did come up for air, the only thing on his mind was her.

Part of me was grateful for his distraction, it meant I didn't have to explain how I was breaking apart inside. How I was caught between secrets I shouldn't know and loyalties I couldn't hold. It was easier to let Michael stay lost in Alessia than to admit the truth: I was terrified.

After Michael and I woke up and got ready for the day, he headed off to meet Alessia for breakfast at the diner. I stood in his room for a long time, staring at the floor, debating whether I should go home. The thought of walking back into that house, of seeing the chaos that might still be unfolding inside, made my stomach twist. I wasn't ready.

Instead, I found myself wandering across the lawn, my hand hovering over Enzo's front door before finally knocking. My heart hammered in my chest. Maybe today I could fix it, or at least beg for his forgiveness.

The door swung open, and at first, a smile stretched across his face. Then his eyes landed on me, and it vanished instantly, replaced by a scowl. "What the fuck are you doing here? Did I not make it clear yesterday? We're done, Antonio. We're no longer friends."

"I...I know. I just...I wanted to talk. Maybe apologize again and explain myself."

He stepped forward, folding his arms over his chest. "Apologize? For what? Betraying me? For thinking you could manipulate me? Because that's exactly what you did."

"It wasn't like that," I said, pleading. "I thought I was protecting you. I...I messed up, yeah, but it was never about you getting hurt. I never wanted to ruin our friendsh—"

Enzo scoffed, shaking his head. "Protecting me? That's rich. You lied to me, Antonio. Lied straight to my face. And for what? Some thrill? Some ego trip to feel important in Joey's world as his pathetic prodigy son?"

"I...I didn't think it would hurt anyone," I muttered, my throat tight. "I didn't know how bad it would get. I thought I would just help clear his—"

"Yeah, yeah. I've already heard your little story...blah, blah, I don't need to hear it again."

"You're being really fucking annoying and for no reason," I snapped. I dragged in a breath. "I wasn't out to manipulate you or betray you! I just...I wanted to make things right, somehow. And it's clear I made them worse!"

"You don't get it, do you? Some things aren't fixed with words. Some things you can't just take back. Fool me once, shame on you; fool me twice, shame on me."

I swallowed, my stomach twisting. "Please, Enzo. I'm asking. I'm begging. I...I need you to at least hear me out. I didn't...I wouldn't do anything to spite you."

"Here's a thought...keep holding out hope. Because after yesterday...I'm done with you. Done with your screwed-up version of loyalty and friendship."

I clenched my fists, staring at him, knowing there was nothing more I could say. If things couldn't get any worse, Sal's blue Thunderbird pulled up to the curb. Enzo stepped out, closed the door, and walked past me straight toward him. I followed, my stomach in my throat, realizing in that instant the thing I'd been dreading was actually happening. I couldn't control everything, and anyone who knew Enzo knew how impulsive he was. There was no amount of pleading that would stop him, but I would try anyway. "What are you doing?" I blurted, panicking. He didn't answer. "Hey! You can't do this, Enzo!"

"You can't tell me what to do," he said, eyes burning into mine. "You can't stop me."

Enzo was a powder keg—angry, impulsive, running on teenage rage. That scared me because I also knew where that road ended: guys like him didn't last long in this life. They were dead before they could legally drive.

"You're making a huge mistake. You're a hothead, Enzo.

People like you don't last in this line of work. You think this is about getting even? It's not. The minute you walk in there trying to prove something, you're already a corpse waiting for a grave."

"God, you're one egotistical motherfucker. You think you can have it all? You think—"

"No! I'm pleading—"

"What kind of hypocrite tells someone not to do something they do themselves?"

"I haven't...I'm not—" The words twisted and died somewhere in my throat.

I turned to Sal, who sat frozen behind the wheel, knuckles white. "And you," I said, voice breaking, "you're an even bigger idiot for going along with this. Do you think he's thought this through? The only thing you two are going to get is your names in the paper under 'found dead in a ditch.'" Sal's head moved slightly—he stared out the windshield but didn't speak.

"I'm not letting you do this," I said, desperation bleeding through.

Enzo's jaw tightened. "You're not gonna stop me."

I squared my shoulders. "Watch me."

Enzo scoffed. "We'll see about that."

Before I could even react, his hand slammed against my gut, shoving me backward with so much force my feet slid out from under me. My back hit the ground, a jolt running up my spine. For a second, all I saw was the blue sky and puffy clouds. All I could think was that Enzo wasn't just pissed, he was too far gone. Enzo was big. Stocky. Built like a kid who could throw a punch through a brick wall, and when you mix that with his short fuse, you've got a walking disaster waiting to happen.

I lay there like a damn fool, watching Sal's wheels spin out as the car shot down the street. My chest burned, not from the shove, but from the sick feeling in my gut. He was really doing this. If I didn't find a way to stop him, the next time I saw Enzo might be in a coffin.

I lay sprawled on Enzo's lawn, the grass damp against my skin, sun warm on my face, trying to make sense of the chaos swirling through my head. My stomach twisted, and every muscle ached from the last twenty-four hours of pure madness. I pushed myself upright, brushed the blades from my sleeves, and froze.

An ambulance screamed down the street, tires shrieking against asphalt, lights flashing. It came to a stop right in front of Michael's house, neighbors spilling onto their lawns to watch the scene unfold. Heart hammering, I sprinted across the yard, in time to see them rush Hector out, pale and unconscious, into the back of the vehicle.

I reached the front steps, catching my breath, when Lucy appeared in the doorway, worry etched across her face.

"Antonio! Where's Michael?" she asked, eyes darting between me and the stretcher.

"At the diner...with Alessia. What's happened?"

"I think...Hector's had a heart attack," she said, panic in her tone, before she turned and bolted down the walkway, following the stretcher as the paramedics loaded him in.

I stood frozen a moment longer, watching the ambulance doors slam shut, neighbors in shock, and the siren fading down the street. My fists clenched at my sides, stomach twisting tighter. The world felt like it was spinning out of control, and there was nothing I could do but watch it all rush past.

Five days after Hector's death

Joey and I barely had time to mend the cracks between us after the last bombshell detonated before another one shook the ground beneath our feet. *Hector was dead, and today was his funeral.*

Joey had left early that morning to talk with Ben, and I was still curled up in my robe, recovering from the tidal wave of tears that had swallowed me whole the days before. I hadn't cried over killing Vincent—*God, no.* There wasn't a shred of remorse in me for that. I cried because I had known the truth for nearly three weeks and kept my mouth shut. Three weeks of silence while Joey walked around with a target painted on his back. *My husband. My protector.* And I betrayed him. That was my sin. One I wasn't sure I'd ever forgive myself for.

I was on the couch nursing a mug of tea when the front door slammed open. Joey barreled in, all the blood had drained from his features, his blue eyes wide with horror, like he'd seen the Devil himself. "Have you spoken to Lucy today?" he asked, his breath ragged.

My brow furrowed as I set the mug down on the coffee table. "No. Why? What happened?"

"Hector." His throat bobbed, his voice full of disbelief. "He had a heart attack." The revelation punched the air out of the room. "Lucy called the station. The medics took him to the hospital, but—" He shook his head. "He didn't make it. Ben came by the shop and told me."

Hector Moretti, the most recent monster in all our lives, snuffed out by his own rotten heart. The irony didn't escape me. Joey didn't even have to lift a finger to make good on the plan he'd been brooding over. Hector beat him to the punch. Nobody thought Hector even had a heart, but I guess he did. Only it was so black, so corroded with evil, it just gave out.

Though the smallest part of me wondered—No, she wouldn't...

At the wake, I watched Lucy. I watched her stand there like a statue, all marble skin and hollow eyes. She had no tears in her eyes. Her hair and makeup were immaculate. She looked like a ghost of the Lucy I knew and loved. I wondered, had the seed once planted in her, the one that had begun to sprout, finally bloomed? I buried the thought as fast as it came. She looked every bit the grieving wife who'd just lost her husband, no matter how cruel and venomous that man had been.

Now...we stood together at *St. Augustine of the Sacred Heart*, the humid wind threatening to ruin our makeup as we faced the polished tombstone:

Hector Moretti

Beloved Husband and Father

What a joke.

The cemetery was thick with black coats. The earth was still fresh and raw where the grave swallowed him whole. Lucy was wedged between Angela and me, our arms draped around her shoulders and back as she wept into a black Chanel handkerchief. Her sobs tore through the winter air, loud and guttural, like grief had gutted her clean through.

The wailing stopped. Lucy straightened, dabbing at her damp cheeks with the square of couture. Her gaze locked on the tombstone, glimmering with something that didn't belong to grief at all. "I finally did it," she whispered, soft as sin, but clear enough for us both to hear. She didn't look at either one of us. Her voice was steady, almost serene, when she said, "I finally killed that bastard."

Angela and I exchange horrific, confused glances.

"I know what happened." Lucy's voice sliced through. "I'm sorry you came to this wretched island only to have Vincent blackmail your son, and this sorry bastard try to take out Joey." Her jaw tightens as her eyes bounce to me, then Angela. "When I heard Joey tell Ben you'd killed Vincent, I couldn't have been happier. If someone had done that to my Michael..." She paused, "I would have done the same."

Her chin lifted again, almost regal-like. "But when I heard their plan...I knew it was a gamble. Hector would have fought with his last breath to convince my father to kill Ben, too. And I thought..." Lucy turned, first to me, then to Angela, like a queen passing judgment on her court. A shadow of a smile played at her lips. "Well, I thought I should be a good wife and make him a nice little afternoon drink."

A sinister smirk bloomed across her face. She shifted her gaze back to Angela, whose crimson lips parted in shock, blinking as if she'd just been slapped. Lucy turned to me, her espresso eyes gleaming like cold steel. "And I'm sorry for being such a shitty friend and not doing it sooner."

"No," I whispered, my throat raw. "It's okay, Lucy. You're not a shitty friend."

"I guess we've all killed a man." Angela's voice slid through the air. She tilted her head, her eyes bore into mine. "Or two, apparently." She leaned closer. "And I would like to know more details about that once we leave here."

"What are you talking about?" Lucy's face scrunched, confusion sharpening into something darker as she swiveled toward Angela.

Angela lifted a shoulder, the corner of her mouth curling with wicked nonchalance. "Oh, honey. I killed my husband, too." The way she said it—like discussing the weather—made my pulse spike. "Well," she corrected, "I didn't pull the trigger. But I had Marco do it."

"Marco killed his own brother?" Lucy choked out, stumbling over the words. "And you've only just now given in to this man?"

"Marco and I..." Angela exhaled like she was releasing years of secrets, rolling her eyes to the winter sky as if even she didn't know where to begin. "...are complicated." A sly smile threatened to break through, but she bit it back, trying to look indifferent.

"Well, that's the understatement of the century," Lucy huffed, her tone sharp but tinged with intrigue.

"Don't worry about Marco and me." Angela leaned forward, her voice dropping to a whisper that still managed to command. "And get to crying like a good mafia wife before everyone suspects you killed the man." She nudged Lucy with her elbow, and a dark glint danced in her eye.

"They'd never suspect me." Lucy mouthed, her grin devilish. "These men think we're only useful for a roll in the hay and to bear children."

"Joke's on them, isn't it?" Angela smirked, and all three of us shared the same knowing grin—the kind that says blood *binds us just as much as it stains us.*

"Are we as bad as them?" The question escaped me before I could stop it. It hangs in the air like gun smoke.

"As bad as them?" Angela repeated, tilting her head thoughtfully. "Debatable." Her red lips curled into something dangerous. "Smarter than them?" She flashed her teeth. "*Absolutely.*"

Joey killed William for me, for all the suffering I endured for years. I killed Vincent for Joey, for every scar Vincent carved into his life, and for the short months he spent blackmailing Antonio. Lucy killed Hector to protect Joey and Ben... and to punish a man who underestimated her. And Angela... well, Angela killed her husband too. But nobody knew why.

Angela's gaze snapped to Lucy and mine. She saw the question on our lips, the same question clawing its way through my chest. *Why?* Her smile was lethal and utterly unapologetic as she said, "One day, darlings. I'll tell you everything. Perhaps, after I'm filled in on Adriana and Vincent."

If there's one thing I know for sure, Angela's story was far from over. Her vows weren't broken. They were reborn as sinful oaths.

Acknowledgments

This book exists because of a small constellation of people who believed in it long before it knew what it wanted to be.

To my family, for being my first readers, my cheerleaders, and occasionally my reality check.

To my sweet boys, for proudly telling everyone at school that their mom writes books for a living. That they can't be too sure what it's about, but something about crime. That's all *anyone* needs to know.

To my amazing husband, for supporting my dreams and always being in my corner.

To my critique partners, Authors Cheyanne King and Nessa Bloom, whose sharp eyes, honest feedback, and enthusiasm kept me moving forward when the words felt stubborn: this story is better because of you both.

To my beta readers (Jay Jones, Sandy Collins, Grace Christian, Deseray, and Jennifer Kingsborough), for taking the time to read and offer feedback that helped shape this book into something enjoyable.

To Nikki, for allowing me to pull you into the dark side so we could debate endlessly over whether Diet Coke or Coke Zero reigns supreme (Coke Zero is better, obviously), and for sharing our unusual love for the man that is, Tony Soprano.

To Frankie, for editing my manuscript with care and a continuous amount of memes.

And to every reader who has fallen in love with the morally grey Romano family—this one is for you. Thank you for being here.

About the Author

Zara's love for storytelling began at the age of nine, when she first plotted a book in a spiral notebook in December 2004. From that moment on, her passion for reading and writing only deepened. With a background in method acting and method writing, she brings emotional depth and authenticity to every story she tells.

Now a wife and mother of three, Zara writes from her home in South Carolina. When she isn't crafting stories or working with fellow writers, Zara enjoys spending time with her family, swimming, and traveling the world.

Sign up for her newsletter to stay updated: www.zara-jadeastrid.com

 instagram.com/zarajadeastrid

Also by Zara Jade Astrid

Sinful Bargains: Sins of the Father Book 1